# The Guardian Temple

## *Demonic Dealings*

*By*

## *Jordan Eilbert and Mimi Jasso*

ISBN  978-1-958788-29-5  (Digital)

ISBN  978-1-958788-41-7  (Paperback)

ISBN  978-1-958788-31-8  (Hardcover)



Publify Publishing

1412 W. Ave B

Lampasas, TX 76550

publifypublishing@gmail.com

# Contents


**SERIES ONE:  Father Thomas** ...............................................................1

Introduction ........................................................................ 2

CHAPTER 1:  Hubris........................................................... 9

CHAPTER 2:  Salvation ................................................... 32

CHAPTER 3:  The Hunt....................................................50

CHAPTER 4:  The Road to Hell .................................... 69

CHAPTER 5:  Redemption............................................. 82

**SERIES TWO:  Sara Baker** ..............................................................**99**

Introduction .....................................................................100

CHAPTER 1:  I Made A Deal with an Angel ............................. 103

CHAPTER 2:  Pros and Cons.........................................112

CHAPTER 3:  Regrets .....................................................124

CHAPTER 4:  Descent .....................................................140

CHAPTER 5:  Hellscape ..................................................158

CHAPTER 6:  Changing Hearts ....................................175

CHAPTER 7:  Lust vs Love .............................................191

CHAPTER 8:  Transference.............................................207

CHAPTER 9:  Uncommon Soldiers ............................. 225

CHAPTER 10: Blackmailed .......................................... 240

CHAPTER 11: Inquisition...............................................256

CHAPTER 12: Hubris ......................................................278

CHAPTER 13: The Life Left Behind ..................................298

CHAPTER 14: Repurposed.....................................................316

CHAPTER 15: Return Voyage.................................................330

CHAPTER 16: Punishment.....................................................351

CHAPTER 17: Old Wounds ...................................................368


**SERIES THREE:  Jason Miller** ..........................................**383**

Introduction ............................................................................384

CHAPTER 1:  Reunion............................................................395

CHAPTER 2:  Night Terrors...................................................409

CHAPTER 3:  Expulsion .........................................................421

CHAPTER 4:  Corruption........................................................441

CHAPTER 5:  Justice................................................................460


Epilogue.....................................................................................478

About the Authors...................................................................490

# SERIES ONE

## Father Thomas

# **Introduction**

I am a Priest at the Vatican City in Italy. I was approached by a Bishop today with something that has to have been a mistranslation. Let me explain who I am, and why I am here:

My name is Father Edward Thomas, I was born in the United States and became a Priest of the Catholic Church when I was twenty. I am an exorcist. I am told I am a very good exorcist, but I do not feel I am. Out of my nearly one hundred and twenty exorcisms, only twenty-five of the possessed have survived said exorcisms. In all cases the demon was expelled, the soul of the possessed saved, but the body can only take so much for so long. Most of the time I have come too late and the family hasn't given proper medical care before my arrival.

Yes, you just heard a priest tell you that if you're possessed see a doctor first, and during your possession. I can heal your spirit and perhaps save your mind, but your body is still a physical thing. While prayer may expedite healing, your body still needs to be tended to by a medical professional, treat it like a temple, my children. I am a spiritual professional, not a medical one.

I even recall an exorcism call where I arrived only to find the young man in question, tied down to a bed, demanding to be released. Why did the family think the young man was possessed? The 'possessed' was suffering from Gender Dysphoria, she felt she was a woman in a man's body. I had her released by the family and brought her to proper medical and mental health professionals. I felt for her, I did, her family felt her condition so odd that they believed it was against God and she must be suffering from demonic possession.. Other illnesses will also get the ill-informed to call me, such as someone with seizures or Schizophrenia.

Misdiagnosis aside, I have always felt that an exorcism where the possessed doesn't survive is a failed one. The church disagrees.

Despite this, I continue my work at the Catholic Church. I do so because I know there are less scrupulous Priests who have the arrogance to believe they can heal in the name of God our Lord, as well as cast out demons. Such a way of thinking leads too easily into pride. An exorcist must be humble, honest, and pure. This is needed because otherwise a demon can feed off of the exorcist's own sin and endanger the soul of the possessed. It's why the old adage calls for "An Old Priest and a Young Priest." The idea being that the young priest can remind the old of his place, while the old shares experience. I am somewhere in between old and young, but I am called when the local priests cannot handle the exorcism themselves.

The Vatican has called me more in the past two years than they have in all the time I was an exorcist before. I have even begun training more exorcists at the Vatican when I myself am not casting out demons. The issue that half of my charges have happened in the last 2 years is not lost on me. These are not false alarms or misdiagnoses. Demons are possessing people at a higher rate than normal, believe it or not.

That led me to the letter I received from one Bishop Bernardo Ricci.


Dear Father Thomas,

Your reputation precedes you, Father. I have reviewed your performance and your understanding of the unclean is beyond reproach. A specialized project has been brought by the Pope himself after the apprehension of a Warlock who goes by the name of 'Immunda.' He is in possession of a highly powerful artifact which we plan to use to summon a demon. You are being requested to lead a group of priests in charge of containing the creature. Please come to me as soon as possible.

The Most Rev. Bernardo Ricci

My Italian must be off, that's how I read it, but that can't be. It must mean that this Warlock, Immunda, has summoned forth a demon that must be sent back to Hell. Frightening as that is, I know I must hurry to the Bishop to aid him. Despite their knowledge, having worked in the field with these creatures gives one a different experience I cannot expect a typical Bishop or even a Cardinal to fully grasp. Again, I do not put much stock in my own skill, but rather fear that their own pride may empower the creature.

I arrive at the Bishop's office, announce myself, and he greets me in earnest, immediately taking me down several long hallways. "Father Thomas, thank God, you made it here swiftly."

"You caught me while I was providing lessons to my fellow priests, Bishop Ricci. I received your letter and came as swiftly as I could." I say in Italian. I speak it far better than I can read it, apparently.

The Bishop stops at the end of a long hallway and then places his crucifix into an indentation in the wall, he turns to me and gives me a serious look. I see an intensity behind his graying eyes, the wrinkles around them, and his forehead showing great concern. "Thank you, Father Thomas, your expertise is required for us to truly address the situation."

As the hallway opens to a secret passage, I'm guided in by the Bishop downward. I adjust my bag over my shoulder, in it, I have all the tools I would normally use for an exorcism, as well as some that I have never needed to. "Bishop, this 'Immunda', what object has he managed to find?"

The Bishop continues down the hallways, LED lights illuminating as we head down several corridors. "He claims he found it in the United States, in a city in New Hampshire, of all places."

I'm confused, "New Hampshire? He found an object that could allow him to summon a demon?"

"It could do far more; we are still studying it. It contains an incredible spiritual power the likes of which we have never seen before." The Bishop explains.

We enter a huge complex down below in what was once a catacomb. Now it appears to be a prison of some sort, a very modern prison. There are plexiglass holding cells and in each is a self-proclaimed witch or warlock of some sort.

The Vatican is not in the habit of restraining your average citizen. Holding a ceremony where you celebrate the 'marriage' of the Sun and the Earth during the summer or winter solstice is a benign thing to us. Heresy, of course, but nothing we're going to hurl someone into a Vatican prison for, nowadays anyway. These cells are reserved for only the most unclean.

The witch in the first cell, for example, who hurls herself at the plexiglass as I walk by?  She has been imprisoned for sacrificing a woman of my congregation to a demon in order to demand he possess her husband. She then planned to have the possessed man impregnate her with his offspring. I cleared the man of the possession before she could finish her pact. The result, of course, was that she lost her wits and her womb, as she failed to meet the bargain of the demon. That is the price one pays for breaking a pact made with a demon.

"HYPOCRITE!" She shouts at me. "YOU DESTROYED THE SANCTITY OF MY MARRIAGE!" She tries to spit at me, but it only hits the plexiglass and slides down the side.

I ignore her as we move toward several cells down. The words of the unclean are not to be paid much mind. Especially those of a woman who would give herself purposefully to a demon. My fingers squeeze the golden ring on my finger, and I think of the Lord God and His glory as we continue.

We stop at a young man's cell. He has a scraggly brown beard and long hair. He wears black robes and has several very old talismans on him. I notice he has a necklace with symbols of each prince of Hell surrounding a central symbol of the Devil himself. Tattoos across his face also convey various pacts with numerous demons, most of which I have heard of. The man is oddly calm, sitting in the room, idly caressing his beard.

Given his age, I assume he must be an apprentice. Such artifacts and carvings I have only seen on some of the most experienced of Warlocks brought into these halls. This means he is dealing with powers he cannot truly fathom.

"He is young," I remarked.

"You are wrong Father, this man is almost eighty-five years of age," The Bishop informs me.

I look at him oddly, no matter what, there is no way he is eighty-five.

"He claims the object he obtained rejuvenated him," The Bishop turns to a dais which stands across from his cell. On the dais, under glass, and illuminated with bright white LEDs is a small red disk, no larger than an inch and a half in diameter. Etched into it, very weakly and recently I notice, are various symbols of a Satanic origin. "That same object is what he plans to use to summon the demon."

I look it over, the object is reddish, and solid for the most part, but the edges of it are translucent, almost like red obsidian. "He found this in the United States?"

"He claims he found it via divination, that its power called him to a burned down house where he found it in a garage, of all places." The Bishop turns to me, "The family of that home cannot be found," He motions to the object before us, "It is concentrated Angel Blood."

I give Bishop Ricci an odd look. "Angel Blood?"

Bishop Ricci nods, looking at the Warlock, "He calls it Sanguine Amber."

I nod, "So we took this from him when he summoned the demon?"

Bishop Ricci shakes his head, "No Father, he says he can use it to summon forth a demon."

I looked at the Bishop, confused, "So then... We have stopped him, and we plan to purify this object?"

The Bishop gives me a stern look. "No, Father Thomas, the Vatican fully intends to summon forth a Demon."

# CHAPTER 1

## *Hubris*

I am flabbergasted as I look between Bishop Ricci and the unnatural warlock behind his plexiglass cage. "Bishop Ricci, you cannot be serious. The demons which I cast out have only echoes of their power." I look to the object before me, the small disk of Sanguine Amber. "But this? To pull a demon from the pit, why would the Church risk it?"

Bishop Ricci looks at me, with a serious tone says, "Father Thomas, you yourself know the increase in demonic activity as of late. You've seen it firsthand. Your reports have shown statements that are most concerning. Mostly regarding the coming of a 'Destroyer'."

I clench my fist but do my best to remain composed, "Bishop Ricci, I have said before that those statements can be from the demon or from the possessed and could simply be the demon pleading to remain inside the victim."

Immunda laughs, overhearing our conversation. He speaks in Latin, "The Demons shall consume your church."

Bishop Ricci motioned for me to follow him into a room at the end of the hall out of earshot of the cell. Here I noticed three other priests, two of which were students of mine from a year ago, and one elderly priest.

"Father Thomas!" An enthusiastic young man spoke, "It's wonderful to see you again." The young man was Father Jason Hammond. He hailed from England. He walked up to me and shook my hand hardily.

A not-so-happy face was that of the other two, while I did not know the older priest, the second younger man was my former student, Father Gerard Charpentier. He was a Frenchman who embodied everything you would imagine a Frenchman should when having to deal with an American. "Mon Père Thomas." Father Charpentier, of course, did not (or rather refused) to speak English.

My French was serviceable at best, but not fantastic. The bane of living in Europe was having to know at least three languages. Knowing the four I did was burdensome enough, learning French for my one stubborn French student five years ago was arduous.

Father Hammond looked to Father Charpentier, "Liven up Gerard, we'll be fine now." He leaned over to me, whispering into my ear, "Father you don't believe a lick of this nonsense, do you? Summoning a Demon?"

I frown and move back to Bishop Ricci, "I would advise against this course of action."

The Bishop motioned to the floor, where a ring of salt was located. Within it was a pentagram with various Satanic symbols around it. "We have taken multiple precautions. A ring of sanctified salt surrounds the summoning circle." He then hands each of us a bottle, "Holy Water, purified by His Holiness Himself after it was filtered through the Shroud of Turin." He looks to me now, "And Father Thomas's expertise."

"I have to protest this insanity!" I shout. "A Demon to be summoned, here, will be a disaster, to say the least!"

Father Hammond's face falls for the first time, "Bishop Ricci, with all due respect if Father Thomas is here for his expertise perhaps he needs to be heeded."

Bishop Ricci shakes his head, "This will proceed with or without Father Thomas's approval. He is here because we need him regardless." He sighs, "Outside this door will be another pair of highly-trained exorcists, the door itself is warded and blessed." He looks up, "And the passageway above is further protected with holy wards, artifacts, and lastly the doorway protecting the passage has been sealed, and only a Bishop's crucifix can unlock it."

I shake my head and turn to my fellow priests, "All of you must be fully prepared, whether you believe in this man's ability to summon a demon or not."

The Bishop looks at the entrance to the room as Immunda is led inside. "We have a purpose. We will interrogate the demon, demand to know what is going on down below, and then we will send it back." He looks at all of us. "I am fully aware of the risks. But the Pope fears that with the increase in demonic activity, we must act. An invasion may be imminent."

I am furious but regardless I bring out my equipment. Silver crosses, Rosary beads, and several charms against possession I give these to each priest. "This is madness, Bishop Ricci." I place my vestments on and look at Immunda. "But if the Church will not back down then I will do my best to prevent this demon from doing its worst." I pull on a pair of heat-resistant gloves and offer the same to my fellow Priests, all of them look at me oddly and do not bother to wear them.

Immunda is grinning ear to ear as the pair of priests from outside hand him the Sanguine Amber. "I shall do this, as you ask." He walks up to the circle, my fellow priests surrounding him.

I close off his path, opening my Bible and laying the chain from its spine over the crease of the pages, keeping the pages from moving. I slide the locks on the sides of it to keep it opened as well. As I said, I am an exorcist, I can count the number of times a demon has tried to close my Bible as I have read from it. I have designed mine to be locked open because of it.

The Bishop leaves with the other two priests following behind him, the door locks behind us. I am aware of the other precautions behind that door, I hope they are not needed.

Immunda laughs and holds the Sanguine Amber in his hands, it begins to glow and levitate between his hands.

Father Hammond is taken aback, and I affix him with a stern gaze. I mouth out to him:

"Be stern in the face of darkness."

Immunda's laughing grows, "You fools... I will not summon a mere demon. With this, the blood of fallen angels, I shall summon forth a Prince of Hell!"

I reach out to stop him but suddenly I am forced back by a mighty wind coming from the center of the circle. The scent is foul and sulfurous. This fool does have the power to summon a demon, I realize.

Father Hammond has fallen to his knees, the older priest I cannot see any longer, but I hear a body hit the ground with a thud.

Father Charpentier is standing along the circle at three o'clock to my six. I point to Father Hammond to go to a nine o'clock position along the circle.

Father Hammond nods, our robes and vestments fluttering in the foul wind.

Father Charpentier is unfazed as he chants a few words I cannot hear over the rush of wind.

I do my own chanting, praying for God's protection, as Immunda laughs hysterically after he completes his own spell.

"Pray all you want to your weakened God! For I, Immunda, shall call forth the brute of the underworld! The Lord of Wrath!" His laughing grows maddening as a green bolt of lightning cracks through the middle of the circle. "Come forth! Come forth, oh, Lord of Wrath!"

A dark figure appears in the center of the circle, and I grab hold of my Rosary beads, green light flashes and the wind stops. A thick miasma fills the room and I smell the sulfur beginning to dissipate.

"Yes! Behold! The Demon I have brought forth for the ruination of this world! An all-powerful," Immunda hesitates with his prattling.

I look ahead of me and squint as I see what is within the circle.

A pair of purple bat-like wings stretches upwards, flapping demurely, pushing the miasma away weakly. Dark purple, almost black horns are seen between auburn hair, long and luxurious. Large green doe eyes glow through the clearing fog, beneath that a feminine nose and plush red lips over pale skin. A rather large bust shows generous cleavage out of what appears to be a purple leather-like corset. A whip-like violet tail waves back and forth wearily, its ending has a spaded tip. The fog has fully cleared now, revealing long legs which appear human-like at first, but at her knees, her legs change to a more goat-like form with black cloven hooves at their base.

"Succubus?" Immunda says, blinking confusedly.

A sweet feminine voice echoes from the center of the circle as Immunda moves closer, "Who... are you? Did you summon me?"

I can almost spot a Boston accent, which confuses me. Most demons speak Latin, Aramaic, Hebrew, and a slang sort of Hebrew I've personally identified as Pit Hebrew. How one of those languages could lead to a Boston accent is beyond me.

Immunda now has stepped into the salt circle. "I do not understand, I summoned a demonic prince of Hell, I wanted to summon the Prince of Wrath! Who are you?"

The woman's voice grows sultry, "Oh, you Summoned me?" She drapes her hands over his shoulders.

"Summoned and bound." Immunda chuckles, he moves his hand through her hair.

I narrow my eyes and shake my head, "Fool."

She now chuckles playfully, "I don't remember hearing the binding words..."

Before Immunda can say anything else she kisses him, her tail wrapping around him and pulling him tight against her. Her wings wrap around him and his body glows green.

I look to the salt circle, grabbing a handful of salt from one of the smaller piles that were left over from the creation of the circle

Father Hammond and Father Charpentier are both transfixed on the perverse display before them, but I'm rather certain what the Succubus wants with Immunda, outside of ensuring her freedom. I'm now certain God chose me specifically for this task due to my own personal sin.

Immunda's body stops glowing and she quickly pushes him away. Immunda collapses to the floor, his feet sliding through the salt circle, breaking it.

She moves to exit the circle as soon as his feet slide through.

I hurl the salt in my hand at the opening.

She screams as she touches the restored border and falls back into the center.

I get to my feet, adjusting my vestments.

Father Hammond laughs after breaking himself out of his stupor, "Good Show Father Thomas."

The succubus in the middle of the room is whimpering in pain.

I look at Immunda, his body looks old and feeble, but he is still breathing. It's odd that she did not kill him. I look at the seemingly twenty-something she-demon in the center of the circle, whimpering and now sobbing inside the prison of the salt circle.

Father Charpentier is about to tend to her before I throw my hand out to stop him, with a stern gaze.

We're silent for a good minute before her sobbing stops.

"You guys are jerks!" She shouts, agitated, "Not even tryin' to help a lady!" She rubs her hand, now pulling her knees to her chest and wrapping her wings around herself, her tail, holding her wings closed over her. She almost looks modest.

I decide I'm done with this charade. Immunda said he was going to summon a demon prince, and the creature before me seemed to be a lesser demon known as a succubus. It must be a ruse. I pull out my holy water. "I compel you, demon, give me your name!"

The holy water hits her wings and fizzles. She yelps, shocked by the sensation of the holy water burning her. "Oh! Shit that burns! Stop Stop! Okay! Sara! Sara Baker! My name is Sara Baker! Fuck, stop that!" She unwraps herself and attempts to brush the holy water off her wings, only to wave her hands in the air, blowing on them to dry the purified water burning her unclean flesh.

I stop, my brow furrowing.

Father Hammond closes his bible, "Sara Baker? What sort of name is that for a demoness?"

Sara turns to Father Hammond, "Well it wasn't my mother's plan for me to be a Succubus!"

Father Charpentier throws a spritz of holy water at her, for good measure.

Sara yelps again, "Owowow! Shit stop it, sorry!"

"Americans." I hear Charpentier mumble.

I narrow my eyes on the whore before me, "Sara... Baker... What do you mean, your mother named you? Do you want me to believe that you were a human before you fell?"

Sara looks at me, an exasperated look in her eyes, "All demons were humans once, don't you know that?"

As I stare at the distraught demoness before me I must remind myself she is a demon. To lie is to breathe for her, so I do my best to ignore her cries. I make my way to the door; I ready myself to inform the others we summoned the monster, much to my great disappointment.

It's at this point Immunda's voice rises from the floor, sounding feeble and elderly at first but growing more vigorous as he speaks. "I was... mistaken..."

Turning to him, I notice Immunda's hand clasping the sanguine amber still. No one had taken it from him during the shock of the successful summoning, I realize.

The Sanguine Amber glows as he draws power from it. He rises to his feet, "The whore should have killed me... now I will bind her," He takes a deep agitated breath, "But first to burn you, priests, to ashes," He points his cursed trinket towards me.

I flipped my Bible open and held my rosary beads before me. I read from Psalm 23.

Immunda laughs at me and he screams, "Haborym Fire!"

I sense the heat of his dark illusion approach me, the flames lick at my brow, but I continue to pray, advancing forward, my faith that God's protection will ward off this dark ether. "Even though I walk through the darkest valley, I will fear no evil, for you are with me; your rod and your staff, they comfort me." I spot Immunda's face, shocked as I exit the fire before him, his spell having little to no effect. "You prepare a table before me in the presence of my enemies. You anoint my head with oil; my cup overflows." The cross adorning my rosary beads is hot enough it now burns through my glove to my palm. I must cool it soon, these gloves can only resist so much, but I have a plan to address this situation.

"What?" Immunda shouts as he stares baffled at the amber in his fist, "How could you be unscathed?"

I push the crucifix into his forehead as the cross brands his brow it cools.

Immunda screams in pain.

I pray over his cries of anguish, "Surely your goodness and love will follow me all the days of my life, and I will dwell in the house of the Lord forever."

Immunda now loses consciousness, I follow him down, cradling his head with the opened Bible to prevent him from striking the stone floor. I do this while still holding the cross to his head. I see the brand left on his head by my cross as I remove it and I stand, brushing ash from my vestments and robes. "Amen."

Father Hammond is the first to speak. "Bloody Hell Father Thomas... I thought you were done for."

I glance to Father Hammond, "Remember to place your safety in God's grace and he will lead you through any tribulation."

Father Charpentier speaks, in English, for once, "I would expect no less from Father Thomas."

I turn to the demoness who is staring at me in shock. "Now, to see if the Church can pry any information from this..." I eye her up and down, "...Succubus."

She pulls her knees to her chest and I swear I hear her whimper.

I sit drinking an orange herbal tea in one of the interrogation rooms. The Bishop sits with me, Father Hammond and Father Charpentier. An outgoing Nun named Fatima Ghazzawi, has also joined us in the room. She was a convert from Islam and a wonderful and caring young woman. "Most excellent tea, Sister."

She smiles, "Thank you, Father Thomas."

I glimpse across the divide separating me from the succubus on the other side, a one-way mirror between the two of us.

She has her hands bound by silver chains attached to a table bolted to the floor in the center of the room. She begins to panic, appearing frightened and looking lost.

Father Hammond speaks first, "This seems cruel... if this girl was once human she must have been suffering whilst in Hell. She surely was coerced into giving her spirit over to the darkness." I could always say Father Hammond is a compassionate soul. However, it was this quality of his that always made me fear he lacked the stomach for some exorcisms.

I keep looking at the Succubus, sipping my tea, "Father Hammond, a pact with the devil must be a matter of free will. Under duress or otherwise unable to think one cannot lose their soul. While a demon may torture someone, they cannot take their soul using torture alone. The torture of others, perhaps, but even then to give your soul over in such a situation is still an affront to God." I place my tea down on the table before me. "Do not pity her."

Sister Fatima looks to Father Hammond, "A blasphemer is a blasphemer. It takes faith to fight the darkness." She looks at the woman before us. "Faith to fight our own demons."

I nod to Sister Fatima as I hold her hand to reassure her. "That's right Sister."

Bishop Ricci now interjects, "Who shall be the first to pry her?"

I stand, "I will interrogate her first."

Bishop Ricci hands me a document, "This is the information we need to know."

The document has the following questions printed on it:

1. When is the invasion planned?

2. How large are Hell's forces?

3. Who leads the armies of Hell? The generals, etc.

4. Why are more people being possessed?

I nod to Bishop Ricci while the others wish me luck, and I enter the room with Sister Fatima in tow.

Sister Fatima lights incense in a thurible and swings it, dispersing the incense through the room.

The Succubus glances at Sister Fatima with a pleading gaze, "Please... Sweetie... You gotta help me."

I chime in, "I am Father Edward Thomas" I sit opposite her, ensuring to draw her attention.

The Succubus turns from Sister Fatima, confusion comes over her face as she stares at me. "Oh, what the fuck? They're making *you people* priests?"

I ignore her remarks, looking over at my phone. "You claim to be Sara Baker, of Boston, Massachusetts, yes?"

The Succubus nods, "What of it?"

With a stern gaze I glanced at her, "Sara Baker, when were you born?"

"March fifteenth, nineteen sixty-nine," she gives me an unnerved stare. "Why am I answering you?"

"The incense fills the room and weakens your demonic aura making it easier for me to compel answers from you," I said, as I looked up her information via the Church's database on my smartphone. This database links to multiple sources which it should not. The Church ensures it has access to such things.

She glares at me, her wings folding behind her. "So what, is this a date?" she scoffs, "Then again I'm not your type."

I peek at my smartphone, "Husband David Miller... Son, Jason Miller. Yes?"

Her face softens. "How the fuck did you know?"

"Interesting that you kept your maiden name." I continue, "You were a student at Harvard University on a full scholarship for Molecular Biology." I say reading the information provided by the database.

She strains against the chains. "Why do you know all these things about me?"

I continued to read what I had found. "The highest marks in the program, one of the most promising students, pregnant at 19, married to David Miller, an excellent catch. A rising star in Harvard's legal program, son to a wealthy billionaire."

She struggles still against the chains, "Stop it!"

I observe the chains, they're still holding, I go back to reading, "They found you dead, on your birthday, March fifteenth, nineteen ninety of alcohol poisoning."

The Succubus now calms her struggling and rests in front of me. Her eyes are wide, tears welling up.

"The day you died, that was the day they sealed your dark pact, wasn't it?" I inquire.

Her voice cracks, "You don't understand..."

"You traded your soul for a wonderful life, it seems. A handsome husband, a beautiful child, a sharp mind?" I tuck my phone away. "It only lasted for so long, now didn't it? The pact for your soul came with its own consequences."

The Succubus shuts her eyes tight, "I didn't realize the real price..."

"But you gave up your soul, regardless," I accused.

"They tricked me." The Succubus whispers. "He said he was an angel."

"A Fallen Angel, but even so one cannot trick you into selling your soul, one must be upfront with the terms, you must agree, knowing your soul will be theirs." I fix her with another stern gaze, "Yet you are not human, not any longer. You're a demon, so explain how that came to be."

She gives me a serious stare now, her eyes still pleading, crying for help.

"What was the pact? Explain." I pry.

She closes her eyes as she heaves a sigh, "I was thirteen." Her eyes opened and rose to meet mine, green doe eyes glistening while she adjusted her arms to present her cleavage. "I was... just a girl..."

Waving my hand, unphased, I confess "You'll find that your seduction won't work on me, Succubus."

Under her breath, I'm certain I heard the word "Faggot" escape her lips. She leans back, no longer trying to entice me, "He promised me beauty and charisma for my soul," Her eyes narrowing on me, "I was always intelligent."

I pick up on something odd about her explanation, "Your will is not your own, yet the owner of your soul doesn't require you to call him 'Master'?"

She looks at Fatima with pleading eyes.

I snap my fingers before her, "Focus please."

The Succubus scowls, "My Master isn't the one who I sold my soul to."

"How did that come to be?" I query further.

"The one who bargained for my soul sold me to my current Master," She admits.

"Demons barter with souls of the damned?" I'm not surprised to hear this.

She nods, "All the Fallen do. We're like currency. The transmuted ones, like myself, are the most valuable." She tosses her hair back as a shampoo model would, still trying to entice. Her form is exemplary. "I fetched a high price, as you can tell."

"Whom were you sold to?" I ask, unimpressed by her display.

"My Master Asmodai," She answers, her eyes seeming to glow brighter as she says his name.

"The Lord of Wrath." I sigh, looking at the one-way glass. "That explains Immunda's issue in summoning. He was attempting to summon Asmodai himself, yet instead, we get the one who leeches off of his power, like a lamprey."

The Succubus looks away insulted, "If my Master came you'd all be very dead men."

"Oh? What is it you believe your master would do to us?" I ask.

A glint of joy enters her eyes. "He would swoop down on his mighty dragon, brandish his havoc blade, and swing into you. Wave after wave of you holier than thou kiddie fucking pricks would come at him as he keeps killing you." She takes a ragged breath, exciting herself. "He'd tear into you all, no matter how many of you there were."

"How can you be so certain?" I pry further.

"I've seen him destroy the forces in his own army when they dared to disobey him." She brags, her breath now more labored.

I inspect Sister Fatima to see her blushing. I motion to her to step out of the room.

Sister Fatima blushes and vacates the room, leaving me alone with the Succubus.

"His own forces? I'm sure there are not that many... We could have much more, yes?" So far I've found her bragging to be informative.

The Succubus bites her lower lip now, her wings hugging herself and caressing her shoulders, "hmm hmm..." She snickers, "My Master commands seventy-two legions of demons, ten thousand strong each. He commands them, they obey, or he destroys them by hand. He is powerful, so powerful, My Master..." She trails off in a slight fit of suppressed moans.

I finish jotting down the information, looking at her with a disinterested view.

Her green, emerald eyes now try to entrap me glistening with an enticing display of verdant hues.

I match her gaze, unphased.

The Succubus now drops her facade and glares at the one-way mirror. "I see why you picked this one to do the talking."

"What are your instructions?" I ask as I notice the incense smell is fading and now being replaced by a scent, not unlike lavender. I assume this is her personal pheromone. It smells rather offensive.

She looks at me while leaning back in her chair, "I didn't understand them. Be happy about that. If I did, I could not disobey them. Something about finding 'The Gate', and I do not know where that is." She fixes a grave stare at me, "Don't tell me if you know."

I shrug, "I know not where it is." I jot down the information, "So... You're tasked with opening the gateway to Hell. How did you know you would be here?"

She shakes her head, "An announcement went out to every demon in Hell, that whoever gets summoned had to find the gate and open it. If they summoned my Master, I'm sure you'd all be knee-deep in shit right now."

I stand, the scent she is emitting has grown far too offensive, "Thank you for your time, if you'll excuse me." I leave the room and head back to the others.

Father Hammond gives me an odd eye as I enter the viewing room.

I turn toward Sister Fatima who has continued to swing her thurible in the room, masking the succubus's fragrance.

Bishop Ricci nods "Good work... So, they knew the summoning was happening. We need to exercise caution if anyone is looking to bring a demon into this world as they will attempt to open a gateway. That explains why she attacked her summoner as soon as she could."

Father Hammond adjusts his vestments with a renewed purpose, "I have a few questions for her myself, things we must have answered." Father Hammond makes his way to the door.

I suggest, "Sister, why don't you aid Father Hammond. Make sure the incense is strong." I hand her an earpiece as she passes me.

As Father Hammond exits the room, she takes it and affixes it to her ear.

I watch as they both walk into the room. The door locks behind them both. I press a button on the small AV system on the table. "Sister, please nod twice if you hear me."

Sister Fatima nods but her face is already flush despite her swinging the thurible faster.

"Do not allow the succubus to touch him. And if your resolve slips, you can leave the room, just nod if you understand."

Sister Fatima nods as she stands behind the Succubus.

"Sara Baker." Father Hammond starts, "Let's start with a few questions, yes? No reason to make this painful."

Sister Fatima continues to swing the thurible next to her.

The Succubus shifts and fidgets in her seat. "Can you get rid of that incense?"

Sister Fatima says, "No, it counteracts your musk."

The Succubus looks Fatima over from head to toe. "What the Hell is someone like you doing being a nun anyway, sweetness?"

As I suspected, The Succubus can only seduce someone if they are attracted to her. Sister Fatima's peculiarity renders her more vulnerable, while my peculiarity protects me.

Father Hammond clears his throat, "Are you treated well... Where you are?"

"It's... Hell." The Succubus answers, sarcastically.

Concerned that the Succubus may compromise her, I appraise Sister Fatima's condition. Praying for Sister Fatima I make sure I keep my eye on her.  My faith in her resolve is strong, and I pray for Father Hammond's as well.

"Can you let me out of here? Please? I escaped Hell already, and it's like you guys are trying to make it seem like Hell on Earth here. The incense is burning my eyes and I want to go outside, just once, it's been so long. I want to see the sun. It's been decades. Please? Father?" The Succubus pleads.

Father Hammond appears nervous, "First we need to have you answer our questions."

The Succubus now looks hurt, "Could you... At least tell me what year it is?"

Father Hammond nods, smiling, "It's the year of our Lord 2018."

The Succubus's face falls, "You... You mean like... 2118? Or... Or 2218?"

Father Hammond shakes his head, "No my dear."

Her lip quivers, "No... No no!" She now cries, tears streaming down her face. "You cannot tell me that was only twenty-eight years!" She sobs. "Only  twenty-eight  ... It seemed like decades upon decades!!" She bawls now, gasping and sobbing in a rather ugly fashion.

I see Sister Fatima place her hand to her mouth, her own eyes welling up.

The Succubus reaches out toward Father Hammond as he offers her his hand.

I shout into Sister Fatima's earpiece, "Do not let her touch him, Fatima! It's a ruse! Get out of there, the both of you!"

The instant I said this Sister Fatima reacted, dropping the thurible, and grabbing Father Hammond's hands.

I unlock the door and Sister Fatima rushes them both to the door.

The Succubus's voice raises in volume, a low growl emanating from her.

I stand up ready, yet, I am not at all prepared for what comes next.

The Succubus slams her hands against the table, it breaks off the bolts on the floor from the initial impact, "No! NO! It can't be! It can't! Belial, that sick fuck Mammon! That bitch Esmeralda! Every one of them! I wasn't there for barely thirty years! I couldn't have! They've tortured me for centuries!"

The Succubus screams, dragging her fingernails across the table, scoring it with her claw-like nails, her wings flapping and her tail lashing about in a fit of rage.

"You bastards! You lying fucks! I was there longer! You can't tell me every year I was in Hell was only a few months! You can't!" She slams her fists down onto the table, cracking it in half, and breaking her chains. Her eyes now glow green as I realize the error we've made. A dark power is swirling around her, amplified by her anger, fueled by her rage.

She was hiding this power somehow, and now it was more than clear. Immunda had summoned a powerful demon.

I dash into the hallway trying to find the best way to warn them of The Succubus's true power, "She's a berserker!"

Father Hammond stumbles into the hallway looking distressed.

The Succubus bursts through the doorway, grabbing hold of Sister Fatima as she does so with an unholy strength. Her glowing eyes now seem to cast a green aura around her, a foul stench fills the halls, and she screams with an ungodly power so loud and piercing it shatters the glass in the adjoining room.

I sense a heat pulsing off her body as she rushes past me, hurling me against the wall and her free hand grabs Bishop Ricci. A burst of wind forces Father Hammond and I to the floor as she flies down the hallway.

I get to my feet along with Father Hammond. Soon Father Charpentier joins us as we rush toward the stairs. I glance to the cells, seeing Immunda still inside, on the way past it I grab the Sanguine Amber, putting it into my pocket as we make our way out of the prison level. I consider that this bauble must be the key to sealing the Succubus back into Hell. At the landing of the staircase, we come to find Bishop Ricci's body.

Bishop Ricci looks battered and broken on the top of the stairs, Father Hammond rushes to his aide as Father Charpentier calls out for someone to call an ambulance.

I rush out into the office near the steps, dread washing over me. I do not see Sister Fatima or The Succubus.

She's escaped. My worst fears have come to fruition.

Father Hammond curses, "She wasn't a woman Father Thomas... You were right... She's far more powerful than we thought. She almost convinced me otherwise."

Father Charpentier frowns at both of us, "Mon Dieu, pardonne notre Hubris."

# CHAPTER 2

## *Salvation*

Father Hammond closes the door to the hidden prison as I examine Bishop Ricci to determine if he is still alive.

I curse myself under my breath, I should never have been a party to this madness!  At this moment a demoness with abilities I can only imagine is now running wild across the Vatican.  Worse yet, we have no one to blame but ourselves.

I stand back as a pair of paramedics rush Bishop Ricci onto a stretcher though I am unsure if they can do anything for him.  Father Charpentier informs them that the Bishop suffered a nasty fall, and for the time being, they do not ask for clarification.  Resting against the now sealed door of the prison level, I do my best to take stock of the situation.

"We left no one down below, did we?" Father Hammond asks me.

"No Father," I say as I shake my head, "The only ones down below are the prisoners." As I say this I am filled with doubt, however, I can overhear the sounds of something scratching at the sealed door.

"Then what is that?" Father Hammond asks.

I spring myself away from the door and face it.  Father Charpentier, Father Hammond, and I ready our crosses and holy water.

Behind the door, I can make out a voice and further scratching noises until the lock clicked.  The door creaked open but a crack. I pick up a Hispanic accent in what sounds, at first, like English but his words seem to shift and change as he talks, regardless I have no issues understanding any one phrase but, as odd as this sounds, I cannot place what language he is speaking in.

"Well that was easier to pick than I thought!" The door opened and I identified a middle-aged man of Hispanic descent.  He's wearing a button-down shirt and jeans, and a pair of boots.  The most noticeable items on him were; a necklace with a strange stone in the middle, and what looks like three round bottles strapped to his belt.

"Who in the name of God are you?" Father Hammond asks.

The man before us looks to each of us in a state of bewilderment before cracking a jovial smile and waving to each of us, "Oh, hello Fathers!"

Again I cannot place what language he is using. I ask now, "Who are you? How did you get down there?"

He appears as if we're keeping him from something, motioning to head down the stairs as he speaks with us. "Oh, well my name is Jorge Chavez! Heh, um... I know this will sound funny but where are we right now?"

Father Charpentier responds, "La cité du Vatican."

Jorge nods, and makes the sign of the cross over himself, "I didn't mean to intrude then... uh... but that makes little sense. We were chasing a demon."

"We?" I interject.

From the steps below abrupt heavy footsteps echo from the stairs at an inhuman pace. I listen as each footfall grows louder and angrier.

Before I can say much else, a man standing six foot three with short black hair and striking blue eyes is standing in the doorway. He wears a black trench coat over a simple white cotton shirt. The shirt is form-fitting, his well-toned muscles show he's a physically fit man. A pair of simple pants and heavy black boots are the last normal items on his person. On his belt are a row of the same strange, rounded bottles Jorge carried, on the other side is a large knife with an ornate handle of brass and ivory.

His voice strikes me with harsh disapproval, "What have you fools done?" He demands.

Father Hammond now moves to shut the door to the office we are all standing in. "Now listen here, whoever you are-" Before Father Hammod can respond, Jorge interjects.

"Oh, this is Saint Timothy Crestfall," Jorge introduces.

Timothy casts a chastising glance at Jorge, "Chavez, we discussed this."

Jorge rolls his eyes, turning to Father Charpentier, "He's modest."

"Saint Timothy?" Father Charpentier asks.

Timothy shakes his head, waving his hands exasperated, "Where is it? Are you hiding it? Or are you all compromised?"

I gaze toward Timothy and try to think how to best answer and decide to play coy. "Where is what?"

Timothy grows frustrated and grabs me by my robes on either shoulder, lifting me up with ease, and forcing my back to the wall. "The Amber. The demons call it Sanguine Amber. Someone used it for something. I need to know what!"

Pinned to the wall and unable to do much else, I reach into my pocket and show the small half dollar-sized disk I had grabbed from the prison below.

Timothy releases me and plucks the Amber from my fingers. "Thank God..."

Jorge also looks relieved, "When we noticed it had power channeling through it, it worried us."

Timothy places it into his pocket, calming as a smile crosses his face. "Yes. The last time this even crossed onto the physical plane a demon prince tried to pull himself into existence." Timothy looks to each of us with relief washing over his face. "I'm glad we found this before someone used it for some dark purpose."

The mood of the room was that of disgrace and silence. Not one of us could speak or admit what we had been culpable to. I looked to the floor, ashamed.

Despite not looking at him, I could tell a grave mood settled over Timothy. "...What happened?"

The first of us to break our silence was Father Hammond, "The warlock, Immunda, he summoned a demon for us to interrogate."

Timothy gazes at me appalled as I nod my head, "We were gaining valuable information until she broke free of our bonds." I soon experienced a fist towards my gut. Father Hammond and Charpentier are flanking me, trying to defend me.

Timothy has moved on after hitting me with a powerful strike. Timothy clenches his fist "Was it a possession or did you fools pull him into our world?"

Father Charpentier answers, in English, "It was a she, a succubus."

"A follower of Asmodai." I gasp as I regain my breath. "She escaped with Sister Fatima as a hostage."

Timothy closes his eyes and I swear I catch a faint voice in the back of my mind. "Sister Fatima? Where are you?"

I peek around but cannot place the voice's source.

Timothy's eyes bolt open and he rushes out of the room.

Jorge, the other priests and myself are soon in tow but keeping up with Timothy proves to be difficult for all of us.

Timothy dodges and weaves through halls of people and objects, traversing with an inhuman grace to each step. We all follow him to a massive room with a high ceiling with ornate archways and artwork adorning the walls and ceilings. Timothy is standing in the middle of the room as we catch up with him.

He glances at us all, "She's disguised both herself and Fatima." He pulls a bottle from his pocket and closes his eyes once more.

I glance around trying to detect the deception. Someone I haven't seen before; someone I do not know or I find out of place.

Timothy's arm lashes out into a group of nuns and drags a dark-skinned woman from the group. He tilts a rounded bottle over the struggling woman's head and steam erupts from her brow as the contents spill out. A familiar inhuman scream echoes through the chamber.

The nun grabs her face and the cloth that was her habit, wrapped around her, turning from black to purple, gaining a leathery texture. The form of The Succubus soon bursts from behind the wings, Fatima's hands bound by her tail. "Will you people leave me..." She takes a deep breath, shouting and with unholy resonance, "Alone!" Her voice echoes through the chamber and I can hear stained glass cracking and shattering in some windows.

Everyone inside the chamber panics and rushes to the doors, many injured by the falling glass, some far worse than others.

Everyone except Father Charpentier, Father Hammond, Jorge, Timothy, and myself that is.

Timothy stares the woman down, his hand on his bowie knife. "No." He declares.

The Succubus now rolls her eyes in exasperation. "Then let me spell it out for you! I'm not going back, not now, not ever! I'm free, if you can't leave me the fuck alone then you will get a free sample of what I'm leaving!" With a deep breath she spews a black flame at Timothy's feet. The fire rushes up to engulf him while the rest of us dive to the floor to avoid the flames.

I roll onto my back and prop myself up with my arms as I shield my eyes from the black flames. The flames swirl and lift from the ground. The flames seem to pass over Timothy's head as they land in front of him, black smoke rising from his ruined trench coat.

It is not the deflected fire that has my attention, however, nor is it the fearful stare that has crossed The Succubus's face upon the flames being blocked by the heavy coat. My attention is on a pair of flawless silvery wings attached to Timothy's back.

My mouth is agape as I observe the image before me. An Angel, Saint Timothy, that is what Jorge meant when he introduced us.

Timothy now brandishes the large blade of his knife. "Submit, demon!"

"Oh, are you fucking serious right now...?" The Succubus's wicked voice has a hint of hysteria. "What the Hell... You guys were all dead! No one down there will stop bragging about it! What hole did you crawl out of?" It seems she's stalling.

Timothy narrows his ice blue eyes, "I liked that coat, demon. I will make a new one out of your wings."

The Succubus looks to her wings, and spreads them, "Oh yeah, those." She jumps into the air, her wings hurtling her toward the ceiling.

Timothy follows suit, his own wings empowering him upwards.

Sister Fatima cries out in fear as it pulls her into the air.

"Release the woman!" Timothy shouts, swinging his blade only to have it knocked back by the Succubus's hoof.

"Sorry choir boy! She's my snack for the trip!" The Succubus reaches the ceiling, by some unholy power standing on it as if it were the floor. Her cloven hoof beats down against the ceiling, causing it to crack. "You're lucky, caroler! If they had summoned me wearing my armor, I'd rip your damn arms off! Instead..." Her hoof crashes down against the ceiling again, portions of it falling apart. "I'll just use your own compassion."

To my shock and dismay, I spot large chunks of the ceiling rushing toward my fellow priests.

The Succubus lets out a vicious chortle as Timothy's flight diverts to the priests and myself.

Timothy pushes Father Hammond and Father Charpentier out of the way.

I felt a wave of relief wash over me until I watched Timothy running towards me. My attention turned upwards just in time to notice a huge slab of the ceiling heading towards me. My eyes shut as I make my peace with God before I catch a crunch, a snap, and a gasp of pain.

I notice Timothy's straining face inches in front of mine. Timothy collapsed after I crawled out from underneath him, the slab on his back. With a yell to Father Charpentier and Father Hammond, I get their help, and with the help of Jorge, we pull the broken concrete off of Timothy.

Timothy's left-wing looks to be bent at an odd angle and his arm appears broken, he wheezes and coughs, though I spot no blood escaping his mouth.

Jorge moves to his side, and helps Timothy to his feet, acting as Timothy's crutch, "Can you walk?"

Timothy nods, but after a step, he falters.

As I rush to his other side I catch him, acting as his crutch for his other side, but being careful of his broken wing and arm.  I give a grim stare toward Jorge, "Where can we take him?"

Jorge grunts, "There's the Temple of the Guardians.  We can heal him there."

"Where is the temple?" I ask.

Jorge frowns "It's at the bottom of those stairs."

After an arduous journey, Jorge and I got Timothy back down into the prison level.  The sight before me is shocking. Affixed to one wall which was bare is a pair of double doors.

"That's the entrance to the Temple," Jorge grunts.

I heave Timothy into the doors, and as I do, I overhear Immunda chortle behind me from his cell.

"Oh, papist… You know not what you will discover.  Your hopes, your dreams, they lay broken behind that door."

For once, I heed the warlock's words.  I regard the room we are now standing in, seeing a pair of massive marble statues illuminated with bright spotlights from the floor.

Before I can assess the room more, Timothy looks to the doors as they shut behind us, Timothy appraises me "None… Of you… Are worthy to enter." He fades out of consciousness.

"We have a way to go," Jorge says.

He is right.  We move to the right of the doors leading us down a series of lengthy staircases and a labyrinth of corridors.  After twenty minutes of walking down yet another flight of stairs, I consider my surroundings, noticing that despite the beautiful marble, the angelic and gothic architecture, there is no one else within the Temple.

"Where is everyone?" My voice echoes against the hallways.

Jorge stares at me horrified, "Please don't Father.  No one hears you here." His expression is that of disappointment, "At least not anymore."

I fear being more and more isolated in this strange temple.  While there is no tomb-like air or scent the atmosphere is empty and the lack of any kind of population inside is unnerving.

Jorge looks to Timothy as he comes back to consciousness again, "Almost there Saint Timothy."

We round a corner and I spot a massive fountain. A fountain is an understatement, but no other word fits. Waterfall? The entire wall has crystal clear water streaming down it into a massive basin. There are steps leading into the water and again it is the clearest water I have ever laid my eyes upon.

Jorge lays Timothy down near the basin's edge and gives him a shove.

"Are you insane? He will drown!" I protest.

Moments later, however, a bright shimmering light bursts out from the water's depths. Timothy breaches the water, both wings spread wide and healed. His eyes are an even brighter shade of blue and he clamors out of the basin, gasping for breath.

"Chavez!" He shouts.

Jorge heaves a sigh of relief. "Thank you, Jesus..."

"Never do that!" Timothy's eyes are glowing and he grabs his head as if his skull is about to burst open and his hands are the only things keeping it from doing so. He grunts in pain, water dripping down his body.

I avert my eyes, his white shirt translucent and displaying more of his physicality than I am comfortable viewing without my sin tainting the image. I speak to both while looking away from Timothy, "We need to call in reinforcements... As it involves the Angels thanks to our foolhardy meddling."

Jorge discloses, "Well... We are the reinforcements."

I hear Timothy groaning in pain behind me, hearing him shift and lament.

"What do you mean?" I inquire as I turn to Jorge.

Jorge motions to Timothy, "You see Father... This is the last Angel on Earth."

I turn now, the gravity of the statement distracting me from all other things. "What do you mean?"

Jorge motions around, "We're in the realm of the Angels. The Guardian Temple of Enoch." Jorge points to Timothy. "That is Timothy of Enoch. Great Grandson of Saint Enoch himself..." The last words reverberate through the empty halls of the temple and strike my nerves to their core, "And the last surviving angel in this temple."

*"The last surviving angel in this temple."*

My ears scarcely can inform my mind what Jorge means before the next phrase escapes my lips. "Angels are not physical beings." I know these saints, angels, and so forth live in Heaven.

Jorge shrugs, "Yes and no?" Jorge heaves a sigh and moves to a small first aid box near the waters. "As Timothy puts it, Angels are of one existence. Man has their mind, body, and soul. Your mental health, your physical health, and your spirit you know?"

"The Holy Trinity." I clarify.

Jorge stops for a moment, eyes going wide in revelation. "Oh, yeah!"

My face falls as now I'm uncertain who is informing whom.

"Well, man has those as three separate things, but for angels, it's all one. If you damage an Angel's body, it harms their soul as well.  If you harm their mind, it can affect their body, and if you harm their soul..." Jorge sighs as he hands Timothy some headache medicine.

I turn my attention to Timothy, who takes four pills and swallows them, without water.

"So, someone..." I begin but am interrupted as Timothy finishes my thoughts.

"Destroyed every Angel's physical body...  They're now trapped in heaven..." He winces, grabbing a hold of his head. "Chavez... we agreed... about the water... didn't we?"

Jorge nods, "Let's get you to bed."

Timothy attempts to walk but stumbles, Jorge moving to him.  I notice Timothy's eyes clamp down in pain, a tear or two rolling down his cheek.  "He... is sobbing... again... I can hear him.  Father... please... stop... I'm trying."

Despite me hearing the term 'Father' often, something tells me I'm not the one whom he is talking about.  "He is sobbing?"

Timothy's eyes are wide and now frightened, "He, who is called I Am."

Jorge nods, "Timothy is descended from Enoch, that mea-"

Before Jorge can finish, I'm by Timothy's side and helping him to his feet.  "He speaks for God."

Jorge nods.

"I can't... I listen to him... I listen to his old words. They're bouncing around in my head so... only after the waters heal me.  I hear everything, his unanswered words, unspoken, for over three hundred years..." Timothy's eyes close as he shouts now, "Tearing my head apart!"

Body, Mind, and Soul all in one, not separate.  That is what Jorge said, so despite the physical injury, they also wound Timothy on the other fronts.  "Where is your room, Timothy?  You need rest."

Timothy shakes his head, "The demon... I..."

"You're in no state to chase demons," I interject.  "You must rest, you cannot run in as you are."

Timothy grits his teeth, "I can push through it... I... I have to.  If I fail... we are all doomed."

His shoulders are burdened by the weight he must carry, and I look to Jorge who helps me carry him onward.  Proverbs 12:25 rings through my mind, '*An anxious heart weighs a man down, but a kind word cheers him up.*' Perhaps between Jorge and I we can tend to his damaged mind and soul. "Timothy, heed God's words: 'Do not worry about tomorrow, for tomorrow will worry about itself. Each day has enough trouble of its own.'"

Timothy turns his blue eyes, burning with intensity, fear, and a glimmer of hope.

For the moment I turn away, feeling a blush on my face. I recall Sodom and now understand why so many were drawn to the Angel's God had sent down to the ancient city.  My lust restrained, as always, as I thought of God's strength.  "Cast your cares on the Lord and He will sustain you; He will never let the righteous fall." I glance back to Timothy, "That means you."

Timothy chuckles though still in pain.

We arrive in a room with a pair of cots.  Jorge and I lay Timothy down on one.  Afterwards Timothy seems more at peace as we leave him to rest.

"I must get to the others in the Vatican," I told Jorge.

Jorge sighs, "Yeah about that, Timothy closed the doors."

"So, let's open them," I explain, making my way to the Temple's entrance.

Jorge follows behind me, trying to explain as he goes, "We can and can't.  Timothy has better control over where they open, but when we open them, they go to the place we desire to be. So, for you if that's the Vatican then it should work but..."

As Jorge and I reach the doors, I go to open them, only to find them locked shut.

Jorge sighs, "They don't always work for us."

Glancing at Jorge, I step away from the door, "Can you?"

Jorge shakes his head, "I'm not able to open them any more than you are." He moves to the doors and tries, but they do not even jostle.

I heave a heavy sigh, "How long before Timothy will be well enough to open these gates?"

Jorge looks to the doors and then back down the corridor we had exited.  "Last time was three days."

A sense of irony washes over me. Three days to rise, that makes sense.  "Well, to a more pressing matter then, what do we do until then?"

Jorge just beams at me despite the situation, "Hungry?"

Perhaps I am a spoiled man, but three solid days of Spam and rice is far too many days of Spam and rice. Regardless, food is not an issue through the three days leading up to Timothy's full recovery. Throughout the time there, he seemed to suffer less and less and even wandered out of his room.

I followed him on one odd jaunt as he walked to an area of the temple, I had not seen him go to. What I saw shocked me.

Timothy standing at the edge of a marble cliff is the only way I can describe it. I looked behind me to see the outside of the temple. Massive was a poor word to describe its towering spires and colossal pillars. But outside of this temple, it all came to an edge, an end so to speak. The marble floor continued until it did not and ended in a massive black void. The sky was full of stars and darkness, and nothing more.

"Where are we?" I ask.

Timothy doesn't address me but stares off into space. "The Expanse. Everything God made is before us."

As I walk next to him, I can see no familiar constellation or heavenly body. "Where is this temple?"

Timothy continues to stare, "The center of the universe. At least the habitable part."

I can only nod and look out in wonder.  Timothy walks back inside.

"I smell Spam," Is all Timothy says as we walk back inside.

As I trail behind Timothy I ask a simple question, "What is Chavez?  A man? Angel?  Are you companions?" I pause for a moment, "Lovers?"

Timothy doesn't stop walking, "Chavez is for all intents and purposes the new curator of the Temple.  He is human, a good man, a God-fearing man.  He keeps me grounded." Timothy scrutinizes me, "He's a companion, a partner, an assistant.  Not a lover." Timothy turns from me as we continue.  "I would have thought you, as a Priest, would be against such things."

Silence fills the air for a few moments as I try to find the most appropriate way to explain myself.  "I have taken the vow of chastity they expect of any priest.  The Church always views the homosexual behavior of two men as a sin. But all pleasures of the flesh are sin." I look to him, "Marriage, however, is not a sin.  Marriage allows for pleasures of the flesh with one's wife or husband." I chuckle as I explain, "The Church also isn't naïve.  We understand most married couples haven't had sex on their wedding night alone."

Timothy seems to be waiting for a point.

I confess, "I am... Well homosexual, but again, celibate. However, I feel that if I weren't if I were to find someone to love well..."

Timothy's stopped walking, and I do the same.

"God is love," I finished.

Timothy smiles and continues his walking. "I love a woman named Sofia. She thinks I'm deployed and human. She's smart, hard to trick," He looks down, face falling. "... If I do ever consummate my love with her, my gifts go to our child. I will lose everything."

My heart skips a beat or two as I realize why there is a line of Enoch. "God allows Enoch children... But all other angels are not."

Timothy nods.

"The Nephilim. You are Nephilim," I realize.

Timothy nods, "Enoch was the only angel allowed to continue to have children, but to prevent what happened before God flooded the world, there can only be one true child of Enoch at a time." Timothy eyes his wings, "If I do what I want, If I do the selfish thing, then the only hope we have has to wait till my child comes of age." He shakes his head, "I can't place that burden on my child. I can't even accept that someone has placed it on me." He looks back into the expanse behind us. "So, I'm also kind of celibate." Timothy didn't speak for the rest of that day.

I did not pry into the matter further.

# CHAPTER 3

## *The Hunt*

On the third day, Timothy emerges composed, wearing another black coat and heading right for the doors before even saying a word to Chavez or myself.

"The time for resting is over. She's gotten enough of a head start," Timothy announces.

I followed Chavez, getting my vestments, "Timothy, if I may: I would suggest we go to the Vatican, I can retrieve my tools, perhaps bless them in the waters here, and then we must make haste to the Succubus's destination."

Timothy glances at me as he opens the doors to the prison, "Are you sure of where she's going?"

"Where she will be," I said with confidence.

We make our way out of the prison level and I see the debris still lying around the floor, construction crews still working on repairing what The Succubus had done.

"I thought they would have been further along in cleaning this up," I mention as I pass by several halls.

"Only a day passed here on Terra while we were in the Temple," Timothy informs.

Chavez nods, "Time is funny in there."

After collecting several tools needed, and informing the other Priests where we were off to, we headed back to the Temple.

Timothy addresses me before he enters the doors, "In order for you to get where the Succubus is, we need to find the exact location in your mind."

"I'm aware of the location, the Cathedral of the Holy Cross in Boston. She will be in the city, and I know that church well enough," I explain.

"Can you remember the basement?" Timothy asks.

"Well enough," I claim.

Timothy then places his hands on my shoulders once we're inside the Temple and shuts the doors. "Think of the location," He instructs.

I close my eyes, picturing the basement of the church.

Timothy opens the doors and before my eyes, we're where I imagined us to be.

We step out into the basement and make our way up to the main floor.

I turn to Timothy and Jorge, "I must explain why I'm here again, I'm sure, but if anyone else asks just state, you're my assistants."

Jorge nods and gives me a thumbs up while Timothy says little.

As we enter the main hall, the priest of the cathedral greets me, to my surprise. I doubt he has had time to get any contact from the Vatican. "Ah, Father Thomas. I'm happy they sent you!" I recall the priest as Father Connor Walsh.

A handshake ensues, and I clarify, "I was in the area, Father Walsh. I am not sure who you're talking about sending for me."

Father Walsh looks to Timothy and Chavez, and then me once more, "Well, the exorcism request."

Confusion crosses my face before Timothy interjects, "Possession? Who is possessed?"

Father Walsh frowns, "It's the young Jason Miller Jr, I'm afraid"

The blood rushes from my face, "Jason Miller... Was his father David Miller? Mother... Sara Baker?"

Father Walsh smiles "Yes. So you received my request?"

"What is their address, Father?" Timothy demands.

A short cab ride later leads Timothy and I to a series of large row homes, all the same, red-bricked buildings, and concrete stoops. I inspect the address on the paper. I spot the proper house number, and with Timothy behind me, I knock on the door.  Jorge remained behind with Father Walsh to ensure no one entered the Temple doors.

Less than a minute passes as someone opens the door.  A middle-aged man with brown hair and familiar green eyes stands before me. "Ah, yeah listen we already go to church so if-"

"They told us that there may be a possible possession here?", I interjected.

"Oh, Jesus Christ, fucking Marie..." The man stops himself, "Sorry Father.  My son's been acting up, playing hooky and shit... She called the church and I have more pressing matters in the house.  I have a few units on the way to button it up, we didn't mean to trouble you."

From his manor to his foul mouth, I am certain he is The Succubus's child. "Jason?"

Jason laughs,  "It's nothing the church has to worry about. Just caught this prowler out in the backyard.  A mental health patient or homeless, she's harmless, I have her cuffed in the dining room.  Like I said, cops will be by to take care of her."

I cleared my throat, "Mr. Miller, if I may, the possessed child is one reason we're here, but the woman is another."

Jason shakes his head, "Father, listen, now isn't a good time."

"She claims to be your mother, yes?  That she has been... Away for some time and has wanted to see you?" I speak hoping I can get by his defenses, I have no desire to have Timothy force his way past the man.

Jason stops for a moment, looking the both of us over. "How the fuck..."He steps back. "Listen if she's yours then... Ah, take her I guess?"

The two of us walk in after being shown to the dining room where we spot the Succubus handcuffed and sitting at the kitchen table. She's in a human form, however, her horns hiding, her clothing looking like those of a vagrant's.

The Succubus addresses us frowning, "Not here.... Please? You know why I'm here."

Timothy has a seat across from her, "And you know why I'm here."

The Succubus closes her eyes tight, a tear rolling down her cheek. "Just leave me be, okay? I have no desire to open the gate, I want to be with my family."

Jason follows us in, "So, eh, 'Sara', these nice folks from the Church said they know you. Maybe you can head back with them?"

The Succubus gives Jason a sweet look, "Jason, honey, you haven't finished telling me about how you became a detective."

"See what I mean Father? She's claiming to be my mother. Who died right after I was born, I might add," Jason says addressing me.

The Succubus continues, ignoring the latter part of Jason's response, "What about your father? I'd like to see him... I'm sure he could also prove who I am to you?"

Jason narrows his eyes, "Yeah sure, why not go visit him, he's out in Forest Hills."

Her face falls, and she looks away from us.

"Where is Forest Hills?" Timothy asks me.

I clear my throat as I inform Timothy, "It's a cemetery."

The front door opens, and I overhear an exasperated woman, "Junior… please… for the love of God…"

We turn to see a woman in her mid-thirties, dirty blond hair, and a rather large coat opening the door as a boy rushes into the house, the spitting image of his father. He runs into the room and stops dead upon seeing all of us in the dining room. The boy's face is still, his eyes looking far away and yet focused with an eerie stare. A stare I am well accustomed to. Out of nowhere, he grins a vicious and unnerving grin. "Hello, Father."

Jason goes to pick up his child but seems unable to lift him off the floor. "Junior, stop this bullshit, okay?"

"Lazy Whore," The child spits out.

Jason now crouches in front of his son, "Watch your mouth there Junior, don't make me pop you one in front of the Father, okay?"

With an inhuman strength, the boy flings his father across the room, he lands on the table before us.

I check Jason's pulse to see he's still alive.

"Jason!" The mother of the child shouts as she runs to her husband.

The Succubus stands up, "Leave them alone!"

"He's going to fuck you in so many new wholes whore," The boy spat.

The Succubus freezes, "… Just leave them alone, okay?  I wanted to be free for a short time."

My holy water at the ready, I fling a good amount on the child.

I can hear his screams, but before I can say another word I hear a sickening crack. The boy has broken his own thumb. "The next spritz… I break another finger…"

My eyes narrow, most demons cause little harm to their vessels, at least not like this.

"Junior, what did you do?" His mother shouts.

Consoling the mother is all I can think to do at this point before the child speaks again.

"Jerusalem, in the Temple Mount, the gate is there, The Seal needs to be broken…" His hand moves to another finger, "…or I break the child."

The Succubus's eyes go wide, "No…"

The Boy grins, "Time is wasting whore," A look of dread washes over the young boy's face.  He looks to his hand and screams in pain, the demon relinquishing his control over the child.

As his mother rushes to his aid, she calls 911 on her cell phone.

The Succubus tries to move toward the child, before the mother picks him up, glaring at her.

"Whoever the fuck you are, get the Hell away from *my* family, you got it?" The boy's mother shouts.

The Succubus glares, "It's my family too!"

The boy's cries stop, and his mother, Marie, glances at his face, finding it turning blue.  "Junior!" She cries.

I rush to her and take the boy, looking for a pulse and still finding one.  He is not breathing, I pull him from her arms and lay the boy on the ground.  "He's going into shock." I turn to the Succubus, hoping to keep her there longer, "Elevate his legs."

Marie begins to explain what is going on to the operator on the phone.

The Succubus does as I ask, and Timothy is standing behind her, preventing her escape.  "Is this my fault?" She asks.

"Yes, it is," I state as I tilt the boy's head back and give him mouth to mouth.  I check his pulse, while weak his heart is still pumping, his chest rising and falling with my breaths.

After my last breath into the boy's chest, he speaks, "Remind you of Father Damascus?"

I freeze, looking the possessed boy in the eyes, he is breathing again, but his eyes are not his own.

"Leave this boy, demon," I demand.

"My master Asmodai has a simple message.  If the slut doesn't leave, the boy dies.  I can kill it if I like, then I'll move on to the father, then the mother," The demon threatens.

My equipment at the ready, I prepare to begin casting out the demon, but the boy stops breathing yet again.  I continue my first aid until a pair of uniformed officers arrive.  The boy starts breathing once the officers arrive, "Father, is that what kissing a girl is like?"

The Succubus gets up, "You pervert! That's my nephew!"

Before I can defend myself I'm tackled to the floor and restrained. Timothy is detained as well as the officers fall for the Succubus's deception.

It's not until Marie has explained the situation multiple times, and the paramedics arrive, that myself and Timothy are out of handcuffs, the officers not letting us go until a good hour of investigation.

Upon our release, Timothy and I cannot locate the Succubus. Suffering yet another defeat we head back toward the Church and Temple gates within it.

"Father Damascus?" Timothy asks as we make our way back. He is fuming but seems to be trying to place his mind elsewhere.

I'm silent for a while before I confess, "He was... A priest when I was a boy. He was not as good as I in resisting temptation."

Timothy closed his eyes, "People like that make me lose faith in humanity."

Concern crosses my brow, "You don't mean that, do you?"

Timothy shakes his head as we get to the church. "This is the second time I failed. The third time's a charm... But the demon isn't alone now. There's a boy possessed."

"Priorities." I state, "The demon is harming the boy too much, he needs to remain at the hospital for now. I cannot perform an exorcism while the demon is this active. After Junior is tended to this demon will be sent back into Hell, I will see to that. But for now, the demon seems more than content to follow Asmodai's orders and may even kill the boy outright if we continue." I heaved a sigh, "I need to find Sister Fatima, however, it appears something separated her and the Succubus at some point."

Timothy's brow creases in thought, "The Succubus took time to get here. I doubt she flew over the Atlantic Ocean on her own with Sister Fatima, they had to have taken a plane."

"Then why wasn't Sister Fatima with her when we visited the Miller home?" I asked.

Timothy gave me a bemused stare, "I have an idea what may have happened. Father, you head to the airport and speak to the security there, I have a good feeling that is where you'll find Sister Fatima."

Timothy had gone ahead to Jerusalem to guard the Temple while I found myself at Logan International Airport, attempting to speak to the TSA there. I have had easier times exorcizing demons than gaining an audience with the security desk.

"Father, I understand you're looking for someone but I can't let you see our detainees because you're a priest," The TSA Officer explained.

Exasperated, I continue, "I am not concerned with the detainees, I'm concerned if you have seen a nun of middle eastern descent. She was traveling against her will, her name is Sister Fatima Ghazzawi, I am here to find her and return her home."

The TSA Officer heads back from the desk and I'm brought to a waiting room of some sort after some time.

Another Officer walks out with Sister Fatima in tow, her face lights up when she sees me. "Father Thomas!"

We embrace as we're reunited.

Sister Fatima explains, "She forced me to buy plane tickets to Boston. She made me spend all of my money, Father. I felt compelled, she had some otherworldly control over me. I was so frightened! When we got here, I knew I had to get away from her somehow, so I did the only thing I could think of, so as to draw the authorities' attention."

"What was that?" I asked.

The officer answered for her, "She shouted 'Allahu Akbar' in the middle of the airport."

Sister Fatima blushed shyly.

A smile crosses my face as I place my hand on her shoulder, "Well done, Fatima."

They allowed Sister Fatima and I to leave after we gave them the Succubus's human description, and the police confirmed that the same woman attacked Detective Jason Miller. I suppose that story played better than his own possessed son knocking him unconscious. We arrived at the

Church, finding the temple doors opened with Jorge waiting for us once we entered the basement.

Jorge addresses us both, "Timothy just got back from the Temple... Um, not good news."

Jorge closes the doors behind us after we enter the Temple.

I find Timothy standing near a pair of colossal doors, looking over the impressive carvings and artwork of Angels triumphing over various demons.  At the top of the doors depicts a lizard-like man, with scaled wings and a giant cross-bearing shield.

"Had she tried for the seal?" I ask.

Timothy shakes his head, "The IDF is outrageous.  They won't let me, an 'American', in and sure as Hell won't be letting a priest or anyone else in right now.  I tried to get specialized permission, but they said it could cause an 'incident'.  The place is a powder keg from what I understand."

"Easier for someone who can disguise themselves with dark magic than for us then?" I frown.

Timothy nods and then looks to Sister Fatima.  "... But some of us could pass through security checkpoints easier than others."

"What do you mean?" I question, glancing to Sister Fatima

Sister Fatima fidgets, "I have no desire to see that creature again."

Timothy nods, "You won't, I promise... But you may need to wear a Hijab."

"Excuse me?" I object, "What are you talking about?"

"Muslim women can gain unrestricted access to the Temple Mount. The Succubus will be posing as one, if Sister Fatima can do the same, all she needs to do is to commune with me, and I can open the Temple doors inside."

Sister Fatima, before we even ask, answers, "If it stops that demon, then I will do it. What must I do?"

Timothy sighs, "But when we find the demon, I still have no clue how to vanquish her."

"Do you still have that Sanguine Amber?" I ask.

Timothy frowns, "I have plenty."

"If you give me the piece you took from us, the one you took with you into the waters, I'm certain I can use it to send her back," I state.

For the better part of a day and a half, Timothy and I wait within the Temple. Timothy's hands are both on the now-closed doors, his eyes rolled back into his head. Last he said was that he was communicating with Sister Fatima, and I am still unsure of what that entails.

Jorge brings me the Amber disk. "Be very careful with this Father. Even purified by the water it's still dangerous if it falls into the wrong hands."

Nodding to Jorge I appraise the disk in my hands. Gone are the Satanic markings and now, adorning the side facing me I notice a cross. A simple cross is the core of the design, outlined by another cross outside, a third with beveled edges encompasses the second.  I look at Jorge, "Did you do this?"

Jorge nods, "It's like the one I recall from my home in Trujillo."

As I turn it over I see an immaculate face of Jesus Christ wearing the crown of thorns, his eyes closed serenely as he accepts his fate as the sacrificial lamb.  I turned to Jorge, "You have a talent, my friend."

Jorge beams, "I was a carpenter when I used to live in Honduras."

I can't help laughing, "A noble profession."

"She's there, and somewhere discreet.  Get ready," Timothy says as he pushes the doors open.

The doors open to a cramped room.

Sister Fatima is wearing a set of robes and a white Hijab, as the doors open out of nowhere, shocking her. "Oh!" She cries, covering her mouth and looking around the corner. "We need to be silent, I'm not sure where we were trying to go, but like you said, I found a place as discreet as we could get."

Jorge speaks up, "Sister, come inside with me, we don't want to get in the way."

Sister Fatima nods, "The sooner this is off of me, the better.  It brings back bad memories of my family." She walks into the doors as Jorge closes them behind us.

Timothy leans against one wall, looking worn down.

"Timothy?" I ask, "Are you pushing yourself too hard?"

Timothy shakes his head, "I'm fine.  I've just never communed with someone for that long.  Almost lost the connection to Sister Fatima a few times."

I place my hand on his shoulder, "Timothy, you cannot do this alone, we are all in this together." I assess the area. "Now where do we go?"

Timothy looks around the corner, "Down."

Another hour or two of wandering through ancient corridors and at last Timothy and I stumble across a modest room with nothing but a mosaic on the ground.  Timothy places a flashlight on the floor and illuminates a dome about thirty feet in diameter.  I recognize the pattern as I pace around in the tomb-like chamber.  "This is... The Secret Seal of Solomon.  I don't understand, this is the most holy of symbols, why would you think this is the entrance?"

Timothy nods, "The seal is the most holy because it seals in the most unholy... Perhaps the entire city is a seal," Timothy continues, "You don't use strong medicine unless you have a terrible wound."

I take in the sight of the seal itself, despite it being ancient there appear to be repairs and other modern touches to it.  Someone has been maintaining this seal over the years, ensuring its integrity.

The outer ring of the seal holds multiple symbols, some simple circles with connecting lines, others more intricate patterns.  Within the central circle is what I can describe as a horizon at the bottom, bisected vertically by a simple line. The central circle also has a line cutting across the center, with what looks like a keyhole in the middle. Flanking either side of the eye of the keyhole is a pair of Greek symbols, one of Mars on the right with a dot in its center, and the other of Saturn on the left. Beneath the top of the keyhole, a semi-circle rests, just above the horizontal line crossing the central circle. A bar of sorts sits on the other hemisphere, just above the horizon, but still across the lower portion of the keyhole.

The Seal of King Solomon, it's meanings and workings a mystery until now.

After my appraisal, I look to Timothy, who has at this point slid himself down along the wall, resting on the floor.

"What now?" I ask.

"We wait. She has to come here and when she does, we stop her," Timothy explains.

Several hours pass and Timothy has since shut the light. It is so dark that I can barely make out Timothy's shape on the other side of the chamber.. Timothy assures me he can see fine enough in the dark. The room quakes out of nowhere, and I hear panic above.

Timothy turns on the flashlight. He is on his feet.

"What is it?" I shout.

Timothy looks weary, "I'm not sure... I do not think it's our demon, however." He asks me, "Can I trust you to stop her if she shows? I will check up top."

I show him the Sanguine Amber in my hand, "I believe I can, God willing."

Timothy soon vanishes down the corridor and I pace about the room. I steel myself and pray to God for guidance and strength for when the Succubus arrives.

As if on cue, once Timothy is out of the room for a short while, I hear the Succubus's voice echo through the chamber. "I thought he would *never* leave." Her green eyes glow from the darkness as she walks into the room.

I have my bible at the ready, locked open, and the Amber in my free hand. "Step away from the seal."

She frowns, looking down to the seal below us. "Just get out of my way. The sooner I crack this seal the sooner I can get Ubiel or Craste out of my grandson." She seems to stop for a moment, "Probably Ubiel now that I think about it. He's got a thing for kids," She shudders.

Steeling myself I move toward the Succubus, thrusting the Amber forward.

She catches my hand, and I interlace my fingers with hers, "Listen, Father, the sentiment is kind of heartwarming but also sad, okay? Choir boy couldn't do diddly and he's a fucking Angel. What are you?"

Sure that my fingers are holding her hand tight, the Amber between us I pray, "I am a man who serves in the name of the Father, and the Son, and the Holy Ghost."

To my surprise the seal beneath us activates, its rings glowing with a white aura.

The Succubus attempts to let go of my hand, but she can't seem to pull away. "What the Hell? Why can't I let go of you?" She tries again, now using her other hand, between our fingers a red aura glows. "What the Fuck!"

"Most glorious Prince of Heavenly Armies," I continue, "Saint Michael the Archangel, defend us in our battle against principalities and powers, against the rulers of this world of darkness, against the spirits of wickedness in the high places."

The Succubus attempts to use her tail to whip at my arms, my face, and her wings flap violently. The two of us fly off the ground and crash to the floor in short order. "Stop it you old bastard!" she protests.

Each blow hurts but does not stop my prayers, the Amber giving me some power over the demon.

I chant what I hope will be the last verse to cast her out. "In the Name of Jesus Christ, our God and Lord, strengthened by the intercession of the Immaculate Virgin Mary, Mother of God, of Blessed Michael the Archangel, of the Blessed Apostles Peter and Paul and all the Saints. and powerful in the holy authority of our ministry, we confidently undertake to repulse the attacks and deceits of the devil. God arises; His enemies are scattered and those who hate Him flee before Him. As smoke is driven away, so are they driven; as wax melts before the fire, so the wicked perish at the presence of God."

The ground quakes again as I spot Timothy coming back to the corridor.

"Father, we must leave now!" He shouts, spotting the Succubus, "Oh of course you chose now to try to open the gates!"

"Fuck off Choir Boy, it's me and the priest who are... Wait, what's happening?" The Succubus complains.

The seal glows, and a wind draws The Succubus into the center eye of the keyhole. She clings to the floor, her nails giving way moment after moment as it pulls her hooves and tail in.

Completing my prayer, I continue, "We drive you from us, Succubus Sara Baker, unclean spirit, all satanic powers, all infernal invaders, all wicked legions, assemblies, and sects. In the Name and by the power of Our Lord Jesus Christ, may you be snatched away and driven from the Church of God and from the souls made to the image and likeness of God and redeemed by the Precious Blood of the Divine Lamb!" I shout over the increasing wind.

Timothy grabs hold of my shoulder, the wind not affecting him in the least.

The Succubus grabs hold of my other shoulder, with her free hand, her wings holding on tight. "Father, if you cast me out, then you're at least going to see what you're sending me back to!" With a mighty flap she rises with me.

I release my hand from hers, leaving the Amber to fall to the floor against the seal.

The roar of the wind is deafening and the Succubus's now freed hand grabs hold of my other shoulder, I can hear Timothy crying out before I feel as if I'm falling a great distance, the wind in my ears rushing faster as the air grows hotter.

The Succubus's face is now in front of me and she grins, "Come on Father, Let me show you Hell."

My eyes go wide as below me I see a sea of flames, as I realize that despite Timothy's best efforts, somehow, the Succubus dragged me down with her.

# CHAPTER 4

## *The Road to Hell*

F alling downward the ground fast approaches. I brace myself, bringing my arms up to my face but still my arms break as I crash to the ground below. My shoulder is next as I roll onto the hard ground and I can sense my hip following suit.

The pain is intense, nothing has gone numb, each crack in a bone is acute, every cut, every scrape. Even more acute is the intense burning sensation which follows not long after. After what was like hours of pain, I could stand.

I inspected my hands, soot covering them, the air was thick with sulfur and earth. Ash fell like fresh snow everywhere I looked. I blink fresh ash from my eyes.

I spot the Succubus gliding down in front of me, she lands a good twenty feet from where I am, her lithe hooves clopping to the ground.

She turns her wings folding behind her, one hoof before the other, sauntering towards me with a sway in her hips, her tail countering each cocked hip. "Welcome..." She says, motioning on either side of her with her hands, "To my humble home," She looks over her shoulder, "Well, the outskirts."

My hands pat at my robes, searching for my tools or anything other than the clothing on my back, I find nothing.

"Ah, that's a shame. Your holy water and crosses didn't come with you?" She stops a few feet in front of me, leaning down to catch my gaze, "Don't even have that Amber shit, huh?" Raising one hand up she continues, "Now you know how I felt. Allow me, Father, to collect my things." In her hand appears a whip, though unlike any I had ever laid my eyes on.

The handle is black and tarnished steel, while the length of the whip looks more like a segment of multiple blades, dispersed between each segment are large barbs. "My babies are coming soon."

I spot two black clouds of ash blasting towards her. The first ash cloud smacks against her back, wrapping around her chest, arms, neck and covering her wings. Her upper body was clad in heavy-looking black plate armor, with green jewels on each of her shoulders. Even her neck appears armored, the plating seeming to blend into the flesh of her cheeks. The jewels on her pauldrons look almost like eyes, and I can even spot the shadows of irises glaring back and forth.

The second ash cloud collides with her rear, wrapping around her hips and down her legs, even swirling around her tail.  As the ash dissipates it clothes her legs in even heavier armor, her hooves even covered in a layer of black metal.  Her tail now looks similar to her whip, with the tip acting as a blade itself.  A pair of green jewels now adorn either side of her shapely hips, I can see the same frantic irises within.

Now armored, she sauntered over "If I was summoned with my babies, Father, I'd have opened the gate in about five whole minutes." Her wings spread, the grinding noise of metal on metal pierces my ears as she now floats, her hooves inches from the ground.  In an instant, she's several hundred feet in the air, and then in another, she is behind me.

The bite of her whip strikes across my back, a deep wound being made, I fall to my knees from the shock.

"You know Father, it's not the constant pain down here that sucks so much.  It's the healing part..." She moves in front of me, her metal-clad wings making a nail-on-chalkboard sound as she closes them.  "That's the real bitch."

I groan as the wound on my back seers in pain, "Why?" The grip of her whip against my chin forces me to face her.

"Because you sent me back here.  You sent me back here after I escaped and I am fucking furious," She growls at me, slapping the handle of the whip across my face.

Blood dripped down my cheek and over my chin.

"You know what these are all made of?  My babies?" She taunts.

"Somehow I feel you'll tell me regardless," I respond, doing my best to not focus on the pain in my back and face.

"These were souls," She boasts, emphasizing her armor and weapons. "Three souls, one in my lovely whip, one lucky bastard gets strapped to my tits, and the other gets the pleasure of caressing my beautiful hips..." She smiles "And more." She brings the handle of her whip to her now black plush lips in thought, "Though maybe if he's wired like you he's not too pleased about it," She laughs.

I staggered back to my feet. I'm rewarded with a slice to my shoulder, sending me back to my knees.

"You don't get permission to stand. Here, I'm your God." The Succubus now places a heavy hoof on my back. "In fact," She pressed on my back, sending me flat on my face, "Kneeling is too good for you, worm."

My face is in the ash and dust, coughing as my nose and throat burn from irritation as I inhale.

"Hm, you know folks pay good money for this treatment." The Succubus snickers. "You're my bitch until that choir boy pulls your soul out of here and considering how green he is you might be here for a hot minute." She giggles to herself, "Hot minute... oh, Sara..."

Gasping I manage a question, "Why make me suffer?"

Her hoof grinds into my back as she explains, "Because all I wanted was to be with my family, and then you all had to fuck it up."

Yet more ash and dust choke me as I explain, "We did nothing... It was you who brought ruin to your family."

She removes her hoof from my back which soon finds itself in my gut. I sail through the air, landing on the hard ground. She was nowhere near this strong earlier, does her armor make her this much stronger?

Next, I see both of her ironclad hoofs slam down in front of me and she picks me up by my robes, "I fucked *my* life up, not theirs!  I set them up for life, my husband, my son, they ought to have been fine without me!"

My feet dangling, I explained myself to her, "Your... husband.... After your death?  He suffered from depression... His law firm failed... Everything you gained with your pact soured." She dropped me, gasping, but I continued, "The riches your father-in-law had invested vanished with the dot com crash in the nineties, he took his life when he lost his fortune.  Your husband died of heart failure a few years later while struggling to rebuild his lost fortune."

"Shut up!" Her hoof yet again finds my gut.  "Shut up you fucking liar!"

The soot makes me wheeze as I try to catch my breath, I gasp out, "Ask the one who bought you... He'll tell you." It's at this point I'm aware of a dull wailing, cries of thousands out in the distance.

"That pact cost too much to just have everything fall apart!  It wasn't just *my* soul after all!" She glared, "I'm five fucking souls worth of demonic power!" Her hoof smashes down on the ground, dust floating in the surrounding air, cracks forming under her hoof, green flames sparking between said cracks.

I manage to sit up, and wheezing again, I ask, "What do you mean?"

The Succubus glares daggers at me, "My soul was part of the pact, but I wasn't the only one going into this body, I was just the core." She growls, "Sara Baker would be the main ingredient, but there were others. The other was the one who gave her body, the porn star heroin addict who sold her body to cultists to get her fix. She sold her soul for a fucking hit and that's when her soul got transmuted into this..." She motions to herself. "The beautiful damned bitch before you... The three cultists who were there were my first snacks, so it took five souls to make the beauty that is me." She marches toward me, her hoofs and hips still sauntering as if it isn't even intentional, but her nature. "You're telling me even after all that, everything I worked for in my life fell to shit?"

I cough to clear my throat as I affirm, "Such is the cost of a deal one makes with a demon."

The Succubus glares at me, "The things you're claiming, they aren't true... Because none of that was part of my pact."

Coughing still I manage, "What was it? What was so tempting that made you sell your soul?"

The Succubus's hand grips her whip, "You wouldn't understand."

I got myself seated before her, my head too dizzy to stand, "Try me."

Breaking eye contact with me she gazes to the ground, "I wanted to be... beautiful."

My brow furrows, "That is all?"

Her hoof crashes to the ground, more green sparks and flames shooting through the cracks made, her eyes burning green. "*That's all?* Yes! Fine! But you don't understand, no one did!  The smart girl in class, the one who's bullied all the time, the one pushed around, who tries to get everyone's approval?  That was me!  Worse yet my life was getting worse by the day!"

Clearing my throat, I figure I may as well taunt more out of her.  "You and I walked different paths when offered the same obstacle."

"Oh please!" She shouts, "At least you had your physical body intact!"

As I Get to my feet, I explain, "Well... Perhaps.  But a gay child?" I narrow my eyes.  "Well, no self-respecting southern family wants a gay son.  I was out on my own at the young age of thirteen...  That's when the Church took me in, and I found God."  I wiped more ash from my eyes, "What did you do when you were thirteen?" I ask.

The Succubus frowns, "I was the smartest girl in my class... Braces? Fine. I get it.  Posture brace?  Fine.  Helped me carry my 'friends' books.  Friends I wanted to impress, wanted to like me." She scoffs, "But then the day my legs stopped working, my arms had issues carrying the books for my fair-weather friends," She spits, "They all left when they heard." She sing-songs, "Amyotrophic Lateral Sclerosis.  A wheelchair at best, likely completely paralyzed.  Oh, and dead by age twenty, most likely."

I winced, "So not just for beauty, but for your health?"

The Succubus rolls her eyes, "But as my dear mother put it... 'It's all God's plan', well God's plan sucked Father! 'You'll have your mind,' A fat lot of good that would do."

"I suppose you'd not be pleased to know a man with a similar diagnosis lived to seventy-six," I informed.

"I'm sure he walked everywhere, huh?" The Succubus says, tapping her hoof on the dirt. "Thanks, but no thanks."

"Yes, suffering in a chair would be much more preferable to... Well, this..." I motion around me, "The price paid for dealing with demons."

The Succubus's eyes narrow, as do the eyes within the gems on her hips and shoulders. "I'll show you the cost, Father." She grabs me by the neck, her gauntlet-clad hand digging claw-like fingers into my flesh. Fresh blood trickles down my neck as she man-handles me.

She brings me near the edge of the cliff and drops me to the ground. She crouches down on her haunches, her hands on her thighs as she survey's the horrible sight before me.

Fiery pits of molten stone and sulfur burn across near-endless planes. Within each fiery lake, massive horrors line the shores. The demons' corral figures I assume are lost souls into the fire or doing horrific things to them should they not fall in. They devour some lost souls, some are dismembered, some chased.

Massive goat-like demons crowd the lakes, others hulking amalgamations of animals and man. Some appear to be half serpents, others fly through the ash-filled air with ease. Each a different nightmare in their own right.

Further off in the distance, all tinged in a red glow of the fires below, no light reaching from above, I see walls and grand structures. Through the air over these walls fly more horrible creatures. Screeches and screams echo across the hellscape before me.

At the center of it all, a giant white spire almost touches the stone roof over the giant planes. Seared red and brown stalactites hang from the ceiling, some massive, others appear smaller and spike-like as if to deter someone from going to the ceiling.

The Succubus seems more serene now as she glances at the central tower, "That's the Blade of Pride. You can guess who lives up there, above all of us."

My eyes go wide at the thought, "God in Heaven..."

"God isn't here, obviously." The Succubus taunts. "It's made of souls too... Everything here is. If they don't break you, you suffer, if you fall apart... Your mind breaks... You become an inanimate object down here. Sometimes you're made into something useful..." She drags her finger across her metal-clad thigh, and I spot the iris's of the jewels on her hips almost rolling back in obscene delight. "Sometimes... You become a brick." She stands, eyes far away, "I sometimes envy the bricks."

As my eyes adjust, I notice one black horror in the sky growing larger. I get to my feet, backing away. To my surprise, the Succubus does the same.

"Are you seeing that giant black dragon coming at us or is it me being paranoid?" The Succubus asks.

"I see it," I confirm.

The Succubus turns, defeat crossing her face as she does, her back to the approaching dragon as the whip slides from her hand. "... Father?"

Blinking ash from my eyes, I look at her in a different light.

Her eyes are watering as tears try to fall but turn to steam as they touch her cheeks.

Even the eyes on her armor now appear to be blinking away tears, frantically looking left-right, and behind themselves somehow.

"Do me a favor, okay? When you get out of here... Please tell my son, Jason, I'm proud of him, okay?" Sara asks.

I nod, hearing the mighty roar of the rapidly approaching beast.

"Kick Ubeil out of my grandson too... He's a fucking pedophile, but one of my Master's most loyal soldiers. He hates water... The stupid fuck drowned in a public pool after some mother tased him for groping her kid. Not shitting you," Sara laughs.

"I will Sara." I agree.

She's taken aback, "That's... The first time I heard you use my name."

"This is the first time you behaved like a human being," I confirm.

Sara looks to the cliff, the giant Dragon seems to keep growing, just as I am certain it's about to land, it is still nowhere near us. "He loves those grand entrances."

Fear grips me, "What is that thing?" To my right, I hear metal vibrating against metal, and as I turn toward the sound, I see Sara is shaking.

"My Master... Or at least... His mount. Hopefully just his mount. Please let it only be his mount," Sara pleads to no one in particular.

Ash and dust burst into the air as a foul odor accompanies the gusts of wind. Decay and acrid ammonia hit me hard enough to rob me of breath.

A massive head of a dragon is before us through the dust the wind has sent into the air.  Its scales are not solid, but rather worn, damaged, and scarred.  The Drake's eyes are milky as well while it would look like a pair of massive horns curl around either side of its mighty head one horn is sheared off.  The head is the size of a tractor-trailer, drool sloughs off the side of its mouth as it snorts a sickening breath through its nostrils.  Its mouth opens and it emits a heinous breath as a booming voice speaks, "Welcome Back, Harlot."

"Always a pleasure Zelletia, you stinky bitch," Sara says, holding her nose, "Here to pick me up?"

The dragon exposes massive rows of sword-like teeth as she grins, "Oh no... I'm Dropping off."

The ground quakes beneath us as we hear a clattering of metal.  Heavy footsteps make their way from somewhere behind the dragon's giant maw.

The dragon's head rises into the air hundreds of feet, its mighty neck making its head vanish into the ash-filled air above, a few steps of massive claws reveal something even more terrifying approaching us.

Black and red plate metal scrapes against itself as the creature wearing it strolls towards us.  Heavy black sabatons cover huge feet that shake the ground with each footfall.  Heavy thick greaves move up thick legs.  A tattered and stained red cloth hangs from a belt wrapped around similar black armor, on the other side of the belt is what may be a living creature attached and dragged behind.

A defanged and lethargic serpent slithers behind, though the size of the thing rivals the largest snakes on earth. I see venom dripping from half-broken jaws, sunken black eyes adorn scales that should have been shed ages ago.

At this mighty figure's hips is a myriad of blades, long swords, daggers, short swords, at least five on each hip. Some swords have blackened handles, some appear to have white and beautiful hilts made of silver and gold, though tarnished they still look like works of art.  A chest larger across than most men are tall leads up to what appear to be three heads.

On his far-left a mighty bull's head, made of metal and thick black leather, its horns, long, and tipped in sharp points. Its eyes burn red as foaming saliva drips from its mouth.  On the opposing shoulder is a similar head, its eyes burning green, though this head is that of a ram, its massive horns ending in a head of metal and matted wool. Between both heads is a helm with a tarnished brown crown crudely welded to its head.  Burning wisps of green steam rise from the eyes behind a slit visor, still more steam rises from the vicious-looking metal mouth. I can see nothing behind the opening in the helm, as it appears obscured by a pitch-black darkness, not even penetrated by the burning light of his eyes.

Behind the creature, heavy and rusted chain-mail clothes, a pair of gargantuan black feathered wings full of ash and black soot.  With every quaking footfall, more soot shakes from disheveled-looking feathers.  As the figure moves closer to us, I see it tower higher and higher over me and Sara, topping out at almost nine feet tall from the base of his sabatons to the top of his crown.

My heart halts in my chest, as I'm certain this is the King of Demons, the Morning Star himself.  I must be faced with Satan.  I try to pray, try to think of a single prayer, but before this horrible creature, this mighty demon lord, my voice fails.

I feel all hope drain from my spirit as his form casts a darkness over me that cannot justifiably be considered a shadow.

His voice echoes from the central head, turning its attention to Sara. The voice is deep, and rumbles forth from his chest, exiting from a mouth hidden under the center helm, and shaking the air and ground around us. "Sara..." It hisses in what I can only call disappointment. "You have failed me."

# CHAPTER 5

## *Redemption*

S ara, shaking, falls to one knee, bowing her head. "Master... Forgive me."

"Forgive?" His voice vibrates both of our bodies as if we were standing near a speaker at a concert. Though he is not shouting, or even raising his voice it seems.

I fall to the ground, in shock, in awe, and in terror.

"You dare ask your Master forgiveness for your failures, Wench?" The Master questioned.

Sara whimpers, "P-Please Master Asmodai..."

My eyes go wide. This is not even the king of demons? This is only a prince? There are seven terrors like this one here, seven more horrors like this fallen before me? This is a single fallen angel?  I think back to the caring and kind eyes of Timothy, his beautiful silvery wings, and compare them to the hulking mass of horror before me.  My body shakes, and despite myself, I can't stop as tears well up in my eyes.

A pair of massive gauntlets rise up to the central helm, lifting it off his shoulders.  As he does this, each head on Asmodai's shoulders follows and then fixes their gaze on Sara. His face is that of a man, his head shaved bald, his face covered in coarse black stubble, his eyebrows matching.

Under his brow, I see his eyes, not soulless, but far worse. His eyes are nothing but blackness, with burning green iris swirling in a storm of rage and anger.  The Prince of Wrath, his eyes an echo of the vengeance of men, of hate, of seething anger.  Within his eyes, I can sense the vengeance I once wished upon Father Damascus.  There is the folly of rage in his eyes, the essence of hatred.

"Oh dear, sweet Sara," His voice continues to shake the ground I am laid upon.  "You are so young, still so very human..." One gauntlet moves to her chin, tilting it up high, forcing her to her feet.  "It is why I favor you.  For in you, somehow, you still have hope to break..."

Sara is now at the tips of her hooves, she is shaking until, to my shock, he pulls her lips to his own, leaning down and kissing her with passion.

Sara's eyes shut as I watched her skin glow green as his corruption seeped into her.

While it renders most men weak or at death's door from such contact with a succubus, it seems Asmodai has the power to spare.

I watch as his hand caresses her thigh, she moans into the kiss, his hand leading up her back and to her cheek. The hand that had guided her chin moves to the other side of her cheek. Asmodai breaks the lewd kiss, and he speaks once more.

"I knew you would fail," His voice seems calm, controlled, shaking the ground and air less harshly. "I hoped Immunda would have summoned anyone but you. You are nothing more than my sex toy. Something for me to fuck when I am weary of rending flesh. I had hoped that the hapless summoner would have called Ubiel... Or even Kaskus, that woeful simpleton would have opened the gate faster than you." He sighs, a putrid wind rushing over me, "But alas, the fool reached too high, he was not powerful enough to draw me... So only drew you, the one who leeches off my grandeur."

Sara sighs softly, "I am so sorry Master," She lays her head against his right hand, nuzzling it, "I'll make it up to you, I promise to please you in every way."

"Yet I had desired that maybe," Asmodai continues, ignoring Sara's promises, "In the least... You would put yourself to the task." His gauntlets move to her horns, "But nay... You tarried." After he says these words, his hands make a quick motion, snapping both of Sara's horns off her head.

As blood rushes out of both of her shattered horns, Sara screams in pain, both of her hands rushing to stop the bleeding, but achieving little.

Asmodai drops the horns in his hands unceremoniously on the ground, placing his massive hands on her shoulders. "That... Was for asking me forgiveness..." He explains. His cold and calm voice shook the air once more, rising in volume. One hand twists at Sara's right shoulder, twisting it further and further.

Asmodai makes the limits of her joints clear as Sara shakes her head panicking, "No... no-no, Master please!" she blinks as blood blinds one of her eyes.

I hear a snap as Asmodai dislocates her arm from her shoulder.

Sara screams, her free hand clawing at his unyielding gauntlet in desperation, "Master Please! Mercy! I beg your Mercy!"

"Mercy?" Asmodai's voice rumbles through the air and quakes the ground, it fills the air with a shock wave of his voice and my heart shudders in my chest. "You *dare* beg me, Asmodai, Lord of Wrath, *Mercy*?" With a motion that can be described as a flick of his wrist, Sara's arm sails off her body, and clatters to the ground, twitching and wriggling within its armor.

Sara screams even louder than before, her free arm grasping at her bleeding and exposed stump.

Asmodai releases her, allowing her to fall to her knees.

Tears burn off from Sara's face as blood gushes from her shoulder. "No more! No more!" She begs.

Asmodai grabs a hold of her left-wing from behind.

Sara wails, "No no no!"

"This... Is for your idleness," He leans down to whisper in her ear, though it is far from a whisper "Reflect on this pain," His voice booms as he rips her left-wing off, casting it aside, armor and flesh all.

Sara falls forward now, screaming in abject pain, her free arm drags her body toward me, "Father…" She whimpers, "…Save me!"

Even more enraged now than he was before, Asmodai grabs Sara's by the hock of each hoof, one in either hand, and lifts her off the ground with ease, spreading her legs apart.

"No! Master! No!" Sara is in hysterics.

"This… Is for your failure." And I can hear a creaking snapping noise as he stretches Sara's legs apart, leaving her spread eagle in midair.

Sara writhes and screams, beating at his hands with her left arm, her right-wing flapping as blood spurts from her open wounds. Another crack and Sara can only grab at her hips, shrieking.

Asmodai, now for the first time, glances at me. "Place your bets, Papist… How will she breach? Left… Or right?"

I only shake my head in disbelief, too horrified to look away.

"Make a wish…" Asmodai taunted with a devilish grin.

Sara releases a blood-curdling yowl that rips her vocal cords to pieces. A horrific sound of screeching broken notes and gurgling echoes out as her left leg splits from her body. A cloud of blood and sinew fills the air near her hips. Her body swings to the right, pivoting in Asmodai's gauntlet. Sara wheezes and gasps, blood gushing from her wounds, yet shock never takes her consciousness.

Asmodai unceremoniously drops Sara to the floor, her head landing with a sickening snap as her neck breaks and her body flops to the ground. He drops her leg on top of her.

Despite the broken body, Sara writhes and twitches in pain, aware of every moment of her suffering.

Asmodai reaches for one of many swords on his waist and draws a broad black blade with green accents along with it.

"Enough!" I shout, finding my voice.

Sara's face turns to face me, blood dripping across her brow, her body coughing and wheezing as she attempts to speak.  Her eyes go wide and her face contorts in a silent scream as Asmodai shoves his drawn blade through the center of her chest.

"Wait for me here, Whore.  While I converse with our uninvited transient," He leaves Sara behind, impaled, gasping and wheezing for air enough to scream, her vocal cords too taxed to continue.  "My Master will undertake a far worse fate for her, Papist, I assure you."

In a panic, I scramble to my feet, though I do not have my bible I close my eyes, "Oh Heavenly Father, hear my prayer, Even though I walk through the darkest valley..."

Asmodai finishes my prayer for me, grabbing me by the throat with one hand and lifting me to meet his eyes, "I will fear no evil, for you are with me; your rod and your staff, they comfort me...."

Even as he says the words of the Lord they sound wrong and tainted.

"O, poor fool.  He hears you, He does.  He sees you, He does." His grip tightens against my throat.  "But He cannot take action here.  He can only watch you suffer.  That, Papist, is the reason for your torment. To make His favored children suffer before His watchful eye.  So He can bear witness, so He can weep.  So He can moan helplessly as His children suffer, as His children betray Him, and serve *our* Lord." Asmodai's heavy footfalls carry me to the edge of the cliff, making me face the Blade of Pride in the distance.  "Your Church desires to know our grand designs, yes?  What musings the denizens of Hell have for your verdant speck among the vast universe?" I'm brought face to face with the fallen's swirling dark eyes, his breath stinks of sulfur and blood.  "I shall grant your wish, Papist.  So pay heed to what I reveal."

I squirm as we are flying in the air, his massive wings unfurled, leaving twin clouds of soot behind them.  Again I cannot help contrast the silvery wings of Timothy.  I long to be near him, to experience the comfort I felt being with one of God's angels, to be back in God's grace.  I recall when Timothy saved my life, his body sacrificed to save mine.

A deep laugh erupts from Asmodai's chest, "Sodomite..."

Horror washes over me as I realize Asmodai can see into my mind.

We land in a field of horrible demons and monsters.  All of them stop as Asmodai lands.  Even the most horrible of horrors slink back from his presence.

"My Legions - Assemble!" His voice is like that of an erupting volcano and echoes through the caverns and plains like a mighty blast.

The demons, in fear, all line up before us.  Hundreds of thousands, each more grotesque than the last, all standing at attention.

Asmodai rises into the air, showing me the vastness of his forces.  "Seven legions of this size or greater await the gates opening… Even now, the Fallen Profit and the Child of Lucifer lay waste to the Seal… And soon the Gates will open. We will wash over our Father's creation like a flood, destroying all life. Burning it down to even the most insignificant of Father's creatures." He takes a breath, "We will burn it all."

His infinite army of nightmares repeats, "We Will Burn All."

"None Shall Live!" Asmodai shouts.

His army in unison, shouted, "None Shall Live."

Asmodai faces me once more, grinning, "Look on my Works, ye Mighty, and despair."

Another figure approaches from the Blade of Pride.

A cloud of yellow and black smoke appears before me. My eyes go wide as another pair of blackened wings soon unfurls before me. They are clad in similar rusted and blackened chain-mail, the feathers seem more pristine but still dirtied with soot.

Of a similar stature to Asmodai is a massive nine-foot-tall angel, but this one is far different. His build is athletic, not hulking, his chest bare. A pair of powerful pectorals and biceps rest underneath near-perfect and hairless skin. Across his middle, a tight leather-like armor wraps around as if it were a cumberbund. He wears a tarnished silvery gorget around his neck while black leather bracers adorn his forearms. His legs have a similar tarnished silver plate covering them, the theme matching down to his greaves and sabatons. As I hate to admit, his face is handsome, his eyes black with swirls of yellow which seem to temp and beguile. His hair is long and black, with a small and sharp goatee.

"Belial," Asmodai says with annoyance. "I have no time for you."

"Oh Brother Asmodai, it's not I who requests you." He grins a set of perfect white teeth. His voice wheezes and gasps as he speaks, "Besides... The Sodomites are mine. You know this. I already sold you the Succubus Sara." He seems delighted, "Oh my... a Priest! Another kiddie fucker?"

Asmodai's gaze penetrates me as I struggle, "Victim, not a perpetrator. Shame. His soul is too clean for you Belial. He must disappoint you."

Belial laughs, causing many other demons to still retreat in fear. "Well then Papist, allow me to introduce myself... I am Belial, Lord of Flesh, and..." he stops, moving toward me, sniffing me. "... Oh... you are friends with that ancestor of Enoch. His stink is all over you." His eyes swirl and the yellow smoke seems to bubble in anger.

Asmodai's smile grows sly, "Oh brother... the Angel who taught a mere mortal man how to cast you out?"

Belial spits as he grabs at Asmodai's chest plate, the shock of the two colliding knocking me out of Asmodai's grasp, and sending the majority of the demons to the ground. "Hold your tongue brother, lest I rip it from your throat!" His voice hissed through the air, blasting shock waves across the plains.

Asmodai's voice quakes the earth and lakes of fire burst forth with geysers of lava, "I would enjoy seeing you try Belial! You may be the Master's right hand... But when an angel needs rending, I am the one he calls!"

Belial now grins, "Unless that call is to open the gates, it seems."

The demons now snicker and laugh.

Asmodai grabs a blade from his left, and another from his right side, and marches toward his armies.

Before they can even clammer to their feet, his blades have somehow sliced through the first three rows, arms, horns, heads, and torsos go flying as the wailing screams of hundreds stain my ears.

The laughter has ceased.

"I'll remind you... That Succubus is *your* creation, Belial," Asmodai's voice rumbles.

"As are most pleasures of the flesh here," Belial grins as he fixes his gaze on me, "Like your Father Damascus. Oh, Father Thomas... You must miss him."

Asmodai's eyes also travel over me, "Brother, is this a contest?"

"Yes," Belial forces his hand forward, and out of a black mist comes a sickening slopping sound. A burst of bodily fluids hits the ground and evaporates in a vile stream as a man of the cloth falls onto the ground. He vomits the putrid contents of his stomach and looks up at me, heaving and struggling to keep breath in his body. "Edward...? Is that... you?"

My eyes go wide as the figure of Father Damascus is kneeling before me. The man had died years ago, and yet here he was before me.

He smiles, his crooked teeth shining, "So... you're here too?" He laughs, shaking his head, "See Edward... Like I said... The temptation is too great for a man of the cloth."

My eyes fix on him as he blasphemes before me.

Asmodai's voice echoed in my mind, my eyes looked to his swirling pools of emerald and onyx. "Such a horrid man. He taints your Church, his own station..." Asmodai offers the blade, "And what he did to you?  To a boy so innocent, cast out, into his waiting arms."

I can only see his eyes, full of hate, full of anger.  The anger flows into me, the hatred fills my heart.

"**Retribution**," The blade's handle is placed into my hand by Asmodai, "His actions **demand** retribution."

My gaze turns to Father Damascus. Squeezing the hilt of the blade a surge of strength runs through my spirit.  Just as the power surges through my arm, I release the blade. My eyes close and I calm myself.  Prayer fills my mind, and I recall my words years ago, after Father Damascus's passing. "No.  I have already forgiven him."

The demons near me hiss and growl in disapproval.

Belial now pressed himself against me, his wheezing voice in my ear, "Of course you did... You enjoyed it, didn't you? So young you were then, too young to know what to do... Had it happened now, however..." His hand roams over my chest, "What pleasures you'd experience?  Oh, the pleasures God has made for your body... To deny them is blasphemy, is it not?"

My eyes shut tight as I tried to resist what Belial was trying to offer, pushing the thoughts out of my mind.

"Why not return the favor Father Thomas... Why not? He never finished you off... So rude... What a poor sexual bedfellow as to finish first and not offer to aid your own desire?" Belial encouraged.

"Get thee behind me, devil!" I shout.

Belial presses his hips against mine from behind, he hisses into my ear, "Is that an invitation, Papist?"

Piercing through the air a bluish light surrounds me, Belial steps back in surprise.

I rise into the air, but Asmodai's hand grabs my robes.

He shoves his hand into my chest, ribs breaking and my sternum cracks as his hand grabs my heart, "Is this weakness all the angel Timothy offers?  I can feel how this drains him... How much he exerts!" He laughs, the ground rumbling again. "All I need to do is hold you but a minute and it will do him in."

Something pulls me hard upward, but Asmodai's grip on my heart causes me to remain, and the pain of it causes my entire body to convulse.

Asmodai's face is now nose to nose with mine, "He is weak..."

A voice blares like trumpets from on high, and I look to the source, a bright light high at the top of the Blade of Pride obscures my ability to see.  "Let him go Asmodai, enough pointless games."

Asmodai's gaze remains on me as I feel his grip loosen.

I gasp, "What... is that?"

"The answer," Asmodai begins, bringing his face to mine, "To the question 'Can God make a stone so heavy, even he cannot lift it?'" Asmodai smiles, "He did."  He releases me in that instant.

My body soars through the air, the pain lingering in my chest from his gauntlet as I hit the ceiling and a bright white light floods my vision.

I bolt upright screaming and covered in a cold sweat, clutching my chest. My eyes dart around me as I survey my surroundings. I see Sister Fatima to my right, Jorge to my left, and Timothy next to him.

Timothy looks exhausted, his hands on my shoulders, his eyes looking weary. "Father... are you... All right?" He heaves.

Accessing my hands and my chest I see no soot. No horrible wound in my chest, but as I blink my eyes, I see the sight of Sara, her body broken and her hand outstretched.

*"Father... Save me!"* I hear her cry.

Overwhelmed, tears flow from my eyes, I reach out and embrace Timothy. Timothy holds me as I sob on his shoulder.

"You're safe Father." Timothy whispers "You're safe."

My body shakes as the shock of my ordeal crashes down over me, the shaking only subsiding when I feel Timothy's wings wrapped around me.

When my bawling subsides, I explain what I saw to Timothy. I spare no details.

Sister Fatima looks away from me and explains, "She... showed her humanity when we were on the plane. She kept looking out the window of the plane, she had never flown before.  Not on earth, anyway.  Her soul is so lost, I pray for her."

With a solemn nod, I agree, "I will as well.  If nothing else... That is all I can do to save her."  I close my eyes, and still cannot rid myself of the image that will haunt my nightmares for years to come.

Father Hammond hands Timothy a glass of water as he greets us all, though concern stains his face.

"Father Hammond..." I smile at him as he gives me a cloth, "Where are we?"

"The Vatican, Father Thomas," Father Hammond states.

I'm relieved, looking around the room, "What happened?"

Timothy takes a deep breath, "I held on to you but somehow the Succubus pulled your soul down with her.  I've spent days trying to pull you out, among other things."

Jorge excuses himself from the room, it seems he's answering a phone call.

Father Hammond explains, "You were comatose for a few days."

Nodding I smile, "Well... Despite it all... We stopped her. We prevented the gate's opening." Despite my words of triumph, I notice no one appears pleased or joyous. "What's wrong?"

Timothy is the first to break the silence, "When I came to get you, they had already arrived.  I got us out of there as soon as I could."

"What happened?" I ask again.

"They attacked," Timothy bemoans.

Before I can complete my sentence a sound of shrieking audio feedback reverberates through the building. The TV in the corner flickers to life on its own accord.

On the screen is a man sitting against a throne-like seat in what looks like a battleship's bridge. He wears a uniform I've never seen of any country, his right hand clad in a golden clawed leather glove. His face looks like that of a man in his early sixties, with graying black hair and a clean-shaven face. What strikes me is his icy blue eyes, eyes I've seen before.

Turning to Timothy I see his face is that of anger, but I see the same eyes in him.

"Yee has been judged and found wanting," The man on the TV begins, "Citizens of Terra, your day of judgment has arrived." As he prattled on of his judgment and humanity's failings, another figure moved into the frame and sat next to him on a similarly sized seat.

Her body was clad in armor that looked like stone, massive white feathery wings close behind her back. White hair is tied in a long braid on her left, and a buzz cut on her right. She leans back, and it's clear she is a strong, powerful, gigantic woman, even sitting it is clear she is larger than the man.

Jorge, explains as he enters the room, "Timothy's mother is a descendant of Enoch. But his father is... well."

"The Fallen Profit," Timothy finishes. "He used to be named Kriggary, but ever since he and the woman next to him killed everyone inside the Guardian Temple he's gone by..."

The man on the screen continues, "Salvation is yours, you need only swear fealty to your new savior, Xyphiel."

The woman's voice chimes in, her violet eyes showing a hint of excitement as she does. Her alto voice, one that doesn't carry many hints of femininity, "Or be destroyed by Ragna. It is your choice."

The Television turns off.

Timothy is silent as hope seems to have left his face, "I barely pulled you out of Hell, barely even touched that Succubus."

I stand, looking at Timothy, "You don't have to face this evil alone."

Sister Fatima chimes in, to my surprise, "I will help you, Saint Timothy."

Father Hammond looks to both of us, surprised, "Sister Fatima, how could you aid him?"

"There is a chapel within that temple Timothy showed me. Someone needs to tend to it," She explains.

A smile crosses my face, "Then I will help you."

Father Hammond says in shock, "But Father Thomas... The Church..."

"Tried to summon a demon which nearly destroyed everything God made! I'll no longer put my faith in the Church, Father Hammond, my faith is with God..." I glance to Timothy, "And His angels."

Timothy smiles, "I appreciate it. I'll need all the help I can get."

Jorge looks to be beaming as if waiting his turn to speak. After a moment of silence, he declares, "Well that's good because your sisters are in the Temple waiting for you!"

Timothy looks at Jorge in shock, "What?  Both of them?"

Jorge clears his throat, "Well... Three of them?  Your mother had a third child."

I'm afraid that is where we are now.  I'll never get the memories of Hell itself out of my mind, that is certain.  Nor will I forget the folly of the Church.  I write this last entry just before embarking on this journey, hoping we can stop Xyphiel and Ragna from opening the gate and destroying all creation. Maintain your faith, trust in God.  This is not the end, not yet, not as long as men have the will to stand up to evil and faith in God above.  If this is the end, however, then good luck, and Godspeed to you all.

# SERIES TWO

## Sara Baker

# **Introduction**

I t is as they say, as it is above, so it is below.

The darkness of Hell is not merely inhuman creatures and horrors upon horrors. While these are there, there are damned souls striving to eke out an afterlife. All Attempting to ease their suffering or endure it.

However, the words before the gates of Hell are clear: "Abandon all hope, Ye who enter here."

Lucifer and his Fallen Angels rule with an iron fist. Their goal is not to torture humans for the joy of torture, or to torment mortal kind. Their goal is to torture the children of God, so He can hear their cries of anguish. To torture God's children whom He loves is to torture God Himself.

To achieve these goals Lucifer has set seven Fallen Angels as Princes of Hell, each an avatar of a deadly sin they most rightly embody.

Belial, the Fallen Angel who convinced Lucifer that a war against God was inevitable.  The so-called Demon of Flesh and Lust.  In Hell, he is the purveyor of flesh, a trader of lust for favors from his fellow Fallen and Damned alike.  Belial remains close to Lucifer, taking the seat as his right hand.  Leader of many a legion in Hell.

Asmodai, The Fallen Angel of Wrath, once known as the Sword of Samael, before the fall of Eden.  Son of the Angel of Thrones Samael and the first woman Lilith.  There his task was to punish those souls who acted in anger and in violence.  Commander of the largest force of Hell's army, he is next only to Belial in Lucifer's eyes.

Mammon, the Fallen Angel of Greed.  Once the dark angel who looked over the sins of man where coin and wealth were involved, now he guards a vault of all the riches of Hell.  From artifacts to damned souls, Mammon is the unholy banker of Hell.  Many legions serve Mammon, and consider doing so, a great honor, as his minions reap grand rewards, but at ever greater costs.

Beelzebub, The Fallen Angel of Envy.  Lucifer's eyes and ears in Hell itself.  Beelzebub has foregone his angelic form while retaining his power. He travels through Hell as a swarm of insects and parasites, listening to the enemies of Lucifer and reporting on all that occurs within the damned halls of Hell.

Astaroth, the Fallen Angel of Gluttony.  Fat, and always hungry, this demon's minions are his slaves in every regard, tending to his every want and need.  Often known to devour his less scrupulous servants.

Belphegor, the Fallen Angel of Sloth.  Lord of Laze and stagnation.  He oversees a bottomless pit in Hell known only as the abyss, where the damned cast themselves in hopes to end their suffering, only to be trapped in an endless nightmare.

Lastly, there is Lucifer, Fallen Angel of Pride, who rules over all others.  Lucifer rules Hell without question, but only due to his power. He is trapped within Hell by a seal upon his chest, but while this holds him within Hell itself, it does nothing to diminish his great power.

Woe to thee whomever crosses paths with these avatars of sin.  This is the story of Sara Baker's woe.

# CHAPTER 1

## *I Made A Deal with an Angel*

"A pact made on one's soul is a pact for one's free will."

H ello, My name is Sara Baker.

First off: I am fucked. I want to break this down as to why I'm fucked, and how fucked I am exactly, and hopefully, after you read this you will never get yourself this thoroughly fucked because I cannot un-fuck myself.

When I was a teenager, I made a deal with an angel. I bet you're thinking: "Oh wow she's pulling our legs", and you're probably wondering if this is some kind of Candid Camera nonsense. As it turns out, selling your soul is some serious shit.

Before you wonder "Well why would you do something so dumb lady?" I'll break down where I was when all this shit went down.

It's the 80s, and I want to say around 1982, I'm thirteen years old. My life, right now? Shitter. I'm limping behind my two "friends" Jenny and Beth. They're fucking beautiful, have long hair, clear faces, sparkling eyes, and their tits are already coming in. Lucky bitches.

Me? I'm carrying their books. Well, trying anyway. I'm wearing orthopedic shoes, a back brace, I've got coke-bottle glasses, headgear for my teeth, a face full of acne, and greasy pig-tails because my sweet mother thinks this is somehow in fashion. That's about when I trip and drop all the books, and Jenny and Beth, so nicely, decide to help out their friend who's been carrying their books for them all year long.

"Holy crap, Sara you're such a spaz!" Jenny chimed in as she got her books off the ground.

For reasons I'm fully aware of, I'm having trouble getting my legs working. Yesterday I was told by my doctor, to my father's dismay and my mother's shock, that I have Lou Gehrig's disease. It started with a weakness in my feet, now it's starting to take my legs. I'm not supposed to be carrying heavy books, but Jenny and Beth asked, so I did it because I wanted them to like me.

Beth is next with the encouragement, "Do you need help, Sara?"

I reach my hand up to take Beth's freshly offered hand before she jerks it away.

"Psyche!" Beth shouted maliciously.

Jenny finds this hilarious.

I've managed to get to my hands and knees by that time my would-be friends are gone. My fist hits the ground and through tears, I glare up at the sky, "Fuck you! What else do you want? Why don't you let me die? Is that what you want?! I won't even make it to college, anyway! That's what the doctor says!" I'm frustrated and shouting at almost anyone who can hear. At this point, again, I basically can't get up.

"Oh, you poor thing," A man's voice wheezes above me.

If I could take a moment to point out that this right here is where I screwed myself. I take the man's hand and he helps me up.

Not only does he help me up, but he collects my books and keeps his hand on the small of my back so I don't fall. "Took a mighty big spill there, young lady. Are you okay?"

I shake my head, "No! No, I'm not!" I stomp my foot, and almost lose my footing again, "My life sucks."

The handsome man smiles warmly at me as he keeps me on my feet kindly, "Oh my. That sounds terrible." He wheezes out. "Young lady," He hands me a handkerchief, "I have a confession to make. I heard what you said, how you're mad. I know who you're mad at."

"You do?" I ask, cleaning up my tears and nose.

He leans in close, and whispers, "You're mad at God, aren't you?"

I glance at the ground, ashamed. I'm pretty sure this guy is going to chastise me somehow.

He's tall, handsome, and he's got black hair and looks like a well-to-do older man in a suit and a tie and he even has a nice fancy hat. He tilts the hat forward and I can see his yellow eyes against the sun as he straightens up. "Well young lady, you aren't the only one. My name's Belial, and I'm an Angel."

"An Angel?"

He nods, "God and I had a disagreement some time ago. I'm not fond of what he does to people like you, Sara."

"You know my name?" I ask in shock.

"Sara, I'm an Angel, and I've been watching you."

I don't see anyone on the street, but I inspect the area just to make sure.

Belial gets down on his haunches so he's eye to eye with me, "I don't think it's fair. A smart girl like you, and you're so disadvantaged. Seems that's the way it goes though, hm?" he slowly pulls the elastic bands holding my pigtails out, "The pretty ones have nothing up top... While the ugly ones need to deal with wits alone."

I pouted at the ground, "Pretty people aren't all dummies." I said, trying to think of one but not really finding a name I could pull out at the time.

Belial laughs, "Oh Sara, that's the way the world is." He seems to stop, "You know... here's the thing... Do you know what a soul is?"

"Is that what goes to heaven when someone dies?" I answer.

"It's more than that little one. You see, your soul is your will, so to speak. It's your spirit, your courage, your personality, your gumption!" Belial seems excited by the end. "Angels like me, we can use a soul or a promise on a soul to do amazing magic."

"Magic?" I ask.

Belial picks up a caterpillar on the ground, laying it in his hand. In an instant, the caterpillar wriggles into a chrysalis and leaves the chrysalis a moment later as a butterfly flutters away. "Magic, like that. Real magic. Powerful magic."

I'm in awe at this point, "Could you... make me pretty?" I grabbed a hold of my head, "But not take my smarts?"

A grin comes over him which, at the time, I was too excited to notice was sinister. "I can. I can make you the most beautiful woman in the world, all while keeping your intellect," He hisses to me, "But it will be at a price."

I frown, "I don't think I want to let you have my soul... If I die, I won't go to heaven."

Belial nods, "You're right. If I have it that is true. But..." He leans over and whispers into my ear, "I can bend the rules. See..." He leans away, "You don't have to sell me your soul now. You can promise me your soul, and I can still make the magic happen. But, since you don't want to lose your spot in heaven, we can make a deal!"

"A deal?" I ask.

"Oh yes!" He's excited now, "Here, for example..." He pulls out a literal contract. "You agree to sell me your soul, unless...

You achieve something specific... Like a life goal! Not something impossible, but not easy either. You're a smart girl, why not name a goal for me?"

I think hard, looking at him, "I want to prove that a pretty girl can be smart."

Belial hems and haws, "Let's be more specific... That's too vague and too easy. You could get up on stage and win a spelling bee to prove that!" He clears his throat, "Is there anything you think you might be able to do with your smarts? I'll even give them a little boost if you like, for free, if you think you could do something for all mankind with them."

My dull legs grab my attention as I think, "... I want to cure Lou Gehrig's Disease."

"How noble! Now you know that when I do this, you'll personally be cured... But you plan to cure others?"

I nod excitedly

"What a lovely and selfless girl you are! Here, give this contract a read, everything is laid out in nice black and white. Nothing complicated, these things don't need to be."

I read the contract, the damn thing is seared into my mind.

I, Sara Baker, agree to sell my immortal soul to the Angel Belial if the following circumstances are not met:

Sara Baker discovers or pioneers a viable cure for Lou Gehrig's Disease.

The Angel Belial will gift Sara Baker with a beautiful healthy female Homosapien form while keeping her person and family ties intact, Providing a modest increase in intellect, and the ability to be financially stable throughout all her years.

If Sara Baker fulfills the above goal, the Angel Belial will relinquish his claim on Sara Baker's soul, and allow for Sara Baker to keep the gifts he bestows upon her.

Sara Baker has until the age of 21 to achieve this goal.

Sara Baker acknowledges fully that the sale of her soul is an affront to God and is entrusting her soul to the Angel Belial.

Sara Baker acknowledges that she is fully aware of the risks of this agreement and knows what happens when a soul is owned by another.

In the event that the Angel Belial is transubstantiated Sara Baker's soul will be transferred to the next highest-ranking Angel.

I face Belial, "What happens if you owned my soul?"

Belial shrugs, "It means you would do whatever I told you to do, and you'd never be able to disagree with anything I made you do." He smiles, "But remember if you make that cure for this terrible and unfair disease that God made... well... You keep your soul and your good looks."

"What if I don't offer you my soul?" I asked.

He lets go of my back and I stumble back onto my hands and knees.

"I do not make such generous offers twice. If you don't at least promise it, I can do nothing. This is fairly standard."

I pant, and read over the contract, "That last part... I don't want to go to any other angel because something happens to you. I don't know what transub... transubstantiated means. I want to stay with you, you're the one I'm making this deal with."

Belial looks at the contract, and back to me, "You are a very bright girl... You know what? I'll leave that bit out. It'll likely never happen anyway, but... For you, I can acquiesce."

The last line on the contract vanishes.

Next Belial hands me a feathered pen, smiling. "Prick your finger, and sign on the dotted line."

I took the quill and jabbed my finger, I signed the contract in my blood.

The next thing I knew it vanished into mid-air and Belial licked his finger before pressing it against my forehead.

I blacked out.

I woke up in my room. Well, it looked like my room, at first, but as I looked around, I couldn't spot my back brace or my retainer. I realized that I also couldn't spot my glasses, but that I could see even better than I could with them. I jumped out of bed and, wow! I could jump! I had sensation in my toes! I looked down and was shocked, I actually had boobs coming in! I rushed to the mirror and was shocked at what I saw.

My once greasy brown hair was a beautiful long auburn. I was rocking a Farrah Fawcett hairstyle after rolling out of bed! I swear I was taller too! Before I knew what was going on my mother called up from the kitchen, "Sara, your friend Jenny is on the phone."

I ran down the stairs because I can run now, and I picked up the phone. "Hello?"

"Oh, Sara! You're home. I am so sorry Beth and I ditched you, I don't know what came over us. We were going to go to the movies later, we wanted to make sure you still wanted to come."

I nearly cried. I was so happy. I rushed up the stairs, got dressed in trendy clothing I never owned before, and rushed down the stairs, "Mom, I'm going to the movies with Jenny and Beth!"

My father called out, "Don't be out too late angel!"

I grinned as I headed down the street to meet up with my friends.

I'm no angel, I just made a deal with one!

# CHAPTER 2

## *Pros and Cons*

**"Free will provides spiritual power for magic
and other acts that are unnatural"**

I was 13, and I just went from ugly duckling to swan.

I was also smart. I mean freaking brilliant. I wasn't a moron in any regard before but after Belial's deal, I went into overdrive. Everything in my life was on Easy Street. I skipped two grades, and I was told to send out college applications at age sixteen. Sixteen! I was hyped up and having the time of my life.

The male population of my school was also having the time of their lives. I was sixteen, but I had the banging body of an eighteen-year-old and the sex drive of a thirty-year-old divorcee. I wasn't stupid though, I used condoms like crazy. I think I spent more money on those than anything else, to be honest. Granted the sexual revolution had already happened but I think I was pushing for the sequel in the late eighties.

What can I say? I was hot, I was smart, I knew how to sweet talk guys. The thing was though that every single guy wanted me to be their girlfriend to show off. I wasn't having that, these guys were around for me, not the other way around. Some folks called me a slut, and I didn't care. I told them I was a female stud.

Sex was something I enjoyed doing, not much else, kind of like a hobby or like watching TV. But I was actually focused on my studies, regardless. Heck half the time I didn't even spend the night at my sexual conquests houses because I had homework to complete.

I later graduated valedictorian of my class thanks to all my hard work. Jenny, Beth and I had a huge party and the two little bitches got me a cake that read "Vala-Dick-Torian". I didn't even know they made penis-shaped cakes!

At least things were going well enough until I had a kind of rough night. See, I had a curfew from my father, he was very convinced that I was his little angel. While I could have given him a lecture about female empowerment and the like I never really got around to it. One night, I was having the ride of my life and lost track of time. Before I knew it I was thirty minutes late for my curfew.

I rushed home as fast as I could, and my boy-toy drove me home as quickly as possible because I told him my father would kill him.

When I got home, I got a scolding from my mother. She said my father was out looking for me for the past hour. She had me wait up for him for another hour or so, both of us waiting in our dining room.

"When your father gets home, you're going to get it, young lady. You may be a bright girl with good grades but we won't be seeing you throw that away for some boy!" She shouted.

"Boys," I said under my breath.

"Excuse me, young lady?"

I shake my head, trying to stifle a snicker, "Nothing mom."

That's when a knock came on the door.

My mother glances at me, "Well go make yourself useful and answer the door."

I sigh, and get to my feet, opening the door I see a cop. "Can I help you, Officer?"

"Is this the Baker residence?" He asked.

"Yes," I answered.

My mother made it to the door after I said "Officer."

"Mrs. Baker?" The cop asked.

My mother nodded, "Yes. What's going on?"

"I'm sorry ma'am, your husband was in a terrible accident. He was pronounced dead at the scene."

To say I blamed myself was a major understatement. Somehow my father wrapped his car around a tree. All while looking for me. Despite all this, mom was super supportive and she never ever let me blame myself. She said it could have been him driving anywhere, and that there was no reason for him to try scouring the neighborhood that late at night.

I was really down in the dumps and I decided that I was going to stop with the sex and be a respectable young lady, in memory of my father.

That worked out for about one week.

I don't know why, but I could not handle it! I'd see a cute boy and despite myself, I just had to have him. I know this sounds insensitive and all, but I legitimately was using it to cope, and it's the only way I knew how to feel good. When I was having sex, I wasn't thinking about my father or how he might have died entirely because of me, I was enjoying the sex. It is probably around this time when I was a full-blown addict, I just wasn't ready to admit it.

It was a little over one year later when I was doing my freshman year in college, Harvard, by the way. As a Beautiful "Kid" Genius in the Biochemistry program. I was still focused on my goal, mostly, the memory of my 'deal' was kind of fuzzy and the more I looked back at it the crazier it sounded. Around campus, I was called 'jail-bait' as I was still seventeen. Before you nuns get all friggin' crazy on me, the age of consent in Massachusetts is sixteen as long as the person I'm banging isn't more than four years older. That meant that college boys were now on the menu.

Anyway, That's when a seventeen-year-old me found a nineteen-year-old Dave Miller. Now I have never been a one-dick gal, but when I met Dave? Lawyer, rich as Hell daddy, and an overall nice guy? Well, I eventually did the whole 'boyfriend' thing. Poor bastard didn't realize I was under eighteen. I can't blame him, I sure as shit didn't have the appearance of a teenager at this point.

Whether Belial tossed something extra into the contract or not, I wasn't sure but I was sporting some fairly large (well I thought they were large at the time) D-cups. So Dave was helpless against my 'charms', both of them. He even convinced me once to go without the rubber, and I did, and man oh man! Apparently, I was doing sex wrong for all my life. That was a Hell of a night.

I did pay for it though. Now, I am a Biochemistry major. When Dave said, "Baby let's ditch the condom tonight?" I had said no plenty of times before, but it was a safe night. There was no way I was ovulating for the next few weeks and I even made sure to get him to fire off before we actually went bareback.

So either Dave has the most resilient sperm in the world or orgasms make me ovulate out of my schedule because two weeks later I'm vomiting into a toilet and cursing Dave's desire for a good time.

"You said it was a safe day!" Dave was shouting at me.

"Well, it was as far as I knew! You've got to have the virility of Genghis Khan or something!" I shouted back.

"My father's going to kill me," He was fretting, "Listen… I'll pay you to get rid of it, how's that?"

"I'm going to blink three times and imagine that did not slip out of your mouth. Roe vs Wade might be a thing, but I'm still an upstanding Catholic girl," I asserted.

Dave laughed in my face, "I found out from my buddies you fucked half your damn chem class!"

"Lies and slander!" I shouted, "Unless you're counting the girls, in that case, it is half, but I think the only one who didn't get a ride was the professor. Also, I'd like to point out you're no virgin yourself, and last I checked you weren't complaining! In fact, you couldn't get enough."

Dave is pacing around now, "My father's going to kill me..."

"Bonus points there Dave, no need for condoms now," I say plainly.

Dave stops and stares at me, and I can tell you right then and there. The boy was in love. "You can't go to school while you're knocked up though."

"I can for some of it," I complained.

"There's no way you'll be able to participate and make all the doctors' visits... Take a semester off," Dave argued.

That was the worst part about the pregnancy to me, having to take a semester off of university. I hated that. I'm eighteen years old by the time I pop the kid out and of course, Dave's dad doesn't want bastard children running around so we get hitched. I keep my name though because I'm a strong independent woman or something. At the time that mattered, now? Not so much.

Jason was born, and he was a beautiful baby. Want to know what else was still beautiful? Me.

I recovered from that kid in twenty-four hours to the shock of every doctor and the envy of every other mother in the maternity ward. Probably should have been tipped off by the fact I still was dressing to show off up to nine months with the kid. I didn't even have stretch marks. I had folks cursing my genetics, and I enjoyed every moment of it.

After that, it was right back to school and hitting the books hard. Now for folks wondering how I was handling being a teenage mother, I'd like to point out when daddy's the heir to a fortune it makes being a teenage mother super easy. Again, I was not sweating it, I merely skipped a step in the whole "The Game of Life" thing.

At this point in my life, between school, the kid, husband, and trying to make sure I never fell behind in my extra-curricular activities, I pretty much forgot about the deal I made. To me, it was some weird fantasy I had when I was a kid. I couldn't have had ALS as a kid! That would be impossible. I was rocking high heels even when pregnant so there's no way I had a progressive neurodegenerative disease. I had to have been misdiagnosed, my parents didn't even remember the doctor's visit.

It wasn't until age twenty-one that I had my rude awakening.

Since my 'Party Girl' status was pretty much dead, what with me being married, and a mom, I had to keep my escapades during college on the droll side. I mean, I guess I got all my wild sex out in high school and Freshman year but I'll be honest Dave really was having trouble keeping up with me. I wasn't about to divorce him, but I was going to start talking to him about threesomes. Vanilla ice cream all day long is boring, you've got to add a scoop of chocolate and some sprinkles to keep things interesting.

Jenny had a private birthday set for me at her place. Just the two of us chilling out on the eve of my birthday and drinking the night away. The nanny had the kid, so why not cut loose? Jenny had bought some vodka, whiskey, brandy, and an assortment of drink mixes.

"Sara... We should fuck." We were a good halfway into our little liquor supply when Jenny came out and said it, drunk off her ass. Jenny was a pretty girl as a kid and she grew up to be a pretty adult. Not going to lie, if I did swing for the other team I'd probably give her a try. Granted it was never off the table.

Me? I've got Irish blood, so of course, I can tell Jenny is sloshed. "Okay Jenny, keep your shirt on."

"No!" She slurred as she tried, and failed, to remove her shirt, "We're sposed' tah 'spermiement when we're in college!"

I'm laughing hysterically at her when she slurs and fails completely at removing her shirt. She passes out in my lap. I turn her to her side, making sure she doesn't vomit in her sleep and choke on it.

We're both on the floor at this point, plenty of booze consumed and some silly board games all over the place when I spot the clock hitting twelve. "Happy Birthday to me." I take another shot.

"Happy Birthday to you..." A familiar man's voice wheezes.

A chill runs down my spine because I knew that voice.

"Happy Birthday, to you," The voice continues.

I turn around and materializing out of nowhere is a man, he's tall, he has wings, and he's wearing a similar business suit as he did before, all white. His eyes are black, with little swirls of yellow where his iris should be. Black hair, a black goatee, and he's floating, disembodied, in the air. I think I can see through him.

"Happy Birthday, dear Sara. Happy Birthday, to you." He grins at me.

"… No," I whisper. This has to be a terrible alcohol-fueled hallucination.

"Yes." Belial hisses. He looks at a non-existent watch on his wrist, "As a fair question, Sara, how's the research coming along?"

I kid you not, I was actually really close to cracking a neuroprotective compound that could have acted as a free radical scavenger which might have reduced oxide stresses on neurotransmitters. Point was, I had barely gotten a formal paper together on it, a question of a hypothesis.

I squeaked out to him, "I need more time!"

His hands clasped together happily, "Oh, Sara! Of course! If you need more time, that's completely possible for you. However… The old deal, I'm afraid, can't be modified. So, how about a second one?"

I'm panicking, "Okay, yeah sure, what do you want?"

"The soul of your son," He replies.

A contract appears in my hands, and I stare blankly at it.

"You have thirty seconds."

My rational brain calculated the pros and the cons of the entire situation, thinking that if I could get my paper all situated in five years. Because my research was solid and it really could have paid off if I managed to get a few of the professors to help out with it. Again, I never had the paper fully written. The compound needed testing, validation, even a grant or two to really get traction.

All that being said, there's something weird that happens to you when you're a mother. When someone puts your child at risk, you stop thinking. I tore the contract in half before I even finished considering how long it would take me to finish the first draft.

Belial smiled at me, "Oh, what a caring mother. Time's up, by the way."

I cross my arms defiantly over my chest and fix him with a stern glare, "Okay... Fine... So...What? I'm yours now?"

Belial floats over Jenny and I roll my eyes as he does.

"If all of this was to watch me make out with Jenny. You should know that might have happened after a few more drinks," I mock.

"A few more drinks?" Belial grins, "That's an awfully full bottle of vodka," Belial points out.

I noticed the bottle of vodka that Jenny and I were doing shots out of, "Yeah. She bought it today, along with the other stuff for mixed drinks. Birthday celebrations, you know?"

"Drink that entire bottle of vodka right away," He commands.

"Are you crazy?" I say as I grab the bottle and remove the top, not noticing what my hands were doing, "You can't expect me to drink all of that–" before I realize what's happening I've got the bottle to my lips, tilted all the way back, and I'm downing a little over a liter of vodka. My eyes go wide as I watch the liquid drain from the bottle as my throat opens up on its own accord. I'm gulping down the vodka like a dehydrated man gulps water in the desert. When it's empty I drop the bottle, gasping, my center of gravity is off-kilter as I catch my breath, "Oh God... I'm gonna..."

"Don't vomit," Belial ordered.

Try as I might, with my stomach and throat burning, I cannot.

"Oh, my... Is that whiskey?"

I'm finding the room is spinning and I am fully aware of my brain slowing down thanks to the spike in my blood alcohol content. "W-wait..."

"Drink that entire whiskey bottle, right now," Belial ordered.

I'm stumbling my way towards it, my stomach is doing backflips, the urge to vomit surged through me but nothing happens, "I-it's full... it's a full bottle... I-I'm already... I've drunk... too much..." I am having trouble breathing but I still see the bottle of whiskey rising up in my vision, I drink it down. Same as before, gasping as it burns my throat and my stomach aches as if it's going to burst. The bottle drops, and I hit my knees, my vision is blurring. "W-Why... Make me... do this?"

Belial smiles, "Your body is worthless, Sara, I need your soul. Goodnight."

The room spins around, I reach out to Jenny trying to breathe but finding myself gasping for breath. The last thing I remember is the floor rushing up to meet me as my vision tunnels, and everything goes black.

I see a white tunnel and at the end a bright yellow light. This will sound crazy but bear with me. The light looks sad. Like the light is disappointed or something. I'm stuck in the tunnel, and in an instant, I'm being ripped backwards.

Before I know what is going on, I'm back at Jenny's place, landing on my ass on the floor. I grunt with the impact and inspect my surroundings, seeing Belial now as a solid being.

He's still in his white business ensemble, but now I can see his legs clearly. He's wearing what looks like very expensive tailored slacks and dress shoes with silver metal tips on the toes and heels. His black wings are closed behind him and it almost looks like the yellow in his eyes is rising out of the sockets like steam. His hair moves like it's underwater for some reason.

"What the hell was that?" I shout.

"What a cute choice of words," Belial taunts.

I get to my feet, march right up to him, and jab my finger in his chest. "What is the big idea making me drink that much! I could have died!"

Belial isn't concerned with my finger prodding, he smiles, "Could have?" He looks over my shoulder.

I turn around looking at what Belial was glancing at. There on the floor is my body, whiskey bottle in hand, passed out right on top of Jenny. While I can see the steady rise and fall of Jenny's chest, I notice my body isn't moving. It's right then and there I realized that I'm dead, and I'm looking at my own corpse.

# CHAPTER 3

## *Regrets*

**"A Soul cannot disobey its owner, its owner is the souls' new God."**

Y ou know that rush you get when you're falling from a very high distance and your stomach lurches as if it's behind you? You know that panic-inducing moment where your body enters fight-or-flight mode but is entirely powerless to perform even the simplest task so it kind of resolves itself to death? That's what staring at your own dead body is like.

I didn't give up though; I rushed to my body and tried to wake up, or dive into it, or something. "No! I'm not dead!" My hands go right through my body and I can't help but scream in panic. I turn to Jenny and slap the absolute crap out of her. To my shock, it works.

Belial even made a comment when he saw her face move, "Oh I picked a ripe one…"

"Jenny! Wake up you dumb slut!  I'm dying!" I shout.

Jenny groans and opens her eyes. As she gets up I get pushed out of the way.

"Ouch! What the Hell?"

Belial snickers, "I love that you say that… But a body that has a soul in it usually resists when an outside spirit tries to get inside. So the average person can push you around, but they can't sense you for the most part. Some are more perceptive than others," Belial explains.

Jenny is rubbing her forehead, "Sara…. Get off me. You're heavy… It's because of your tits I bet… You bimbo," She groans and tries to move my body.

I try waving my hand in front of Jenny's face and she doesn't notice. "Oh damn it, Jenny, why couldn't you be psychic like that kid from The Shining?"

"That film portrayed the afterlife so terribly," Belial shakes his head in shame.

I shoot Belial a glare, "Oh, really? What movie got it right?"

"Personal favorite? The Exorcist," Belial grins.

"What kind of fucked up angel are you?!" I scream.

Belial's black wings spread wide, "Sara... Come now, you're smarter than that. You knew all along."

I glare to the floor and stomp my foot, "Right, an angel who disagreed with God. A Fallen Angel..."

Jenny appears startled at the sound of my foot hitting the ground, she starts to push my body with her foot, "Sara... Get up you slut."

"You knew that Sara, I know you did," Belial mocks.

"I knew... But I figured I'd hit my goal before it mattered, or that it was all a dream." I frowned, "You knew it didn't you? That I wouldn't do it?"

"Sara?" Jenny shouts, shaking my body frantically, "Oh my God!" Jenny's feet cause the floorboards to creak as she runs to the phone, dialing it frantically.

"Sara, I should be honest, I targeted you from the start. You were a powerful young woman, strong, able-minded, confident, and destined for greatness," Belial admitted.

I grimace as I face Jenny as she screams into the phone, "What do you mean?"

"You would have found the cure for a few diseases, to be honest," He chides. "The ALS cure would have been your first discovery, followed shortly by a breakthrough in immune system response therapy. You either would have discovered a cure for cancer or AIDs, depending on outside factors. You would have discovered one while investigating the other and cured both."

Jenny is yelling, "She's not breathing, get here fast!" She hangs up and starts performing CPR on my body.

"Yes, Jenny!! Come on! Revive me!" I shout.

Belial laughs, "How long do you think you've been dead Sara?"

"Huh?" I turned to Belial, confused.

Belial shakes his head, "Your corpse is quite cold there dear, for you to be outside of it like this you need to have been brain dead for some time."

"But people have out-of-body experiences all the time!" I shout.

Belial laughs, "Yes... On an operating table, while trained doctors are working the instant of death to revive them."

I grab either side of my head as I watch Jenny do chest compressions on my lifeless body.

After a few compressions the contents of my stomach bubble out of my body's mouth, causing Jenny to retch. Jenny turns my corpse over to its side. Jenny hugs her legs and is rocking back and forth freaking out. "Oh, My God..."

Watching Jenny I walk over to her and hug her, even as the paramedics come to the door and rush in. I don't know if Jenny notices me holding her but she seems to be freaking out slightly less, or she's going into shock.

I watch in horror as one of the EMTs shakes his head and looks to his partner, "Calling it man. She's cold."

Jenny straight up screams at this point.

The EMTs tried their best to calm her down while also bagging my corpse.

Everyone eventually leaves, Jenny is escorted by police for questioning, and I turn to Belial.

Belial is sitting happily on the couch grinning ear to ear as he watches the whole thing, "That was lovely. She's completely and utterly broken. Jenny is absolutely never going to be the same," He stands proudly, "She's positively suicidal!"

"Fuck you!" I shout.

Belial glares down at me, "You need to apologize with all of your heart."

My knees hit the floor and the sensation of absolute regret over what I've said washes over me. The emotion isn't mine, I can tell, but it is mine now, my new reality, "I'm so sorry, Master."

Belial nods, "Very well, on your feet, Sara."

I get to my feet, "Why did I call you Master?"

"Your soul is mine, meaning I am your Master and you are my thrall," Belial explains.

"So now what?" I ask.

"Excellent question!" Belial takes my hand, "We're off to fetch component number two!" He stops as if realizing he left the gas on somewhere, "Which is... late. Lovely. Well, apparently we have a week while my..." He grumbles, "*Servants...* Prepare the vessel."

"I had a perfectly good vessel wrapped up in that body bag about an hour ago, you know!" I shout, stomping my foot.

Belial shakes his head, "No no. Your spirit is what I was after.  While your body looked lovely it only did so because of an overuse of my magic. The vessel has had much more subtle changes made to it."

"Subtle changes?" I give Belial a wary stare.

"Only mild physical changes with little rework of the entire nervous system. For you, dear, I had to rewrite your entire body from the ground up, not good for the purpose I need," He gives me an absolutely demonic grin, "Count yourself lucky young Sara, by the time I'm done you're going to be a demon."

"Over my..." I was about to say 'dead body' but stopped myself.

Belial snickers at me. "Well we have some time to kill it seems, so we can do some sightseeing."

Belial snaps his fingers and we're in a funeral parlor instantly.

I see friends and family from both Dave and I's sides. "... That was fast."

"Not really, it's been about five days," Belial clarifies.

"Wait, how?" I ask.

"To skip ahead in time is easy in this realm, can't go back though. Short jumps are nice and simple though." Belial slaps his hands together, rubbing them excitedly, "Now, let's do some eavesdropping, hm?" Belial hisses as he walks me over to Dave's father. "Oh wow, this is interesting..."

I take a gander at Dave's father, normally he's a fairly heavyset fellow with a gray mustache and a bald head and a perpetual nasty grimace on his face. He's the sort of fat cat you'd see in a stuffed suit smoking a cigar and drinking brandy with the 'Good ol' boys.' However I noticed a weird mark on his forehead, it looks like a coin of some kind, and it's glowing red.

"What is that, Master?" I curse under my breath as I find myself calling Belial that more and more. Worse yet, I'm actually starting to experience a weird devotion to him growing inside of me. It's like the longer I'm near him the more I want to please him. I hate it.

"That is the mark of my brother, Mammon. He's the avatar of greed. Seems Dave's daddy didn't get where he is now on his own."

I shudder, at least I'm not the only one doomed here. Though I was taken first, apparently.

Dave's father, who if I remember right was named Maurice? I think he went by Murray or something. I'll call him Murray. Murray is standing with Dave and he's none too pleased.

"I told you, boy, there are women you fuck and women you marry. You don't marry the woman you're supposed to only fuck," He grumbles to Dave.

"Father, please, not here? You didn't know her as I did," Dave says, defending me.

"Oh please! Don't pretend as if you had her to yourself! That girl was the town bicycle wherever she went, everyone had their damn ride. You think she suddenly only let you ride her once you knocked her up? She saw you as a meal ticket and nothing else." Murray grumbles to himself, "It's better it ended this way Dave, it is. You have a son and no horrid wife who would divorce you for your riches later in life."

"She wasn't like mom," Dave walks away from his father at this point, bringing Jason in a carriage along with him.

I march up to Murray and poke him in the throat which seems to cause him to cough, "I never liked you either, old man."

Belial grabs my hand, "Wait, this part should be juicy."

In the next instant, I'm standing before my mother.

She's wearing all black, her hands in her lap. She looks emotionally drained. Her eyes have a far-away look in them and they seem to be looking past the casket.

My aunt sits next to her, "How are you doing, Deb?"

My mom snaps out of her blank stare and turns to her sister, "Oh, doing as good as you can expect, Marie."

My Aunt Marie nods, "So, terribly?"

Mom nods.

"I mean... First Hank now Sara? If you need anything, you can live with me and Frank for a while."

Mom shakes her head and is silent for some time. "They say... She drank it all on purpose."

Aunt Marie looks away.

"She blamed herself for her father's death. I know she did. I... I thought she could get past it. She always seemed so strong and independent, I never asked," Mom lamented.

My Aunt Maire shook her head, placing her hand on my mom's shoulder, "Deb, it's not your fault at all."

Belial snickers, "Oh, is that what you think Auntie Marie?"

I turn to Belial as he places his hand on my Aunt's head.

Even with her mouth not moving, my Aunt's voice echoes. "The little trollop partied too hard on her birthday and you think the bimbo actually felt bad for driving Hank up the wall? Jesus Christ Debbie, you are one gullible bitch! That slut slung her cunt on anything that was dick-shaped. She probably fucked her way through school to get those grades! Not your fault? Bad parenting is what got her in that casket."

"What the Hell is that?" I shout.

Belial smiles, "It's her true feelings." Belial places his hand on my mother's head.

I flinch for a second before a soft caring voice echoes through the air.

"Sara, I miss you so much already. I'm still proud of you, I don't believe a word they say. Not one. I know you were a smart girl, I'm sure you had so much joy in your life you got carried away. My sweet girl, be with God."

Belial pulls his hand away, "Ugh, well isn't your mother just a saint?"

I'm drying tears away when I glance at my hands, seeing the teardrops on them, "Wait, I'm dead how am I crying?"

"Physical representation of the soul dear, anything your body could do your spirit can do. Anything your body could experience your soul will experience. Heck, you'll even bleed and sense pain in the same way." Belial explains as he looks around, grinning again.

"Oh no, what is it now, Master?" I dread what is next.

Belial leads me to the back of the room where Jenny is, or at least I think it's Jenny.

She's wearing huge sunglasses and her hair and head are done up in a scarf like she's trying to hide her identity.

Belial's hand lands on her head.

"Sara, I loved you and you ran off with that rich boy Dave! It's my fault you're dead, I thought if I got you drunk enough you would fall for me and we could run off together. But don't worry Sara after today I'm going to come to join you. I'm coming with you, my sweet Sara," Her voice echoes through the air.

"What the Hell, why didn't she ever say anything like that to me before?" I glare at her, "For fuck's sake Jenny! You were such a bitch when I was ugly but once I'm pretty I'm suddenly your girl-crush?"

Belial laughs, "Oh, this is rich. Want to watch her do it?"

"What?" I ask, shocked.

"Oh, yes, I think we're going to watch her 'off' herself," Belial muses.

A priest who looks very concerned walks past us, he reaches my mother and says a few things. I walk over to catch the rest of their conversation.

The priest is speaking to my mother as I draw near, "I want to let you know that honesty with the dead is important, so please I beg you to consider this as I speak. I mean no disrespect to your daughter."

My mother nods, "Of course Father."

Belial smiles, walking behind me, his hand on my shoulder, "Oh, this is going to go over swimmingly."

The priest stands at the front of the room, placing his bible open on a podium. "Good afternoon everyone," He begins, "Firstly, my condolences to Debra Baker. Bless each and every one of you for being here today to support her during this trying time."

The crowd murmurs and my bitch of an Aunt rubs my mother's shoulder.

I glare daggers at my aunt.

"Secondly, to Dave Miller. Dave, to lose a wife and mother of your child after such a short marriage, is a terrible thing. My condolences." The priest opens his bible. "Sara Baker, a brilliant young woman, cut down in her prime. While many can talk about the circumstances which led to her death, more are concerned with the state of her spirit after a life lived so full."

There's actually a chuckle from someone on Dave's side.

"But I want us to remember John 8:7, 'Let him who is without sin among you be the first to throw a stone at her.' For everyone sins, some sin more so than others. But we must remember that God forgives. Sara's reputation was sordid before, yes, but when she met her husband, Dave, had her child, she was a devoted wife and caring mother." He flips a few pages of the Bible, "Let us also recall Luke 7:47, 'ThereforeI tell you, her sins, which are many, are forgiven for she loved much. But he who is forgiven loves little,'" The priest now looks to Dave's family, specifically his father. "I listened to many depraved tales of Sara's youth, and I even now hear many in this room whisper ill of the deceased. So again, I ask each of you, whoever is without sin, cast the first stone."

The room was dead silent.

The priest began again, "Lord Jesus Christ forgives us all, for we are only human, now let us pray."

Belial rolls his eyes and snaps his fingers, "This became rather dull.  They don't make priests like they used to, it seems."

We're instantly in Jenny's room, it's the evening time. "Wait, that 'Jesus saves' stuff... can h-"

"If you hadn't sold your soul, yes," Belial clarifies.

"Okay, did you 'jump' us forward in time again, Master?" Ugh, I swear I almost asked it in reverence at this point.

"Yes... Because the show is about to start." Belial says, taking a seat.

"Show?" I ask bewildered.

Jenny barges in through the door, locking it behind her. She throws her scarf off her head and throws her glasses at the wall. She looks around the room and runs to her kitchen. Before I can react she grabs a knife and presses the tip to her throat. She screams for a second and drops the knife.

"Good Girl Jenny," I say.

Jenny looks to her balcony and throws the blinds open. She undoes the lock to the sliding glass door and opens it, stepping out into the cold.

"Oh shit, no no!" I shouted as I ran over to her.

Jenny gets up on the edge of the balcony, standing unsteadily.

I rushed over and hugged her legs tight, "Don't do it! Please don't do it!" I plead.

Jenny puts her arms out on either side of her and closes her eyes.

I hold on as hard as I can and watch in horror as Jenny's body falls three stories down to the ground, her leg snapping and her body tumbling down on her shoulder and rolling onto her back.

I scream, "Jenny no!"

Jenny's voice is above me, I see her standing on the railing, "Sara? Oh my God, Sara!" She jumps down from the railing and hugs me tight, kissing me full on the lips. "I knew it... I knew we'd be together."

I manage to free myself from her hug with a bit of a struggle, "Damn it, Jenny! You dumb slut! Why did you do that? And why aren't you down there rather than up here?"

Belial chimes in, "Jumper's spirits leave their bodies before they hit the ground, Sara. You see, once they resolve themselves to their fate... well... They're already dead."

Jenny looks to Belial in shock, "Is... is that the angel of death or something?"

I whisper to Jenny, "Worse... Jenny... Listen to me, get out of here, get back to your body, and live, okay? Live a long life. Forget about me, okay? I fucked up. That's not a good angel, and he owns my ass now. Okay? Please... Go."

"But I already..." Jenny begins.

I push her off the edge of the balcony and toward her body, as I shout, "Live Jen! Live for me!"

Jenny falls until she hits her body where she vanishes. Her body suddenly starts gasping for breath. Someone had been next to her giving her CPR.

In shock, I watch as he comforts her and he shouts for someone to call an ambulance.

Belial peeks his head over the balcony and turns to me, "... You were a catch, Sara. To redeem a jumper even after you sold your soul to me? By my Father you are a special one." He placed his hands on my shoulders, "I am quite pleased you're mine."

Either it was the praise, the close contact, or how long my soul was in his possession but genuine happiness washed over me as he praised me, "Thank you, Master." I shake my head, "What the..."

"Oh, don't worry Sara, that's your devotion as my newest thrall showing through." He tilts my chin up, "You see, I'm the avatar of lust. At some point I will have you, you see, and when that happens you will be absolutely elated."

A shudder runs through me as he says this, and I hate to say but I'm somehow genuinely looking forward to that.

"Well, things should have finally moved along to the point where we can begin your ascension, or Descension, rather," Belial states. Belial moves his hand up for another snap.

"No no, wait!"

Before I know it, we're in a dank basement of some kind. There are nasty pentagrams all over the walls and the smell of mildew everywhere. There are the skulls of several dead animals and a large altar in the middle of the room. I'm also pretty sure there's a rotting animal corpse somewhere in the room but I can't find where it is, my attention is drawn to the altar.

On the altar is a woman, or the caricature of one, anyway. She has long blond hair, huge ruby lips, tits the size of her head pushed up into a corset. She's also got an impossibly tiny waist and ridiculous hips. She is wearing fishnets and platform heels and looks like she's got a number of tattoos on her upper thighs, each a pair of puckered lips.

"Wow and I thought I was a slut..." I remark as I appraise the bimbo before us.

Belial interjects, "Actually she's a whore. Well, porn star. Also a heroin addict. That's a key component. The rest, well, base materials."

The woman on the slab mumbles, "Guys... It's three hundred if you're gonna run a train on me, or I'll do you for free if I can get a fix. You promised one or the other."

Three men in brown robes walked in, one with a needle, "Fine fine, quit yer bitchin'." He injects her.

"Oh!" The woman shouts, "That's good shit! Oh... oh yeah... but uh... mm. You guys should have saved that for... Later cause... mm...." She seems to zone out, moaning and shivering on the slab.

The second guy looks at the other two, "So, you guys are sure?"

The first guy with the needle nods, he has a mustache, "I told you, the voice of the demon spoke to me. He said to bring her here, lure her with the heroin, and to stab her in the heart with the icepick." He looks to the third man.

A third man nods, showing the icepick, "That's what he said."

"Nothing else?" The second guy asks.

"Nope, just that we're going to have a demoness serve our every sexual desire for the rest of our lives," Says the first guy. He looks to the third guy with the ice pick, "Come on man, let's do this."

At this point Belial grabs me by the back of my head, grinning, "I'm rather excited, Sara." I'm looking down at the drugged-out whore below me.

"Why?" I can't move away from him, his hand on the back of my head still.

"Because," Belial says with a hint of madness, "It has been almost a century since I created a new succubus..."

# CHAPTER 4

## *Descent*

---

**"Human souls which give in to darkness fail to remain human, and demonic corruption takes them as they commit more atrocities in the name of their masters."**

---

"**W**ait, what? A Succubus!" I shouted.

"Don't worry, she's a little older, but when her soul burns away and becomes your body, your youth will return and you'll be an even more perfect form of lust than she is now," Belial explains.

"Wait, okay, let's just talk this over, okay? How about I just haunt people for you?" I reasoned.

The third man holds his ice pick over the right side of the whore's chest. Belial growls, moving his finger over to the left, a small round burn mark showing on her skin.

The first guy laughs, "Holy shit! Our Demon Lord is guiding us!" He moves the third guy's hand over to the new spot. "Don't miss!"

The third guy nods, and stabs the pick into that spot once, pulling it out.

The woman gasps as she's stabbed.

"In you go!" Belial shouts.

"Wait! Wait! Can't I get a countdown or-" He shoves my head toward the hole in her chest, and I'm sucked into her.

My eyes shoot open and I glance around me, seeing the three men looking down. I'm tied to the altar and I turn to my--well the whore's chest, the wound healing rapidly. With a grunt, I try to pull myself off the table, but the straps hold me down tightly. My heart is racing and my vision is blurring.

"Is... Is she a demoness now?" The third guy asks.

I'm about to spit on the little bastard when pain wracks my entire body from head to toe. I scream.

It's like someone is ripping my toes off, one by one. The high heels I'm wearing tear apart as my toes change into a pair of cloven hooves, and my feet stretch out longer and grow a layer of purple fur. The pain subsides in my legs for a moment and then changes into a strange tugging sensation- -my legs are toning themselves, losing any form of fat that I had. The tattoos vanish as my hips somehow grow even wider, snapping the underwear I'm wearing. Steam is evaporating off of my skin and everything was way too hot! As if I'm burning from the inside out.

I scream again because someone is tearing my spine out through my back. A thin and long-tail bursts out of the small of my back, and I raise it up to my field of vision. Before my blinking eyes, I watch as the tip of the tail suddenly splits into a spade I groan -- now my midsection is being crushed, ligaments are snapping and reattaching audibly as this happened. I realize the corset isn't tight on me anymore, my waist is now actually that tiny. With my hourglass figure pretty solidified, a new intense burning pain radiates from behind me. I scream as a pair of huge purple wings tear free from my back, knocking two of the three men over.

Finally, I sit up from the intensity of all the pain, snapping the restraints as if they weren't there. I stagger to my feet, or hooves at this point, this strange power washing over my body.

My skin tightens and it grows smoother and clearer. My hair changes color from blond to a deep auburn. I gasped as my nose cracked and adjusted and my brow changed shape. It's as if someone is molding my face with their hands, cracking cheekbones, and pulling at muscles, all reshaping the size and shape of my head.

I gasp; thinking every change must now be done. I turn to my would-be captors, heaving breaths as I inspect each one.

Without warning an incredible pain rushes to both sides of my head. I grab either side screaming, my ears filled with a cracking grinding noise. A pair of ram-like horns push out of my skull. Just when I think they're done, they crack and creek another few inches, curling around from the front of my head to the back. They finally stop, curled near my ears, the points stopping just at my earlobes.

All the pain finally subsides. I shake my head, my long and luxurious hair falls between my new wings. I flex them experimentally. My vision is clearer than it has ever been, I can see every little thing in the room, even some things that aren't physically there.

I can see a kind of aura around each of the runes and pentagrams on the walls. Some animal carcasses have a black glow forming over them, which I can tell is a curse or at the least, the beginnings of one.

I sniff the air. Amidst all the mildew and dead animal parts, I can smell something else, something that smells oddly appetizing. I smell men, three of them. Now I'm seeing these three men in a vastly different light, I realize I don't want them, I need them. I licked my lips and noticed my canines have gotten a little longer, and my tongue-- I can stretch it far longer than normal.

Belial stands next to me, "Oh my, aren't you beautiful. Tell them to show you a mirror."

I turned my eyes to the third guy who had the icepick, "Sweety, mind fetching me a mirror?"

The three men stood there, dumbfounded until the third guy finally dropped the ice pick, rushing up some stairs.

The other two men hugged each other, "It worked!" They shout in unison.

"I can't believe it worked!" Shouted the first guy.

While they are celebrating, I'm appraising each like meat. "Master... Why...? Why do I want to fuck them?"

"Oh, Sara, that's the addiction part of this body. During your transmogrification, it changed from a heroin addiction--" He grins, "Into your sexual addiction."

I stared at both men and even considered the absent third, licking my lips, "I'm so hungry."

"Yes, you're starving right now, your transformation is not yet complete," Belial explains, "These three men were promised a sexual servants for as long as they lived."

The third guy comes down with a flimsy full-length mirror and pops it in front of me.

I appraise my new appearance, and I must admit I'm like raw sex appeal on a pair of goat legs. It's weird to say but as I stared at myself, I must admit I'm hot. My face is my own, my hair as well, but everything else is like a younger version of the whore's body. My skin is completely flawless. My fingers are perfectly manicured with purple nails coming to fine points. They don't appear painted, they're about an inch long each. Experimentally I loll my tongue out of my mouth and find it hangs out almost eight inches. I flex it and curl it in on itself, and giggle at the possibilities as I pull it back into my mouth.

I notice the three men are staring at me slack-jawed. I wink at them, "Oh boys... I have to admit... despite being a bit shocked myself, you are looking rather yummy."

Belial walks in front of me, "Before the fun starts and I excuse myself, I'll give you your orders and training. Firstly, your goal is to entice, seduce, and destroy anyone who would be attracted to you. If you're going after heads of state, you're to ruin their marriages and enslave them if possible. Serve yourself while on earth as long as you continue to do this. You're free to target the clergy whenever you like, but be careful not to get yourself stuck in a church. Your powers don't work on holy ground."

I nod to Belial, seeing his body makes me weak in the knees, and I suddenly want nothing more than to please his every desire. "My powers, Master?"

Belial licks his finger and places it at the center of my forehead, "Your training my dear..."

Through some horrific screeches and other images soaring through my mind, it's as if someone compressed all of my classes in my life in a second.

From this, I became completely familiar with my body, the wings, the tail, the horns, everything. So I'll recap before we continue.

First, I can fly with my wings, which is literally the least they can do. I can wrap them around myself and by doing so, I can appear to be wearing anything or appear as anyone. Little old lady? Your high school crush? Yes, to both. Doesn't even need to be female, apparently.

My tail, surprisingly, has some cool tricks. The tip leaks a poison that, when ingested, completely paralyzes someone for up to an hour. My tail is also much stronger than you'd think: I could choke a man with it and use it to even drag someone behind me. Which was handy on my way here.

Eyes have some cool tricks. If I locked eyes with you and you do the same with me, I can give suggestions. As long as they're of a sexual nature and you're aroused by my physical body, they will take. However they are weak suggestions, you'd only do them if you would have anyway without asking. For example, I can't make you walk off a bridge or stab someone by looking at you.

That being said, I can ask you to kiss me and if you're so inclined, then all bets are off. If I can get my lips on yours, I can do a few neat tricks. I can draw strength from your body, leaving you helpless in my arms, or I can completely enthrall you. At that point, I should say that if I do kiss you, I could make you walk off a cliff singing the Russian anthem.

However, I won't let a nice snack get away from me. Sex is the next thing, and if we have sex, I normally have control over how much and fast I can leech the life force out of your body. Unless I'm starving, then you are toast.

Speaking of toast! The three guys in front of me are doing rock paper scissors trying to figure out who gets the first go at me.

At this point, my starvation is overruling every other thought in my head and I saunter over to the guy who stabbed me. Me? Or the whore Trixy? Oh, I know Trixy's entire life story, it's in the back of my head, but let's focus on getting me (her?) a little revenge, shall we?

"Oh boys," I purr, "you have the rest of your lives to fight over me. So I'll pick for now." I pull him by his robes, "You two wait here."

Once we're out of the basement and heading up the stairs, I wrap a wing around him and stare into his eyes. "Take me to a nice secluded room."

His eyes dilate a bit and he nods, taking me through a pretty disgusting house. It's small and the entire place is covered in revolting trash and rotting food. I can smell everything but my hunger is overriding my other decisions. Soon I'm taken to a ratty room with a threadbare bed.

Once we get there, he grins, "I want to do you from behind."

I snicker and turn him to face me. I pull him in for an intense kiss. When I break it, his eyes are blank and he's entirely in my power. "Strip below the waist, get on the bed, and stroke your cock till it's as hard as it will get, sweetness."

He does what I ask, and I do have to say I'm very disappointed in what I have to work with. But any port in a storm as they say.

I mount him without much ceremony and I do have to add that my body's nervous system is wired for extreme pleasure. Despite guy number three's meager size, I'm at least satisfied enough to already approach a climax. That, of course, if I let it happen on its own in the state I'm in, will drain him completely. After a few minutes, I can sense that guy number three is about to burst and I leaned down and whispered into his ear.

"Are you ready for the last moment of your life?" I taunt.

Guy three's face contorts as confusion washes over his face, right before he crosses his eyes in ecstasy.

His essence poured into me and I cry out in something between raw sexual pleasure and a cold drink on a hot day. His energy and strength surge into me. I watch as he's surrounded by a purple aura and grows thinner and thinner. He struggles weakly against me, his thinning arms and increasingly boney fingers clasping at my body, trying to push my hips off his.

The power trip is unreal, his life is fading faster and faster as I grow stronger with each passing second. My wings grow larger, my horns push another inch or two out, and my tail wraps instinctively around his neck and starts to squeeze with ever-growing strength.

"Yes.... Give it to me... give me everything!" I shout in rapture.

Eventually, the guy stops moving and as he does the surge of energy turns to a trickle and then stops entirely. He looks like a dried-up mummy at this point. I dismount him and poke at his dried-up corpse.

"You in there, spunky?"

He's stone dead.

Whether because I was still starving or it was due to my transformation, I feel little to no sympathy for him.

"You dumb shit. You should know better than to trust demons."

I reflect on the irony briefly before I pick up his corpse and drop it under the disheveled couch in the living room. Then I go downstairs to grab guy number two.

Both men were still eager, apparently having heard the commotion upstairs.

"So that's one man with the ride of his life... who's next?" I ask.

From here, it was like rinse and repeat. After guy number two, I grew even stronger. My hunger was almost sated, but I found that I was physically stronger. The strength of my own body, plus the other two men were surging through me --I was absolutely drunk on the intense power from the whole experience. So when it came time for guy number three, I decided to test my strength.

"My turn?" The mustached guy asks with anticipation.

I grab him by the shoulders and force him to the ground with ease.

He starts to panic and tries to struggle against me. I grinned down at him as I completely overpower him.

"Your turn, little man."

"Wait... you... you're ours! You're the gift Lord Belial gave us!"

My tail snakes over to his mouth and shoves past his lips as his eyes grow wide. I lean down and whisper to him as he goes rigid as the poison takes hold, "No... you're the gift he gave me!" With this, I tear away his pants and start my final ride.

Despite being paralyzed, the little fucker keeps crying out for help. "Jake! Taylor! Help me! Where the fuck are you?" I think those were their names, I can't be sure.

As I ride him, a grin crosses my face and my tail snakes around his neck, "Oh honey... they're already dead."

His eyes grow even wider if that's possible. "... Oh no."

"Your sexual pleasures... I'll serve them... until your dying days," I groan. "Now feed me, honey... give me everything you've got and more."

With that, he screams, unable to move, as I suck the life out of him.

It is at this point that things go entirely off the rails for me. Apparently, the three stooges were supposed to lure the whore to their house where they would do their deed. No big issue, right? Well, the dinguses had instead snatched her off the street in view of folks who knew her. Those folks called the cops. Those cops got the plates from the moron's van and tracked it to their house because of course, they did this in their house! So, now, while I'm riding the first guy to his death, a policeman kicks the door into the basement and spotted me.

"Okay get on the... what the fuck..."

Frustrated, I give a final effort and finish him off with a growl, rolling off of the altar.

The officer shouts into his radio "I've got a body... and... a perp... she... uh... she's in some kind of sex costume. I need backup."

After composing myself, I take a nice deep breath and close my wings around myself. I make myself out like a human woman, wearing the outfit I had on when the three morons brought me down here (or her, it's kind of jumbled up in my head).

I stagger to my feet, "Oh... Officer... Thank God." I pretend to be very unsteady.

The officer was startled as he saw me and looked at the body, not dropping his gun, "What happened... to him? Why were you on top of that... corpse?"

I faked some tears, looking him in the eyes, "Oh, they made me do it... they made me jump on that terrible thing. They said if I didn't, they'd kill me." I add a few sobs in there while working my power and looking into his eyes.

The officer drops the gun down, walking towards me, "Oh... okay, I believe you. Just... let's get you out of here, okay? Do you have any ID on you?"

I keep my eyes on his. "You don't need my ID, honey. Just get me out of here without anyone else seeing me."

"I... I can't do that."

I'm close enough at this point, I kiss him deeply, pulling him close. He struggles for a moment but eventually, he relaxes. I pull back, looking him in the eyes, "Get me out of here, safely, and without anyone seeing me."

He nods mutely and picks up his gun as we walk up the stairs. At the top of the stairs is another cop.

"Ramirez, who's that?", A woman's voice asks.

I whisper into his ear, "No witnesses. Kill her, get me out of here, you'll do anything for me."

Officer Ramirez aims his gun at the officer at the top of the stairs.

"Hey! Holy shit Ramez stop!" She shouts.

I see Ramirez shake his head slowly, "Can't!" He pulls the trigger three times.

We make our way up the steps before I notice the woman isn't there.

"What the fuck?"

Ramirez looks to the left--and is suddenly body checked into the wall by the woman. Both of them are blocking my way so I try to push past them. I have a little issue doing this, as I've got the strength of four people. However, me forcing my way through knocks Ramirez on the head.

"Freeze!" The woman shouts.

I turn to her, trying to enthrall her with my eyes.

"Okay whatever crazy bullshit you're doing with your eyes, stop now! On the ground!"

"Fuck you, pig!" I shout and rush toward the back door.

"I will shoot!"

Part of the knowledge that Belial gave me told me that I couldn't die by a mortal weapon, but it would mess with my camouflage. I decided to chance it, and I did my best to run to the door. That's about when the bullet struck my shoulder, then another in my chest. I roar in pain. It's not a human sound, and it startles me and the female cop. My disguise drops, wings unfurl, my tail swings out, and my hooves push me up another foot taller. I glance down at my chest and see yellowish fluid leaking out of the holes. Both seem to be slowly closing but I'm weakening as they do.

"What the fuck!" The female officer screams.

I face her and charge her.

She unloads the rest of her clip into me, and one of those bullets hits my head. Everything goes black, and I hit the floor.

All I see now is black as the female officer's voice echoes somewhere near me.

"She took two fucking bullets and then turned into that... thing! She's not fucking human! It's not a fucking costume!"

Another man's voice is overhead, "Officer Ramirez described her as a normal woman."

"She was controlling him!"

Ramirez's voice cracks in, "Captain, Judy, you shot her dead right?"

Judy, the woman, chimes in, "I put one between her eyes."

"Then why is the body bag rising and falling like she's breathing?" Ramirez asks.

Oops!

Soon I see light as the zipper to the body bag I was in is opened. I blink as I see Ramirez, Judy, and another officer staring down at me. I decide to try to reach out and grab the superior officer, and my arms tear through the body bag I'm wrapped up in without much issue. In short order, another bullet rips through me, as the superior officer plants it between my eyes. Apparently getting shot in the head is inconvenient for a succubus and I'm passed out again.

By the time I've regained consciousness, I'm staring at the inside of another body bag. I struggle but I'm strapped down hard to something. I mean really strapped, my head, neck, shoulders, chest, waist, hips, legs, and feet.

"Jesus, the fucking thing came back!" Judy shouts.

Ramirez is next, "Who the fuck is she?"

"It!" Judy shouts, "That's not a woman!"

"Fuck you!" I shout. "Let me go, pigs!"

Ramirez continues, "She's a fucking Barney for Christ's sake, you heard her talk?"

Judy interrupts, "Hang a left here. We're going to the Church."

A third male voice speaks now, "Is that why we're heading to Copley?"

"Yes, we're going to Trinity Church. We need a priest, not a doctor," Judy continues.

"Okay, whatever." The driver says.

The vehicle turns and I shift with it, ever so slightly in my restraints. I remember my kiss on Ramirez. My eyes close tight and my horns heat up as I concentrate on giving him another order. "You want to save me. They're trying to kill me. Crash the truck. Set me free."

Judy suddenly shouted, "Ramirez, what are you doing?"

"Hey! What the fu-" The driver shouts before three shots go off. The vehicle swerves and crashes. The gurney I'm strapped to falls over as I try to free myself. There's a struggle in the vehicle now that it has come to a stop.

"Ramirez! Stop!" Judy shouts.

"You're trying to kill her... I need to save her." Ramirez drones.

"Don't... don't reach for it. Ramirez. Put it down! Ramirez!" Two gunshots ring out.

I'm grinning ear to ear, still strapped down. In a moment I'll be unstrapped and free. The gurney gets set right side up, and the zipper to the body bag is removed. However, I'm not too pleased with what I see.

It's Judy and boy, does she look pissed. Her face was bloodied and I can somehow tell it was not all her blood.

"You made me shoot my partner, you bitch! I'm going to send you straight to Hell."

Before I can do anything, the bag is zipped up and I'm being wheeled up some ramp, Judy grunting with each tug as I do my best to make things difficult for her. Once we're at the top of the stairs, however, a strange sensation comes over me. The unending hunger leaves me. What did Belial tell me? "Be careful not to get yourself stuck in a church. Your powers don't work on holy ground."

Judy's voice screams, resounding through what I assume is the inside of a church, "I need a priest! Seriously! I need a priest!"

A moment goes by and an older man's voice echoes as if we're in a large room, "Child... please... this is the house of God. He hears all, there is no need to shout."

I close my eyes and concentrate on hiding my shape, trying to pick something innocent, but it doesn't seem right. I can see again as she unzips the body bag.

"Jesus, Mary, and Joseph…" The priest says, shocked.

I'm confused, and I realize, as the priest touches my horns, that I didn't change shape. "What the fuck?" I locked eyes with him, trying to get him to unstrap me.

Judy's hand goes over my eyes, "Don't look at her eyes when she does that… she… she took over my partner… he… I had to… oh God, Father… he had already killed someone for her, he was going to kill me. She… She's some kind of…"

"Demon," The priest says plainly. The body bag is zipped up. "I have a call to make. Take her to the courtyard."

It's a few minutes of silence before I hear the worst thing I've heard all day. "I just called, we have to burn her. Only holy ground"

"Fuck off!" I shout.

Judy's voice is next, "Okay I'll get wood."

"How about you just let me go!" I shout.

Before long, and after a lot of really frightening sounds of wood being piled up somewhere, I'm wheeled on top of something.

"If you bastards are going to burn me, could you at least knock me out first?" The body bag unzips entirely and Judy's face is in mine.

"I'm gonna listen to you burn, bitch, for what you did to my partner."

I narrowed my eyes, all bets off, "Your partner wanted nothing more than to plow me eight ways to Sunday, and all I did was kiss him once."

Judy flicks a lighter, "Go back to Hell, bitch."

I grab her hand tight with mine, hugging her close to me. "Are you willing to go down with me?"

Judy tries to tug away from my hand, but an echo of the strength of the men I drained is still there, and she can't budge me. Judy puts the lighter out, and goes for her gun, I grab her other hand. I squeeze both of her hands until bones break.

"Try lighting me up now, bitch!" I shout.

Judy screams, and looks behind me, "Father! Light it!"

"But you're still–"

"Do it!" Judy shouts, interrupting him.

Heat surrounds us, but I still hold on tight, "See you down there."

"I don't think we're going to the same place," Judy says before she screams as the flames consume us both.

# CHAPTER 5

## *Hellscape*

"Wounds heal in Hell, but they inflict pain while doing so.  For every horrific wound suffered, a more horrific healing pain will follow."

Burning hurts. The fire, your flesh peeling back and muscles searing. The worst part is how you can feel what parts have just been cooked. You go numb, you choke on the smoke of your own skin and hair. It's... a terrible way to go.

Also, as a side note, I took that policewoman with me. There are… some regrets after I realized how painful it is to burn to death.

However, the next thing I remember is going down a dark tunnel. Soon a foul wind is blowing through my hair and I open up my wings to stop myself from falling. As I circle around, I dodge a few unfortunate bastards falling past me. Down below, there's a huge hill. I head towards it only to find it is most certainly not a hill.

The people falling are smacking into a huge pile of bodies. Most everyone is naked, and each hit makes a sickening snap and smacking sound. It looks like blood is pooling underneath the giant pile, so I land a good distance from it, taking in the fairly sickening sight. I notice the blood is evaporating a few feet from where I land. The people in the pile are all screaming and moaning in pain. For some reason, as I hear the screams, I experience no empathy for them. Instead, I'm relieved that I'm not them. I take to the air again and inspect at the top of the pile.

I'm mostly looking for Judy the police officer, she's not near the top or falling. As I land, I spot something flying toward me. I dread that it may be my Master Belial, but what lands before me is another succubus.

Well, another succubus would be a terrible way to describe her. Each horn on either side of her head is almost four feet long. They curl out of her head and point near her back. Massive red wings close up behind her. I notice her hooves are covered in some kind of bronze boots, which run to her thighs with crimson leather. Her crotch is covered with a bikini bottom, leathery-looking with a bronze triangle covering the front. The red leather motif continues up her waist as a full corset that covers her torso. A posture collar wraps around her neck. Her arms are also covered in red leather. However, this appears to be part of the dress where the front basically doesn't exist. The dress seems connected to the posture collar as well. Her lips are full and black, blue eyes, and her hair is black as well.

"Sara Baker, I assume?" She speaks with a posh British accent.

"Who wants to know?" I ask.

She heaves a sigh, "Bloody Hell, you sound like an Irishman."

I narrow my eyes. "Fuck off!"

She shakes her head and holds her hand in front of her, an image appearing in front of her with writing on it.

"I'll orientate you quickly: Welcome to Hell. I am Esmeralda, I am essentially the Queen of the Succubi, answering only to Belial and of course to our Lord." She motions to a huge white tower in the distance.

I sneeze from the ash falling in the air. "Wait, so you're... my boss or something?"

Esmeralda nods, "I get that this is difficult for one of your social statuses to grasp, what with you being of slave ancestry, but please try to keep pace."

"I'm a fucking Harvard student, okay? I'm not some moron," I chastise.

Esmeralda produces a whip from nowhere, and it snaps across my face.

Pain sears across my cheek and I fall to the hot ground.

"What the fuck was that for!?"

"Disrespect.  I am your Queen, and I will have none of that. Now up, wench! I'll show you to your new quarters," She says as she takes to the air.

I follow her, as the body pile doesn't seem terribly enticing at the moment.

As I fly through the air, pools of lava are below us, demons marching around, and what looks like humans being horrifically tortured. Some are drawn and quartered, thrown into pits of boiling lava, that sort of thing. Esmeralda lands in a fairly not-so-on-fire location. There's a series of small huts that each have a door with a sturdy lock

"Welcome to the fields of Lust. Here you and your fellow succubi will do favors for Belial's indebted. Occasionally you will go out and feed on some lost souls. I suggest avoiding any of the lesser demons or anything else out there of similar or greater standing." Esmeralda closes her wings as she approaches me. "We succubi are at the bottom of the barrel here. We are the lowest form of demon, we do not garner any respect. We need to stick together to survive."

For the first time, I sensed some sincerity, "Is Master going to punish me?"

Esmeralda shakes her head, "You did what you could with what you had. Murdered two officers, an EMT, and devoured the essence of the three dolts who helped to create you. Had you actually not been in a situation where human authorities were shooting you the moment you were created, perhaps you'd have done more."

Esmeralda looks out to the large white tower, "Lord Belial is in the Blade of Pride right now, torturing those three dullards. They failed him in a way that is indescribable."

Then she looks at the end of the row of small huts and raises her hand up. From the ground, a new structure appears.

"Your quarters," Esmeralda says simply.

I walk towards it. When I open the door, there is nothing but a slab of dirt as a bed, with no covers or pillows. There's a small window in the corner. "This looks like a prison cell..."

Esmeralda chuckles from behind me, "My dear... this is Hell, after all, what did you expect? Royal accommodations?"

At this point, Belial lands near Esmeralda and me. He's no longer wearing the suit and hat. Instead, he's shirtless, wearing a silver gorget and medieval leg armor. He is much larger than I remember, towering above me and Esmeralda at almost nine feet tall.

Esmeralda falls to one knee, her tail wrapping around my neck and pulling me down, "Bow before our Master, Wench!"

My knee hits the hot ground as I'm robbed of breath. At this point, I also assume my new name is apparently 'Wench'.

"Sara, how unfortunate to find you down here so soon," Belial growls.

"Sorry, Master... I... I failed you," I say. I don't know why but actual sorrow washed over me for not doing what he asked of me.

"It is not your fault Sara," Belial sighs.

A wave of relief washes over my body. A weight lifts from my shoulders and a shiver of pleasure runs through me as he speaks. I noticed that Esmeralda is in the same state I am with our Master before us.

Before my eyes, the three morons who created me are thrown to the ground.

"These idiots... are to suffer. Sara... I think this a wonderful first assignment for you," Belial begins, "Devour them over and over again, and when they request reprieve, give them none, fuck them until they cannot give another ounce of their essence, and then do it again and again until I tell you to cease."

I lick my lips as I am given my orders, "Yes, Master."

The three men whimper in front of me.

"And Sara..." Belial growls, "Be dominant, give them no pleasure."

For the next few weeks, I make each of those guys regret having cocks. A weird thing happens when you drain a soul in Hell. The normal mummification thing happens... but they kind of 'puff up' again, but painfully. Over time I notice that they are getting less and less talkative. To be completely honest, I never learned their names.

One day, after a rousing session all three men started to act oddly.

All three had stopped talking entirely, just laying around all day doing little or nothing outside of breathing. My orders from Belial were the same, and I continued to ravage them, drawing less and less essence by the day. Finally, after a particularly intense "draining," one of the guys didn't just dry up into a mummy--instead, he continued to shrink, his body crumbling into itself until he was nothing more than a brown orb with a dim light in the center. I was confused but followed my orders on the other two until the same thing happened to both of them. I stared, confused, at the three dim orbs sitting in my little hut. I walked out, not too sure what to do. The orbs aren't men to drain or devour, so I figure I can call Esmeralda. She hopefully would know what was going on.

I clear my throat, "Yo, Esmeralda!"

A few succubi around me stop and stare at me oddly. They scoff, ignore me, and move on.

"...Oh God, it's middle school all over again." I think to myself.

I see Esmeralda approaching me casually. "At first I thought boulders were careening down the cliff sides to land upon a particularly unlucky serpent, causing a hissing cry of anguish..." She stops a few feet in front of me, with her whip at the ready, "but it was none other than my crass bog-trotter."

I clear my throat, mocking her accent, "My good lady, I hath a question to pose to you."

Esmeralda squints as if I just dragged nails over the chalkboard, "Never... ever attempt to speak King's to me again. I rather your bastardized Gaelic than that." She adjusts herself, "Now, what is it?"

I show her the three orbs in my room.

"Where did you get three soul cores?" she asks, kicking one with her gilded hoof.

The orb lights up for a moment before going dim again.

"Those were my charges," I say, looking at Esmeralda, "Now what do I do?"

Esmeralda closes her eyes, and I watch as her horns glow, an aura extending around them before it pulls back. "We await our Master."

A shudder runs through me as I think of him, "ugh…" I say out loud.

"You'll eventually learn to deal with his presence," Esmeralda explains. "He'll take his time, of course." She walks into my little hut with me and closes the door.

"So what's a soul core?"

Esmeralda gives another one a small kick, rolling them into each other. "Think of them as the absolute lowest point a soul can get to. The raw building block, so to speak. Strip away one's identity, one's will, their individuality and all that is left is their base existence."

I shrug. "So I drained these guys till they were nothing?"

"Doubtful. This happens when one's spirit breaks. A Succubus has never caused such a thing. We may give pleasure and drain essence but to draw away someone's identity is… well, unheard of," Esmeralda explains.

I lean against the wall of my little dirt hut, grumbling at how every surface can manage to be uncomfortable.

Belial eventually enters, looking to both Esmeralda and me, "Well, if it isn't my two favorite harlots. What is this?" He motions to the orbs.

Esmeralda swoons, "Master, Sara was doing your bidding, as you commanded, and her charges suddenly changed into Soul Cores. We had to consult your intellect before we did anything."

My body is on fire as I move closer to Belial. "What shall I do with them, Master?"

Belial grumbles to himself, "He would be rather agitated if I did not inform him of this." Belial looks me over, "Sara, you're going to meet my Lord."

Esmeralda swoons again, "Oh Master, shall I come with you? Last time Lord Lucifer's lust rose, I attended to him, he was oh so grateful and appreciative of my skills."

"I doubt he will be in the mood Esmeralda, but if you wish, I can see if he'll want you later," Belial scoffs, "Perhaps you could soothe him." Belial narrows his eyes at the Blade of Pride in the distance. "Come with me, my Sara, and gather up those baubles."

As I move to pick up the three orbs, I grumble about how large they are. They're the size of bowling balls, but about a quarter of the weight. "Little shits couldn't be smaller, could you?"

To my shock, they grow smaller, suddenly the size of marbles and now much brighter "...okay, weird." I walk out holding them in one hand.

Belial lifts his eyebrow. "They weren't that size before."

"They are now," I say simply, sliding them between my cleavage.

Belial takes to the air and I follow behind him.

After a few minutes of flying, we reach the very top of the Blade of Pride. The closer I get to it, the ivory white tower appears less solid white and more a mass of many white building materials, few in a straight line. A massive balcony juts out from the top with an ivory-like railing around the edges. I notice that the rails within appear to be made of bone, and it appears the rest is constructed from the same material.

As Belial lands, he gives me a stern talking to, "You do not speak unless spoken to or requested to speak, do you understand?"

"Yes, Master."

"And do not, under any circumstances, disrespect Him, do you understand?" Belial continues to lay down the law.

"Yes, Master." I drone.

With this, the two of us walk into the massive darkened chamber connected to the balcony.

Inside I'm greeted with a gruesome sight. A man of middle eastern descent hangs by his neck from the ceiling. The rope digs into his flesh harshly as he dangles. His gasping and rasping voice echoed through the darkened room.

The room itself is cavernous, a ceiling so high I cannot see the top as it stretches into the darkness. Across the room, the dark is broken up by streaks of red light from outside. On the floor and wall in between is a massive throne. The throne's back is as tall as the ceiling. Etched into the white human ivory is an ornate pentagram. Directly under the pentagram, I see a pair of violet swirling eyes, like

Belial's, but somehow burning brighter, stronger, more imposing.

The head they are in starts to move toward the hanging man.

"Forty virgins..." He says flatly. He walks into the light.

A handsome face, the features look like they are carved from marble. Power radiates from his form, his build athletic but contained within tarnished silver armor. Across his chest is a pair of glowing white chains crossing at the middle of his breastplate. The chains look as if they have seared the metal of the armor, yet no steam or any indication of heat is visible. Behind him is a pair of huge black wings with flawless feathers, unlike Belial's which are covered in soot. He has long blond hair, flawless hair. Everything about him is flawless, perfect-looking. He looks like the ideal male, standing nearly ten feet tall. He looms over me and even Belial.

Out of sheer instinct, I kneel.

A smile cracks across the beautiful angel's face and his laugh fills the room, but it's not joyful laughter. It's filled with malice and a tinge of hate.

"Forty virgins! Allah shall grant you for the vicious murder of innocents! Yes!" He shouts, "Yes! What fools are you, to think killing unarmed innocents in the name of God is justified?"

His hands go onto either shoulder of the man. His tone shifts drastically, "The decadent delights I have for you will make you regret ever speaking his name in my house."

The man squeaks out two words, "Allahu...Akbar..."

Lucifer backhands the man, sending him flying into the air while remaining tight at the end of the rope. He hits the apex of his swing and then flies back, his toes coming within an inch of the floor before he swings in the other direction. At this point, Lucifer seems to notice us.

"Belial, to what do I owe the pleasure?"

Belial has been kneeling this whole time, "My Lord, I have an interesting development."

"More interesting than asking me for a portion of my power to place your shadow upon the world to create a seductress of men, only to have her slain in less than a day?" Lucifer says flatly.

"My Lor-"

Lucifer's voice radiates off the walls and back at us so loud, it's as if I'm at a rock concert.

"Do not regale me of your pitiful excuses Belial! Succubi in this plain are worthless as the ash that falls from the cavern ceiling!" Lucifer is still for a moment, his eyes tracing to me. "Are you parading your failure to me as mockery, Belial?"

"No Lord Lucifer, I would neve-" Belial is cut short as he is jolted up from the floor. He flies forward until his neck collides with Lucifer's outstretched hand.

"I was very clear, Belial, was I not? I informed you that you were never to drag that pathetic creature before me." Lucifer squeezes Belial's neck, Belial's gorget creaks from the pressure.

Belial gasps, "My Lord, she has proven... extraordinary."

Lucifer releases Belial without much ceremony. "Then speak of this anomaly and leave me."

Belial wheezes and motions to me, "Show him the cores."

I reach into my cleavage and pull out the three marble-sized cores. I place them in front of me.

"Soul cores. What of them, Belial?" Lucifer says without paying me any mind.

"She made them, My Lord," Belial says ominously.

Lucifer walks toward me, each footfall reverberating around the room and back to me and then again. He picks them up in his hand, and as he does, they grow dim. His eyebrow raises. As he moves them toward Belial, they remain dim. As he brings them toward me, they begin glowing again.

"Speak your name whore."

"S-Sara Baker," I managed to stutter.

He places the orbs on the ground before me, and then pinches my chin between his thumb and forefinger, leaning down to me. "Now, Sara Baker... what are you, exactly?" His eyes swirl faster and fill my vision entirely.

It's as if I'm being stripped naked. But it doesn't stop at my clothing, it continues, growing more invasive, as if he is stripping me of more than that. Layer after layer of my mind, my heart, my soul are peeled back. I shake and quiver under his gaze as it bores into me, as no secret of my life is left untouched, He sees things I didn't even know about myself.

When he is done I slowly piece myself back together.

Lucifer slowly raises back to a standing position, turning his focus to Belial. "A word, brother."

Lucifer's wing extends toward Belial quickly and then jabs into his chest, a metal-like ringing through the air as it pierces Belial's flesh.

Belial gasps, grabbing at the feather impaling him. The feather doesn't budge, as if it were made of steel. Belial steadies himself for a moment, "What... is the meaning of this My Lord?"

"Did you know what she was, Belial? The soul you took... What sort it was? It's destiny?"

Belial whines, "Only after I had taken it, My Lord."

The feather slides deeper into Belial's chest as I look on in horror.

"You're a greater fool than I thought you to be if you want me to believe one like her fell for your transparent ploy."

Belial winces, "There's less spirituality, fewer miracles, more disease. All since your daughter ravaged the temple of the Guardians, My Lord, the humans are less enlightened!"

Lucifer's feather rips out of Belial's chest.

Belial takes a knee as he hits the ground, bleeding.

"The three halfwits are the only proof I need of that. No adversaries make for foolish human servants..." Lucifer seems to spit the word 'human' out of his mouth as if it leaves a bad taste.

From behind us, the hanging man whimpers again, "Allahu...Akbar..."

Lucifer turns and in an instant is by the man, his massive hand inside the hanging man's mouth.

"I will rip your tongue from your head," Lucifer threatens as flesh and sinew snap as he does just that, "Every time you speak His name." He raises the man's tongue above him so the man can see it. "And then I will shove it back down your throat!"

Lucifer's hand dives down into the man's mouth, his jaw cracking and dislocating as Lucifer's gauntlet bulges and breaks the skin. Bone fragments pierce through the man's cheeks as he chokes on the tongue now lodged in his throat.

Lucifer starts to rant, "Favored of Our Father... Made in my image to mock me!" He shouts. "Given free will, as I gave to my own children, whom He slew!" The whole temple shakes. "All for these monkeys!" He turns to Belial and me, the violet eyes surging with power and rage. "You, Sara! What do you think of humans? Having been one recently."

I consider my place for a moment, but I remember my father-in-law, my aunt, my 'friends'. How my aunt was a two-faced bitch, my father-in-law's opinion of me. I think back to Jenny and Beth's treatment of me, how it led me down this path. "I hate them."

Lucifer's eyebrow raises.

"They're greedy, small-minded, hateful creatures," I say plainly.

There's a moment of silence. Then Lucifer approaches me and smiles. It is a horrid grin despite it appearing gleeful. It's full of malice, wickedness, and pride. "I rather like you."

I shudder in relief.

"Belial, pick yourself up and bring me those hapless fools you called your servants. I have some tortures I'd like to try," Lucifer chuckles. "Small-minded..."He repeats.

Belial stands slowly, his wound surprisingly still opened, "My Lord, those three are the soul cores. I had ordered Sara to torment them as punishment for failing me."

Lucifer looks to the three orbs, "After so short a time?" He appears to be in thought for a moment or two, "Belial, she gets to keep them. They have an affinity for her, for some reason, so they won't be much use to anyone else."

"My Lord-" Belial is interrupted.

"I said she keeps them," Lucifer repeats, "Not you, her!" he points at me. "Now both of you leave me and send me Esmeralda. Your Succubus Queen is the only one whom I can take pleasure in," He eyes me curiously, "for now."

"At once, My Lord," Belial says as he limps out of the throne room.

I gather up my orbs, place them in my cleavage again, and help Belial to walk. Once we're outside, I look at his wound. "My Master... why does it not heal?"

Belial grunts, "Wounds inflicted by Lucifer's hand... do not heal as others do. If he so desired, he could slay my soul entirely, such is our Lord's power."

I try to hide my excitement, "Master, are you dying?"

Belial laughs. "I am wounded but I shall not perish from Lucifer's chiding."

Damnit, I think to myself. Belial's death would set me free. Well, at that time it would have. You see, my Master isn't

Belial anymore. That all started when Esmeralda came to all of the Succubus years later.

"Whores!" Esmeralda shouted at us, as we were lined up before our little huts, "We are now in for a very important task!"

I look along the row, seeing a few faces I'd grown familiar with.

"Lord Belial has promised one of you unfortunate wenches to a very important client."

I can hear Mara, a friend of mine, start to whisper to my right, "Not again..."

Esmeralda announced, "Lord Asmodai."

# CHAPTER 6

## *Changing Hearts*

"A pact made on one's soul is a pact for one's free will." "Sin is life in Hell.  But God is Love. As such, the only thing considered a sin in Hell is Love."

"No! No! I won't! I can't! Not again!" Mara hysterically cries out as she falls to the ground.

Esmeralda looks her dead in the eyes and I swear, I saw the daggers lash out and crash into the shrieking girl.

Mara whimpers. "He picked me last time... He... He... ripped off my arm... and... he..." She breaks down sobbing.

Esmeralda looks at me, "Sara, help her up."

I nod and kneel down to grab her by the arm.

"So that's all, my Queen?" A middle eastern voice says plainly, "That's all it takes to avoid the ravages of Lord Asmodai?"

Esmeralda glares at her, "Hold your tongue, Khairunnisa, or I'll ensure Lord Asmodai chooses you!"

As I help Mara back to her hooves, Khairunnisa continues, "At least replace Mara, my Queen. Why not let Sara onto the docket?"

There's some murmuring among the others.

I'd been left out the last two times Asmodai had called. Poor Mara was chosen both times.

"She's not too green now," Khairunnisa continues. "She's as good as any of us. Apparently better, being Master Belial's favored."

Esmeralda pulls out her whip, "Our Master prefers none of us over the other. Now silence yourself before I crack you across your throat!"

Esmeralda coils her whip and connects it to her hip as I continue to struggle to get Mara up.

"I don't care, add me to the docket," I say as I stand up in line, propping up the hysterical Mara.

Khairunnisa just grins at me, snickering.

I glance at her, spotting her brown eyes and yellow horns. Her leather is a mix of reds, blues, and yellows. She's likely the most experienced succubus outside of Esmeralda. "What are you laughing at, Ghazzawi?"

Khairunnisa shakes her head, "You're a smart girl, Sara, but you lack wisdom."

Esmeralda shouts at both of us, "And yet you're both here. So shut it!" She heaves a sigh, "It is I who chooses who will be part of the selection."

Belial lands near her, and all of the succubi swoon, Esmeralda less than most, "You are not the only one, my Queen." He grabs at Esmeralda's rear.

Esmeralda staggers for a moment, "My Master... I was preparing our... stable for Lord Asmodai's choosing."

Belial lets go of Esmeralda and looks over all of us, focusing on Mara, "What is it, dear Mara? Can you not serve me well enough today?"

"N-No, Master. Lord Asmodai was cruel to me... n-not like you, Master..." She trails off.

I let go of Mara and stepped back, as the Succubus to her left did the same.

"Repeat that whore," Belial demands.

"He... he... I meant to say, you've never treated me--"

"Would you like me to? Clearly, if I haven't treated you as poorly as Asmodai can, then I must be doing something wrong," Belial spat.

She shudders, half in dread and half in lust-fueled desire, "No-No he... he just made me feel more pain than... than you have..."

Open mouth, insert hoof! That was a stupid comment to make to Belial. I learned very quickly that while Belial paraded us around to every demon with soul cores to spend, he also prided himself on being a Prince of Hell.

Belial's perfect mouth turns up at either end into a million-watt smile. The kind of smile a lawyer gets when he wins a multi-million dollar case when his client is guilty. It is a predatory smile.

"Mara, is it?"

Mara nods cautiously,

"I want you to experience barely imaginable pain, feel it, embrace it, through every pore of your skin. As if every nerve in your body was experiencing the pain of birth that first stupid whore Eve gave all of you little twats."

Mara screams and falls to the ground, grabbing at her body and writhing in such an extreme and intense way, it looked like she'd crack herself in half.

"I have got a lovely stable of whores, and your task is to perform. Perform for those who I give you too. I do not care what they do to you, because at the end of the day, you'll still be my beautiful, perfect representations of lust!" Belial barks, Mara's screams acting as a backdrop to his speech. "You have an eternity of horrific tortures, don't go losing your mind just because someone screws an opened wound. Next one who gets uppity will get tossed into the fire until I remember you're there... which reminds me, I think we have a whore who's been in there for some time now."

"Bertha, my Lord, shall I pull her from the fires?" Esmeralda asks, bowing.

"How long has she been in there?" Belial asks.

"Forty years," she replies.

"Eh, what's the point, why not?" As he walks off, he states, "Your Queen will be collecting the lucky 'winner' once his choice is made. You all have ten hours to submit your most alluring portraits to Esmeralda." Then he left through a portal that opened out of nowhere.

I could think straight again, we all could. Mara's screams were starting to get to me. Luckily Khairunnisa managed to gag her so now we just heard muffled screaming.

The charred skeleton of Bertha was whipped onto the floor by Esmeralda.

Her bones were blackened by the fires but slowly seemed to 'unchar' and turn white. Her flesh slowly grew back next. Then her vocal cords strung themselves back together; the screaming from her picked up nearly as loudly as Mara. She didn't scream for as long though, once her skin reformed and her wings and tail grew back. She was panting heavily and completely naked, struggling to get up onto her red-furred hooves.

I moved to help her up, along with the Succubus who was next to Mara at the time, Britney I think her name is?   I generally don't socialize much with the other succubi-- like I said, middle school all over again. Bertha looks at us, visibly shaking, her deep green eyes, bloodshot at the moment, darting around like flies.

I figured I'd ask, "Bertha, you okay?"

Her hands are around my neck in an instant, her clawed fingers pushing into the back of my neck. "I... burned... forever! Okay?! OKAY! How. Fucking. Dare You!" She lets go of me and collapses on the ground, now sobbing. "Oh, why...?"

Esmeralda cracks her upside the head, knocking her to the floor, "Shut up and get dressed, whore. Be happy enough that Lord Belial recalled your existence! Now get your worthless cunt into the dressing halls and put on something alluring!"

Isn't she a sweetheart, folks?

The other succubi scurry along. I help Bertha up to her hooves.

She stands unsteadily, looking up to me. Bertha wraps her wings around herself and shudders, then looks to the ground. "Sorry." She squeaks.

I sigh and place my hand on her shoulder, walking us toward the multiple huts. "I asked for it."

Bertha mopes off and I look to Esmeralda. There isn't a whole lot of comradery between us succubi. The fact that, at the merest request, Master Belial could simply ask one of us any information he wanted and we would tell him, doesn't really help out with that.

I walk up to her, "I'm ready for the portrait."

Esmeralda looked me up and down, raising a perfect eyebrow. "Like that, Sara?"

I nod.

"I know you have been spared a goodly amount of all of the suffering. You are smart enough to keep your nose clean and you've been one of his more favorite acquisitions."

I keep silent, waiting for her to get to the point I know she wants to make.

"In case you have not taken heed to the signs... Lord Belial likes you. For some reason, your soul must have been worth quite a lofty sum to him, how I do not know," She looks to where Belial had arrived from, the Tower of Lust--a huge black spire reaching into the air which, honestly, I always thought looked like a giant black stone dick but that might have just been a coincidence.

"But offend him and you will end up worse off than that unfortunate one." She gestures to Mara who was still writhing in so much pain, I heard a limb snap as she writhed around. "Obedience is going to be the sole way you can survive and so far you have been well enough to be good and obedient."

I raise my eyebrow.

"Well, as 'good' as one can be down here. You have to realize there are worse fates."

I looked down at my own leather-clad hooves. "It's still Hell."

"Obviously Sara. What do you expect? Take my advice and make the best of the worst situations. Keep your head down and mouth shut. How is it you think I rose to this position? As he collects more whores, he may be seeking out another to work under me but above the others. While he has not said so, my assumption is that he would either choose you or Khairunnisa, but you must remain vigilant and proper. Do not cross his good graces, bog-trotter."

This might not sound motivating, but down here it was the closest to a 'Ra-Ra-Ra go Sara!' I was ever going to get.

"I understand... Still, just take the portrait." I look up, smiling with my pouty lips, wrapping my wings around me, lowering them ever so slightly to give a bit of cleavage, just a tease. My hair is a bit wild as I look ahead alluringly, giving a smoldering gaze to my Queen.

Esmeralda holds her thumb to her pointer finger and does the same with the other hand, making a rectangle out of her fingers. She lines them up and then a thin vestige of me appears within her fingers. She turns her palm open and then looks at the smoky and burning image before closing her hand around it.

"Drag Mara to her quarters. I'll talk to Belial about ending her torment by the days' end."

As much as I hated Esmeralda, she was the only one who seemed to give a rat's ass about us. Some would claim she only did it because it meant she didn't have to screw Belial's clients. I knew better, deep down, I think she actually cared. She never showed it though.

I shut Mara into her quarters, just as Khairunnisa shows her face.

"You will be a broken woman, Sara Baker," she says, taunting me.

"So what? Then I'll be you, 'Khairunnisa Ghazzawi,'" I taunt back.

Khairunnisa laughs, "You're a foolish girl, you know that?"

"Not my fault the summoners got me killed after a few hours of my 'rebirth'."

Khairunnisa scoffs, "Always an excuse with you, Baker. When I finally passed, it was only because an entire city had accused me of being a witch and adulterer." She smiles as she reflects. "My original husband turned to an incubus at my behest. So many little wives from him and enthralled husbands for me. Our harem was truly haram." She chuckles at her stupid joke. "I made polygamy a tradition in my family and country, that is how true the lust I spread was." She looks me up and down, "What did you do again?"

I say nothing as I try to walk away.

"Ah yes, you fed yourself to the wolf," Khairunnisa taunts.

I turn to face her, "Why are you so certain Asmodai will choose me?"

Khairunnisa laughs, "When Asmodai was on earth, he murdered all seven fiancés of a young woman. He coveted her and he slew any and all men who dared to have her." She grins. "It took the summoning of the Angel Raphael to cast Asmodai back."

I shrug. "What's all that have to do with me?"

"Her name was Sarah," Khairunnisa said menacingly.

My eyes go wide as I realize.

"He'll choose you, Sara, he'll choose you and he'll torture you and rend your flesh. He'll break you because you are weak and green."

I look around to see if I can spot Esmeralda. Maybe she can take me out of the running or Belial might not want Asmodai to have at me. Ever since we had visited Lord Lucifer he had been overly protective of me. Before I can go anywhere, however, Khairunnisa's tail is in my mouth. My eyes go wide as the sour poison touches my lips.

Khairunnisa is standing over me after I collapse. "You look tired." She grins, "Don't take it personally Sara... but with the possibility of Esmeralda becoming a full-fledged demoness... that means the position of Succubus Queen may be open. You and I are in the running for Belial's favorites... as I said, my dear. You're smart, but not very wise."

Her tail wraps around my throat and she drags me to my hut, placing me on my dirt bed.

"Sleep tight." she grins.

I lay on my bed staring at the ceiling for the next few hours. Khairunnisa's poison was potent, for some reason I had a very hard time fighting it off. Maybe she was saving it up for weeks for me. "*How long was she planning this? That bitch.*" I think to myself. By the time I manage to get enough strength to roll over off my bed, every joint is stiff and aching.

When I do manage to get out of my hut, I spot Esmeralda. "E-Esmeralda... I need to talk to you."

Esmeralda glances over to me, always looking at her floating notebook, as I came to refer to it, "Sara. I was wondering where you'd wandered off to. I assumed you were on the prowl to feed off a few of the damned souls while we waited." She sighs, "So many orders I had to put off while waiting." She glances at me, "Basically everyone is now on hold while Lord Asmodai makes his choice."

My eyes go wide, "He's choosing?"

"As we speak," Esmeralda states, "Oh don't worry, Sara. Lord Belial would raise the price paid for you, making you less likely to be chosen. He considers you, his most recent acquisition, rather special."

While I'm mildly relieved, I have a sinking feeling that Khairunnisa has done some other nefarious work against me.

Esmeralda lets out an exasperated sigh, "Mara, ironically, is the only one working."

"Belial released her?" I asked.

Esmeralda nods, "And she's doing everyone's work in order to make up for being off Asmodai's plate."

I consider complaining about Khairunnisa but decide to explore the other curious thing. "So, you might be leaving us?"

Esmeralda looks me over, "Word travels too swiftly down here." She sighs, "I might, I might not. It's not my decision." She looks up to the Blade of Pride, "It's **his**."

I must have looked concerned.

"Oh please, it's not like my tasks are more difficult. I only monitor who has been loaned to who and when they are due back. Then collect them if someone hasn't returned our whore," Esmeralda explains.

"You're basically a pimp," I remark.

"I'm unsure what a 'pimp' is, Sara." She sighs. "How much has the world changed since last I was in it?"

"When were you last in it?" I ask.

"The year was 1374, at least that's the year I was sent to Hell. I had been on earth for a good two hundred years prior." She looks at me, "It's funny, I've never asked any of the girls this."

Shrugging, I try to list some changes, "We have steel ships, humans can fly in vehicles called planes... uh... no one uses horses anymore, we have cars that we can drive that run on gas. We landed on the moon, which was cool."

Her eyes go wide, "Landed... on the moon? As in man has... Set foot up there?"

I nod.

"Why?" Esmeralda asked.

"We had a fight with Russia over who had the best economy and... We figured we'd try and get to the moon first," I explained.

Esmeralda looks to her notepad, perplexed, "In my time the most difficult task in a war was determining alliances and what family could and couldn't be trusted." She chuckles. "Traveling to the moon to prove your superiority. What an odd thing to do." Her book flashes for a moment and I see my portrait appear. Esmeralda gives me a serious look.

"I... I thought you said Belial would raise my price?" I asked.

Esmeralda glances at the book, "Seems he did." She grimaces, "And Asmodai paid."

My mind was reeling and I had to catch my breath. I felt queasy and every other form of nervousness I knew I could feel but shouldn't.

Soon Belial was next to both of us, "Well that was an excellent negotiation! Sara, spruce yourself up, you've got 48 hours with the Lord of Wrath."

I turn to face him and am about to speak before his finger pressing into my lips.

"Tut tut tut," Belial starts, "You don't get to object, Sara, you are mine, remember? Now…" He places his hands on my shoulders, "You will serve at his pleasure. Do whatever he wants. If he wants to tear a hole in your chest and slide his cock into your heart, you merely open to him as you would your legs." He grins sickly to me, "Understand?"

I nod, slowly, on the verge of tears.

Belial then kisses me hard on the lips.

The kiss has the same effect on me as an hour of foreplay. Tears are the last thing on my mind as I shiver in pleasure.

Belial breaks the kiss, taps my hair, which straightens it, and runs his fingers over my eyelids and then lips, adding make-up I was unaware of. "Flawless. Now go." Belial turns around and snaps his fingers, a portal opening to a dark room before me. "The Halls of Wrath awaits, and your charge, the venerable Lord Asmodai."

As I walk toward the portal I glance at Esmeralda.

She looks away but looks troubled. I can tell she wants to speak but can do nothing. This is how I know she actually cares about us.

I look ahead and walk into the portal. It closes behind me and I'm left in a dark room.

I can make out a window with bars on it overlooking a high wall. In the distance, I can hear the sounds of armor and swords clattering against one another. Much closer I can hear the sound of a whetstone on metal. I turn and see three sets of eyes. From left to right, one set was red, another green, and the final pair yellow. All six eyes look up to me from the darkness.

I take a step back and kneel immediately. I've never seen Asmodai, but I've heard rumors that he has three heads.

I hear the snapping of fingers as torches are lit in the room.

Along the walls are all manner of weapons and armors. Horrible axes, spears, swords, daggers, polearms, and halberds. Armor of all sorts, all with holes in them from one weapon or another.

Asmodai is standing tall, a bull's head on the left with burning red eyes, snarling, and a ram's head on his right shoulder doing the same. In between is the bald head of Asmodai. His fiery green eyes look angry.

"You're the *Sara*?" Asmodai asks, his voice rumbling in his massive chest.

I nod, "Yes my Lord," I answer quickly.

He looks me over, "Are you frightened?"

I discovered very quickly that lying is a very bad thing in Hell, no matter what, and half of these fallen angels and demons get a hard-on from power trips, "Terrified, my Lord. Mara spoke of your violent tendencies."

He was silent for a moment, "Stand. You're small enough without kneeling."

I stand and find him a good two feet taller than me. I remain silent, as does he for a few moments.

"My Sarah had black hair," Asmodai says, running a hand through my hair.

Closing my eyes, I hope he doesn't suddenly break my neck or tear it off my shoulders. I can feel the strength in his hands, the harshness of his gauntlet. After a few moments of this, I ask him, "What do you wish of me, Lord Asmodai?"

He removes his hands as he speaks. "You are young. You still have hope to break." He looks me over some more, "Remove my armor, Sara."

Standing, I start by running my hands up his huge breastplate, stretching up to fiddle under his shoulder armor. As I do, I find the clips holding them on, and undo them. I manage to catch the spaulders, each with the head on it, and set it on the ground carefully.

"They have taken the blade of the Archangel Michael and spat off shattered bits of Hope Steel after breaking it. They are not fragile," Asmodai states.

Keeping eye contact, I reach under his armpits and remove the latches for his breastplate, the back and front clattering to the ground.

Asmodai nods in approval as I do this.

Next, I remove each gauntlet. I notice his powerful arms and chest. My hand traces over his abdomen and I feel my face flush as I stare at his impressive muscles.

"What is this?" His hand brushes my cheek.

"W-what?" I ask.

Asmodai tilts my head up to face him, "Your cheeks are flush. Why?"

My cheeks get redder, "You're... A very powerful... Man, er Demon, uh, I mean - Angel! I-I just, touching you excites me..."

Asmodai's green eyes scan me, looking over my body. His hand moves to the front of my corset, his other on the back. With a swift motion, he tears it off me. My corset falls to the ground in two halves.

I gasp as he does this.

"Look at me," Asmodai says sternly, his voice not rumbling now, but a quiet bass, "What I am about to ask you does not leave this room. Nor your lips, do you understand?"

I nod, "Yes, My Lord."

A strange look comes over his face, "On earth, were you married?"

"Yes, My Lord."

Asmodai's eyes stop swirling, becoming still, "Do this for me and nothing else. Make love to me as if it were our wedding night."

My heart skips a beat. I hadn't heard the word 'love' in what felt like decades.

# CHAPTER 7

## *Lust vs Love*

---

"A Succubus always draws energy from their lover. The wherewithal to survive depends on the strength of the victim."

---

Asmodai's request wasn't lost on me at all. I looked him over; I certainly have been forced on worse. The disgusting fat belly of Belphegor, the sick delights of Abaddon. Verrine liked to have a whole harem of succubi and would sometimes just give each of us a thrust or two and be done with it, and that's just the Fallen! But Asmodai? He looked solid, like climbing a mountain of muscle.

Shortly after he asked me, I had to accept and so I slid my arms around his neck while pulling myself up slowly to kiss him with passion.

To my absolute shock, he returned it! His hand wrapped around the small of my back and he pulled me up hard against him, his hands roamed over me and caressed me.

I hadn't been touched with any sort of affection in so long, I think I had tears as I continued with nothing more than gentle caressing. This wasn't something I wasn't used to at all. Again, I was just a whore for the most part. Kissing was unheard of for me, let alone foreplay.

Shocking me further, Asmodai broke the kiss and started to trail soft wet kisses down my neck.

My hooves were dangling, he had me lifted so high and my body shivered against him. I bit my lip to keep from moaning as he licked and sucked at my skin trailing down to my breasts, and yet a single soft moan escaped me. Again, something I haven't felt in years. "Take me, My Lord."

"Not 'My Lord'," He chastised, as he had me wrap my legs around his waist so he could carry me to another room, "Just say my name."

He carried me in such a way that only a precious woman--er well succubus, in this case--would know. The strength of his arms around me and the way I had to tightly hold my legs around him is something I never experienced, even with a man like Dave and he only carried me over the threshold of our house after our wedding.

In the room was a bed. Over it were the heads of multiple strange creatures, stuffed and mounted. The bed itself was covered in odd leathers.

Asmodai dropped me on the bed. He slowly crawled over me, his hands sliding up my calves toward the inner part of my thigh in which he peeled my thong, tortuously slowly down my legs.

I watched his every movement, relishing his fingers caressing against my skin as he bared me to him.

I took a chance and placed my hands on his chest to sit us both up, I didn't give him an opportunity to stop me and gave him a look to roll onto his back. And ho ho ho surprise, surprise! Someone likes a dominant woman in the bedroom--he obeyed with just a look!

Asmodai eyes me warily as he goes along with my desire and rolls onto his back, looking at me with a little glowing hint of excitement, and yes, we demons can have some emotions other than chaos.

Now that I have him on his back, I slowly crawl my way up to his long muscle-toned body and straddle his thighs. I undo his pants and pull out his massive cock--oh yes, ladies, no joke, massive! Now, fellas, it's okay the fallen have it better!

"Asmodai," I whispered, then I bent down slowly, staring into his eyes while licking my lips to wet them before running my tongue along the tip of his cock.  I needed to taste him. I swear, I heard him release a deep breath as if he held it until I tasted him. Asmodai growls at me, and it ignites a fire in me that I thought had gone out years ago.

I spent some time tasting that long thick cock until my jaw felt like it would detach if I didn't stop soon. Thankfully, he gently pulls me from his cock and slides my now wet pussy onto him. His hands are placed firmly on either side of my waist as he guides my bouncing body above him. His thrusts grow more powerful as we come together as one. Oh yes, you heard me, as one! This is unheard of in Hell, there is no love, but here we are, a fallen angel and a succubus making love.

I'm on cloud nine as my body sings a song I haven't heard in years. He continues to thrust, and just as I feel I'm nearing the edge, Asmodai grabs me by the neck and pulls me down to him for a searing kiss.

"Do not release until I give you permission, we shall be one at the same time," I almost orgasmed right there but to my amazement, my body listened, and instead, I moaned against his wet lips. I rode him for two days straight and I'm tellin' ya that has got to be some kinda Hell record because whoa, it hurt after!

As we climaxed together for what felt like our fiftieth time in two days, this last time was something different altogether. Our bodies were pushed to exhaustion at this point, but something in us either broke or grew, I can't tell. Our hearts connected because we seemed to have no boundaries: it was never enough for either of us, this need to feel like we were one was beyond words. This last release had me curling anything and everything. We knew this was the last one and with that knowledge, his strong hands held me down hard against him. I felt my tail whipping around wildly as the pleasure overcame me and I screamed out his name.

Now I know what you must be thinking, "Where can I get me one of those fallen angels?" Well come on down to Hell, there are plenty!

Anyway, after that last mind-blowing orgasm, I lay against him trying to catch my breath and him doing the same, still attached below the waist if you know what I mean. Oh, and ladies, if an Angel, fallen or otherwise, asks you to make love, I highly recommend it! He was tireless in his desire and the only thing that kept me going was my ability to drain bits of his energy, which he willingly gave me. Despite this, he never slowed, never tired, never stopped and that is exactly why you ladies need to find yourselves one of them hottie fallen angels! Or, for you goodie two shoes, get a regular angel.

It felt as if we were making love for days. When we did stop, he did something to me no one else has done since I was human. He pulled me tight against him. I figured he might want to go another round after our connection but when I reached for his cock again, he stopped me, catching my hand and bringing it to his lips to press a kiss.

"No... Just stay like this for a little while. I need the calm," Asmodai said as he smiled at me.

"You... Want to... *Cuddle*?" I ask, shocked.

"Why are you surprised?" He asks.

"You know damn well why I'm surprised." I give him a light slap on his chest.

He looks at my hand and then at me, his smile not fading. "You are bold. I saw that in your eyes when I looked at your portrait."

I blush. "My Queen told me I was being foolish."

His hand brushes through my hair--he was actually stroking my hair! I know this seems so mundane but to me, I was so happy I could cry. "I like foolish."

Nuzzling my face against his chest, I just purr and kiss his skin, "I should thank Khairunnisa after all... Had I known you were like this, I'd have volunteered."

His smile fades.

Mine goes with it, and I shiver, "Did I say something–"

Asmodai squeezes me and continues to play with my hair, his hand roaming over my horns. "It's important you don't tell the others. This was for you alone. You looked different than the others. Their eyes were dead, but you still had a twinkle of hope behind yours."

I frown, "I cannot keep a secret from my Master."

Asmodai nods, understanding, "You let me handle Belial." He sighs. "If you promise me to hide this from them, then I promise you, I will choose you again."

I blush more, "Again? You want me again?"

Asmodai smiles, "For as long as your cheeks burn red."

I snuggle against him, my leg draped over him as I do.

Asmodai's fiery green eyes stare up at the ceiling while I look at him. He appears lost in thought. We remain like this for hours. Just cuddling in silence, the chaos outside reminding us what we were avoiding.

Finally, Asmodai closes his eyes, "Our time is nearly up."

As Asmodai rises I pull the covers over myself. He looks at me oddly and chuckles, "I've seen and kissed every inch of you. Why hide, girl?"

Playfully I drop the sheet, thrusting out my chest, "Better?"

Asmodai's smile doesn't last however as he gets to his feet. "You cannot lie to your Master. This we both know. Nor can you lie to your Queen."

I slowly get out of bed, confusion on my face as I follow him into the weapon room.

Asmodai takes hold of the sword that he had been sharpening when I first saw him. "So our only choice to survive is to make sure you're not a liar."

With trepidation I walk into the next room, looking at all the weapons around us, "I see." I say simply.

Asmodai holds the blade to my navel, "Best you do not redress yourself."

The sword touches my skin gently but I notice he doesn't force it in. Asmodai's face contorts and twitches as he holds the blade unnaturally steady.

"I understand, you have to," I say softly.

"Have too?" The green wisps of smoke in his eyes swirl in anger, his voice rising, "I do not have to do anything! I am the Lord of Wrath! There is only one that is stronger than I! Do not tell me what I can and cannot do!"

My eyes narrow at him, "Then stop being a pussy and do it! Stop making me wait!"

His own eyes narrowed, "What did you call me?"

"I called you a pu–" I am interrupted as the blade digs into my stomach. I gasp in pain.

"One encounter and you talk down to me, girl!" His voice booms.

My hands are on the sword's blade, and I whimper, "I-I thought..."

The blade is pulled out of my stomach and the broadside of it smashes against my left hoof, snapping it and sending me to my knee. My hands are clutching at my stomach, blood pouring out of me when the pommel of the sword smashes down on my forehead. Before I know what's happening next, I'm on the ground looking at the ceiling.

Asmodai comes into my vision again with a mace in one hand and a club in the other.

My eyes tear up now, as I realize why Mara was so traumatized. I don't protest, or stop him.

Asmodai hesitates for a moment before he slams the mace into my face, and busts my knee with the club. The club crashes into my face next and the mace crushes my arm, pulverizing it. I scream in pain as he bludgeons me. The pain continues for far too long. I cannot even follow the next few blows as I feel ribs snap and my vision blurs as I taste and choke on blood. I'm fairly certain my intestines are on the outside at this point.

My ears are ringing as I hear Asmodai say something, then I'm kicked and as I sail through the air, I land on hot dirt with a sickening thud. I think another bone cracked. As my hearing returns, I hear one of the Succubi scream.

"Oh Hell, Queen Esmeralda! It's Sara! She's... Oh..." I hear a Succubus shout.

I whimper as my vision slowly returns, as it clears I see Esmeralda over me.

"Deep breath Sara, come on, bite down through the pain," She encouraged.

I swear I can feel my teeth start to crack as my body heals painfully, bones snapping themselves back into place and my organs sliding back into my body. Tears boil-off of my skin as I finally heal enough to stand. I feel nothing but a burning searing rage burn through me.

"I'll kill him! The bastard! That sick fuck!" I shout as I slowly get to my hooves.

Esmeralda backs away from me, confused, "Sara, calm down!"

I glare at her. "*You* calm down! *You* didn't just get torn to pieces!" I slam my hoof on the ground and to my shock, the ground shakes.

Esmeralda narrows her eyes at me and then grabs me by the chin. "Enough, Sara! Settle down!"

Esmeralda lifting me up like a child pushes me over some kind of edge, and I grab her wrist and snap it, forcing her to release me. I hurl her into the air. I was fuming at this point until I saw a shadow directly over me. I look up to see Esmeralda flying above.

Her wrist snapped back into place, I saw her horns had a violet aura around them. Her eyes were closed at this point. When she opened them they were also glowing violet. "You little Bog-trotter," She hisses.

My eyes went wide, "Oh... Shit..." I think this is the most common phrase someone says before they die. Had I not technically already been dead, I probably would have.

Esmeralda dives at me, her hands grab me by the wrist and slams me hard against a wall.

My head knocks against the wall and I feel woozy and disoriented. My vision is filled with Esmeralda's burning violet eyes as she rams her horns against my head, finally knocking me out.

When I came too a few moments later, I was in my hut, the door shut with Esmeralda standing over my bed. "...You drank from Asmodai too deeply, wench!  You forget your place."

Rubbing my head as I sat up slowly, I winced as my ears slowly stopped ringing. "Yeah... I had to, in order to keep up with his demands."

"That horrid then?" Esmeralda asks.

Thinking of the tail end of the evening, and contrasting it with the beginning I nod. Great idea Sara, fight with the guy right before you have to leave, I think to myself. That will make him ask you back. I wipe a tear from my eyes.

"You went berserk when you came out due to his essence," Esmeralda explains.

"I was pretty pissed... I'm never that angry normally." I look at her, "What made you go all...uh... nutty?"

Esmeralda sighs, "You drank from Asmodai, Lord of Wrath. Whom do I service most frequently, Sara?"

My eyes go wide.

She nods, "That power can be intoxicating at times. Worse yet, he demands I drink from him." She looks out the window. "I fear the next time, what I draw will overwhelm me and I'll lose myself in that raw power."

Even as she talks about it, I see her eyes tinge violet.

"My ascension to a full-fledged demoness, like I said, was not up to me."

"Will you forget about us?" I ask.

Esmeralda nods, "Most likely." She turns to me, "Using what I had stored to restrain you was difficult, but when you attacked me, I had to retaliate."

Her eyes glow again and I watch as she clenches her fist, a portion of my floor lifts up and is crushed into a ball.

"Testing my strength helps, but I can feel it even now at the edge of my control." She releases her fist and the newly minted rock clatters to the ground. "I don't know what I'll be, who I will be if it ever happens." She glances at me, "It's why I wanted you to take my place."

"I don't think I'm up for it, Esmeralda," I confess.

Belial soon opens the door to my hut, obviously knocking is not a concern of his. "Sara! Excellent!" He glares, "What the Hell did you do?"

I swallow hard, "I... I did as Lord Asmodai asked."

Belial grins, "Well, you performed excellently. He wants you again... I'm merely working out the terms."

My eyes go wide, "W-what?"

Belial snickers, "I saw the lump of flesh and bone you popped out as. As Asmodai said: 'Her cries were like music to my ears. She still had hope to break. I must have her again.'"

Belial cackled, "He'll pay out the nose for you. This is a lovely day." Belial then turns to Esmeralda. "You, I need to have a word with. *He has* requested you again."

Esmeralda's face actually looked concerned, "Yes Master, we must speak of that."

It was a few days later when I was before Asmodai once more. I had stepped into the portal, and the second it closed, Asmodai was in front of me, on his knees.

"Forgive me," He says, pulling me close to him.

I am confused as I look down at him, "Wait, what?"

"I know you were goading me, but I feared I had gone too far and offended you."

I shook my head, "Wait for what? I thought I got you mad at me and you never wanted to see me again! At least not li-" before I could finish, his lips were on mine and we didn't speak for at least a day and a half. Unless you count moaning as speaking.

During the cuddling that occurred afterward, Asmodai tells me of his plans. "I am negotiating your soul from Belial."

I looked at him, shocked, "Wait, you can do that?"

"He owns your soul, he can transfer ownership at his discretion."

"But... But I thought he couldn't transfer my soul to someone else!" I say, confused.

"You'd be free if he were destroyed or rendered mortal. Which is forbidden by Lucifer for us to do to one another, unfortunately. Otherwise, I'd have already torn him to pieces for you."

I'm blushing again as Asmodai grins at me.

"You just need to act as if you are horrified at the prospect of being mine, and I'll keep you locked inside the Halls of Wrath, mine forever."

I smile at him, "That sounds... nice."

Unfortunately, it was rinse and repeat when we were done. I am looking forward to a time when my lark with Asmodai doesn't have to end with me being bludgeoned and tossed back into the fields of lust with half my insides out.

When I am well enough to stand, however, I see a rather disturbing sight. Holding the little notepad, looking quite proud of herself, is Khairunnisa, "Ah, Sara, I see your favored is done with you?"

I stagger to my hooves, "Yeah well... I'm stronger than you thought."

Khairunnisa smiles, "Stronger than you thought, 'My Queen'."

"Where's Esmeralda?" I demand.

Khairunnisa shrugs., "Not sure, but she is our Queen no longer. That honor is now rightfully set to me."

I look at the Blade of Pride in the distance, feeling rage burn through me. Without thinking. I take off toward the Blade, not really sure what my plan was.

It isn't until I am nearly at the balcony that Belial appears before me and catches me, one hand over my mouth, the other binding one wing. "No no, Sara. You're still mine, for now, I'll not have you doing anything as foolish as this. It would reflect poorly on me, and I'll not earn Lucifer's wrath again."

I struggle but Belial easily brings me back down to the fields.

Belial growls, "Khairunnisa, it is your task to reign them in!"

Khairunnisa frowns, kneeling, "I'm sorry, My Master. It will not happen again."

"It would make sense that no other could handle my former station. Do you fail to even reign in a single succubus properly? You shame the title itself." It was Esmeralda's voice! At first, I was happy to hear her voice, although it was very different from what I had last heard. I look up and am shocked at what I see.

Esmeralda's face was there but covered in deep violet skin and her entire body was dark purple. Her wings were massive and black now. She let the air out of both her wings and landed on the ground with a quake. Her hooves were larger, much more like a Clydesdale horse with flowing fur to match running all the way to her hips.

A black cloth hung from a belt, covering her crotch, and it had a white skull-like symbol on it somehow. Her horns were huge, at least her old ones were, curling back over four feet long, with another set of shorter horns curling out of her forehead. Her eyes burned with violet light, the irises and pupils gone. Her teeth looked sharp and vicious, her hands were massive and clawed. Her small spaded tail was replaced with what looked like a serpent's tail, scaled and thick, covered in black and purple stripes. She was a terrifying sight to behold.

Belial smiles, "Esmeralda, you look lovely."

Esmeralda grins a toothy smile to Belial, "Lord Belial." She bows. "May I discipline the whore? I saw her let a succubus charge toward the Blade of Pride. She clearly is failing you if you were required to intervene."

My eyes are wide now as I hear her speak, her voice echoes and her form looks absolutely inhuman. Her chest is covered in black armor, little of her feminine form showing behind her face and long, but now wild hair.

Belial laughs, "Why not."

"I am the Queen o-" Khairunnisa is interrupted as she's lifted off the ground as if she were bound by ropes tying her arms and wings tightly to her body.

"You are the Queen of nothing but Sluts and Whores... Hardly a queen at all," Esmeralda is holding her hand out, purple smoke rising from her eyes, "Lose control of your charges again, and I'll do far worse than this!"

Khairunnisa scoffs, "This is nothing!" She suddenly chokes as her arms crack, and her ribcage collapses.

Esmeralda had merely clenched her fist to do what she had done to Khairunnisa. She releases her fist, leaving Khairunnisa to crumble to the ground, broken.

"E-Esmeralda?" I stutter.

Esmeralda grins as she looks at me. "Wait...." Her eyes scan over me for a moment, "Yes!" She hisses, "The bog-trotter. Yes yes, Sara!" She chortles, "How do I look? Our Lord saw fit to grant me more of his power, and I ascended! I'm a true demoness now! More powerful than ever before! Do you like it? My new form?"

I shudder as I examine her, "You're... You look very powerful, Esmeralda."

She licks her lips with a black forked tongue, "It's intoxicating. I broke Khairunnisa with hardly a thought." She cackles, "I must go, there's so much power coursing through me, it feels a shame to not use it!" She launches herself into the air, her wings unfurling when she's at the apex of her jump, cackling madly as she dives toward the lakes of fire.

I watch in dismay as she joins the other demons in the lakes, torturing and rending the flesh of the damned like the other horrors.

Belial wheezes, "She's now a private in my unholy legion. She may rise quickly too. She's quite proud of her new form, as you can see. If you play your cards right, Khairunnisa, you may join her."

Khairunnisa staggers to her feet, looking horrified, "I-If you wish it... My Master."

Belial leaves us, snickering to himself.

Khairunnisa looks at me, "Sara... I... I don't want that to be me. She was..."

"A monster," I say quietly.

# CHAPTER 8

## Transference

**"A soul owned can be transferred to another as long as the master of that soul wills it. A trade is often requested, but not always required."**

My time in Hell was somehow mixed. I had found a lover, of sorts, and one of my friends was barely hanging on to what little humanity she had left. So when Belial showed up grinning ear to ear I was somewhat nervous.

Belial popped into my hut. "Well Sara, I've got some news."

I was looking in a mirror. My eyes had a green glow to them. I was getting worried. I feared if I kept drinking from Asmodai's essence, I'd end up like Esmeralda. "What now?" I ask, trying to keep my attitude in check. Normally with Belial, it wasn't an issue. Today, for some reason, I felt snappy, nor did I feel the admiration for him I normally felt.

"I've made a lovely arrangement with Asmodai--you are now his," Belial announced.

I turned to him in shock. I began to cry tears of joy, but I could tell by the look on Belial's face that he thought they were tears of dismay.

"What? Did y-you sell me? To Asmodai?!" I whimpered.

Belial chuckled, "Yes, you'll be his new pincushion, I'm sure. Now get your shit and get out. I've found a new method of minting a Succubus and if she happens to arrive here, there needs to be empty space."

I grabbed my three soul cores, drying my eyes, "You are truly a cruel creature."

Belial places his hand on his chest, "Why, Sara... Flattery will get you everywhere." He snaps his fingers, a portal opening. "Suffer well!"

He gives me a shove into the portal. As I enter, I look around to find Asmodai in his full armor and regalia.

He turns to me and removes his helmet, smiling. "My newest thrall."

I blush, bowing. "My Master."

Asmodai shakes his head.

"Only when we're in the company of others will you call me Master," Asmodai orders.

I feel a wave of relief come over me. It's as close to being free as I could get.

Asmodai's smile is strange but genuine.

"Something you will learn of my thralls, we are not in the business of pleasing others." He draws a blade, "We're in the business of war."

I frown a bit. "I'm not a fighter."

"You only lack the tools and training," He says proudly. "I'll secure for you a few suitable soul cores, and make for you some true demonic armor."

I look away from him. "You want me to become a demon, like Esmeralda?"

Asmodai's sword is sheathed and he picks me up in a hug, spinning me around.

"I wouldn't change a single hair on your beautiful head," Asmodai praised.

Hugging back after he says this, I relax a bit, "Why do you need soul cores?"

"They can be forged into armor and weapons for you by Sabnock. We'd just need to find some cores with an affinity for you," Asmodai explained.

I reached into my cleavage and produced the three "moron cores", as I had started to call them. They are each glowing brightly now.

"These are pretty attuned to me I think," I offered.

Asmodai picked them from my hand, noticing they dimmed in his, and when he handed them to me, their glow returned. He takes them back from me. A portal opens and he slips the soul cores inside.

"You're full of surprises aren't you, Sara? Your role will change slightly under my care," Asmodai chuckles.

"Care? Really?" I asked.

Asmodai dons his helmet as he exits the room. I follow him, and the sight is fairly horrific.

Thousands of demons of all shapes and sizes are in different formations, some fighting each other, others practicing.

"Forcas!" Asmodai bellows.

Asmodai's voice reverberates through his troops. All of their training halts and they all look to the top of one of the larger buildings. An angel with long white hair, a medium-length beard, and wings looks down from a watchtower of sorts. As he lands, I watch light armor shift on his body. He has a sword at his side and on his back, his eyes are black, mostly, like Asmodai's, but with a calm white at their center.

"My liege!" The angel kneels, "The troops are improving by the day."

Asmodai speaks in a loud voice, "Excellent to hear, Forcas. I have a charge for you." He turns to me, "An experiment of sorts for me. This is Sara, she's a succubus once owned by Belial, now my thrall."

Forcas nods to me. "Greetings Sara. I am Forcas, commander of the 290 legions of the infernal armies. Your Master's right hand, as it were."

Asmodai's voice is still in what I'll call its grand-standing tone. "You are to train her to fight."

Forcas stands slowly. "To fight, my liege? She is not a concubine?"

Asmodai looks at me from behind his helm. I can feel his grin, "Not merely a concubine."

Forcas nods. "Very well. You, Girl, come here," He motions to me.

"Wait! Right now?" I asked.

Asmodai bellows. "Yes! Now, **wench**!"

I blush. Of course, he has to treat me like everyone expects him to. "Yes, My Master."

Forcas moves down toward the training grounds. A few demons scoff at us. One, in particular, Ubiel, stands in Forcas's way.

Ubiel is a massive red demon, with long black horns, heavy hooves, and monstrous wings. "Where are you going with our little treat?"

Forcas's thumb pushes his sword out of its sheath by the hilt slightly. "Ubiel, back to your training."

"I'm stronger than you, old man." Ubiel grins. "I've not had a woman for some time, and this one looks scrumptious."

"Forcas!" Asmodai shouts, the sound alone causes me to stagger. "Stand aside."

Forcas's sword slides back into its sheath and he steps away from me.

Suddenly Asmodai swoops down in front of me, the ground quaking as he lands, "Ubiel. You've grown a spine? How surprising."

Ubiel roars at Asmodai, who doesn't move an inch. I cover my ears from the roar, his foul breath wafting over me. Asmodai's ram head sneezes, the bull snorts.

"Are you done?" Asmodai asks.

Ubiel growls and pulls out a massive sword from his back. It's almost ten feet long, a giant sword for a giant demon. He flies straight up into the air. "I'll show you my power, 'Master'! I shall be the first greater demon to smite a Fallen!"

Asmodai doesn't move, the green wisps of his eyes producing twin streams of green smoke rising above his head.

Ubiel flaps his wings, a black aura surrounding him as he dives at Asmodai. The giant sword crashes into Asmodail's head, the impact causes dirt and dust to fly into the air.

I scream out, "Master!"

Ubiel's hands are shaking as he drops his blade, the massive thing cracked in half.

"I'm surprised." Asmodai bellows.

Ubiel wrings his hands in pain.

"I did not think you had the guts," Asmodai's hands moved over several swords at his hip. "What blade shall your comeuppance be handled with?"

Ubiel growls, grabbing at the remains of his sword.

Asmodai growls back, then he whispers, "My Havoc Blade should do," and vanishes.

Ubiel stomps about confused, then takes to the air, "Show yourself, coward!" Ubiel shouts.

An explosion or something like it sounds all around us. Then, speeding down from the ceiling, his wings propelling him toward the ground at an incredible rate, Asmodai attacks. "**Cry, Havoc**!" Asmodai shouts as he makes contact with Ubeil's already broken blade.

A sound like that of a thousand swords smashing against each other reverberates through the air. The blade in Asmodai's hand glows with a green aura, but the aura seems to project forward, past the blade.

My eyes grow wide as I watch Asmodai's sword slice through Ubiel's like butter. After it passes through the sword, blood sprays into the air from thousands of gashes that rip through Ubiel's body.

Asmodai lands, the caverns, shaking beneath me as he does. He stands, Ubiel's corpse falling to the ground.

"This thrall is mine. If you are fortunate enough that I should gift her to you, so be it, but she is mine, not yours," Asmodai declared.

I'm staring in disbelief at Asmodai's power. I can barely stand because of how weak I am in my knees. He could take me before every soldier in his army and I wouldn't complain.

Asmodai glares at his armies. "Now get back to your training, you maggots! One day you will taste living flesh and feast on the dismembered wings of Angels! Now act like it and fight!"

A shiver runs through me. Through all the lovemaking and sex, I nearly forgot what a horror Asmodai was.

Asmodai sheaths his sword, looking at me, "Now train with Forcas."

I stagger to my hooves, "That was…"

"A sorry display," Asmodai begins, "I used this trinket I took from a lesser demon who had failed far too many times. I use it to chastise my more disobedient troops… When I am not feeding them to my mount."

Forcas laughs as he walks back to us, "Where is your mount, my Liege?"

Asmodai grumbles, "Belial now owns it."

Forcas seems surprised. "Belial? For what did you trade the twin-headed chimera?"

Asmodai glances at me.

Forcas raises an eyebrow, "Ho ho… For her?"

Asmodai walks past us. "Prove not to be a poor investment, wench."

He walks back to the main building, closing the door.

I frown. It's difficult to tell if he is acting or not. I'm fairly insulted, however, that I was traded over a mode of transportation. A frivolous one at that, since the Fallen can fly anywhere they want.

Forcas snaps his fingers, bringing my attention back to the present. "Come along girl. I assume I must teach you how to handle yourself in battle. Be honored Lord Asmodai has chosen me, his Master-at-Arms, to train you."

I nod. "I'm very honored."

I follow Forcas to a more secluded training area, where he forces a heavy chunk of metal that I could barely call a sword into my hands.

"Basics, first," Forcas says to me matter-of-factly. From there a very brutal training regimen begins.

After the first day, I dragged myself to the door Asmodai had walked out of, knocking at first and eventually just opening the door. My body ached all over, my arms and legs especially. Forcas demanded I learn how to handle the weight of a sword. I didn't even learn how to swing the stupid thing, just going through the motions of holding it while doing various aerobic exercises.

"Master?" I plead. "I need a break."

Asmodai is standing near a window in his weapon room, his helmet off but his armor still on. He turns to me and looks me over, "Seems he was rough with you." He turns away from me. "Good."

I frown, "Mas-"

"We spoke of this. We are alone now, are we not?" He boomed, not looking at me.

"Asmodai," I correct myself, "I'm not a fighter."

"I know," He says, "You're an experiment."

My heart sinks, "I'm just a-"

Asmodai interrupts me, "I need a new mount. It looks ridiculous for the Lord of Wrath to arrive on the battlefield under his own power." He looks at me. "Would you like to seek one out with me?"

I'm still taking in what is basically heartbreak, and it must have shown on my face.

"Consider it a *date* of sorts." Asmodai says as he grabs his helm, "Afterwards, I can give you a gift."

As he walks by me, I try to protest, before I remember how pointless that would be. I follow him as exits through another door.

"Follow me, Sara, we have got a long flight ahead. It will be shorter, of course, on the way back," Asmodai informs.

I groan as he takes flight, my body already exhausted from training, and now a long flight. Flying into the air after him, I do my best to keep up.

After what feels like hours, a fresh horror is before me.

Hundreds of damned souls slowly march toward a vast black pit. The thing is huge but doesn't appear to be a cliff, like most others. This is against what you could call the far wall of Hell. The pit looks like nothing but the end of the ground and the beginning of blackness. I notice some of the souls turn away halfway there, but there are others who hurl themselves in.

Asmodai has landed near the edge and appears to be looking for something.

I land next to him, and I watch a man, sobbing, in tattered clothing, limping toward the edge. He looks at me with hopeless eyes as he reaches the edge. He hesitates, shaking and sobbing.

Asmodai glances at him, "Pathetic mortal, either hurl yourself to the void or go back and suffer our Lord's punishment as you have been."

The shattered man just turns to us, tears streaming down his face, "I don't deserve this!" He whimpers.

Asmodai laughs viciously, "I do not care."

The man then closes his eyes and hurls himself forward.

As he vanishes into the endless blackness, Asmodai bellows out a sickening laugh, "The fool!" He shouts, "The void is no reprieve. It's a prison, your senses go blank and all you have is your thoughts. It drives men mad."

I wrap my wings around myself as I see a few other souls turn back, walking back what must be miles, some pleading with others after hearing what Asmodai said.

"Master, why are we here?" I can feel the despair from the damned souls, and hear a strange call from the blackness to hurl myself in.

Asmodai takes my hand. "We're going to get a mount." Without another word, his hand in mine, we jumped in. I scream as we fall, no end in sight as I look up and see every light vanish. I can barely even see Asmodai before I hear his voice.

"Don't let go, if you do I may lose you."

I grab onto his arm with both hands, shaking like a leaf. "I don't like this!"

"I'd be surprised if you did," Asmodai counters.

After a very long way down, we stopped. We haven't hit bottom. I can feel us floating. Asmodai must have stopped us somehow.

"There it is," He says.

Before us, slowly coming into view, is a Dragon. I'm not talking like a figurative one, no--there is literally a massive beastly dragon curled up in some kind of fetal position, its wings and claws twitching, a look of pain on its giant face.

My eyes adjust to the light Asmodai is casting on the blue dragon, and I see hundreds of people in the same state. Each of them floating aimlessly, curled into a fetal position, all look as if they're having a nightmare. I bump into one of them and they merely flinch, floating away from me. The more I see, the less I want to be here.

Asmodai holds out his hand, the huge dragon floating towards us.

"Uh... what if it wakes up?" I ask.

Asmodai says nothing as we begin to rise up, the dragon in tow. I hang on for dear life as we rise faster and faster until finally, I can see light again. Well, the red glowing that I call light. Asmodai lets the dragon fall to the ground outside of the pit. As it does, several people run in fear and some even hurl themselves into the pit faster.

I suppress a desire to stop them, but I'm more concerned with the huge beast that is groaning before us.

The thing is massive, its head alone is the size of a tractor-trailer, though one horn is missing. It growls and slowly I see its milky eyes opening. A strangely feminine voice echoes from its huge maw, "What... Happened...?"

"Greetings, I assume you're a Rex Dragon, yes?" Asmodai asks plainly.

The dragon, or dragoness(?), lifts her head wearily, "Who are you? I... I had a horrific dream, I was..." She looks around, "Oh by every God it wasn't a dream."

Asmodai smiles, "I am Asmodai, Lord of Wrath."

The dragoness growls, "I was told the void was an option, should I feel I could no longer tolerate your horrific tortures!"

"It still is," Asmodai gestures to the pit, "However I'm sure you've experienced the void for long enough to understand what it truly is."

She narrows her milky eyes at us. "Aye, trading you horrible things for my own demons."

"And how did that exchange work for you?" Asmodai queries.

"Poorly..." She looks away.

"I have an opportunity for you," Asmodai offers.

She turns to us, lowering her head, "I am listening, Fallen."

Asmodai grins. I require a mount. For your soul, I will keep you from the void below, and keep the other demons from torturing you. In exchange, you will be at my beck and call to ferry me, or my troops, wherever I desire."

"So you want my pride and dignity sullied?" She huffs.

"I could always leave you to rot in the void again," Asmodai rebuts.

She's silent for a moment, "Fine Fallen. I'll be your ferry."

Asmodai snaps his fingers and a rather familiar piece of paper appears in front of him. "What's your name, dragon?"

"Zelletia," She says, as she scratches something onto the paper with a massive claw. As she does she suddenly writhes in pain. Her blue scales turn black, and a foul odor comes off of her. She roars, her teeth grow longer and sharper, and a horrible breath hits both Asmodai and me.

I stagger back; Asmodai doesn't move. When she's done roaring, she opens her wings and lowers them back to us.

"Climb aboard, My Master. Where must I take you?" She asks in a docile tone.

"So... what she's a slave now?" I ask.

"Only to Master, Wench!" The dragon growls.

I hate that word more and more each day.

Asmodai says nothing, merely gesturing for me to climb on board. He speaks to Zelletia, "Fly toward the Blade of Pride, then bank to the left, toward the Halls of Wrath. When you drop us off, fly about and get a lay of the landscape. Then return to the Halls."

We take off in an instant, and as we fly I can see we're going a lot faster.

I'm pinned between the foul-smelling dragon and Asmodai, and my exhaustion gets the better of me. I lean back against him, closing my eyes for a moment. To my surprise, Asmodai wraps his arms around me and holds me tight against him.

The mixed signals are killing me, but I take what I can get for now.

After we land, I spot another Fallen Angel. He's similar to Forcas, but unlike Forcas, he wears a black blindfold over his eyes. His clothing is not armor either, rather a simple set of slacks, a shirt, and heavy leather apron and gloves. His feet are bare, dirty, with long and gnarled toenails.

Asmodai walks towards him "Sabnock, I assume you have what I requested?"

Sabnock snickers, and turns to me, "Oh, the boys are quite excited that you're here. Yes, yes!" His voice is sniveling and grates on my ears like nails on a chalkboard.

"Your gifts, Sara." Asmodai grins at me.

"Firstly…" Sabnock begins, holding a black and green ball in his hand, "The upper armor." He chucks the little ball into the air and it bursts into black smoke.

The smoke swirls around me and then fuses to my skin. It feels strange for a moment as if someone is groping me all over but then solidifies. When it's done, I look down, no longer seeing my cleavage exposed, but rather covered in a black iron-like chest piece. I turn and my wings are covered in metal as well, though I can flex them still. I look at my shoulders and shriek, each one has a huge green jewel that looks like an eye! The dark pupils inside, dart back and forth.

"What the Hell?" I shout.

Asmodai grins his approval. "Fitting Sabnock, well done."

"The lowers." Sabnock begins again.

I protest, "Wait, wait, give me a damn–"

Before I can continue, there's smoke swirling around my legs and bottom. I gasp as I feel, again, like someone just groped me all over. I appraise my leg, sticking out my hoof to see it's covered in black metal as well, even covering my hoof itself. It's like I'm wearing shoes over them. I see a similar set of jewels at either hip, the irises almost pleasing. My tail is also covered, though the spaded tip is now showing a blade on each edge, with the tip itself still exposed, likely so I can still use my poison.

Asmodai looks me over and nods, "Very good, Sabnock."

"So do I get a helmet next?" I ask, thinking of the three cores.

Asmodai shakes his head, "We've covered up enough of your... Assets," He explains, "A helm would hide your eyes and lips. Both are potent weapons for a Succubus."

Sabnock cackles, "Yes, yes! Besides these were brothers My Lord, and they lusted after this succubus with a passion. Making them into an armor set was easy! The outlier, however, was difficult. What weapon does one make for a succubus, yes? A whip is the normal fare, but not as useful..."

I frown. "Master I... I don't know how to..."

Sabnock snaps a third black orb.

The smoke spills out and collects around my hand. Suddenly a sword with a black hilt and a green jewel in the center appears in my hand. The blade has an ornate blood groove down the length and is about four feet long.

"Okay that's kind of pretty," I admit.

Sabnock snickers. "Press the jewel with your thumb."

I do so, and the blade suddenly falls apart, or at least it appears to. It breaks into segments, all linked together, now almost twice the length.

Asmodai's grin is now vicious, "Oh marvelous. Belial's newest demoness won't know what hit her."

I turned to Asmodai, surprised, "Wait, what?"

Sabnock smiles now, a smile full of yellow teeth. "That sword won't break when solid, it fuses you see. A flawless transition from chain sword to bastard sword. It will even play to her old strengths."

I glared at Asmodai, "What do you mean that Belial's newest demoness won't know what hit her?"

Asmodai smacks me across the face, "Do not take that tone with your Master, Harlot!"

My eyes closed, I did my best not to scream and shout, remembering we were in public.

"I am sorry Master..." I calm myself, "I just don't understand what I need this stuff for."

Asmodai smiled., "My dear... You are an experiment. Lucifer feels the Succubus are useless, and as we prepare for a war on Earth and Heaven, we need soldiers, not seducers."

I frown, "I'm an experiment?"

Asmodai nods. "Lucifer purposefully transformed the Queen of the Succubi into a greater demon with his essence. I proposed a different avenue."

My heart is starting to break as he speaks.

"Imagine a soldier on the field of battle, who can entice an enemy with a look, enthrall him with a kiss, and force him to slay his comrades at her desire... then she can drain him of strength to heal her wounds and continue to fight!" He shouts. "And in a weeks' time, Lucifer and I shall pit our experiments against each other!"

I hold back tears, "I... I don't understand."

"In one week, Sara, you will face Esmeralda in battle," He smiles at me, picking up my chin, "and you shall win."

# CHAPTER 9

## *Uncommon Soldiers*

"Lucifer seeks out every advantage in war.  He does not wish to repeat the mistakes of old in the new war with Heaven."

Forcas, at this point, is swinging his sword at me, and I'm still having issues parrying and avoiding his strikes. "Dodge!" He shouts.

I, unfortunately, didn't. I'm laid flat on my back and grunt as my tail is pinched under me.

Forcas stands over me. "Why didn't you dodge?"

Narrowing my eyes at him and grumbling through gritted teeth, "I felt like taking a break."

Forcas laughs, offering me his hand.

As I take it, I ask, "How the Hell did you wind up here? You don't seem like the typical sociopathic angel."

Forcas looks to Asmodai who is busy eviscerating Ubiel again, and feeding bits of him to Zelletia. "Hmm." He sheaths his sword. "Afraid I was on the wrong end of history."

"I'll say," I agree.

Forcas strikes me in the head swiftly with his training sword. It's blunted but still hurts.

"During the war, I had a choice, and I chose to try and save lives. I suppose I didn't realize that, in the end, God's plans were far different."

"Save lives?" I look at him incredulously.

Forcas rests his sword on his shoulder, "Humanity is not the first intelligent lifeform on Earth, Terra as it is referred to in the grander scheme."

"So... like Dinosaurs?"

Forcas, looks to Zelletia, "Where do you think she came from."

I look at Zelletia. "I... don't know I thought dragons were make-believe."

Forcas, shakes his head, "Old, yes. A myth, no." He laughs. "God made many creatures like that on Terra at first. And when he made Lucifer, Lucifer requested his own experiment. So, on Venus, another civilization occurred."

I look at the Blade of Pride, "Wait, so there was an entire planet of Satanists?"

Forcas, laughs at me. "In a way. They just called him their God, and some prayed." Forcas frowns. "Some did not."

"And Lucifer punished them?" I ask.

Forcas shook his head, "No. He did not. Freewill existed on Lucifer's version of life, it did not exist on... His." Forcas looks up. "Needless to say, we discovered an interesting thing about prayer."

"Prayer?" I ask.

"Yes," Forcas begins. "Gods and ethereal beings like them thrive on prayer. The more prayer they receive, the stronger they are, and the longer they last."

"Okay... I'm following." I rotate my shoulder. It hurts like Hell.

"So the fact is that prayer from someone who can choose to not pray is more powerful than a prayer from someone who has no other option but to pray," Forcas explained.

I take a moment, and Forcas seems generous enough to give me the time to think that over. "So... Lucifer started to grow in power?"

Forcas nods. "And then... Well... Lucifer was informed his experiment was over. That his world would no longer be habitable, and as a result, Heaven divided. Some felt the extreme reaction was just the Almighty being paranoid." Forcas sighs, looking up to the Blade of Pride, "I only joined his side to protect. Then... after the war was almost over, Lucifer was cast out, he fell... and he fell to Terra, destroying almost all life out of spite." Forcas looks to me, "In the end, Lucifer destroyed far more than he preserved. And the Almighty started over on Terra, restoring it after the calamity."

"They don't teach that in school. Wait, when you say calamity what do you mean?" I ask.

Forcas thinks a moment, then offers, "Well, he did most of the damage by landing from Heaven. However, he stalked around on the surface for a short while before he was finally bound by a prophet."

"That's a prophet I don't want to meet," I state.

Forcas chuckles. "It's funny, you might."

Before I can ask anything else, Asmodai's voice booms across the training fields. "Forcas, Whore! You're both done for the day."

I snap my fingers, causing my armor and sword to return to their blackball state. I slide them into my cleavage where they usually go and head back toward Asmodai.

He walks inside before I even manage to cross the training area.

I frown as I eventually get inside, closing the door.

Asmodai is nowhere to be found.

"Master?" Silence. "Asmodai?" I wander around for a bit, eventually making my way to the bedroom where I find him sitting on the edge of his bed.

He's no longer wearing his armor and looks me over. "In a few hours, you're going to face Esmeralda. I figured you could use some time to recover."

I wrap my wings around myself, looking him up and down. "Recover as in rest, or recover as in drink?"

Asmodai looks at me. "Whichever you prefer."

I walk over to the bed and slide up next to him, my hand moving over his chest. "After all the training these last few weeks, I am utterly exhausted! Every part of my body hurts."

His hand moves over my arm, where he feels a slight muscle. "You've been benefiting from the training, it seems."

I flex my arm, but then smile and pull out one of the little black balls, snapping it in my hand, the top portion of my armor wrapping around me. With a hard push, which was almost all of my strength, I managed to force him onto his back. "Is that a turn-on for you, Asmodai? For me to be strong?"

Asmodai grins, "I see the armor is amplifying your-"

I push my fingers to his lips, "Shush... this is my time to recover. Let me use you how I want."

Asmodai just smiles and leans back as I kiss over his abs and chest.

I finally make my way to his mouth and kiss him deeply, drinking in his essence. While I had sipped at him before when I grew tired, this was the first time I was intentionally drawing from him. It felt like drinking from a firehose! I had to stop, shivering a bit as I processed what I had done, but despite myself, I wanted more.

Asmodai grins. "Did that whet your palette?

I grab both of his hands, pinning him down to the bed, "Yes," I hiss and kiss him again. I control the surge of energy better this time, my body aches vanishing as I'm replenished, my strength feels like it's doubled as I squeeze Asmodai's wrists tighter.

He's like a drug, I can't get enough of him but I know too much will be terrible for me. I remember what happened to Esmeralda and finally break the kiss, shivering as I lay on top of him. I've riled myself up a bit too much and tried to calm myself down.

"Are you alright?" Asmodai asks me.

I nod. "Yes, just... I want more but I'm afraid."

Asmodai laughs and kisses me on the cheek, "After you win, you and I can spend endless hours celebrating."

My cheeks blush as he says this, or at least blush deeper. "How long until I'm going to fight her?"

Asmodai chuckles. "We don't have long."

"One for the road, then." I kiss him once more, with him kissing me back with passion.

Asmodai and I were on the balcony shortly after. I have my armor on and I'm feeling very nervous. Belial seemed to be late for some reason, much to Lucifer's agitation.

When Belial shows up, he appears riding on a strange creature. Its fur is matted and foul, and it has furry but clawed feet. Its neck was lizard-like and long with a feline-like face on it. Huge leathery wings folded on either side of the creature.

Belial dismounts, looks to Asmodai and grins. "She's quite a fast little creature. I still feel I got the better deal of the two of us."

Asmodai smiles a bit. "Did you see the ancient black Rex Dragon at the base of the Blade?"

Belial's face falls. "...Yes."

Asmodai grins wickedly, "That's mine."

Belial looks to me, then to the balcony. "Well, that's mine."

A huge demon landed on the balcony of the spire. I assumed it was Esmeralda behind him.

Her form was even more monstrous. Her hooves were even larger, yet they were caked in filth. Her arms were so large, she was basically hunched over. They were muscled and burley, covered in fur. Her hands were massive and looked like they were large enough to grab my entire body. Her mouth was so full of sharp teeth that it appeared she couldn't close her lips around them; thick drool sloughed off her mouth as she growled. Her eyes were still glowing purple and she snorted in my general direction.

Asmodai leaned down to me as she marched in before Belial. "Remember, victory is when your adversary is no longer able to attack you."

I nod. "Yes, Master. I remember what Forcas told me."

Asmodai looks around and then whispers, "Good girl" into my ear.

I shuddered.

"Fashionably late, Belial, Trouble with your charge?" Lucifer asks.

Belial bows. "My apologies, my Lord, Esmeralda is a bit... Wild at the moment. Your power courses through her and continues to corrupt her form."

Lucifer nods. "I see..." He looks at me and Asmodai. "Let us not forget the purpose of this battle. We are determining the usefulness of the Succubi. Belial, should your charge win this fight I will ensure that every succubus in Hell drinks their fill of Fallen essence, preparing for our invasion on Terra." He looks to Asmodai. "Asmodai, should your charge claim victory, then we will begin to train the Succubi in combat and provide them armors, as you had suggested."

I look at Asmodai. "Wait if I lose then...?"

Asmodai nods.

Glancing at Esmeralda and shivering, I try to remember everything I learned from Forcas. "It's only been a few weeks."

Asmodai smiles a sly grin. "Just trust your training." He glances at Esmeralda, "And do not forget what I said." He walks away from me.

Belial looks toward me and scoffs, "A pretty sword and some armor and suddenly you think she's a warrior, Asmodai?"

Asmodai looks at Belial. "More respectable than to whore your way to power."

"**Enough**!" Lucifer shouts.

Belial steps away from the monstrous Esmeralda.

Esmeralda growls at me and through her teeth, she spits out, "I'm going to rip you in half..."

I frown, imagining Mara and the others all transformed into hideous creatures like this. I grip my sword and take a readied stance.

Lucifer looks at the two of us. "**Begin**."

I wait, remembering what Forcas had told me.

"*Never be the first to strike. It's like showing the enemy what you're made of. Let them make that mistake,*" I recalled Forcas's words.

Esmeralda roars, and charges at me, moving to her hind legs as she builds up speed. She dips her head down to gore me with her horns.

I wait until she is a few feet in front of me, and then jump to the side, using my wings to propel me, Forcas's words in my head: "*You're small, your speed is your best asset. Your strength only makes your blows swift, your movements fast. Do not use long blows, you cannot fall her by force, you must have a victory of a thousand cuts.*"

Esmeralda barrels past me, using her huge claws to slow her down.

As she passes, I manage to get a good slice at her left leg.

As Esmeralda starts at me again, her left leg slips.

I dodge her again, jabbing into her right thigh. This doesn't work out too well, as she flexes her thigh, and my sword gets stuck. "Oh, shit..."

Esmeralda turns with her huge hand and goes to crush me.

I managed to pull my sword out of her thigh just in time and hold it up horizontally, her hand stopped by it. In order to keep myself from getting cut, I have the broadside of the sword facing her palm.

Esmeralda pushes harder against my sword, cackling as she does, "I'll crush you, you tiny thing!"

Forcas's voice is in my head again. "*Never forget, you're in Hell. Honor is unheard of here.*"

I press my thumb against the sword's jewel, my sword breaking into its chain form.

Esmeralda falls forward, her hand hitting the ground as I step back.

I pull the tip of the chain sword closer to myself, and then release it, pulling hard on the handle. The chain rips through her wrist and removes her hand.

Esmeralda roars in pain, she stumbles back and I take the moment to jump on her chest.

I swing the bladed chain behind her head and pull her to face me. I kiss her on the lips as best I could, feeling her lips on mine--or mostly. I looked her dead in the eyes and put so much effort into them that I could feel them burning in my sockets.

"Esmeralda, remember who you are! Remember why you sold your soul! Remember all of it and stop being such a ravenous beast!" The last part might not have stuck as I felt my vision start to tunnel. I jumped off her, and blinked, trying to clear my vision, but I had definitely overextended my eyes.

Esmeralda roars, then I hear her groan, and then another roar.

I turn around quickly to make sure she isn't trying to charge at me.

Instead, her massive hand is grabbing a hold of her horn as she thrashes about wildly. "I... I... Stop... I can't..."

I narrowed my eyes to see better and then had a simple thought. In a mock English accent, I shout, "Oi, Love! Looks like you've got a spot of a headache!"

Esmeralda roars again, her head slams down into the floor, her horns connecting and reshaping. The two pairs twist together, yet start to shrink slightly. Her entire body begins to shrink, however, and I notice it seems like something was being pulled into her. She groans, breathing heavily. "Can't... hold..."

"Yes, you can!" I scream. I drop my sword and run up to her. I lift up her head in both of my hands and I can see her irises behind the now dim glow of violet. Her teeth are still sharp but they're smaller, I can see some humanity on her face. "You can handle it. Believe in yourself." I whisper.

I'm knocked back by her tail, her wings fold around herself as I hear more grunting and groaning. Finally her wings open again. Though they're just as black and large, I notice her face looks like a woman's, and her form is sleeker and more feminine. Her hooves are still massive and fur still coats her legs and arms completely. The massive chest piece now follows a trimmer waist. Her tail, while still huge, is now more fitting to her smaller form. She staggers, falling to one knee, heaving, and struggling.

"Esmeralda?" I asked tentatively.

Esmeralda holds up her arm with the missing hand: it's rapidly growing the hand back with a pointed finger, "Bogtrotter..." She looks up, her irises returning, the glow changing the color of her eyes, her skin changing from violet to the original pale white that I was used to seeing, "*Never... Speak Kings... again.*"

I smile, "Okay..."

Esmeralda slowly gets back to both hooves and then turns to Lucifer. "I... am unable to contain the greatness of your essence, my Lord... Sara defeated me because I could barely think." She winces, placing her hand on her forehead, "Sara's... Control over me is all that is keeping me together."

Lucifer raises an eyebrow, "Sara used her enchantment on you? Aren't you a woman? Belial, explain." Lucifer looks to where Belial was, but he's nowhere to be found. "...Where is Belial?"

Esmeralda looks back to Lucifer, "All Succubus and Incubus are Bisexual, my Lord. As for my Master... I know not."

Lucifer walks up to Esmeralda until the two are at eye level. He evaluates her. "Seems with your wits about you, you're far stronger."

Esmeralda nods. "I don't know how permanent it is, my Lord."

Asmodai appears to be looking around for Belial, looking rather confused. "Could he not stand the sting of defeat..."?

Esmeralda finally seems to be in her right sorts as she walks over to me. She still towers over me a good three feet, even a foot over Asmodai. "...You're still a *tiny* thing."

I smile. "Welcome back."

She smiles a bit as well, though her teeth are still razor-sharp. "I wasn't all gone, Bog-trotter." Esmeralda soon makes her way to the balcony.

Asmodai approaches me, "Well done, whore."

Lucifer then shouts, "**Beelzebub**!"

A black swarm of insects suddenly flies into the room. It swirls around in front of Lucifer and forms a man with black wings. "My liege." His voice buzzes and clicks as if it's being made by insects.

Asmodai leans down to whisper to me, "Beelzebub, the Avatar of Envy, Lucifer's spy."

"Where is Belial?" Lucifer demands.

"He is possessing someone, it seems," Beelzebub hisses.

Lucifer narrows his eyes, "Now? In the middle of..." He suddenly closes his eyes, when he opens them, they are swirling in anger, "The Guardian Temple is opened...? By who...?"

Lucifer waves his hand before him and an image appears. He stares in confusion as there appears to be a construction crew or something inside some kind of temple. "...Who is doing this?"

Asmodai looks at Lucifer. "My Lord, did your daughter not lay waste to every guardian angel in that temple?"

"Yes she did… It was a glorious bloodbath. I enjoy re-watching it at times." He glares. "There are no angels left… Belial had assured me he corrupted the last one… Where is he?" Lucifer looks around. Lucifer waves his hand again, "There is exactly one… wait… Four…?" Lucifer snaps his fingers and four images appear before him.

One image is of a young man, with black hair and blue eyes. He's wearing a trenchcoat of some sort and is standing in the temple in the original image.

The second image is of an older woman, roughly in her fifties. She has huge white wings and is surrounded by two female guards. She wears all manner of finery, jewels, robes, and even a small crown. She has long red hair, and blue eyes, though they look tired and drained.

Third, there's an image of a young girl. She has red hair and blue eyes like the woman. She is wearing a smaller crown, similar to the woman. She has similar robes, though hers are simpler. She's reading a book and looks to be in her teens.

Lastly, and the image that is largest, is a young girl, maybe a year younger than the last girl. She's also got huge wings and is wielding a sword. She appears to be training with a full-grown woman in full armor. However, she seems to be knocking the woman around with ease. She has short black hair and bright violet eyes.

Lucifer's eyes swirl. "Rachel had children…? The line of Enoch is unbroken…?" Lucifer eyes the fourth photo and grins, "Well done Ragna… You've somehow found a way to have a child after all… With Rachel. Intriguing… A descendant of Enoch… and Lucifer." He grins, "That will be an interesting occurrence indeed. The first Cherubim born outside of His desire." Lucifer's anger returns, however, as he looks to Beelzebub. "Beelzebub, find Belial and find out what that boy is doing in the Guardian Temple. Now!"

"Of course, my liege... But I have something else to report." Beelzebub bows, and then looks to Asmodai and me, "These two..."

My eyes go wide and a chill runs down my spine.

Beelzebub smiles, his face made of insects that are constantly crawling. His voice echoes through my ears as my stomach drops, "Are *lovers*."

# CHAPTER 10

## *Blackmailed*

**"Hell is a prison.  Lucifer is the strongest inmate. Dissension is dealt with by those both fearful and loyal to his power."**

Lucifer motions for Asmodai and me to approach him. Lucifer narrows his eyes on Asmodai. "Asmodai...."

Asmodai removes his helmet, kneeling before Lucifer. "I can explain."

Lucifer looks at me. "You bought her soul from Belial under the pretense you would perform this 'experiment'. You grew on her and now you feel a more potent connection. So much so you risk everything, your station, and even your mere existence to have her."

Asmodai is speechless, staring at Lucifer.

I do the same, also kneeling.

Lucifer places his fingers on the bridge of his nose, rubbing it in frustration.

I'm petrified.

Lucifer looks to Asmodai. "I will put this very plain, Asmodai. You are one of the strongest Fallen I have. You are the leader of my armies. The Sword of Samael.  Should Belial begin the coup I think he is trying, you are likely to be whom he will reach out to."

Asmodai begins, "My Lord I would never--"

"No." Lucifer says plainly, "No, you would never. Because, if you did..."

I suddenly can't breathe--it feels like someone's squeezing all the air out of me, and I feel a few ribs snap. More so, I feel like something is draining out of me. I can't describe it, but it hurts. It hurts like no pain I've ever felt. It hurts deep in my heart like I'm dying.

"I will destroy *her*," Lucifer says simply.

Asmodai's eyes grow wide. "My Lord... I am your faithful servant for eternity! I would never serve Belial, under any condition!"

I fall to the ground, coughing and wheezing. The pain from my injuries remains, and I do not feel myself recovering. I feel weak and feeble. I'm shaking at this point.

Asmodai rushes to my side.

"If you want to accept that weakness, Asmodai, then so be it. She will worm her way into your heart and if she ever leaves, she will leave you a shell of what you once were. Remember that," Lucifer growls.

I wince, looking up to Lucifer, "I'm... sorry my Lord..."

**"Silence**!" The tower shakes with his voice and I see the wisps of purple smoke rise from his eyes. "The only reason I do not destroy you now is that Belial has gone rogue. Right now, I need loyalty." He looks to Asmodai, "And you being held hostage is the easiest method by which to guarantee it." Lucifer looks at Beelzebub now. "Beelzebub, thank you for bringing this to my attention. I trust I am the only one you have brought this information to?"

Beelzebub stands. "Of course my Lei–"

Before he can finish, Lucifer's hand is on Beelzebub's face.

A horrible screeching and scratching noise is heard as Beelzebub's form shifts and almost falls apart.

Lucifer removes his hand as Beelzebub's form coalesces. "Beelzebub, your only task now is to assist Asmodai in finding the root of Belial's plans. His whore will assist as well, being one of Belial's favored Succubi, she should have access to his operation's inner workings. Am I understood?"

Beelzebub bursts into a swarm of insects and disperses.

Lucifer looks to both of us with agitation. "It appears this experiment was not just a ruse to purchase your whore. Belial used it to distract my attention." The tower shakes as his eyes swirl again, "Go. Now. Before my mercy runs out. Discover Belial's treachery and I may consider allowing the two of you to continue to exist as you are. Otherwise, I will debate only between ending your entire existence or hurling you both into the endless abyss."

Asmodai nods, helping me to my feet. "Right away my Lord."

I stand, my hooves slipping as I have trouble with my footing.

Asmodai narrows his eyes to me as we get to the balcony. "You acted suspiciously."

"I did no such-" I tried to argue.

Asmodai slaps me, hard.

I tumble to the floor, whimpering as the sting of the hit still lingers.

"Are you trying to get yourself destroyed?" Asmodai growls to me in a hushed voice, "Do you think I enjoy hurting you? I don't... I hate myself more each time I must do this..."

I roll over so I'm sitting on the ground, looking up to him. "It's not like I enjoy it either."

Asmodai clenches his fist to the point I see blood dripping from his hand.

"...Master, stop, please," I say softly as I manage to barely get to my hooves, climbing up his leg for support. "I don't know how Beelzebub found out... I'll be more discreet." I close my eyes, "But it also means you need to be more... forceful."

Asmodai is silent.

I open my eyes, looking at him defeated, "No one smacks their whores here. No one just yells at them. I wasn't the one acting suspiciously."

Asmodai looks away. "We need to do what he ordered us first. We'll discuss this later." Asmodai growls, "Now go to your Succubi whores and find where your old master went, or I'll string you up before my army and let the lot have a go at you till you can't feel your tits."

I bow and as I walk by him and whisper, "That's better."

Asmodai whispers back to me, "I'd never..."

I leap into the air before he can finish, flying toward the Fields of Lust, making sure to take the most direct route possible.

I landed eventually, much to the surprise of the Succubi around me.

Khairunnisa is one of the first to greet me, "Sara... you're... what are you wearing?"

I look down at my armor and scoff for a moment, "The armor my Master wants me to wear."

Khairunnisa frowns, "Oh Hell... are we expected to fight?"

I nod. "It's better than the alternative."

Khairunnisa shudders for a moment. "Luckily Lord Lucifer hasn't asked for me yet."

"Speaking of our respective masters..." I begin, "Where's Belial?"

Khairunnisa frowns. "I don't know where he is," She says simply.

I cleared my throat, "Do you think maybe, you know who might?"

Khairunnisa narrows her eyes at me, "Do you think if Belial were to be up to something, I would just tell you?"

I think for a moment, and then grab Khairunnisa by her cheeks and kiss her deeply.

Khairunnisa resists for a moment, but my eyes are on hers first, and I focus as I did with Esmeralda.

"Who would know where Lord Belial is?" I question.

Khairunnisa appears stunned and glances to her floating clipboard flicking her finger through it., "Mammon has been receiving a very heavy discount on his pleasures."

"Mammon?" I asked.

Khairunnisa nods.

I fly off to find Asmodai.

Asmodai and I walk down many hallways into the Labyrinth of Greed.

I glance at Asmodai as we head down the long staircase, "So, I know he's the avatar of Greed but does he have any other qualities?"

Asmodai grumbles, "He and Belial share similar traits. Lust and Avarice often mix and mingle."

I roll my eyes. "Never seen a rich man have trouble with women."

Asmodai nods. "Also never seen a rich man take his riches with him when he dies."

"Or his women," I chuckle.

"That I have seen," Asmodai says simply.

I shudder as we get to the main floor. The air stinks of heavy incense, and the smoke burns my eyes slightly.

Asmodai, as usual, is unphased as he makes a right down a maze of hallways.

I follow along and make sure not to lose Asmodai as he makes many turns and twists through the long basement. Finally, we get to a large room.

The room is filled to the brim with weapons, armors, soul cores in chests, and I can hear a Succubus somewhere in the corner, gasping and gagging.

I shiver as I remember the odd desires of Mammon.

Asmodai heads toward the sounds, with me in tow. We eventually get to the throne. On it, I spot the succubus, Britney, a blonde girl with baby blue eyes. She's covered in filth, a foul stench somehow overpowering the very strong incense.

Britney rides Mammon reverse cowgirl style as he sits on his throne, feeding her filth as she does so. His hair is slicked back in a ponytail that goes down to his waist and he is naked from the waist down. From the waist up, he has a leather shirt with golden buttons, a gold necklace, and multiple piercings on his nose and lips. On his hands, I notice there are multiple gold and silver rings on each finger, as he reaches for another bit of filth on Britney and slips it past her lips. His wings are gilded, the brown feathers at the crest of his wings golden, as are the tips of the feathers at the edge of his huge wings.

Britney gags as she continues to bounce on his dick.

"Swallow it, whore. You are filthy, both outside and in. Wallow in that. Yes..." Mammon groans. "Asmodai..." he asks, without breaking his rhythm, "Brother, what a pleasant surprise. Care to have a go at her? Blood may mix well with everything else here."

Asmodai's lip curls in disgust. "I'd rather not sully my 'blade'."

Britney gasps and then cries a bit.

"Then how may I be of service...?" Mammon lets out a groan and gives a few final thrusts into Britney.

Britney cries out. I can't tell if in pleasure or in disgust, but I go with the latter.

Mammon grins, slapping Britney on the back of her head. "Off with you slut, go on. I have business to get to."

Britney falls forward, gasping and pulling her clothing over herself. She wretches as she tries to speak, recovering shortly afterward. "Thank you, Lord Mammon..."

Mammon waves her off as he stands before us, naked from the waist down still.

From simple observation, I discovered that Mammon was made from a different mold than Asmodai, thankfully. Britney had to suffer twice, it seemed.

"Brother brother, why do you barge into my parlor unannounced?" He claps his hands. "You need a loan for the war effort? I can strike a nice little deal here... Especially if that whore's on the offering table."

Asmodai takes a deep breath. "We can negotiate the price of my whore another time."

Mammon snickers, "She looks very cute in that armor get-up. I've requested my charges to wear many kinky outfits. It is only fitting that our Lord of Wrath and Grand General is fond of his concubine in armor."

I look to Asmodai and hope he can maintain his composure.

Asmodai glares. "Enough pleasantries Mammon... What is Belial up to?"

Mammon's face falls. "What makes you believe I would be aware of his activities?"

"Because he's giving you a crazy discount on every succubus you order. That's not normal." I add, "Belial *never* cuts anyone a break."

Mammon narrows his eyes on me, "Who told you that? What little lying whore would dare to sully *my* name and defy her master?"

I decided not to answer him.

Mammon grabs me by the throat, "Answer me. you little harlot!" He screams.

Asmodai growls and shoves a blade through Mammon's chest.

Mammon wheezes and falls to his knees, "Brother... Why?"

Asmodai then snaps his fingers: a gag, hood, and chains appear in Asmodai's hands, "Because our Lord requires your presence."

Mammon is kneeling before Lucifer now, his hands and wings chained, his head covered in a hood.

Lucifer scans Asmodai, Mammon, and I, "Let him speak."

Asmodai pulls the hood off and removes the gag from his mouth.

Mammon spits, "The outrage! My Liege, Asmodai has lost his mind! He came barging into the Labyrinth of Greed just to bully me! You know I am at your beck and call, My Lord!"

Lucifer growls, "**Silence**!" The tower shakes. "Asmodai stated you are in some sort of pact with Belial. Belial, as it were, is not here." Lucifer looms over Mammon, "What is he planning?"

Mammon grumbles, "I am unsure of what he is planning at this moment, My Lord. I had an agreement regarding his holdings and planning their purposes."

Lucifer looks at me. "Mammon, if he is guilty, is not going to just confess, Girl."

Asmodai glares at me. "If you are wrong about this slut, I will rip your intestines out through your mouth and force them back up through your ass."

While I dwell on that colorful image, a thought occurs, "My Lord?"

Lucifer looks to me, and I wilt slightly under his mighty gaze, "What?"

After I composed myself, I started again, "Who was it who began to offer the idea of making Esmeralda a demoness?"

"Belial." Lucifer says simply, "The suggestion was a strange one, considering it would harm his prospects. But I had thought, for once, he wanted to aid the war effort."

"Did he offer anyone other than Esmeralda?" I ask.

Lucifer shakes his head. "No, he said only his succubus queen was the one he felt I should..." Lucifer's face relaxes as he has an epiphany, "I see." He closes his eyes for a moment and opens them again, "Esmeralda will be here shortly. However, if she is the one who was instructed to do this, she is not going to defy Belial so easily."

"Yes, she will," I corrected.

A pin could have dropped and it would have excused itself for making such a commotion.

Lucifer broke the silence with a slow inhale from his nostrils, "Girl... I am not a fool. I know that as Belial is her Master for eternity, she will not give him up without a decent struggle."

Esmeralda soon lands outside the balcony, making her way towards us, "I came as quickly as I could, My Lord."

Lucifer looks at me. "I will destroy you, in an instant, if you cannot draw the information out of her."

I shudder a bit and walk over to Esmeralda. "Hey... can I ask you something?"

Esmeralda raises an eyebrow at me, "What is it, bog-trotter?"

I whisper something too low for her to hear.

Esmeralda bends down. "What? Speak up, you are tiny-"

I kiss her deeply, locking my eyes with hers, keeping my lips locked to hers until I feel her kissing me back.

Esmeralda gasps as I break the kiss. She leans in again for another but I stop her.

"No, no, pet... listen to me... What were Belial and Mammon scheming? Tell our Lord and I will give you another"

Esmeralda licks her lips, a far away look in her eyes, as she looks to Lucifer. "My Lord, My Master instructed me to provide Mammon with all the succubi he wanted in exchange for a secured vault which would hide away Belial's wealth. Mammon, in exchange, kept tabs on all powerful artifacts that may move into his reach. Their goal was to pull themselves to the surface and dominate it. Master told me to drink heavily from you whenever I could, even to the point where I could not sustain the energy. I know not why."

I add, "Because if she was a mindless Hellbeast, she wouldn't be able to tell anyone of Belial's plans."

Mammon glares at Esmeralda, "You dumb bitch!! What sort of succubus cannot resist mind control from a weaker succubus?!"

Asmodai growls, "She is my succubus, not Belial's, and as such, she is stronger."

"Also Esmeralda isn't a succubus anymore", I add, sheepishly, "She's a Greater Demon and I can control the demons with my powers of seduction."

Mammon laughs, "Nonsense!"

Esmeralda whimpers, "S-Sara... you promised..."

I blush, "Oh, right... uh... just a sec." I turn to Esmeralda and kiss her again. She picks me up as I do this. Before things go too far, I break the enchantment, looking at a confused Esmeralda.

"...What... what did you... do to me?" Esmeralda looks at Lucifer and then kneels, "My Lord... I... I had no choice but to follow Lord Belial's request!"

Lucifer ignores her and turns to Mammon, "So she speaks the truth, of course?"

Mammon whimpers, "My Liege... I..."

"I will order Asmodai's armies to raid the Labyrinth of Greed and pull from it every bauble, every trinket, every single soul core within it, and dump them into the abyssal void if you do not tell me, precisely, why Belial is possessing someone on Terra at this instant," Lucifer threatens.

Mammon's eyes go wide, "No, No my Lord! Of course. Belial had the idea, I merely supported it! I always keep an ear and eye out for powerful relics and... and one created by your daughter fell onto the Earth!"

"What was created by my daughter, Mammon?" Lucifer shouts.

"I named it myself! It's leftover angel blood from when Ragna tore through the Guardian Temple!" Mammon blabbers.

Asmodai barks, "That's Lord!"

Mammon blinks, looking at Asmodai.

"Lord Ragna! Do not disrespect her heritage!" His voice booms.

Mammon gulps, and nods, "Y-Yes, when Lord Ragna slew the Guardian Angels, their blood coalesced in a pool within a gash she left in the floor. After centuries, it solidified into what I call Sanguine Amber."

Lucifer closed his eyes, "How much of this Sanguine Amber was there?"

Mammon thinks for a moment, "Several pounds of it, My Lord."

Lucifer grits his teeth. "And Belial seeks it even now? Who has it? What power possesses the Amber now?"

Mammon frowns, "A... a simple sinner, My Lord. He cleans up after murderers for a price, as his sin is greed I'm very familiar with him."

"Does this mortal have any affinity for the Almighty?" Lucifer queried.

"Less than most, My Lord. I nicknamed him 'Red Fred', as he cleans up the blood of deeds performed by murderers and adulterers." Mammon whimpers, "I beg you, oh Lucifer, Lord of all Hell, great Morning Star, please take pity on my insolence!"

"Pity?" Lucifer nods then gets down on his haunches. "I will not harm you, Mammon. You came clean... told me all I wished to know." He looks to Asmodai. "Raid the Labyrinth. Your legions shall have their free reign over any and all spoils within it."

Mammon's eyes grow wide. "N-no, M-My Master you-"

Lucifer grabs him by the neck, "You will watch as Asmodai's legions fumble through your vaults, steal to their heart's content, and ravage your precious collections." Lucifer grins. "And you can thank Belial when he gets back."

Asmodai flies off immediately, shouting and commanding his army to do as Lucifer ordered.

Mammon skulks off, leaving me rather awkwardly with Lucifer.

"Esmerelda, get out of my sight." Lucifer ordered with a scoff.

Esmerelda makes haste to leave, standing, bowing, and flying off without a word.

Lucifer moves to his throne, sitting on the huge thing, and looks to me, "Girl, come here."

I walk up to his throne, and kneel, "Yes My Lord?"

"Belial, at this moment, is trying to use this Sanguine Amber to pull himself into the surface world with his full might. From there, he will draw his armies, and then he would more than likely have summoned Mammon." He pauses, looking out toward the Labyrinth of Greed as Asmodai's armies ransack it. "From there I can only assume he would guard the gate and prevent us from ever opening it. With us so close, I, of course, want him to fail."

"Of course, My Lord," I responded.

"Enough kissing my ass," Lucifer refutes, "You're a bright girl. You were on to Belial's ruse and the plan behind it well before I noticed. Likely because I was so concerned with the idea of ridding myself of the Succubi. They are so... human at times... it's sickening."

I frown. "It's either us or fucking the she-beasts in the lakes of fire."

Lucifer laughs, and stands, "I knew I liked you. Fair enough girl, here is my bargain: Remain loyal to me, along with Asmodai, and I will allow your farse to continue."

I smile.

"Under the condition that Asmodai stops pussyfooting around with you in public. Those backhands to your face may as well be kisses on the cheek."

I blush.

"And stop that," He growls, "It's ridiculous to see a Succubus blush."

I nod. "I will do my best My Lord."

Lucifer then walks toward the balcony, overlooking the chaos below, "Loyalty is now in question in Hell. I must flex my power and show my true superiority to all below." He turns to me, "You, Sara, and Asmodai, shall be my new inquisitors."

# CHAPTER 11

## *Inquisition*

"A punishment from a demon in Hell is a nightmare. A punishment from Lucifer himself is a tragedy."

Lucifer had put Asmodai and me in charge of rooting out anyone who wasn't loyal. We weren't terribly popular, as you can imagine. I found out some interesting things about my abilities though.

One: I could use my enchantment on just about anyone... except for Princes of Hell. Tried that on Belphegor and he was super pissed, mostly because Asmodai forced him to actually stand. Belphegor is, apparently, the Avatar of Sloth.

Two: My powers even work on the Succubi!

In the end, I think that this whole inquisitor position may have been a punishment all of its own. Mostly because no other Fallen were in cahoots with Belial: only a few greater demons in his armies. He played this very close to his chest, apparently. But I did pity those demons, I did. We had delivered them all to Lucifer, but I never saw any of them again after we did so.

I remember one demon, Azazel. He was apparently one of the original demons, or as Lucifer called him, a Dei? Apparently, that's what the race on Venus was.

Azazel was about six and a half feet tall, not counting the straight black horns. He would have been a burly guy if he had been on earth. His skin was red, and his feet were horse-like hooves. He lacked a tail but did have bat-like wings. He was surprisingly, what you'd expect of a stereotypical demon--I guess that's what the Dei looked like? I'm not sure.

Azazel had flown with us to the Blade of Pride, entirely under my enchantment. When we landed, however, he started to act out of sorts.

"Hey, sweet cheeks..." He flexed a bit, leering at me, "When are you going to lay another one of those hot Succubi kisses on me, huh?"

I narrowed my eyes, "Okay: We can not and say we did," I snapped my fingers, breaking the enchantment. I didn't even have to seduce him for the first kiss.  He was just a complete and utter slime-ball.

Asmodai was silent as he glared at Azazel.

Azazel just shook his head for a moment when the enchantment wore off. "Woah... uh... wait, why are we at the Blade?"

Asmodai pushed him forward, "You have an appointment."

Azazel stumbled forward and scoffed towards Asmodai, adjusting his clothing. Oddly Azazel didn't wear armor. He wore a black pinstripe suit, black tie, and even had several blackened rings. The pants remained pinstriped right up until his feet turned to furred hooves, and even then they were all very expensive looking. "No need to rough me up, big guy, I hear you." He walks forward. "So what's all this about?"

Lucifer stood from his throne as Azazel walked through the archway into the throne room. "...not you too, Azazel."

"Me too, what, My Guardian?" He asked, kneeling with his fist to the ground, looking to the floor.

Lucifer shouted now, his voice deafening, "Do **not** take me for a fool! Belial's hand has been shown!"

Azazel sighed, "Is this about the vault?"

Lucifer stormed up to Azazel, "That whore behind you is not in Belial's service, she is in Asmodai's. I have been rooting out treachery against me..."

Azazel looked up, his expression that of shock.

"And they brought you before me... Which means you either have information on what was happening..." Lucifer's wing straightened, and from it, he pulled out a long feather. He slammed it down next to Azazel and it cut right through the floor. It seemed hard as steel, if not stronger somehow.

Azazel looked at the feather, and then to Lucifer shaking, "It's just--you have to admit, we've been down here a long time. When we first started the war, you promised you'd free Dei and rule over all creation," Azazel shrugged. "And it hasn't quite been a good ride. Belial gave me a better offer. If he succeeds, he'll pull me and my legion out of Hell."

Lucifer's breathing was slow, even and calculated. Without warning, he started to laugh.

Azazel smiled nervously, laughing along with him, "I-it's kind of funny, right?"

Lucifer's laughter grew in tempo and tilted off the deep end of madness as he grabbed the feather. "Do you know what's funny?"

Azazel slowly got to his feet, "What's funny, My Guardian?"

Lucifer shoved the blade through Azazel's chest, "When Belial tries to summon you... He will get nothing..."

Azazel grabbed at the feather-sword in his chest, writhing, "W-what do you--"

Lucifer grabbed Azazel by the head, and started to saw the sword through him, "Because for the first time in over a millennium..." Lucifer looked him directly in the eyes, grinning wickedly, "I'm going to destroy a soul."

Azazel gasped, "W-wait... W-why not throw me in the pit, or hang me fr-"

Before Azazel could finish Lucifer lets go of his head, ripping the feather-sword through him from his chest to the top of his skull.

A white light glows out of Azazel, and what looks like a soul core came floating between his bisected cranium.

"Nephesh chayyah he'evadeti," Lucifer whispers as his feather is thrust through the small orb.

It shattered into bits and pieces and the remains of Azazel disintegrated into dust. An intense wind blew past us as he did this.

Lucifer narrowed his eyes on the dust, "Goodbye, my little one." He looked to both Asmodai and me, "Was he the last of them?"

I nodded, looking at Asmodai whose eyes were wide.

"Azazel is..." Asmodai whispered.

"No more," Lucifer said simply. "Do not think I hold reservations about doing that to your precious succubus." He walked toward the throne, "Now get out of my sight. Your concern for her is sickening."

We didn't linger.

Asmodai and I had gotten back to the Halls of Wrath. For once he was still angry with me when we were inside. He grumbled as he removed his armor.

"Asmodai, do you want me to help you with that?" I ask.

Asmodai growls to me, "It's fine, I handled it fine before you arrived, I can handle it now."

"What's wrong?" I ask.

Asmodai narrows his eyes, "Lucifer destroyed Azazel and threatened to destroy you. And yet, despite that, I still cannot stop seeing you kissing the letch!"

My jaw drops, "Are you *kidding* me?"

Asmodai is silent, though still fuming.

"You amazing jerk!" I shout, trying to keep my insults tame because, well, he could eviscerate me at any moment. "I was once under Belial, that means I was literally *under* Belial, and countless other demons! You're angry about some kisses?"

"That was when you were his. You're *mine* now," Asmodai heaves a sigh, "Besides, Azazel seemed to genuinely enjoy it."

I march up to him, pushing against him as I do, well pushing my bust against him, getting to the tips of my hooves to try and get as close to his face as possible, "I may be yours but it's my lips that saved our asses because you pulled your punches while we were in public." I poke his chest, "And for your information, *everyone* enjoys it when I kiss them--that's the point!"

There was a moment of silence, I saw the green swirl in Asmodai's eyes and I flinched as he roughly grabbed my hair, tilting my head back. In an instant, his lips were on mine, and his other arm was holding me tight against him.

I shudder and kiss back, melting in his arms.

He then forces me against the wall, pulling my armor off my legs and ripping through my underwear.

I gasp, "Wait, wait-OH!" I cry out in shock as he roughly thrusts into me, "Oh! Asmodai!" I gasp.

Asmodai growls, "You've been frustrating me all day, kissing everyone you pleased... You need a reminder that you're **mine**!" He continues his rough treatment of me, and I am not one to complain in the least.

While pinned, I do manage to pull him close for some light kissing, but he's mostly just a mechanical bull now, thrusting into me with power and rage and taking all of his frustrations out on me. While I prefer our more intimate and softer moments, I can't say I'm not enjoying myself as he plows into me.

Maybe I was delirious from the mind-blowing power Asmodai was pouring into me, but as we neared our climax, I just cried out, "Yes, Yes! Oh, Asmodai, I love you!"

I collapse on his shoulder, shivering in the afterglow.

Asmodai slowly lets me down, sitting with me in his lap, my legs around his waist and my arms draped over his shoulders. "...You too."

I am catching my breath, blushing, "I... uh... what?"

Asmodai's face twists oddly and he whispers into my ear, "...I love you too."

I nuzzle into the crook of his neck, "You just got frustrated, huh?"

Asmodai nods.

"...You sure you're not the avatar of envy?"

Asmodai chuckles a bit, stroking my hair. "I won't lose you."

I smile at him, and kiss him softly, "I am not going to go anywhere."

Don't make promises you can't keep.

It was a few weeks later when some kind of insane commotion occurred at the Blade of Pride.

A huge swirling vortex of dark clouds was hanging over the balcony with a rumbling sound of trumpets and a choir of sweet voices filling the air.

Asmodai is wearing a shit-eating grin as he looks out at the Blade of Pride. "Want to watch?"

I frown. "Watch what?"

"Belial getting his comeuppance?" Asmodai explains.

A smile that is legitimately evil crosses my face, "I wanna go, I wanna go right now!"

When Asmodai and I landed at the Blade of Pride's balcony, Lucifer was already waiting.

Lucifer's smile was downright vicious, "Bring him to me already."

A massive black creature dropped from the vortex. It had voluminous scaled wings that blotted out the sky and an endlessly long, scaled black tail. Around its enormous head swirled a pair of short white horns. A long neck sprouted out of its broad shoulders and chest and both of its feet were giant lizard-like claws. Shining armor covered its legs, continuing up its monstrous body, up to his lizard-like maw, over its broad chest, and down its heavy arms. Each hand was scaled and clawed, and one of them grasped Belial's neck.

Lucifer grins as he greets it. "Brother Enoch. My, it has been a long time."

Enoch snorts, "You left this one on the wrong plane."

He drops Belial before Lucifer.

"So I did." Lucifer slowly walks toward the black creature, "How is Father? Doing well, I hope?" Lucifer mocks.

A sound that is almost like singing grows from the creature's throat; however, it sounds like angry singing. "Father is well."

"Your great-grandson?  He's quite the inspiration." Lucifer smiles as he walks over to Belial, grabbing him by the scruff of his neck.

"M-My Lord..." Belial wheezes.

"Silence," Lucifer growls. "The adults are talking."

Enoch's tail swishes back and forth in agitation. "My Great Grandson is none of your business."

Lucifer chuckles, "No, no, no... of course not... but... your Great Granddaughter... is... well, my Granddaughter." Lucifer corrects, grinning wickedly. "What does that make us, Brother?"

Enoch's tail slams on the balcony. "Your blood will not corrupt her as you think it will."

Lucifer starts to chuckle and then begins a hearty laugh, which transitions to maniacal laughter.

Enoch looks up, then turns to me, frowning. I see no pupils in his eyes, just a soft white glow from empty sockets.

Lucifer's laughter dies down. "Yes... look at that one. I corrupt all, Enoch. Nothing is safe from me. Not your Guardian Angels, not your children, not theirs, not theirs after that."

Enoch looks away and whispers, "You will not win."

Lucifer grins, "Enoch. Don't be foolish." He changes his grip to Belial's throat and tightens it, smiling proudly, "I've already won."

Enoch merely jumps into the vortex.

Before it closes, Lucifer shouts, "Give my regards to Father! Tell him his Terra will burn beautifully once again! This time, the fires will be twice as hot!"

The vortex closes, but I'm pretty sure I can still hear a choir of some sort.

Lucifer then looks to Belial. "Belial! Please--you appear tired from your arduous journey! Let's take a load off those tired bones of yours... and have a nice chat about your trip!" Lucifer says jovially.

Belial winces and grunts as he is dragged into Lucifer's throne room.

I follow without invitation.

Lucifer stops to look at me. "Why are you here?"

I look at him and without blinking, I blurt out, "I want to watch Belial suffer."

Lucifer smiles and looks to Asmodai, "You're rubbing off on her Asmodai. I like it. Come along, you vengeful little minx, you can have a front-row seat."

Belial objects, wheezing, "No... You and I can discuss this in private."

Lucifer laughs loudly, "No no Belial! Not at all! Why spare anyone the lovely conversation we are to have."

He hurls Belial before the throne, where he lands flat on his face.

Lucifer holds out his hand: black mist swirling around his hand before a huge sword appears in it. The blade's tip clashes down into the ground and cracks it, and as it does I can swear I hear faint screaming.

The sword is almost as long as Lucifer is tall and the massive blade has a fuller running from a few inches below the tip to the hilt. The hilt is huge. It looks like a single cross, but the crossguards, each appear to be an angular wing, I realize the main guard of the sword looks like a beak biting into the blade as if the sword was exiting the beak itself. The pommel of the sword has a Nazi Swastika for some reason.

Belial's eyes grow wide, "Why... My Lord... have you drawn the Puriel Blade?"

Lucifer swings the sword and points it to Belial's throat, the tip cutting his skin slightly. "Why oh why indeed. Belial... explain yourself."

Belial gasps as the blade tip touches his skin, "I... planned to... take Terra for myself." He seems short of breath for some reason.

Lucifer inhales slowly through his nostrils, "Do you know what I've done to Mammon?"

Belial winces as the sword digs a little deeper into his throat, the skin around it blackening, while veins along his skin and throat appear to turn black or purple. He seems to be in great pain. "I... Assume something... appropriate...."

Lucifer pulls the blade back from Belial's throat.

"I am extremely unsurprised, Belial. I suppose all these eons of you being faithful were... well... I guess to lull me into a state of false security. But, I have purged the entire Hellscape of your treachery and we have found every one of your conspirators." Lucifer smiles, "Unluckily for you, they shared your loyalty." Lucifer places the sword to Belial's shoulder, "By all logic, I should transubstantiate you now, and hurl your newly minted moral soul into the lakes of fire to be broken into a soul core that I would then have Sabnock smith into a toothpick..."

Lucifer leans down to be eye to eye with Belial, "But it would be a waste of effort."

"Thank you, my Lord," Belial wheezes, his hand on his throat even as more veins along his face turn black. It's like poison spreading through him.

Lucifer grins wickedly, "Oh no Belial, do not thank me yet." He walks to his throne.

Belial turns slowly, "I... I'm not sure what you mean my Lord." He's looking woozy and unsteady even on his knees, and his face looks paler than normal.

Lucifer speaks softly, "Pittura infamante." He says simply.

Suddenly from the black void of the ceiling, several ropes fly downward, wrapping around Belial's legs and hoisting him up into the air.

"My Master! Wait! No! You don't need to do this!" Belial is now hanging upside down by his feet, unable to undo the ropes on his feet, but desperately trying to do so. As he struggles, blood leaks from his mouth and eyes as the blackened veins on his face spread further and further across. The ropes tighten and then do something odd, looking as if they are fusing with his legs. Belial screams, his eyes rolling into the back of his head as blood runs out of his eyes.

"Reflect on this pain, Belial: reflect, surrender, and consider breaking some of your old habits." Lucifer leans back to his throne as suddenly Belial's movements halt entirely. "I think a century is a fitting punishment for you to remain in accelerated suspension."

Belial's hands move behind his back, and he disappears into the ceiling as his screams die down. The blood on his face freezes, blackens and looks like it hardens immediately.

My eyes grow wide. As Belial is hoisted into the air, I suddenly see there are hundreds of others suspended from the ceiling. Each is in a frozen state of screaming, their faces contorted in suffering. Some have both legs tied together; others have a single leg with the free one lax, sometimes hanging off their body, looking as if it's about to fall off. No one has blood on their face or blackened veins like Belial.

Lucifer interrupts my horror with a sigh. "The price you pay for being a traitor. Those have been up even longer. Despite my saying so, only a few years will pass here... but to them?" He smiles at the ceiling. "To them, hundreds of lifetimes are passing, with them hanging, dying, and being hung again. Belial will experience his defeat on Terra and down here in an endless loop for a century, all in the span of a year's time."

I swallow hard. "Fitting, My Lord."

Lucifer snaps his fingers again and the image of the younger girl from before is shown. She's using a training sword against a boulder, said boulder breaking as she hits it with almost impossible force.

I figure to ask, "My Lord, who is that girl?"

Lucifer grins, flipping the image, "My granddaughter. Her name is Zepherina."

Looking the girl over, I notice she has black hair and purple eyes. "She has your eyes."

"I see you noticed." He grins.

As I recall, the granddaughter of Enoch was shown to us before, when Belial's plan was first found out. I start to wonder how there's a granddaughter between them if both only have daughters. "Uhm, My Lord, if you don't mind, may I ask how this girl is your granddaughter?"

Lucifer grins. "My daughter's quite brilliant, isn't she? She is a lesbian herself, and unable to conceive a child on her own." He leans back in his throne, "But through a debasement of science and natural law... she managed to sire a child with Rachel, granddaughter of Enoch." He laughs.

"Our houses joined, and the first Cherubim born without God's consent has been made."

The little girl's training sword breaks, and out of frustration, she smashes her fist on the boulder, shattering it to bits.

"Such power!" Lucifer says proudly.

I swallow hard. Your... daughter must be proud, my Lord."

Lucifer's face falls slightly, "Unfortunately she doesn't know of the girl's existence yet."

"Oh," I say. "So... she's growing up without her mother?"

Lucifer nods. "Well, one of two but yes. I'm sure you can relate." Lucifer motions for me to come closer. "I will end you, should you share this information, you understand, yes?"

My stomach drops and I fall to my knees. "Yes, My Lord."

Lucifer leans back and waves his hand: a picture of a woman at a bar materializes.

She has long black hair, half of it buzzed off, and massive white wings sprouting out of her back. She wears a tank-top of sorts that does little to hide the massive burly muscles that make up her arms. In her hand is a bottle of some kind of hard liquor. Her head rests on the bar now, she's heaving heavily, and alone.

"I hate love," Lucifer starts, "It worms its way into the strongest of us and when it leaves, it leaves behind nothing but a hollow shell of what they once were."

Another image materializes a scene of the same woman swinging a pair of swords through countless other angels. There is no sound but she is laughing, blocking blades with one hand and shattering shields, swords, and bone with the other. Blood sprays from the slaughtered angels and she appears to be laughing maniacally as she slays them.

At some point in this gruesome scene, she shoves the two swords into a pair of angels, then reaches behind her to draw a massive claymore with a clear blade, like a diamond. She takes it in both hands, turns her stance, and swings it like a golf club, slicing a huge gash into the floor and bisecting three angels in one strike.

Lucifer motions to the first image which now shows her drinking from a fresh bottle.

"From destroyer... to drunk... all over a woman." He growls, his fist clenching, "All for love... disgusting... filthy... degrading... love..." He glares at me. "I am also burdened by it. I can see, but I cannot console, cannot touch, cannot do anything but watch her waste away."

I frown. "I'm sorry My Lord."

"I know you feel similarly, not being able to see how your family is, being helpless." He sighs, waving the images away. "Be happy that you are currently in my favor. Without you, I would still question the loyalty of my generals--but now I know where they all stand." Lucifer drops the Puriel Blade and it vanishes into a puff of black smoke. "Go on, Sara... go to your lover. These matters are done for now."

I nod to him, "Thank you, Lord Lucifer."

As I get up, I look at the hanging people and back to him, speeding my way out.

Right before I leave, I hear Lucifer's voice, "Oh, and one last thing..."

I turn to face him again, "Yes My Lord?"

"You are to train the succubi to fight."

I bow, "It would be my honor to serve you."

Lucifer merely dismisses me with a wave and leans back on his throne.

Asmodai is chuckling, "I enjoyed hearing him beg."

"We should go..." I whisper.

I trained with Forcas more over the years. In turn, I trained the other Succubi: we had broken it down to a one a week session where I would have them spar against each other. Eventually, Belial was released and Khairunnisa was rather pissed.

She had been running things pretty well on her own. She had even gotten all the succubi armor and weapons like mine, though most of the others preferred whips. Belial wasn't pleased about that but he had little choice in the matter.

For the most part, as I was well behaved, Asmodai and I led a pretty nice afterlife. It sure as Hell wasn't pleasant, to say the least. Hell is Hell, after all. But having someone to share it with was nice. Asmodai was hard on me when we were outside, but I was harder on him when we were in private to make up for it.

It was a few years later when I discovered I had a new ability, of sorts.

While training with Forcas, he was getting pretty touchy about my form.

"Your riposte is horrid," He said simply. He stood across from me, "Strike at me, forward."

I grumbled in complaint, "But we've been at this for hours!"

"And yet it seems you can not riposte! Now, I will show you. Strike!"

When I thrust my sword at him, he parried my sword and lunged at me, striking my shoulder. "See? Again."

We repeated this five more times, he kept hitting the same exact spot.

Finally the sixth time I grabbed the training sword. I'm fuming, and I feel a sudden surge of strength rush through me. I feel angrier by the second and I snap the training sword. I charged at him, shoving my training sword into his shoulder.

"How do you like it huh? How's my riposte now?!" I realized my voice is echoing somehow, and everything seems tinged in green.

Forcas, then thrust his training sword into my throat, his foot on the back of my head, "Down, girl!"

This just gets me even more agitated, and I feel another surge of strength through me. I pushed myself up enough to move Forcas's foot, and I tackled him to the ground, squeezing him tightly. I'm trying to squeeze the life out of him, or break something, it's hard to tell as I'm in a rage.

Forcas grunted, struggling. "Sara..."

I barely hear what he says and I redouble my efforts in snapping him in half.

Forcas's eyes glowed white for a second and I felt dizzy.

I shook my head and rammed my horns against his forehead.

Forcas managed to pull himself out of my grip and I charged at him again. Forcas, blocked my horns with his sword, "Sara! Enough!"

I'm pushing with all my might, and I feel even more strength coming the angrier I get.

Suddenly Asmodai's arms were under mine and he was holding me tight to his chest as I writhed and kicked.

I shouted and snarled some unintelligible curses and slurs while I'm held. Eventually, I calmed down, heaving in Asmodai's arms.

Forcas got up, dusting himself off "She went berserk."

Asmodai released me, I grunt as I fall to the ground, "I... I couldn't control it." I heard a sword being drawn.

Forcas frowned, "My Liege... please show some mercy... her actions were not her own."

I turned over only to get a sword shoved into my chest. I coughed, blood spurting out of my mouth.

"This is mercy, Forcas," Asmodai glared at me, "Do not strike your trainer, harlot."

He pulled out the blade and I fell forward. Blood gushed from my throat as I gasped for air, convulsing as Asmodai walked away.

When Asmodai was out of sight, Forcas leaned over me and placed his hand on my wound. Ensuring no one is looking, he started to heal the gash in my chest.

After a few minutes, I coughed up all the blood I could.

Forcas leaned me up against an armor rack. "You alright?"

I grumbled, "The answer to that is never going to be, 'I'm super thanks for asking,' you know?"

Forcas stood, sighing, "We're done for today then."

I managed to get up on my hooves, "Sorry… for charging you."

Forcas frowned, "I did not want to hurt you by fighting you off…your master seems less concerned with such things."

I looked down, "Yeah… Well, he's my Master so…"

"Indeed," Forcas sighed, "be safe Sara, until our next session."

I walked back into the Halls of Wrath, finding Asmodai in the bedroom, cleaning the sword he had run me through with. He looked at me mournfully, "I still do not like this."

I settled next to him, moving his hand away from the sword, "It's what we have to do. I will suffer an eternity of pain to be with you," I kissed him softly.

Asmodai returned it. "So I'm doing well then, yes?"

I nodded. "Yes… well enough where Forcas seems to think you're mistreating me."

Asmodai laughed, pulling me close as we lay down on the bed.

As I lay with him I was less than pleased, but I just closed my eyes and reminded myself: This is as good as I can get here. I've got to accept that.

It was several years after this, ten after Belial's failed coup, that something weird happened again in Hell. Throughout the fields, the caverns, and all of the various lands we all heard a voice chanting some weird dark words.

Asmodai was looking out of the window as it happened.

At the time I was dressing, my armor balls were sitting patiently on the nightstand by the bed. I was adjusting my corset, "What's going on out there?"

Asmodai looked at me as I wiggled myself into my thong, "Not sure. It sounds like a summoning ritual, but I've not heard one of those in over three hundred years."

I frown, "Belial isn't up to anything again is he?"

Asmodai shakes his head, "It's too weak to summon forth a Fallen. Maybe some lesser demon is being summoned as a familiar."

Lucifer's voice then rang out over all of Hell. **"Denizens of Hell! Hear my command!"**

I walk to the window, leaving my armor behind, listening closely.

**"One of you is being summoned! I know not who, but know this: Whoever is summoning you, your first task is to kill them, or entrance them to release you! Do not be bound**

**to their will! When free, your only goal is to break the seal on the gates of Hell! Today we have been given the key!"** His voice echoes through the air, **"You will be that key, to unlock the gate! Ready yourselves! Prepare, for soon we will destroy all of His works!"**

There's cheering, shouting, screaming, and roars of all kinds occurring all over Hell.

Through it all, however, Asmodai's eyes are narrowing as he listens to the summoner's voice. "What is he..."

I frown, "What's wrong Asmodai?"

A voice rings throughout the caverns, "I, Immunda, shall call forth the brute of the underworld! The Lord of Wrath!"

# CHAPTER 12

## *Hubris*

---

"A demon can be summoned forth from Hell by a skilled summoner.  One must have the desire to sacrifice themselves or someone else, or have an object of great power to do so. The power of the sacrifice determines the power of the demon summoned."

---

Asmodai growls, "The fool... he's not strong enough to summon me."

A green light suddenly surrounds me, and I look around, confused as I see runes lighting up at my hooves, "Uh... Asmodai..."

Asmodai is still looking out the window, "His spell likely won't work... Lucifer is going to truly destroy him if he bites off more than he can chew."

I shout, "Asmodai!" The green light all around me is growing and blinding.

Asmodai turns to me just before my vision is cut off, "No! No anyone but you! Get away, Sara!"

I try to move, but I can't escape the light that's all around me. I try to get down to the ground and mess with the glowing runes that are under me, but they don't move.

"Come forth! Come forth, Lord of Wrath!" I hear the voice of Immunda shout.

The last thing I see is Asmodai's hands reaching into the light before they fade away. As I see past the runes, the ground below me suddenly changes to the roof of the Halls of Wrath, then all of Hell, and then darkness. Through it all, I can hear Asmodai screaming for me. All the while it feels like I'm speeding toward the top at breakneck speed.

In an instant, the first thing I notice is that the air isn't hot. That's a welcome surprise. Then I hear a voice not too far away.

"YES! Behold! The Demon I have brought forth for the ruination of this world! An all-powerful..." Immunda's voice hitches.

I stand up, stretching my wings as I do so, looking ahead of me.

For reasons I can't really explain, there's a priest and a warlock in the same room. In his hands, the Warlock has some little red disk and a black beard and is covered in weird tattoos. His black robes stink and are tattered looking. He's staring at me in confusion.

"...Succubus?"

I pour on the charm as I spot him. "Mmm, who... are you? Did you summon me?" I glance down, noticing a binding circle. In his confusion, however, he didn't say anything about binding me to him or any kind of requests yet. My orders from Lucifer were pretty clear: kill the summoner and then break the seal. So I start working my initial entrance with my eyes, hoping to lure him into the circle.

"I do not understand! I summoned a demonic prince of Hell! I wanted to summon the Prince of Wrath! Who are you?" He asks as he walks into the circle I'm currently stuck in.

"Oh, *you* summoned *me*?" I purr as I slide my arms over his shoulders and around his neck, moving closer.

"Summoned and bound," The idiot says as he runs his hand through my hair.

I try hard, so hard to remain composed because that hair is my Master's to run through, not some two-bit mortal with a fancy disk that can summon demons.

I think I hear one of the priests call him a fool as he does this. I agree, he is a fool.

I just giggle at him. "I don't remember hearing the binding words..."

The look on his face is priceless as I pull him in for a kiss.

Funny thing, I think being summoned makes you thirsty because I am suddenly so thirsty. I drink deep from him, with the intent on killing him. Drinking from Asmodai is like sampling a fine vintage wine. It's a dry, delicious taste that tingles as it goes down and when it hits your stomach it warms your whole body and leaves you wanting another sip. Drinking from this mortal was different: it was sweet and tasty, sure. I'd say refreshing even. Basically, it was like drinking a Coke-- nothing special, but still tasty and satisfying. When I feel pretty much nothing left in my little soda can/summoner, I push him out, making sure his feet hit the circle so it breaks and I can get out. Wouldn't you know one of the priests saw through my plan and blocks me?

I grasp that you're all humans, but when a demon gets summoned, even a succubus or lesser demon, and they try to exit their summoning circle without being told? Ouch! It hurt like Hell. Well, less than Hell, but it still hurts! This marks two times I've been on earth as a Succubus and both times I'm stuck in a church. I'm none too happy about all of this, plus I know these priests are only human, so I make sure to simper and whine in the center of the circle. Also, as a point of order, I'm a Hell of a lot more powerful than the first time I came to town, so to speak. I can tell already that holy ground alone isn't limiting my abilities.

"Good show, Father Thomas!" I hear a British accent. It reminds me of Esmeralda. If he calls me a bog-trotter, I'm going to strangle him.

Despite my whimpering, I notice none of them are buying it, so I just pout, "You guys are jerks! Not even tryin' to help a lady!"

Of course, the main priest isn't too happy with this. I'm pretty sure he's not buying it. Why? I don't know. He starts trying to get me to say my name. He tosses holy water at me and it burns like a bastard!

"Oh! Shit, that burns! Stop! Stop! Okay! Sara! Sara Baker! My name is Sara Baker! Fuck, stop that!" I shout, hoping that puts an end to Mr. Baptizer.

"What sort of name is that for a demoness?" The Brit chimes in.

"Well, it wasn't my mother's plan for me to be a Succubus!" My sass gets me more Holy Water, of course. "Ouch! Shit, stop it! Sorry!" I shout.

I think there's a French dude somewhere who mutters something about Americans. Makes me want to rip his throat out while humming the Star-Spangled Banner.

"Sara... Baker... What do you mean, your mother named you? Do you want me to believe that you were a human before you fell?" The first priest asks.

I roll my eyes. I figured a priest ought to know this shit. "All demons were humans once, don't you know that?"

The priest ignores me and it looks like they're ready to walk out, leaving me here stuck in a summoning circle. The jerks! But then I notice Immunda getting up, which is impressive because I drained him dry!

At first, he looks pretty worse for the ware but then the guy starts looking younger. "I was... mistaken..."

He's got something in his hand. I'm not sure what it is but it's glowing red.

"The whore should have killed me... now I will bind her, but first to burn you, priests, to ashes!" Immunda threatens.

Okay, I'm on board if he can manage it. Maybe then he'll make the same mistake twice and I can escape the circle.

Immunda points his glowing disk at the main priest and shouts out, "Haborym Fire!"

I roll my eyes. That's probably the weakest fire spell in Hell. Listen, as a demon, you eventually meddle in magic and such. It's pretty basic if you're already what they call an 'ethereal being'. As a mortal, you're supposed to call upon fire spirits and such, but when you're a demon, you basically are a fire spirit. Nonetheless, this dude just whipped out Hell's 'firestarter' spell that I might use to light a cigarette.

I had to suppress a laugh because the main priest not only isn't phased by it, it seems to have heated up his cross to the point where he can brand Immunda with it. I didn't want to give myself away, however, so I was quiet while the priest did his thing to Immunda.

When the priest is done with putting out the world's worst summoner's campfire, he looks to me, and the next few minutes are all "Bind her hands" and "Don't look into her eyes" and all the other nonsense that experienced people would expect. I'm expecting to be hurled onto a fire soon and sent back to Hell.

Honestly, I'm looking forward to it. I really am. Instead, they pop me into an interrogation room. I have no idea what they're going for here. But the entire time I'm looking for a way out.

The priest from earlier walks in, brown hair, kind of middle-aged guy, brown eyes. I try my normal little tricks on him, but he doesn't even glance at my tits. I'm a bit surprised but then, holy shit is that Khairunnisa? Did she get summoned too? She's clearly in disguise because she's dressed as a nun, so I try to see if she'll work with me.

"Please... sweetie... you gotta help me," I say, pleading.

The priest interrupts me before she can respond, "I'm Father Edward Thomas..."

That's when it hits me as I look him over, and look at the woman who Khairunnisa is impersonating. I can still feel desire for me from her, but I feel nothing at all from him. Which of course means that he's not attracted to me at all. "Oh, what the fuck. They're making you people priests?" I've never heard of a queer priest, did something change in the 90s?

I was seriously freaked out with how much this guy knew about me, just from my name and my date of birth.

As he's grilling me and I'm answering in ways I'm not comfortable with, I look to Khairunnisa incognito, hoping for some aid here. She keeps swinging that stupid incense thingy and it keeps producing the smoke that makes me talk.

But the weirdest part of this whole interrogation is that I do not remember half of what I said. It was like there was some other part of me talking, a part of me I really barely seem to remember having control over. I'm not sure what I said but I felt like I was crying. I hadn't cried in years, I mean my eyes might water when Asmodai strangled me in public or shoved his sword into my gut, but not like this. Emotions I hadn't felt in a long time.

The whole time, it was like someone else was doing the talking. I'm trying to pay attention to what I'm saying but it's difficult.

I start to get really nervous toward the end. I keep talking about Asmodai and I'm so scared I'm going to spill the beans about our real relationship. However, talking about Asmodai seems to get me back into my normal mood.

"My Master Asmodai..." I can control myself again!

"The Lord of Wrath." Father Thomas laments, "That explains Immunda's issue in summoning! He was attempting to summon Asmodai himself, yet instead, we get the one who leeches off his power, like a lamprey."

That gets me pissed off to no end, "If my Master came, you'd all be very dead men."

"Oh? What is it you believe your master would do to us?" He challenges.

Oh, what Asmodai would do to you, I get hot just thinking about it. I smile to him, "He would swoop down on his mighty dragon, brandish his havoc blade, and swing into you. Wave after wave of you holier than thou kiddie fucking pricks would come at him as he keeps killing you. He'd tear into you all, no matter how many of you there were." I am on fire right now.

"How can you be so certain?" He asks me.

I remember how he took care of Ubiel, Mammon, and everyone else who gave us a hard time during our inquisitioning days. "I've seen him destroy the forces in his own army when they dared to disobey him." Remembering how he took me after the inquisition gets me going again.

He motions for Khairunnisa in disguise to leave, and I'm running out of options.

I guess my body was turning her on.

"His own forces? I'm sure there are not that many... we could have much more, yes?" Father Thomas must be an idiot.

But I get that far away feeling again so I start to talk about Asmodai again. "My Master commands seventy-two legions of demons, ten thousand strong each. He commands them, they obey, or he destroys them by hand. He is powerful, so powerful, My Master..."

That faraway feeling grips me again, but mercifully Father Thomas finally excuses himself before I say something stupid like that I'm in love with Asmodai, "Thank you for your time. If you'll excuse me."

I heave a sigh of relief and just lean back in a terribly uncomfortable seat. I'm very certain that, now that they got what they wanted from me, I'm going to be hurled onto a bonfire and sent back to Hell. Again at this point, I would almost welcome it. The incense is burning my eyes and skin and it just hurts.

A minute or two passes, and the British priest walks in, "Sara Baker. Let's start with a few questions, yes? No reason to make this painful."

Painful? That's an understatement. But this guy is straight. Maybe I can influence him. He's a priest though, so he's not stupid, so I start small. "Can you get rid of that incense?"

"No, it counteracts your musk," I hear Khairunnisa in the nun-outfit say, which is funny because the more she talks, the less she sounds like Khairunnisa. I look her over and I realize that she's not. The incense isn't bothering her like me, and I can't see any demonic aura around her. But she looks exactly like Khairunnisa; she's even bisexual. Well, at least bisexual enough that I can tell she's attracted to me. But she's in a nun outfit. I decided to take another approach. "What the Hell is someone like you doing being a nun anyway, sweetness?" Maybe I can seduce the nun and get her to get me out of here.

The priest chimes in with by far the dumbest question that a human has ever asked in the history of dumb human questions, "Are you treated well... where you are?"

"It's... Hell..." I answer mockingly. I redouble my efforts on the male priest, hoping to counter the incense with sheer will. "Can you let me out of here? Please? I escaped Hell already, and it's like you guys are trying to make it seem like Hell here on Earth. The incense is burning my eyes and I want to go outside, just once, it's been so long. I want to see the sun. It's been decades. Please? Father?" I gave him the cute puppy dog eyes. Asmodai can never resist the puppy dog eyes, so this mortal has no chance in... yeah.

"First we need to have you answer our questions," He starts.

More questions! Burn me or get me out of here, but no more questions! I'd rather be in Hell. But I do have a question for him, maybe he'll answer me. "Could you... at the least tell me what year it is?"

"It is the year of our Lord 2018," The Priest said.

2018! I am trying to do the math in my head. It has felt like decades upon decades and I've only been locked up for less than half a lifetime? That can't be right. "You... you mean like... 2118? or... or 2218?"

The priest shakes his head. "No, my dear."

I feel my heart sink. It's only been a few short decades. I have to get out of here. Now I don't want to go back to Hell. I start to try and appeal to the priest's soft spot. I force some tears welling and soon I'm sobbing. I'm blubbering incoherently and I reach out for the priest's hand. I'm hoping my pathetic display may at least get me a snack-- I could go for another coke, you know?

Just then the would-be Khairunnisa rushes the priest out of the room.

At this point, I've reached my limit. I'm not going to be in this room another second and I let my anger take hold. I start to channel my Master's power inside of me, letting my anger and rage overflow, driving me into my berserk state. I slam the table hard, breaking something.

"No! NO! It can't be! It can't! Belial, that sick fuck Mammon! That bitch Esmeralda! Every one of them! I wasn't there for only thirty years! I couldn't have! They've tortured me for centuries!"

I drag my claws across the table, as I can feel new strength surging through me.

"You bastards! You lying fucks! I was in there longer! You can't tell me every year there was only a few months! You can't!"

I slam my fists down again and now the table breaks. I'm feeling more rage and strength flow through me as I pull my hands apart, snapping the chains. Feeling my rage boiling up,

I shoulder-check through the door. I grab the would-be Khairunnisa and rush past Father Thomas, making my way down the hallway. I see an older man in robes and grab him as well as I rush down the hallway. I do my best to control myself and I glare at the old man, "How do I get out!" I shout.

The old man shakily points to a set of stairs, which I dash up. I reach a locked door and I look at him. He shakingly pushes his Crucifix into the door with just a look.

I grin and drop him hard on the ground. I think I hear a few of his bones break. The nun in my arms whimpers.

I look at her, my rage subsiding. At this point I know I have to get out of Dodge. So I smile at her, pouring on the charm, "Sorry about all that ugliness, sweetness. What's your name?"

She stutters, "Sister Fatima Ghazzawi."

I snicker, "Ghazzawi? I think I know a relative of yours or an ancestor... Khairunnisa."

She frowns. "I-I know no Khairunnisa."

I grin. "I'm sure you don't. Now you're going to be very quiet, or I'm going to break you in half, okay, sweetness?" I wrap my wings around myself and transform into a nun as well. Before holy ground was a problem for me, but with all the training I had in Hell and the power I had from Asmodai, that wasn't a problem anymore. Holding her hand, Fatima's appearance changes as well. I start pulling her out and look around for an exit.

There are tons of priests and nuns everywhere. "How do we leave, sweetness?" I whisper to Fatima.

"T-This way..." She points

"Good girl," I compliment her and we make our way towards the exit.

From here it would have been smooth sailing if not for a little brat getting in my way. Someone grabs my arm and dumps water over my head. Only it's some kind of holy water and man, does it sting! I scream as I feel my disguise break.

"Will you people leave me alone!" I shout, and even to my surprise, my voice echoes through the room.

So standing in front of me now is some cocksure kid, who can't be older than thirty or so. He's got a Bowie knife and a trenchcoat, ice blue eyes, and black hair. I'm certain I've seen him before but I can't put my finger on it at the time. "No." is all he says. So dramatic!

"Then let me spell it out for you! I'm not going back, not now, never! I'm free, if you can't leave me the fuck alone, then you will get a free sample of what I'm leaving!"

I breathe deep and grin as I think of a middle-of-the-road fire spell, one that Immunda probably couldn't dream to cast. It's called dark flame. I breathe out and cover him in the stuff.

Black flames engulf the twerp and I just giggle to myself, happy that I'm not getting sent back quite yet. I have plans, after all, and not all of them are what Lucifer wanted me to do.

Except my joy is ended pretty quickly as the guy gets up, throwing his burning trench coat aside to reveal why he's unscathed by my unholy dark flames: He's a friggin' angel! Huge white wings spread from his back, so large I wonder how he even kept them concealed under the coat.

"Submit, Demon!" He shouts.

"Oh, are you fucking serious right now?" He looks young too, and his white silvery wings look so nice, kind of like Lucifer's but not as grand. "What the Hell... you guys were all dead! No one down there will stop bragging about it! What hole did you crawl out of?"

"I liked that coat, demon. I will make a new one out of your wings," He taunts.

He is just so over the top, I kind of like him, you know? I desperately want to seduce him, he's cute, but more importantly, I don't want to go back yet and he just reminded me: I have wings! I jump into the air carrying the nun with my tail and head towards the ceiling.

"Release the woman!" The angel shouts at me, as he takes to the air after me.

I get to the ceiling and land, both hooves clicking on it as I hold myself to it using another neat trick I picked up in Hell. I grin at him as I stomp on the concrete ceiling.

"Sorry, choir boy! She's my snack for the trip!" I give another good stomp, "You're lucky, Caroler! If they had summoned me wearing my armor, I'd rip your damn arms off! Instead--" I give one last hard push as I feel the ceiling give way, "I'll just use your own compassion."

I watch as the angel rushes down to protect the people below, and then I crawl out of the new hole I made in the ceiling.

I look at Fatima and smile. "Hold on, sweetness, we're going for a ride." I slide down a domed roof of sorts with the sister clutching me tightly. Once we land, I disguise ourselves again and look at Fatima. "So get me to the airport now. We're going to take a little trip to Boston."

Fatima shakes her head, "No, I will not help you!"

I sigh, and kiss her deeply, not a draining kiss of course, and wait for her to kiss back.

Fatima moves toward me as I break the kiss, wanting more.

My fingers go to her lips, they remind me so much of Khairunnisa. "Not yet, sweetness. Right now, you're going to get me on a plane, okay?"

She leads me out from a few buildings and down several streets. All of the buildings are of a large marble and feature huge columns.

"Sweetness, where are we?" I ask.

"Vatican City, love,"She says dreamily. "Isn't it beautiful?"

I nod, "Very pretty." I see her tapping on a small flat piece of glass for some reason. "What the hell is that?"

"My phone?" She asks, showing an image of a small car on it.

"That's a phone?"

She nods.

"Where... do you plug it in?"

"In the outlet, to charge, at night," She says, still in a trance.

We're now standing near the street, and I glance around, wondering what we're waiting for. "Why did we stop sweetness?"

Fatima turns to me, "I called an Uber."

"An Ubiel?" I say, raising an eyebrow.

Fatima shakes her head, "No, an Uber."

Suddenly a car comes up to us and Fatima checks her phone and walks towards it.

I follow her.

As we get into the car, she looks to the driver, "Aeroporto di Fiumicino?"

"Sì sì! Nessun problema, Sorella," The driver says.

I don't speak Italian. I turn to Fatima as we sit in the back.

"So I have a friend in Hell, also a succubus, probably an ancestor of yours... Has to be because you're a dead ringer for her. Anyway, what are your parents' names? I'm curious."

She's quiet for a moment, "I have no parents, love."

"You... Don't have parents?" I ask, confused.

"I disowned them. They wished me to marry a man and be one of his wives. So I ran away with the help of my Uncle," The nun explained.

I laugh, "Well, damn, girl! Way to go!"

"Thank you, love... can I..."

"Oh, sure, I'm feeling hungry... But I still need you so just a sip, okay?" I kiss her again, sipping at her essence, but not too much. It's funny, she tastes more like seltzer than a coke.

By the time we get to the airport and Fatima buys our tickets, we're off waiting on a flight for a few hours. This is about when I realize that we are both hungry.

We stop to eat, and even as I watch her eating a Gyro of some kind, I'm still hungry, but not for the food she's eating. I think to myself about how, for the most part, I haven't eaten food in decades. Even now, with it right in front of me, I have no real desire for it. The smell doesn't make my mouth water; the image of it doesn't really entice me at all.

However, what does look absolutely delicious is the young man sitting across from us who keeps giving me looks.

He's got long blonde hair, looks to be about twenty years old, and is undressing me with his eyes.

I smile and wink at him.

He winks back and blows me a kiss.

I look at Fatima, "Honey, you wait here, I'm going to go grab a bite."

Fatima just nods.

I saunter over to him, as I do I change my appearance a bit, enough where I wouldn't be recognized when someone starts looking for this guy. I walk up to him, smiling, "Hi there, handsome... Please tell me you speak English?"

He laughs, "A little English... A little..." He looks me over, "Bellissima, Molto Bellissima."

I brush some of my red hair over my ear and lean down to kiss him. I smiled standing up and motioning to him with my finger. He smiles dumbly and I lead him to a broom closet I manage to spot.

I pull him into the closet, lock the door, and I undo his pants and turn around, dropping my disguise, and pull my thong to the side. I rub my rear against him and he eventually takes the hint.

He thrusts into me... And I miss Asmodai already. I sigh and let him do his thing, drinking more and more of him as each thrust grows weaker. I swear I want to yawn!

Eventually, I hear him gasp, "Mio cuore..." His voice sounded much more tired and old.

I turn to look over my shoulder and grin as I see the life leave his eyes. "Thanks for the meal, Cutie."

His mummified corpse slumps over and he falls out of me. I don my disguise and waltz out of the closet. After I get near Fatima, I assume my normal human disguise, which is just me before I got transmuted.

Fatima seems to be coming out of her enchantment a bit. "How was your meal?"

I frown, "Well he was tasty but his dick was a bit small for my taste. Still, I'm satisfied."

Fatima looks disturbed.

I'm about to reaffirm my control over her when she interrupts me.

"That's our gate. We need to go..."

We both get up and board the plane. I made her splurge on first class. It's not my money, after all. Needless to say, I got the window seat. Halfway through the flight, I'm very much enjoying the view. "You know Fatima... I've never flown on a plane before. I assume you have?"

Fatima is quiet.

"I haven't done a lot of stuff, you know?" I look at her.

Fatima looks scared of me.

frown, imagining what Esmeralda looked like to me when she was a demoness. "I'm not going to hurt you."

Fatima whispers, "You are a demon. How can I trust your words?"

I lean back in the comfy leather seat, "I don't know... Have faith?"

"I have faith in God. Not a demon," She responds.

I chuckle, "Hearing that from your face is so strange..."

"No one in my family is a demon."

I roll my eyes. "Well, someone up along the ancestry is, honey. You look just like her. She's Queen of the Succubi now."

Fatima pulls her arms across her chest. "I did not appreciate you kissing me."

I chuckle. "I heard no complaints when I was doing it."

Fatima glares at me, "You seduced me... You raped me."

I sigh. "I kissed you - I can only make you do what you wanted to do deep down before the kiss. Deep down, you wanted it."

"The deepest part of my lust? Yes... you're beautiful. But you're a beautiful poison."

My heart sinks at that, and I look at the view out the window. After some time, I whisper, "Sorry."

Fatima speaks up, though I'm not looking at her, "What?"

"I'm sorry for kissing you. You were my only way out, okay?" I admit. "You forget about things like rape when the whole world around you is nothing but violence and horrors."

Fatima is silent for a short time and then breaks in with, "I forgive you."

I look at her, and she's smiling oddly. "What's with you?"

"I didn't know a demon could ask for forgiveness. Maybe there is hope for you."

I scoff. "My soul isn't mine. It's not getting saved, Sister, don't get my hopes up."

"Hope is all someone like you must have to survive," Fatima continues.

I sigh. "I gave up on hope. I just make do with what I have." I'm silent for the rest of the trip.

When we finally land and deplane, I head out holding Fatima's hand. I look at her oddly as she pulls her habit up over her nose and mouth for some reason, pulling the top of it to cover her forehead. "What are you, cold?"

"Allahu Akbar! Allahu Akbar!" She shouts.

# CHAPTER 13

## *The Life Left Behind*

> "When a Demon takes a soul, the deal struck often has lasting repercussions. Demonic magic is not magic that comes easily, it often comes with a great cost."

Suddenly everyone around me is panicking and I see cops rushing toward her. I let go and make a mad dash into a crowd of people as she's tackled by security officers and people start shouting into radios. Luckily, it's absolute chaos in the airport and I manage to get out of the place.

Outside there are a few people pushing past cops who are working to ensure everyone is leaving in an orderly fashion. I rushed to one cop, clutching at his uniform, locking eyes with him. "You need to help me out. I'm very important, my mother is sick. Help me get into town."

I watch as the cop's eyes go glossy and far away and he takes me by the hand, "Follow me, Miss... I can give you a ride to town."

Soon I'm whisked away into a squad car, passenger seat of course, and my eyes are wide at all the changes I see as we drive along.

Electronic billboards? Signs? Even the traffic lights look different! I see fashion has changed like crazy since I was human.

Once I see we are near Copley Square, I tell the cop to let me out, and I head towards the Library. I figure I can look up where David is in the White Pages. Right now, all I want to do is find David, find my son Jason, and figure out what happened to everyone after I died.

I am doubtful my mother is alive, I'm rather certain she's passed. It would be nice if she was still alive, I'd love to give her a proper goodbye, explain what happened, and so on. But I try not to get my hopes up.

As I walk into the Library I head over to the information desk, "Excuse me...?"

A young teenage girl looks up at me. She's got acne, thick glasses, and greasy brown hair. It's almost like I'm looking into the past at me before I sold my soul.

She stares at me in complete disbelief for a moment.

"Hi," I say, smiling.

"H-Hi. Are you famous?" She stammers. She has braces. Poor dear.

I grin at her, "Oh, thanks for the compliment sweetie... No, I'm not famous." This doesn't stop me from flicking my hair over my shoulder, "I'm trying to find..." I try to think of the best way to not sound like a stalker, "...My son, actually. I lost his address and I only have his name." I chuckle, "I know it sounds crazy."

The awkward girl stammers, "Uh, well... You could check online."

"On...line? On what line? Like a hotline?" I ask.

She frowns, "What's a hotline?"

Clearly, I've got a bit of a communication gap. I lean over, motioning at her with my finger, "Sweetie, come here for a moment."

She leans over to me, "Yes?"

I licked her ear and whispered a small incantation I picked up in Hell. It should help me pull information from her mind.

I hear her gasp and groan.

I feel a burst of information rush into my head, smartphones, computers, the Internet, whatever memes are. I pull away before I get too much information. As I do, I notice the girl's face is flushed and she's panting softly.  I smile at her, "You okay honey?"

"I...I..." She hugs her shoulders, "Oh... I feel all tingly..."

I smiled at her, "You should take better care of your hair, stop eating greasy food, get into shape, and start looking for a hunk darling..."

"B-but I'm not pretty—"

I grab her hand, sliding my thumb over her palm, "Oh honey, I used to look like you when I was younger... You need to dedicate yourself to your body, taking care of it, and you'd be amazed what you can get from it." I wink, "At your age, give it just a few months, you'll be drop-dead gorgeous to any guy."

I let go of her and head over to the computers.  I wonder if the girl's going to take my advice, I never cast anything on her, so I'm hoping she can make better decisions than I did.

I sat down at the computer and after a moment or two, I managed to find Jason's information!  I even got his address.

Not having any cash, I figured I wouldn't get too far.  I headed out into a nearby coffee shop and found some guy wandering around with a laptop. I smiled and slid my hand up his arm, locking eyes with him, "Hey cutie... Can you help a girl out?"

I watch his eyes fog up for a moment and he nods dumbly.

I sit down at a table, guiding him with my hand on his.

He sits down across from me.

"Do you have any cash on you sweetheart?"

He shakes his head.

I frowned, "Well... What are you going to buy coffee with if you don't have any cash?"

"Debit Card." He says.

Oh! Right, I didn't really connect that info but apparently, no one carries cash nowadays. How funny. Well, I don't care what form it's in, this fellow was going to be my meal ticket for a little bit. I leaned over the table and gave him a deep kiss, which got us a whistle or two from a few tables over. I winked at the older man, making a mental note to come back here and grab him if I burned through The Coffee shop guy too quickly.

The Coffee Shop Guy looked at me as if I was a Goddess and just smiled warmly, "I'll do whatever you want..."

I smile, "I know..." I moved closer to him, "I need you to cancel any plans you had for today babe... And clear a space for me at your house. Do you have a girlfriend? Wife? Kids?"

He shook his head, "No."

"Oh good," I knew how to pick them! "I'm going to need you to buy me a phone. Seems I'm going to need one," I thought about the phone Father Thomas had and I curse under my breath how dumb I was. He looked up all that information about me on his phone! So I would need one of those too. Besides, I would need to be able to keep my new "toys" on call.

The Coffee Shop Guy just nods and closes his laptop. He stands up and points across the street, "I can get you a phone there."

I smile, "How generous..."

A few minutes later I got a shiny new smartphone.  The Coffee Shop Guy is carrying my bags and I'm pretty sure he's close to fully tapped out financially.

"Hey, babe, how much money do you have left?" I asked.

He thinks for a moment, "A couple of hundred bucks I think."

I grin, I'm feeling a little hungry at this point.  "Let's head back to your place..."

Excited, he took my hand and started heading down the road, towards his house.  Oh the poor bastard, if he only knew what was about to happen to him.

We had just gotten to his house and I gave a quick look around to see if he had a roommate.  I see him plop his laptop down on the floor.  "Hey cutie, wanna give me that Laptop when we're finished?  It would really help me out."

He nods dumbly, "Yes. Anything. Anything for you..." He looks to me curiously, "I'm sorry, I didn't catch your name."

I saunter up to him, pressing myself against him with my arms draping over his shoulders and around his neck, "Sara."

He groaned, his hands finding my hips, "Sara..."

I smile, thinking how Asmodai would rip this mortal's arms off and shove them through his sternum if he could see us now.  I slide down his body and undo his pants.  I frown as I see his meager hard-on. Maybe I didn't know how to pick them after all.  I sigh, Oh well.  As they say: "Any port in a storm."

I hear him moaning as I start to suck on his pencil dick.  I feel it swell slightly in my mouth but nothing that would make life any better for me.

I soldier on, wondering if I can drain a guy from oral sex alone.  I give it my all, using all my skills.

I feel his hands on my head, his breath catching in his throat, "Oh, Oh God... t-too much!  I'm gonna... l-let go I'm gonna cum!  Oh, God!  So hot!"

I suck harder, sliding my hands over his hips and squeezing his ass, taking his whole length into my mouth easily, teasing him mercilessly with my tongue.

"Stop! Oh shit!  Oh shit!  It-It's hot!  Your mouth is so....so hot! Oh Fuck!" He shouts and I feel him release in my mouth.

I double down on my sucking, pulling his hips tight against my face and growling as I drink.  I feel my wings slide out as my disguise disperses as I begin to feed.

"Holy shit! W-What the... What the Hell are you?!  Stop! It h-hurts!  Hurts so... fucking good... oh... shit..." I feel him getting weaker, his thrusting continuing but getting weaker with each push.

I feel myself filling up as I suck harder and harder on him. This is the first time I've drank someone down like this, and it feels so satisfying.  A salty and savory taste on my tongue, and a fullness in my stomach as I pull his essence into myself.

"Ha...Oh... shit..." He moans, "I can't... stop cumming... s-s-stop sucking... oh... I don't feel so... good... please..." His voice starts to grow raspy, "Please...stop..." He gasps for breath, "W-what's happening... to me...?"

I glance up at him as I see his thinning frame. I flap my wings, giving him a powerful suck as I make eye contact.

He wheezes and fails to scream as I watch his skin dry up, his eyes rolling back into his head and shriveling up before he gives a final thrust into me.

I let go of his shriveled cock with a pop of my lips, grinning as I notice it's somehow even smaller than when I started. I let go of him and he falls to the ground with a light thwack, like a bail of hay.

"That was pretty satisfying... It's always fun to try new things, you know?" I smile and change back into my human shape, changing my hair and clothing to match the current period a bit better. I pulled out my new phone and punched in my son Jason's address. The little GPS app gave me walking directions.

I popped the headphones that came with the phone into my ears, grabbed Coffee Shop Guy's laptop in its laptop case, and headed out, making sure to lock the door behind me with his keys. I force his keys back inside through the mail slot and head out.

After a long and wonderful walk, I finally found the house. I'm surprised, given David's inheritance, I expected a bigger place. Instead, it's a normal row home, brick, nice porch, lovely hedges out front. I see some tasteful drapes and an American flag hanging by the front door. I'm not sure why that's there, but I notice most folks have an American Flag now.

Funny, I thought only a patriotic nut job would have the flag on his house, but whatever, times change I guess.

I ring the doorbell, and wait, hoping to see David, but I'd be happy enough to see Jason.

I see someone looking through the window of the door and then it opens.

I spotted Jason, a grown man, but still my son! He has to be! He has my green eyes and his father's brown hair. He's about as tall as his father and he has some of his rugged good looks, but my father's chin.

"May I help you?" He asks.

I beam at him as he looks me over, likely shocked to see me. "Hi," I say as I move some hair from my face, hoping it sparks some recognition.

"And you are?" Jason asks me.

I can't help but laugh, maybe I was wrong, maybe he isn't Jason? "Are you Jason Miller?"

"Detective Jason Miller," He says sternly.

My heart jumps, oh he's a police officer! I'm so proud of my Jason! "Detective? Oh!" I can hardly contain myself, "That's wonderful Jason... Can I come in? It's been a very long time after all." I start to walk in.

He shakes his head to my disappointment, stopping me at the stoop. "No... You can't come in. Mostly because I don't know who the Hell you are and that is sort of an important prerequisite to coming into my house."

I frown, "So... You wouldn't let me in, no matter what?" I try looking at him with my eyes, pouring my power into them.

I hate to have to use my abilities on my own son but I really have no choice. Besides, I'd free him the second he lets me in.

To my surprise he shakes his head again, "There are three reasons I can't, sweetheart." He sticks his hand in my face and starts counting his fingers at me, "One? You're too fucking pretty. So no matter what you're selling, I'll never hear the end of it from the Misses."

I feel my cheeks flush at my own son telling me I'm pretty. Also: He's married? Now I need to meet his wife too! So much catching up to do!

He counts his second finger at me, "Two, I have no fucking clue who you are."

My face falls as does my stomach. He doesn't recognize me? How? How doesn't my own son remember me? I know he was young when I died but surely David has pictures around the house, doesn't he?

A third finger goes up in my face, "Three? See reason two. Now have a nice life." He slams the door in my face.

I'm stunned into silence. How could my own son treat me this way? Why was my own son this rude? Did David raise him like this? I am still trying to reconcile how he doesn't recognize me. After a few moments, I head down from the doorstep.

I look around and figure that if he isn't going to let me in, I'll just let myself in. I look around and head around the block, counting the houses and making sure I can circle back into his backdoor. I sneak behind the back alley, hopping over the small fence that protects the little garden behind the house. I double-check that I've counted the right number of houses and then make sure no one can see me.

I sneak my tail out from under my waistband and kneel near the frame of the door, sneaking my tail up and around the doorknob. I grin as I feel the deadbolt and unlock it. Next, I finesse the other doorknob and smile, sliding my tail out from under the door  slowly quietly opening it.

I step inside quietly and smile, sneaking around. I don't see Jason right away.  I decided to see if the family habits are the same as I shut the door silently behind me.

I head up to the front of the house and see if there's a coat closet.  Bingo!  I slide it open and look above the coats to see if I can find a photo album.  David usually kept them in the coat closet, so if he raised Jason right then that should mean... ah! I am correct, as usual!  Here's the family photo album!  Oh, wow it's heavy!  There are bound to be some photos of me!  I sneak it down from the closet and I head into the dining room and kitchen combination.  I drop the photo album down on the kitchen table hard and pull a chair out.

I start to notice how tiny the house is.  David should have been able to afford something much bigger.  Why is Jason stuck in this little house?  No matter, I open up the photo album and spot Jason, a woman, and a little baby as the first photo.

I've not felt warmth running through my heart in a long time.  I felt my heart swell and I just smiled as I realized I had a bouncing baby grandson!  I was a grandma!  A Hot grandma, of course.  Is that a GILF?

I start flipping through the album, checking for some photos of me.  I do see some photos of David, and frown, wondering where the photos of me would be. That's when I hear a click from the stairs.

"Don't fucking move," I hear Jason say.

I turn to him. Shit, he did say he was a cop, of course, he'd have a gun in the house. He looks pissed off, reminds me of his father. "You don't have a single photograph of me, Jason." I'm not worried about the gun. There are at least ten spells I can think of that will handle the bullets. It's one of those things I learned from Forcas. Last thing a great demon needs is to waltz up here only to be taken out by a mortal weapon. I mean, honestly, I could probably take a few hits and heal them within an hour, it's not like I have to worry about vital organs or anything.

In a rather aggressive tone Jason states, "I can't imagine why I would, you see that's a family album. If you're looking for photos of yourself, most people just check their fucking *Instagram*. So, get up, and get out, and maybe I won't call the cops on you."

I huff, ignoring him and trying to flip through the photo album some more. "Somewhere in here, you must have a photo of your father and me from college or our wedding day? I rocked that wedding dress." I did too, so there must be a damn photo of me in the thing. Once I find it Jason can stop doubting who I am. I can't blame him for freaking out so far.

Jason pulls the hammer back on his pistol, "Lady, put the fucking photo album down, and get the fuck out of my house."

I just turn to him, glance at the gun, and roll my eyes at it. I go back to flipping through the album, "That won't work on me." I scoff.

"Okay lady," Jason reasons, "Why don't I just call the police, and maybe we can get this straightened out." He warns.

I just shake my head, "That's no way to speak to your mother, Jason." I'm done playing coy with him. He's my son, so he needs to know where he stands in this. "Jason, I know it's been a long time, but it's me, your mother." I look at him, smiling warmly.

"Get out now, or I'm going to shoot you. Do you understand? I'm a cop—I've seen cops shoot people for less and get away with it. I've given you plenty of warnings." He is now absolutely pissed.

I just shoot him a bemused look and lean back in the chair, "Jason, honey, you can pull the trigger if you really want to, but I don't think it's a good idea."

I hear the safety of the gun click off. I guess he's really going to do this. "Oh, it's not a good idea? What's not a good idea is breaking into a cop's house, claiming to be his dead mother, who died thirty years ago, I might add, and expecting to not get shot."

Jason can't be that bad at math, "Twenty-eight" I chide.

"What?" He says, getting more agitated.

"I died twenty-eight years ago," I corrected him.

He just frowns at me, then moves his finger to the trigger, "I'm going to do it if you don't get the Hell out of here."

I stand up and prepare the spell in my head. I'm thinking something to slow time around me, not anything to reflect the bullets. Something simple and quick. "I'm telling you the truth, Jason," I explain, concentrating on the spell, making sure not to miss any part of it. Getting shot is painful, and I've been enjoying a few hours without any searing pain so far.

"Get down on the ground!" He shouts, like I've seen in every cop movie.

"I just want you to hear me out. It's me, Jason, it's mom," I try to explain.

He isn't calming down, "My mother's in heaven, Bitch, but if you want to meet her, keep talkin' about her!"

I frowned again. "Oh, Jason, it's sweet you think that, but..." I started wondering if I should break that illusion or not.

Apparently, that was the final button and Jason lets a bullet fly.

I should have been expecting it but I feel it strike my right breast. I look down to find the bullet there, it's like a bee sting but hasn't even bruised me. I pick the bullet up, looking it over, "Wow. Last time, they at least broke the skin." I took the bullet and flicked it at him.

Jason catches it before it hits him, and he looks shocked. He pulls his magazine out of his gun, checking the bullets, and looks at me in disbelief.

I smile, "Will you start to believe me now?"

"I'm gonna start to believe they're making fake tits a whole lot sturdier!"

I shot him a glare, "These are real!" I crossed my arms over my chest. I mean, they were not silicon tits, they were real, magic maybe, but real. "Is that any way to talk to your mother?"

"No, because you aren't her!" He slides the magazine back into the gun.

"Haven't we been over this?" I ask.

Almost without warning, Jason just starts shooting.

I'm not pleased, but I was prepping the spell for a reason. I'm surrounded by shadows and the room darkens. I see the bullets in the air and I pluck them out, making sure to break their momentum as I do and collect them in my hand. I let the spell end, feeling the hot bullets in my hand. It's funny how their heat doesn't bother me in the least.

Jason is still pulling the trigger, the gun clearly spent. Jason's fear is clear on his face

"I know you're scared, but I can prove it if you just get a photo of me. Er, a photo of your mom," I said, attempting to assuage Jason's fear.

"I just... that was a full mag. What–"

To interrupt him I just opened up my hand and let the bullets fall to the ground. "Mortal weapons won't work, Jason. Now, if you'll go get a photograph of your mother, I can talk to you. I smile at him, "I just want to catch up."

"Okay... uh... I'll be right back." He says as he heads up the stairs.

I sit back down at the kitchen table and keep flipping through the photo album. I start seeing photos of them at an amusement park, I think it's Dorney Park. It's been a long time, but I'm very certain that's it. I hear Jason coming back down, hopefully with some different photos, with me in them.

"How old?" I ask, looking at the photo.

"Last year," Jason says as he sits down next to me.

I roll my eyes, smiling, thinking that he must finally have found that photo and now knows me, "I was talking about Junior here, how old is he?" It's funny, I noticed my grandson was named Jason Jr, which was so sweet.

"Listen, that's my kid, don't you dare try anything."

"I know, you've got that protectiveness from me.  I was like that with you, you know?" I say, remembering when Belial tried to give me an extra bit of time for his soul.

Jason suddenly seems very pissed again, "Oh?  So 'Mom' I have a question for you, if you were so protective, why did you kill yourself?"

I frown, how do I tell him? "I didn't, I... well okay, I did drink that stuff but I was forced to, okay?" I sigh heavily, remembering my last mortal moment.  "I know how to handle my liquor, and I knew my limit."

"So, if you didn't kill yourself, what did happen?" He asks with legitimate curiosity.

I turn from him for a moment.  How do you tell your own son you sold your soul to a demon for vanity's sake?  I decided to change the subject, "I'm... listen we could talk about me all day, I want to know about you." I turn to him, feeling my eyes wet with tears, "I've missed you."

"Oh, you miss me?  Do you?" He laughs at me.  "Listen, lady, I am not your kid.  You have to be attached to something to miss it, and you only had me for two years before you croaked."

"Two years and four months," I correct.  I'm still unsure if he thinks I'm his mother or not, and I'm noticing he doesn't have a photo with him.

"So... You're saying that you're somehow my mother?  A waitress at Denny's named Daisy who picked up my dad one night?"

I'm pissed off now.  I narrow my eyes at Jason, "I will smack Dave upside the head if he ever said I was just some fucking waitress!  I was going to Harvard with him, dammit! Did he say that to you?  That I was some waitress?  Who the fuck is Daisy?  My name is Sara, you damn well know that! Oh... You better know that or I will sock Dave right in the balls!" I realize I'm ranting.  "Listen, if you're trying to probe me, I get it. But I was in Harvard, with your father, I majored in Molecular Biology, my best friends were Jenny and Beth from South Side, and your Grandfather's name is Hank Baker."

Jason seems rather shocked by all the info I just tossed at him.

"Mind telling me why you became a cop?" I hope maybe I can redirect the conversation.  This isn't how I imagined my reunion with my family would be going.

"I, uh, well I wanted to help people," Jason says, rather shocked.

"That's so nice, so how did you decide on being a detective?" I got a bit worried, "You don't put yourself in danger much, do you?  You have a family, you know?"

Just then there's a knock at the door. I looked at the door wondering who else he was expecting, when I felt Jason cuff me to the table.

"Really Jason?" I ask exasperated.  I could snap the handcuffs easily enough.  But I think I've scared the shit out of my own son enough for one day.

"Yes, Really.  Those are probably the cops I called who can take you away to a nice padded room somewhere, you loony." He says as he heads to the door.

My heart just breaks, after everything, he still didn't believe me?  I sit there waiting for him to come back with police officers who I'm debating I can seduce and devour.  I need to find out where Dave is, that way I can get him to help me convince Jason.

I hear Jason and two other men walking toward the kitchen.  I assume this is the police officer but as I look up my face falls.

It's that fucking priest and his Angel Buddy.

# CHAPTER 14

## *Repurposed*

"A soul owned cannot resist the instructions
of its master, or the master of that master.
For that soul's will is no longer its own."

I looked at Father Thomas and the Angel he was with, "Not here... please? You know why I'm here. No one is getting hurt." I pleaded.

The angel sits right next to me, "And you know why I'm here."

I hate this guy with a passion. I thought I left him crushed under a pile of rocks in Rome. How has he recovered so quickly? I feel so frightened that they're going to send me back to Hell, I can't stop myself from tearing up, "Just leave me be, okay? I have no desire to open the gate, I just want to be with my family!"

Jason starts, "So, eh, 'Sara', these nice folks from the Church said they know you. Maybe you can head back with them?"

I looked at Jason sweetly, "Jason, honey, you haven't finished telling me about how you became a detective?" Maybe I can still sway Jason to my side.

Jason looks to Father Thomas, "See what I mean, Father? She's claiming to be my mother. Who died right after I was born, I might add."

We've been talking so much about me, I had to ask Jason about Dave. "What about your father? I'd like to see him. I'm sure he could also prove who I am to you."

"Yeah, sure, why not go visit him, he's out in Forest Hills."

My heart sinks. Forest Hills is the local cemetery, meaning that Dave is somehow dead. But he's too young to be dead! My mother, sure, I'd expect her to have passed. She'd be in her upper eighties by now.

The angel asks, "Where is Forest Hills?"

Father Thomas answers him, "It's a cemetery."

The door opens again, this time I hear a woman's voice in the foyer, "Junior, please, for the love of God…"

Jason makes his way to the woman who I assume is Marie, Jason's wife.

I see Junior walk over to Jason and stare at him blankly, "Hello, Father."

A chill runs down my spine. I can tell, instantly: That's not my grandson. I fix my gaze on him and I can see something is possessing him. Someone I might know... There's a shadow over him that I almost recognize.

Jason gets down on his haunches, "Junior, stop this bullshit, okay?"

"Lazy Whore," Junior says.

I know who it is now. I can see the shadow over my grandson, his grip on Junior's throat, Ubiel. What is Ubiel doing here?

Jason then gives Junior a stern look, "Watch your mouth there, Junior, don't make me pop you one in front of the Father, okay?"

Junior or I should say, Ubiel in Junior's body, grabs Jason's arm and hurls him into the air, landing him on the kitchen table. Jason knocks his head on the kitchen table and he's out cold.

Father Thomas check's Jason's pulse.

"Jason!" Marie cries out in shock.

I get to my feet, snapping the cuffs off of myself quickly, "Leave them alone!"

"He's going to fuck you in so many new holes, whore," Ubiel threatens through my grandson.

I freeze, Ubiel's working directly for Asmodai, isn't he? "Just leave them alone, okay?  I wanted to be free for a short time," I say, hoping Asmodai can forgive me.

Father Thomas hurls some holy water on Junior.

Junior stumbles back and screams a mix of a child's scream and inhuman cries of anguish.

Okay, go Father Thomas!  Get that sick fuck out of my grandson!

Suddenly there's a sickening snapping noise, Junior's thumb is snapped, and Ubiel opens Junior's eyes, growling, "The next spritz, I break another finger."

Marie is shocked, "Junior, what did you do?"

Oh, Momma Marie, that's not Junior. Before I can say anything else, however, Junior's eyes turn to me.

"Jerusalem, in the Temple Mount, the gate is there, the seal needs to be broken..." His hand moves to another finger, "...Or I break the child."

"No..." is all I can say, my eyes wide as I see Junior's hand move to another finger.

"Time is wasting whore," Ubiel says through Junior's mouth.  Then Ubiel releases him.  Junior looks horrified and starts screaming bloody murder.

The poor baby!  My heart breaks, but now I can't stay, I need to get to Jerusalem and find the Temple Mount.  I can't unset myself to my mission now, there's no more time to waste.  I feel the new desire in me, the new purpose overrides everything I ever wanted to do.  I have to get to the gate, I must open it.  That was the command.  With everything in me, however, I try to at least console Junior, moving toward him.

Marie snatches him up suddenly, "Whoever the fuck you are, get the Hell away from my family, you got it?"

I glare at her, I get that she's in momma bear mode but that's my grandson, "It's my family too!"

Suddenly Junior stops breathing.

Marie looks scared as hell, "Junior!" She screams.

Father Thomas rushes over to Junior and pulls him out of Marie's arms, "He's going into shock," He shouts as he lays Junior down on the ground, he turns to me, "Elevate his legs."

Marie pulls out her phone and is dialing 911.

The mission is burning in my mind, I try to help, lifting Junior's legs, but more and more I can feel my concern for him being overpowered by the task I must complete.  I must open the gate, I must go to Jerusalem.  It's pounding louder and louder in the back of my mind.  "Is this my fault?" I ask, trying to distract myself.

"Yes, it is." Father Thomas says bluntly.  He starts to give Junior mouth to mouth.

Junior gasps, but then Ubiel's voice comes from his mouth, "Remind you of Father Damascus?"

Father Thomas looks like he's seen a ghost, "Leave this boy, demon."

Ubiel starts again, "My master Asmodai has a simple message.  If the slut doesn't leave, the boy dies.  I can kill it if I like, then I'll move on to the father, then the mother."

I shiver, Master Asmodai's name being mentioned makes my body ache for him. I feel myself growing flush, I can feel my desire to serve him, to please him, rising hard and fast. Master will kill them if I don't go. I must go.

Junior stops breathing again, and Father Thomas starts doing rescue breaths.

At this point, two cops rush into the house through the opened front door.

Junior breaths again, but Ubiel's voice comes out one last time, "Father is that what kissing a girl is like?"

My instincts to leave are strong, I need to bog the Angel and Father Thomas down, and Ubiel just gave me a perfect window to do so, "You pervert! That's my nephew!"

On cue, the cops tackle Father Thomas and The Angel.

I rush out the front door. I ran out quickly, dashing down the street and running toward the airport. I know I am unlikely to be able to get a ticket myself, but right now I'm escaping, as Master wanted, so that I can make my way to Jerusalem.

I pull out my phone and open up the map application after I find myself a decent enough distance from Jason's house. I punch in "Temple Mount, Jerusalem" It doesn't help at first until I realize there's a flight option. I click that and it shows me where I can go, across the ocean.

While I certainly cannot fly right now, I do know one thing I can do, so I head to the Port of Boston. I searched along the port for a large fishing boat. I only need the thing to get me halfway across the ocean. I'm sure I can fly the rest of the way. That's when I spotted it, a huge fishing boat, covered in nets, rigging, and with three guys loading it up for departure.

I walked over to one burly fellow who just slammed a large barrel down onto the deck.

He turned to me, smiling, "Hey little lady... what are you doing here?"

I flung my hair over my shoulder, bringing my finger up to my lip, "Oh... well I saw you carrying that heavy barrel and it just turned me on so much..." I gushed.

He smiles, walking up to me, he smelled heavily of body odor and fish, but I had smelled much worse. "Well, we don't ship out for another hour... I could give you a heck of a fun time before I head out into the waters," He boasted.

I giggled, "Oh you don't need to wait..." I say, sliding my hand over his shoulder, locking my eyes on his, "Why don't you take me with you... I'll fuck you and your buddies..." I kiss him softly, entrancing him.

He just nods, "Yes.... You should come with us..."

I smiled, "I'll be your ship wench." I hated that word but I figured that's the term for a salty sea vixen.

The fisherman nods.

"Why don't you show me where I can lay down? And then when you leave, you can head to Europe, Spain specifically."

He nods, "We need more fuel... Won't have enough."

I smile at him again, moving in close, just about to kiss him but just falling short, "I know... You just need to get me close enough, lover... I promise to make every minute up to that point heaven for you."

He groans and shows me down into the crew cabin.

I flop down onto his bed, and undo my shirt, showing him my tits, "Here's a preview baby.  If you hurry up, you'll get to play with me."

He nods, heading above deck.

I relax, closing my eyes, hoping we ship out soon.  There's some arguing above deck, and I wonder if I managed to get the captain or not.

Apparently I didn't, because storming down into the cabin, interrupting my relaxation time on the bed, is an angry short fellow who is all fire and fury when he gets down.  He has a fairly solid beard and had rubber boots and slacks on over a tank top. He had a pair of rubber gloves on as well. Graying red hair and blue eyes are glaring at me.

"Who the fuck is you?" He shouts.

I sat up, letting my tits flop out, which disarmed his anger immediately.  "Oh, my *goodness* you fishermen are so *eager...*" I saunter over to him.

He stammers, "W-We aren't taking you anywhere... S-Sure as shit not to Europe... Our boat... Holy fuck those are nice tits..."

I smile, hefting them in my hands, "Wanna hold them, babe?"

I get close enough and he drops his gloves off, he gives my breasts a rough squeeze, "Holy shit..."

I moan, "Oh yes baby... Feel me up..." I lean against him, quickening my breath, "Feels so good..."

His eyes are getting hazy as he kneads my breasts in his hands.

I lean over to him, pressing against him, my breasts flattening against his chest, my lips so close to his, "I just need a ride hun... Can't you give me a good... *Hard*... Ride?"

He nods dumbly.  Men are so easy.

I kiss him sweetly, entrancing him.

His eyes go full glassy and he just nods, "We'll store as much diesel as we can carry.  We'll get you there honey."

"Good boy," I whisper.

He shudders, "W-when will you... When will you fuck us?"

I smile, "Oh baby, keep yourself ready, once we head out, I promise I'll fuck you... I'll do the captain first.  I promise." I slide my finger over his lips, smiling sweetly.

Just like that he ran off, and there's more commotion as my two new thralls start prepping the boat.  I can hear some argument from the third guy, and I peek up above deck.  I changed my outfit into a flowing sheer white dress, heels, and a choker.  I also make sure my make-up is fantastic as I peek up to the deck, spotting the third man.

"What is wrong with you Dawson?  Cody?  What the fuck..." He turns, eyes fixed on me.

I motion to him with my finger, smiling.

He walks over, "W-who are you...?"

I smile sweetly, "I'm Sara. I'm here to attend to your carnal needs while you're sailing... Come down with me," I back my way down the steps.

This guy follows, getting down into the crew quarters with me.

"What's your captain's name, sweetness?" I ask.

"C-Cody. And Dawson's the first mate." He explains.

"Aw... Are you just the lowly deck-hand?" I tease, walking slowly toward one of the beds, shifting my hips seductively.

"Y-yes... My name is Terrence. But everyone calls me Terry." He stammers.

I bend down, pretending to pick something up, and I moan softly, "Oh Terry... I'm so needy, so horny..." I turn to look at him, my ass wiggling in front of him. "How bad do you want me?"

Terry walks right up behind me, grabs my hips, and pulls them against his.

I gasp in mock surprise, "Terrance! How forward of you!" I straighten up, pressing against his hard-on. Oh! Finally! Terry has some meat! I gyrate my hips against him, "Oh my... Terry... Is that your fishing pole...?"

He lifted my dress upward.

Oh, he was forward, I loved it. "Oh... Terry... Are you going to help yourself to me before your bosses?" I ask.

He grunts, "I don't care what they say, you're too hot to resist... I'm sorry Jackie."

I shiver as I feel his cock sliding over my pussy lips, "Oh Terry... She'll forgive you..." I gasp as he slides his thick cock into me. "Oh... With a cock like that I know she'll forgive you..." I press my hips back, sinking more of his cock into my pussy. I grunt, "Oh! A girl can't hog a dick like this all for herself..." I bend over, grabbing a pole for support  as he begins to thrust. I arch my back, gasping, "It's not fair to the rest of us!" I shout.

Terry keeps thrusting harder and harder into me, his hands on my hips holding me tight. He stops occasionally, but only to give my ass a hard and firm slap.

I shout, "Oh fuck yes!" I loved what he was doing, every bit of it. I was doing everything I could to not suck the life out of him. One, I needed him to help the other two with the boat, and two, I was thoroughly enjoying myself. "Fuck me, Terry! Fuck me!"

His thrusts just got stronger, and soon one hand snaked up along my side, giving my breast a rough squeeze.

I moaned as his rough hand fondled me, his fingers pinching my nipple. "Oh, God!" I cried out.

"You like it rough don't you slut?" He said, thrusting harder.

I moaned, "Yes baby... Yes I like it rough."

"Are you my slut?" He taunted as he thrust harder.

I moaned, "I'm... Oh fuck... I'm not... Yours..." I gasp

He spanked my ass hard, "You will be when I'm done!" He shouted

Oh, my oh my! What a passionate man, little did he know he was about to be all mine. I clenched my Kegels hard, pinning his cock inside me, and gave him a good tug.

He moaned, grabbing my hips for support, "Holy fuck!"

I groaned, "Oh, not quite cutie..." I gave him another vise-like tug with my pussy, "Oh... But it is a good fuck... Come on baby... Don't stop now just..."

He started thrusting again, going harder than before. Several hot minutes of this and I can tell Terry's thrusts are getting weaker, which is fine, as I can't take much more without drinking him to death.

I cried out in pleasure, "Fuck me stud!" I commanded.

He grunted, gripping my hips for all he was worth, "I-I'm gonna...", His thrusts peaked as he gave harder and slower thrusts.

I moaned, "Fuck stud, cum for me!" I squeezed him tight. "Cum for me like the hot stud you are! Be my stud!" I say, grinning.

He grunts, and gasps, "I'm... oh...fuck!" He shouts, blowing his load into me.

I moan as well, feeling an orgasm wash over me, making me shake in bliss. I lose control of my human form, my wings and tail coming out. My tail wraps around his waist instinctively as my wings close tight against my back. I turn to him, grinning.

His eyes are wide as he slides out of me, panting heavily.

I smile, kneeling before him, licking at his huge meaty cock. I taste the salty cum on the tip, sucking it into my mouth.

Terry's shock vanishes, and his hand rests on my horn. "W-what are you?"

I pop his cock out of my mouth, licking along its length, and sliding it over my cheek. This is the best human cock I've had in a long time, "What are *you*?" I asked.

"I'm your stud..." He said dreamily. "Wait, why did I say that?"

I smiled, sucking the tip of his dick into my mouth, swirling my tongue around the head.

He groaned, his other hand grabbing my other horn. "S-sensitive... I-I just...Came..."

I don't stop sucking. Instead I go even harder.

He gasps, "I-I'm... Gonna..." He groans, "C-cum for you... I-I'm your... Stud... I cum for... mistress..." He gasps, filling my mouth with cum. He's panting heavily as I drink him down.

I swallow down his cum, standing up slowly, towering over him, "The others are just mindless limp-dicked slaves for me Terry... But you're going to be my stud for the trip..." I smiled, dragging my nail over his hard cock. "Understand?" I smile, letting some of my lust magic work its way into his flesh.

He groans, his cock getting harder and even thicker after my magic touches him. I watch as his muscles swell slightly. His eyes go milky white for a moment.

I smile, he's all mine now. "What are you?"

"I'm your stud." He says confidently. "I'm your stud until you're done with me."

I nod, "Good boy, now go help your friends get ready."

He nods, slides his cock away, and heads up above deck.

I laid back against one of the beds, feeling the boat vibrate to life as its engines began.  I needed the sex to distract me, but now I was nervous they would be going the wrong way. After a few minutes, I head up above deck, wearing a normal human form as I do so.  "Hello boys," I say as I come up.

They look to be infatuated.

"We're heading to Spain, right?  Or can we make it all the way to Jerusalem?" I asked.

Captain Cody looked at me, "We can get three-fourths of the way there... After that, we will run out of food, water, and fuel."

I nod, "Good..." I smiled at them, "How long?"

They looked at each other, "About a week."

I frown, "Well, make good time."

# CHAPTER 15

## *Return Voyage*

**"The Seal of Solomon is both a lock and a key.**

**It seals the demons within Hell below, if**

**broken the gate is opened."**

T erry thrust into me again, "I... I am... going to..." He grunted.

I moaned, the ship's fuel had run out this morning, with little ceremony, I had drank Cody and Dawson quickly. Neither was a good fuck for the week we were all on the boat, and I was saving my strength for when I was going to need to fly the remaining leg of the journey.  I saved Terry for last, he was the strongest of the three men anyway.

I moaned as I gripped him tightly, "I'll miss that thick dick of yours Terry… mmm… Harder baby… It's the last thing you're going to do." I smiled up at him, my legs over my head as he gripped my hips tight.

He groaned and began to jackhammer into me.

I rolled my eyes into the back of my head in pleasure as he gave me his all, "Oh fuck baby!  I'm gonna miss this dick!  Thank you, my rugged stud!"

He somehow found some extra strength to thrust harder into me for his final three thrusts.

I'm not going to lie, I came on the second thrust.  I let my body pull at his energy as hard as it could.  I wanted to make it fast for him.

"Oh…Fuck!" Terry shouted as he rapidly deflated in front of me, his body shrinking and withering in seconds.

I screamed in pleasure at the mad rush of power, strength, and passion. "Oh, Terry!" I gasped, shivering as I felt his cock shriveling inside of me.  It was a damn shame.  Granted, I made good use of that thing over the last seven days.  I pushed Terry's dead and withered corpse off of me, stretching and luxuriating in the afterglow of my orgasm.

I headed up above deck and found the sun setting.  The perfect time for me to head out.  I was in my succubus form, as once we got to the open sea there was no reason to waste energy hiding what I was.  I pulled my phone off the charger and checked what direction I should go.

Without much ceremony I spread my wings and leapt into the air, flying high over the ocean water.

I quickly discovered that the wind of the ocean made flying fairly easy, as I was mostly just gliding.  Either way, holding my wings open for several hours at a time was tiring.  I was going to need to feed once I landed on dry land.  My three meals were basically me eating all of my food to give me the energy for this flight.

Just when I worried, I might have to swim for the rest of the trip, I saw lights.  I checked my phone and smiled, I was coming to shore.

I landed on a fairly rocky shore.  I looked at my phone, seeing that I was in Portugal, which was a good start.  I also needed to charge my phone.

I walked along the beach, getting increasingly tired when I spotted someone along the shoreline.  I smiled, it was a man. Perfect!

I changed my appearance to a small attractive woman, wearing no shoes and tattered clothing.  Making myself out to be some kind of ship-wrecked woman.  I cried out, "H–help!"

The man turned to me and rushed over.

"Ai meu Deus, o que aconteceu com você?" he asked.

I pretended to faint, and he caught me.  Sooner than later he's carrying me across the beach and up to a truck I assumed was his.  As he's about to place a phone call I grab his hand, pulling him towards me. My hand massages his dick through his pants and I feel him grow hard. I moan into his ear, "I want you..." nothing impressive in his pants, it seems.

He gasps in surprise.

Lick along his neck. Before long I manage to fish his cock out and I swing my legs over his.

Not thinking clearly, he grabs my hips and thrusts into me.

After a week with Terry, disappointment is my main sensation. Without any ceremony, a groan, and clenching onto his little dick. I grind down against him and shiver as I drink hungrily from his essence.

He barely manages to squeak before he climaxes inside of me.

I feel myself sink down into the seat as he withers beneath me, my tired body re-energized for now. I pull his wallet and ID, take his keys, and study him closely. I change my appearance to match his, push his corpse out of the truck, and started making the drive towards my true destination.

After following the directions on my phone for the better part of a day I finally ran out of money. Well, I shouldn't say that. I think they found this fellow's withered corpse and deactivated his cards. I notice at this point that everyone is speaking French, and from what I can see I managed to get to the city of Nice. While I don't need sleep, I do need to eat. This traveling and holding different shapes is draining on my body.

I groan, ditching the truck at some parking lot. Of all the things I manage to see as I walk around the city, I'm kind of shocked to see a McDonald's.  Really France?  A McDonald's?  Upon seeing it though I can't help but feel a pang of regret.

I imagined my life if, maybe, I had never become a succubus.  Spending time with my husband and my son Jason, seeing his wedding, maybe taking my grandson to McDonald's and spoiling him.  I hug my shoulders looking at the golden arches and I can't help but feel my heart sink into despair.  I can't help it as a tear rolls down my cheek.

To my surprise, I hear an English accent right next to me, "It's a damn shame, I know."

I turn to face a black man in a rather fashionable outfit, slim fit clothing, well-kept, a rather handsome man, despite being so thin.  "Oh, yes.  You speak English?" I smile at him, drying my eyes.

Dear God, this man hands me a handkerchief!  "Yes." He smiles sincerely, "I couldn't help noticing you staring at it, American I assume?"

I nod, "Yeah, Boston."

"On holiday?" he asks.

I nod, offering my hand, "Sara."

"Fredrick," he says, extending his hand and shaking firmly.  He looks to the McDonald's, "Care to come in?  I was going to grab a bite, might be nice to hear some of the King's for a change, yes?"

I smile, "Sure." Poor bastard.  He seems nice.  Maybe I'll keep things polite and not drain him completely.  Granted I'm not actually sure if I can eat normal food.  I think my body is designed for just eating men at this point.

Regardless, we head inside. I'm a bit shocked as some of the photos don't really match what I would expect to see in a McDonald's.

Fredrick heads to the counter and turns to me, "What do you fancy?"

I look over the menu, despite it being in French, I can figure out most of what is up there. I'm not hungry for any of this food, of course, I'm much hungrier for Fredrick. I frown, it's a damn shame because he seems nice. "I'm not too hungry..."

"How about something to drink? A frappé?" Frederick asked.

Odd that he's so adamant about me having something, but I shrug, "Sure."

Fredrick orders, pays, and as we wait he strikes up a conversation. "So how long will you be in town?"

I laugh, "Oh not long. I'm on a road trip." Honestly, I am.

"Where's your destination?"

"The end of the world," I smirk.

He just grins at me, "So just a wandering American in the big world around her, is that it?"

I nod, "Yep, just me, myself, and I."

Our order comes out, I notice he's also only gotten a drink. He hands me mine and we head to a booth in the back, near the bathroom of all places. He settles in, placing his satchel next to him as I sit across from him. "Staying anywhere?"

"Oh, not yet, I just rolled into town."

He nods, "Perfect." He hands me my drink, "Well, to adventure."

I nod and drink. I swallow. Now I am fully aware of what vanilla tastes like, I'm also aware of what milk and sugar and everything else taste like. I can taste all of that and something else. Something tart and sour. I take another sip, giving Fredrick an odd look.

Fredrick's face doesn't change from his disarming smile, "Surprised to see a McDonald's out here, right?"

Something is in this that shouldn't be. I drink again, it's hard to place. Whatever it is, I can tell it should knock a normal woman out. It's odd how I can tell, but it's as if, as I swallow it, my body feels the would-be-effects, and ignores them because, well, I'm not human. "Yeah... listen this tastes a little sour, try it?" I offer.

Fredrick drinks his own, "We ordered the same thing, Sara. Feeling alright?"

Now I don't feel so bad for what is about to happen. I feign being dizzy, "Oh... I... I don't actually."

Fredrick gets up, helping me to my feet, keeping his satchel with him. "Come here dear, let's get some water on your face, you're looking green at the gills."

How many women has he done this to? This bastard! It's all an act! I pretend to stumble against him, grabbing his shoulders, "Oh... Fredrick I think I need a doctor..." maybe, just maybe he's not the culprit. I should remove all doubt, right?

Fredrick shakes his head, pulling me into the bathroom, "Nonsense dear, it's just a dizzy spell..." and into the bathroom, we go. He gives me a push onto the floor and locks the door.

I pretend to fall and remain there, groaning and putting on a fairly convincing 'drugged up girl' act.

Fredrick pulls a damn tarp out from his satchel, lays it over the tile floor, and then rolls me over onto it. He proceeds to wrap my legs up in the tarp, and even cup the thing around my shoulders.

Dropping the act, I ask, "Fredrick, what are you doing?"

He's taken aback, "Oh, just about to gut you like a fish you American twat." He smiles, "You should be down for the count any moment. Then I'm going to play with your pretty insides."

As he's talking about gutting me, I have snuck my tail out from the tarp and moved it behind him. I tap his shoulder with it.

He turns quickly and as soon as he does the tip of my tail finds its way into his mouth.

I pump my poison relentlessly down his throat. Within seconds he collapses onto the floor, gasping for air.

I pull my tail out, and stand up slowly, kicking the tarp away, "How many women did you trick with your good looks there Freddy?" I ask as I slowly straddle his hips, looking through his satchel to find surgical equipment.

He gasps for air, "A-about nine... you'd be... number ten..."

I let my horns come out, dropping my human form completely. I slide my hoof up to his head as I straddle him, undoing his belt, "Fredrick, do the girls feel it?  When you cut them open?"

He's trying to scream now, but he can't get above a whisper, "W-what are you?  What are you?  Get away from me!"

I fish his hard cock out, "Did they know they were going to die?"

He whimpers, "Yes!  T-they're awake for most of it!  Let me go!  I won't do it again!"

"Oh, Freddy..." I smile at him, pointing to the horns, "See these?  These aren't 'Forgiving' horns. They're demon horns. I'm a succubus, you see?  I don't forgive." I slide his cock inside of me, "I punish."

He shudders, "W-what a way to go."

I shove a knife from his kit into his shoulder.

He screams, unable to move.

I smile at him, draining hard, my heart racing.  This is turning me on, giving me a thrill as I watch the fear wash over his face.  "When you get to Hell, tell them Sara Baker sent you. It might give you some extra special torture..." I scrape my hoof against his temple, scraping some of his scalp off the side of his head.  "You piece of shit."

He starts to wither.

I grin, leaning down, "I guess this isn't the first time someone from Boston showed an Englishmen how to get properly fucked, huh?"

His eyes sink down into his head until I have a lovely idea. I stand up, knowing he doesn't have much time left.  He looks like an eighty-year-old man.  "I think I'll let you expire on your own..." I change back to human shape.  "I'm going to leave you in here, bleeding, dying, and helpless on the floor."  I tower over him, smiling, "Nice meeting you Freddy.  Enjoy your holiday..." I lean down, whispering, "Tell my Master Asmodai, I miss him."

He gasps, his throat dry and his body absolutely useless.  Even without my poison in his veins, he wouldn't be strong enough to stand.

I walk out, closing the door discreetly.  I toss both of the drinks into the trash, heading out of the McDonald's.  I search through Fredrick's satchel, frowning as I see multiple women's IDs and passports.  Their wallets and some cash.  Well, Freddy wasn't lying, he had done this before.  Seems he kept trophies as well.

I figure the last leg of my trip should be in style.  I get all the cash in the satchel together and head toward the airport.  They don't have a direct flight that day, but I manage to have a lovely set of first-class trips, from one airport to the next.  Landing in Cairo.  I keep telling myself flying on a plane is much faster than wasting energy flying myself, and in each first-class area, I find so many men willing to lend me their fortunes for my little day trips.

On the way to Cairo, one lovely gentleman was sitting next to me, smiling the whole way.

I had chosen a very upper-class model-like body, wearing an expensive skimpy little dress, fashionable heels, and top-notch make-up.  I even managed to fake some expensive-looking jewelry.

The olive-skinned fellow next to me smiled warmly and offered his hand, "Saleem Mohammed Amari." he said. He has a number of very nice rings on his fingers. He's dressed in a very nice suit and tie, nice shoes, and looks to be a rather wealthy man.

I smile, taking his hand, "Sara Baker." As I touch him, I can tell he's more than a little interested in me. He wants me badly. I can also get a hint of his sins, he's an embezzler, stealing from his own non-profit organization that's supposed to feed people in need.

As I let go, I wonder if as a succubus, I am drawn to men who sin. Is it just like a radar? I happen across men whose souls are dark and evil? That would explain Fredrick.

"You must be an actress," he starts.

I just smile, leaning over to him, locking my eyes on his, "I'm a model, actually..."

I watch him actually resist my initial enticement.

I grin, "What do you do?"

He smiles, "I work for a large charity, actually. We build homes for needy families impacted by the war in Syria."

I let go of his hand, leaning back as the stewardess fills my wine glass, "How noble of you.'

Saleem nods, getting a refill himself, "So what business do you have in Cairo?"

I flash a million-watt smile at him, "Oh, I'm doing a shoot in front of the pyramids."

Saleem laughed, "Ah, I see!" He took a swig of his wine, "I wonder what the Pharaohs of old would do, knowing their tombs are nothing but the backdrop for beautiful women the world over."

"They would probably want to fuck us all," I grin, "Them being kings, after all."

Saleem laughs, "What is that American saying, 'it's good to be the King', yes?"

I nod, "Yes." I frown a bit, "Though I am so very bored of these shoots.  I get to travel all over the world and I never get new experiences..." I slowly uncross my legs, my foot sliding up his calf as I do.

"Oh, new experiences?" He asks.

I smile, leaning close to him, "...I've heard people call me a whore." I slide my fingers over the back of his hand slowly, "But wouldn't you know?  I've never ever been paid for sex..." I squeeze my thighs together, "It would be such a rush to be paid for sex... if a man... a wealthy man... were to offer... I'd have to take him as a client, like a common whore." I lean away, smiling, "Why... I'd even let him have me in the lavatory of a plane."

He grins wickedly, "A woman of your beauty would be an expensive whore..."

"Mmm..." I purred to him, "How much would a wealthy man like you pay for your expensive whore?"

He thinks for a moment, "Ten thousand dollars."

I grin, and force myself to blush, "Oh that would be such a rush..."

He pulls out a checkbook, jots something down, and then offers it to me, a check for $11,000.

I bite my lip, and look at him with giddy excitement, "Oh... my...." I shiver, leaning in to give him a kiss, but he stops me.

"Go to the lavatory, and wait for me, I will knock three times, and then fuck my whore," He instructed.

I gasp, forcing myself flush still, and then stand, heading into the lavatory in first class. Once inside I drop the experimenting rich girl act and look at the check. I smile, he only wrote the number, and signed it, he never actually spelled out eleven thousand. I wondered if I could get more out of him. I probably could once his dick was in me.

Three knocks come, and I get back into character.

I gasp, and open the door slowly, backing up as he comes in. "I can't believe I'm doing this..."

He grins, "Oh, but you are my whore."

I shiver as his hand roams up the hem of my dress. "Oh, yes sir. What do you want your whore to do?"

Saleem flipped me around and made me face the mirror. I grinned, then turned to face him as he flipped my dress up over my hips. He gave me a hard slap and I yelped in a mix of pain and pleasure.

Note to self, have Asmodai give me a good spanking when I see him again. I shudder at the thought.

Saleem seems to think this is his doing and undoes his belt, "You like that don't you?"

"Yes..." I hiss.

"What a bad girl you are…" his hand drags down my back as he presses his cock against my vulva.

I groan, "You have no idea…" I gasp as he thrusts into me. My God!  Surprise!  He's huge!  "Oh my God, you're so big!" I gasp again as he pulls out and thrusts in again.  It's rare when a man's confidence matches his dick size.  Saleem was very confident.

He grunts and keeps thrusting, as he does, I can see his eyes get a faraway look.  "Yes… that's right whore…"

I press my hips against him and clench down painfully hard on his dick.

Suddenly he gasps in pain.

I look back over my shoulder, my eyes meeting his, "One hundred grand… and I let go… and you can keep fucking this whore…"

He groans, "You're a harlot… I like it…"

"Love it…" I say.

He shudders, I can feel him twitch inside me as he pulls out his checkbook, "How much to buy you… whore…?  I want you forever…"

I grin, "If you want to buy this whore for the rest of your life, then it'll be half a million."

He groans, writing the check, "Done… Done and done! Now… You're mine, my new concubine…" he grins.

I smile as I take the check, "Oh yes… I'm all yours, for as long as you live…" I shiver as he starts thrusting again.  I decide to let him ride me until he's ready because he feels quite good inside me.  Dare I say almost as good as Terry.

Saleem really gave me a pounding for quite some time before he grabbed my hair and pulled back hard, "I'm cumming whore! Take my seed!"

"Yes! Yes, I'm your whore! I'll take it all!" I shout, nearing my own climax.

Saleem reaches his first, as expected, and floods me.

I groan and shiver as I feel his essence start to pour into me, his flesh weak and easy, his energy flowing into me like a floodgate opening. I scream in pleasure, shuddering as I slam my hips against him, his strength flowing into me in such a mind-blowing fashion. I cannot believe how good it is to feed on mortals, living mortals that is.

Saleem gasps, he can see himself withering in the mirror.

I smile in the mirror, and let my true form show in the reflection for him, "Stealing from the poor to give to yourself... Saleem... So *naughty.*"

His eyes go wide as he struggles against me.

I moan, shivering in bliss as I feel the last of his life surge into me, "Mm.... See you in Hell, Saleem..."

Saleem's eyes roll into the back of his head as he completely shrivels up, his corpse slumping against the toilet.

I dress myself and fix up my hair and make-up. I look at his corpse and frown, "Well this wasn't very well thought out..." I frown, poking him.

His skin is dry and flakes off his body.

I try to think of a way to dispose of the corpse, considering some of the magic I know of. I could do some kind of portal. Normally I can walk through a wall with it. Granted if I put one in the side of the plane the whole thing would go down. I look to the floor and smile. I made a little hole to test, and just as I thought, it looks like a cargo hold. I slide Saleem's body into the hole, after making it slightly bigger, and close it back up.

As I walk out of the lavatory, I shut the door behind me, I get a knowing look from one of the other passengers who is nearby the lavatory.

I wink at him and make my way back to my seat, looking over the check I just got. I had plans for this money, primarily to wire it right away to Jason. I'm sure he could use it. I settle into my seat as the voice-over states we're landing. Despite my orders, I know I can take five minutes to wire Jason the money.

After I hop off of the plane and find an exchange bank to properly wire the money, the man at the desk was oh so helpful after I forced him to comply, I headed off to my final destination. My last flight was going to take me to Tel Aviv, from there it was a short flight to the city of Jerusalem.

When the last plane landed, I was happy to see it was still dark. I pulled out my phone, pulled up the GPS, and took to the sky once I was out of view from any prying eyes. It's funny, as I get closer and closer to my goal of opening the gate, I feel more apprehensive. I'm more and more concerned about Jason and my family. I hope the money may help, but if the world basically ends due to all Hell spilling out, money might be the last thing on their minds. I need to talk to Asmodai, I'm sure he'll spare them, maybe put them under his protection.

As I reach the city, I land and ensure I take on the form of a Muslim woman, which is helpful as women seem to like to cover up around here. That's when I found the Temple Mount in the distance. There's a line of people who are going in to worship. I slide up to one man walking alone, lock eyes with him, and soon I'm walking inside easily.

Once inside, I ditch the man and stealthily sneak off from the tour groups. I can feel something deep inside the temple drawing me to it. As I walk down several corridors and stairs towards the familiar power, I find my disguise breaks on its own, causing me some concern. The temple must have some kind of defense against demonic powers. Great, this is going to suck.

I finally feel that I'm on the same floor as the seal. I am so close. But damn it! As I get close enough to it I spot Father Thomas and his Angel butt-buddy standing near it. I hide in the corridor outside, and I decide I'm going to wait them out.

They have to leave at some point.

I guess taking the boat gave them a head start. Which is terrible. Now I'm stuck here hoping they leave.

It felt like hours waiting when suddenly a huge explosion from outside shook the ground. I got to my hooves in time to see the angel rushing out of the sealed room. I grinned, knowing only the Priest was inside, I could handle the Priest easily.

"I thought he would never leave," I taunt as I walk into the room, finding Father Thomas praying. I can feel the power beyond the seal, and it seems to invigorate me.

Father Thomas has his bible at the ready, locked open, and some little red disk in his free hand, "Step away from the seal."

I frown, looking at the seal, "Just get out of my way. The sooner I crack this seal the sooner I can get Ubiel out of my grandson," I sigh, "He's got a thing for kids," I shudder as I remember why Ubiel was in Hell to begin with.

Father Thomas thrusts his hand at me with the red disk, I catch it easily, lacing my fingers with his.

"Listen, Father, the sentiment is kind of heartwarming but also sad, okay?  Choirboy couldn't do diddly and he's a fucking Angel.  What are you?" I taunted Father Thomas.

Father Thomas grips my hand tighter, which I find odd, "I am a man who serves in the name of the Father, and the Son, and the Holy Spirit."

To my left, the seal starts to glow white! I can feel myself weakening as I realize the damn thing is radiating with holy energy.  Was this a trap?  I try to free myself from his grip, if I can get away, I might be able to find a way to break the seal when Father Thomas isn't there.  As I attempt to pull away, however, I find I'm stuck fast to him.  "What the Hell?" I shout, "Why can't I let go of you?" I grab his wrist with my other hand but for some reason it's like his hand is welded to mine, a red glow pulses from between our hands, "What the fuck?" I shout.  I can see a powerful aura from between us, and I start to feel a burning sensation against my palm, some kind of holy energy, and it's sapping my strength!

I try to whip at him with my tail, while not strong, if I can get him to just back off and let go, I'll be able to regroup!  I was so worried about the damn angel, I never thought that a simple priest would be so challenging for me!

Father Thomas starts to pray, "Most glorious Prince of Heavenly Armies Saint Michael the Archangel, defend us in our battle against principalities and powers, against the rulers of this world of darkness, against the spirits of wickedness in the high places!"

I feel the heat grow from the object that's holding me tight, I need to escape and fast or I have a sinking feeling I'm going to get sent back to Hell without opening the gate as ordered. Deep down, however, along with the sinking feeling, I feel a bit of relief. If he stops me, then I can say I tried my best, right? Thinking of trying my best, I flap my wings hard, hoping to maybe pull myself from his grip. This only winds up sending both of us to the floor, "Stop it, you old bastard!" I scream. I keep smacking him with my tail, and even beating him with my wings. While I'm hitting him hard in some places, it seems his resolve is firmer than my ability to hurt him. I feel weaker and weaker as he continues to hold my hand as if I'm losing all the energy I drank.

Father Thomas now looks me dead in the eyes and starts to pray, "In the name of Jesus Christ, our God and Lord, strengthened by the intercession of the Immaculate Virgin Mary, Mother of God, of Blessed Michael the Archangel, of the Blessed Apostles Peter and Paul and all the Saints, and powerful in this holy authority of our ministry, we confidently undertake to repulse the attacks and deceits of the devil. God arises; His enemies are scattered and those who hate Him flee before Him. As smoke is driven away, so are they driven; as wax melts before the fire, so the wicked perish at the presence of God!"

The ground shakes suddenly, and I'm not sure if it's Father Thomas or something else, but I see the angel standing in the doorway to the room we're in.

"Father, we must leave now!" I hear him shout, he then looks at me, "Oh, of course, you chose now to try to open the gates!"

"Fuck off Choir Boy it's me and the priest who-" I feel something pulling me downward, as if the floor is no longer solid beneath me, "Wait what's happening?" I turn to look and see a huge seal covered in intricate runes I've never seen before. It's almost twenty feet in diameter, and I realize that's the seal I should have been breaking. Problem is, it looks like it's been activated. The seal meant to hold the forces of Hell at bay has just been turned on, and in the center of it a symbol glows bright white. I realize I'm being dragged towards it!

That bastard Father Thomas managed to activate the seal, and I'm about to be sent back to Hell.

"We drive you from us," Father Thomas continues, "Succubus Sara Baker, unclean spirit, all satanic powers, all infernal invaders, all wicked legions, assemblies, and sects."

Now the seal is really pulling at me, so much so that I have to grab hold of the floor with my free hand, my claws digging into the ground, but not stopping me from getting pulled in.

Despite the wind and the chaos around us, Father Thomas keeps praying, "In the Name and the power of Our Lord Jesus Christ, may you be snatched away and driven from the Church of God from the souls made to the image and likeness of God and redeemed by the Precious Blood of the Divine Lamb!"

My hand slips from the ground, and I decide if I cannot stop myself from being sent back, then I won't be going back alone. I grab Father Thomas's shoulder, making sure that I'm not just grabbing his body, but grabbing a hold of his spirit. "Father, if you cast me out, then you're at least going to see what you're sending me back to!" I flap my wings and rise up with both of us, I can tell I'm pulling his spirit from his body.

He finally lets go of my hand, and I see a small red amber disk fall onto the seal.

I grab his other shoulder, lifting his spirit up from his body. The wind is deafening as I'm pulled towards the center of the seal. I grin at Father Thomas's soul, seeing his translucent face looking at me in shock, "Welcome to Hell!" I shout as we're both pulled into the seal.

# CHAPTER 16

## *Punishment*

"An owned soul cannot ignore orders but following orders haphazardly can lead to failure. Intentional failure is punishable."

$A$h, the unfortunately familiar smell of sulfur and ash. I did not miss it, I didn't miss the heat, I didn't miss the distant screams and the color of red tinting damn near everything around me.

I released the priest and let him fall, figuring I would allow him to have a taste of suffering. I was truly agitated that he had sent me back.  I was actually having a good time on Earth!  I might add, I was also cleaning the place up too, one sicko at a time.  Okay maybe they weren't all assholes and murders, but the last two definitely were.

I watch Father Thomas land with a hard thwap on the ground below as I glide gracefully to the ground near him.  Oddly this isn't the same body pile that I had landed on when I first got to Hell.  It seems we're on a distant cliff overlooking the greater portions of Hell.  I can see the blade of Pride out in the distance, the Halls of Wrath before it, and even the Fields of Lust.  It's funny, I never knew this place existed.  Not like I ever had time to really go exploring around here.

I land lightly on my hooves, walking seductively towards Father Thomas as he slowly gets to his feet, his wounds healing painfully, "Welcome," I say, adding some flourish with my hands on either side of me, "To my humble home," I glance at the cliff's edge, "Well, the outskirts."

Father Thomas is patting himself down, likely trying to find any of his stuff.  Poor fuck should be happy enough he has clothing at all.

"Ah, that's a shame.  Your holy water and crosses didn't come with you?" I lord over him, locking eyes with him, "Don't even have that Amber shit, huh?" I raise up my hand, calling my armor and weapons to me, "Now you know how I felt.  Allow me, Father, to collect my things." I feel my whip hit me first, unfurling in my hand and uncoiling around me.  I look it over, grinning wickedly, "My babies are coming soon." I can feel the armor following not too far behind. They wrap around me, covering me, head to hoof in my beautiful armor.  I feel strength surge into me as my armor completely covers me, my whole body feeling as if I could hurl a boulder.

I saunter around him some more, towering over him, feeling far superior in every way now, "If I was summoned with my babies, Father, I'd have opened the gate in about five whole minutes," I taunt, spreading my wings. I shiver as I hear the metal scraping noises that my upper armor makes as my wings spread wide. I know it grates on a mortal's ears, but it almost sounds like a song to me. I feel myself floating above the ground, my armor empowering me further, they must have missed their mommy. I soar into the air, nearly to the top of the cavern, and then rush down right behind Father Thomas, showing him my true power.

I whip him hard across his back, the blades of my whip digging hard into his back and gouging a deep wound exposing his ribs. Watching him bleed gives me a satisfying feeling. Now he can suffer at my hands. He falls to his knees immediately, in shock from the pain.

"You know Father, it's not the constant pain down here that sucks so much. It's the healing part..." I taunt, walking around the other side of him, closing my wings. I smile as I watch him flinch at the grinding metallic sound that occurs as they close. "That's the *real* bitch."

I watch as the wound slowly closes on Father Thomas's back, he whimpers and groans, "Why?" he asks.

I push the hilt of my whip against his chin, making him look me in the eyes, "Because you sent me back here. You sent me back here after I escaped and I am fucking furious," I growl, giving him a good smack across the face with the hilt of my whip. I grin as I see his face mangled and bleeding. "You know what these are all made of? My babies?" I asked rhetorically.

"Somehow I feel you'll tell me regardless," the smart-ass replies.

I ignored his little quip, boasting, "These were souls, three souls, one in my lovely whip, one lucky bastard gets strapped to my tits, and the other gets the pleasure of caressing my beautiful hips..." I grin, feeling my armor caress me lovingly along my legs and crotch as I mention him, "and more." I grin, bringing the hilt of my whip up to my lips in mock thought, "Though maybe if he's wired like you he's not too pleased about it."

Father Thomas manages to get back to his feet, his wounds nearly healed.

I give him another good slash to the shoulder, sending him to the ground, "You don't get permission to stand. Here, I'm your God." I press my hoof on his back, "In fact," I kick him to the ground, "Kneeling is too good for you, worm."

Father Thomas falls face-first onto the ground, coughing on the dust and ash.

"Hm, you know folks pay good money for this kind of treatment," I snicker, "You're my bitch until that choir boy pulls your soul out of here, and considering how green he is you might be here for a hot minute." I can't stop myself from snickering at my own joke, "Hot minute... oh Sara..."

"Why make me suffer?" Father Thomas gasps.

I grind my hoof into his back as the question really gets my blood boiling, "Because all I wanted was to be with my family, and then you all had to fuck it up!"

Father Thomas coughs and wheezes, "We did nothing... it was you who brought ruin to your family."

I see red, and give him a firm kick to the ribs, sending him flying and landing a good twenty feet or so away from me. As he lands I leap into the air, landing right in front of him, just barely missing his face with my armored hooves. I bend down and grab him by his robes, bringing him face to face with me. "I fucked my life up, not theirs! I set them up for life, my husband, my son, they ought to have been fine without me!"

Father Thomas's body dangles in my hands, his body bruised and battered, but he begins to speak, weakly, "Your... husband... after your death suffered depression. His law firm failed, everything you gained with your pact soured," he explained.

I dropped him harshly on the ground, "Shut up!" I kick him in the gut before he hits the ground, "Shut up you fucking liar!"

Father Thomas clutches his midsection and gasps, choking on the ash in the air, "Ask the one who bought you... he will tell you." Father Thomas seems distracted by something in the distance.

"That pact cost too much to just have everything fall apart!" I shout, feeling frustrated, mostly because Father Thomas is probably right. Belial likely did make sure my deal left my family in ruins. I just did not want to face the truth. "It wasn't just my soul after all!" I glare at him, spreading my wings, "I'm five fucking souls worth of demonic power!" I slam my hoof on the ground, cracks forming under me as I do so, green fire pulsing from my body through the cracks.

"What do you mean?" Father Thomas wheezes.

I fix him with an angry glare, "My soul was part of the pact, but I wasn't the only one going into this body, I was just the core." I growled at him, "Sara Baker would be the main ingredient, but there were others. The other was the one who gave this body, the porn star heroin addict who sold her body to cultists to get her next fix. She sold her soul for a fucking fix and that's when her soul got transmuted into this." I make a grand movement with my arms, my tail swaying behind me as I spread my wings straight up, "The beautiful damned bitch before you... the three cultists who were there were my first snacks, so it took five souls to make the beauty that is me." I saunter over to Father Thomas, slowly folding my wings, "You're telling me even after all that, everything I worked for in my life fell to shit?"

Father Thomas clears his throat, "Such is the cost of a deal one makes with a demon."

My rage is starting to subside and get mixed with sorrow, I only doomed myself. That's why I didn't take Belial's extension. I didn't want my son or husband harmed. "The things you're claiming, they aren't true," I say simply, trying to suppress tears. "Because none of that was part of my pact."

"What was it?" Father Thomas coughed, "What was so tempting that made you sell your soul?"

I grip my whip tighter, trying to dig the hilt into my palm to stop my eyes from watering, "You wouldn't understand."

Father Thomas gets himself sitting upright on the ground, clearly still dazed from my kick to his gut, "Try me."

I look away and to the ground beneath us as I feel my heart quivering in my chest. What did I do it all for? To escape a wheelchair, sure, but would that have been so horrible a fate? For the first time in a long time, I feel regret creeping into my mind, "I wanted to be..." was this it? The real reason?

"Beautiful." I shivered a bit as I said it. I burned for beauty and vanity, that was my sin. I thought I did it for more than just that. It had all been so convenient at the time, so wonderful when I first got my pretty face. Jenny liked me, Beth tolerated me, I wasn't the school freak.

"That is all?" Father Thomas asks.

My heart sinks as he says it because maybe it was. I stomp my hoof on the ground, no! I did it for more than that! I know I did! "That's all?" I mock, "Yes! Fine!" I shout, accepting it myself, "But you don't understand, no one did! The smart girl in class, the one who's bullied all the time, the one pushed around, who tries to get everyone's approval? That was me! Worse yet my life was getting worse by the day!" I'm shaking, my rage burning away any sorrow I had as I recalled how I was treated by my old 'friends.'

Father Thomas clears his throat, "You and I walked different paths when offered the same obstacle."

Now I swear he's trying to piss me off! "Oh please!" I shout, "At least you had your physical body intact!"

Father Thomas slowly gets to his feet, "Well... perhaps. But a gay child?" he narrows his eyes on me, "Well, no self-respecting southern family wants a gay son. I was out on my own at the young age of thirteen." He explains, dusting himself off, "That's when the Church took me in, and I found God." He wipes some ash from his face, "What did you do when you were thirteen?"

My heart sinks as I reminisced, "I was the smartest girl in my class. Braces? Fine. I get it. Posture brace? Fine. Helped me carry my friends' books. Friends I wanted to impress, wanted to like me." I scoff at the thought of Jenny trying to get into my pants, "But then the day my legs stopped working, my arms had issues carrying the books for my fair-weather friends," I spit at the ground thinking of how they left me on the sidewalk all those years ago, "they all left when they heard." I give a little sing-song voice, "Amyotrophic Lateral Sclerosis. A wheelchair at best, and completely paralyzed, but death by age twenty most likely." I remembered that death was something I feared too, it wasn't just beauty I sold my soul for, I was also staving off the grim reaper!

"So not just beauty, but your health?" He asks.

I roll my eyes, nothing is good enough for this bastard! "But as my dear mother put it, 'It's all God's plan', well God's plan sucked Father!" I shout. "You'll have your mind,' a fat lot of good that would do."

"I suppose you'd not be pleased to know a man with a similar diagnosis lived to seventy-six." Father Thomas informed me.

"I'm sure he walked everywhere, huh?" I taunt, tapping the dirt. So, death wasn't a risk after all. Well, this day is getting worse and worse. "Thanks, but no thanks."

"Yes, suffering in a chair would be much more preferable to, well, this." Father Thomas motions around us. "The price paid for dealing with demons."

Who am I kidding? I could have dealt with a wheelchair, I'd deal with it all day compared to my time in the pit. I tap my hoof nervously on the ground. Regardless I narrow my eyes and fix them on Father Thomas, "I'll show you the cost, Father." I grabbed him by the neck and carried him to the edge of the cliff, my gauntlet's claws digging into his skin as I dragged him over the edge.  Rather than drop him off, I plop him down near the edge.

Father Thomas's eyes go wide as he looks over the horrors below, all the molten pits and the creatures ripping damned souls apart and either feasting on them or hurling them into the molten lava.

"That's the Blade of Pride." I explain as I look out at it in the distance, "You can guess who lives up there above all of us."

"God in heaven..." Father Thomas whispers.

"God isn't here, obviously." I taunt.  I look back at the Blade of Pride, "It's made of souls too.  Everything here is.  If they don't break you, you suffer, if you fall apart, your mind breaks, you become an inanimate object down here. Sometimes you're made into something useful." I drag my finger across my armor-clad thigh, looking at the eyes inside the jewels as they roll back in pleasure.  I felt the armor squeeze me ever so slightly as if to return the favor. "Sometimes, you become a brick." I look out at the Blade of Pride, wondering what it would be like to just sit and stare thoughtlessly.  "I sometimes envy the bricks."

In the distance, I'm pretty sure I can see Zelletia, the black dragon that Asmodai always rides in on.  I can feel the pit of my stomach start to drop.  I was so very concerned with taunting Father Thomas, I kind of forgot that I had failed my mission, and now I was here, about to be punished for said failure.  "Are you seeing that giant black dragon coming at us or is it me being paranoid?" I ask Father Thomas.

"I see it," he says simply.

I turn from the cliff's edge, staring at the far wall of the cavern. I let go of my whip, a sinking feeling crossed my entire body. Terror grips me hard as I fear what Asmodai will do to me. "Father?" I ask meekly.

Father Thomas looks to me, blinking ash from his eyes.

I feel the tears I've been holding back start to surface, they drip out of my eyes and burn away as they touch my cheeks, "Do me a favor, okay? When you get out of here, please tell my son, Jason, I'm proud of him, okay?"

Father Thomas nods.

Zelletia roars in the distance, sending shivers up and down my spine all the way to the tip of my tail.

"Kick Ubiel out of my grandson too. He's a fucking pedophile but one of my Master's most loyal soldiers. He hates water, the stupid fuck drowned in a public pool after some mother tasered him for groping her kid. Not shitting you." I chuckle through my tears.

"I will, Sara." Father Thomas says.

I look at him, half in shock, "That's the first time I heard you use my name."

Father Thomas is silent for a moment, "This is the first time you behaved like a human being."

My humanity, I honestly thought I had lost so long ago, did I still have it? A small glimmer of who I was before I became a succubus? I turn to face the cliff's edge and I see Zelletia nearing the cliff, her size really being showcased, "He loves these grand entrances."

Father Thomas is shaking like a leaf as he looks out into the distance at the giant black dragon, "What is that thing?"

I'm shaking too, I can't lie.  "My Master, or at least, his mount." I try to steady myself, hugging my shoulders, "Please let it only be his mount," I whimper.

Zelletia flies over us, causing us both to move back from the cliff's edge as dust and ash are kicked up into the air.  I smell Zelletia's foul breath and the scent of her general 'decay' as she lands.  Her huge head lowers next to me, "Welcome back, harlot."

"Always a pleasure Zelletia," I start, waving my hand before my nose, "You stinky bitch."  I pinch my nose shut mocking her, "Here to pick me up?" I asked, hopefuly.

Zelletia grins wickedly, her rows of dagger-like teeth showing, "Oh no, I'm dropping off."

I feel the ground shake and hear the clattering of armor sliding against itself.  My heart sinks as I see my Master Asmodai walking toward me, dismounting Zelletia.

He's in his full armor, his shoulder guards with the bull and ram head-on, he's even wearing a dark helm.  There's a bronze crown attached to the top and I cannot see his face or eyes behind the black shadows cast by it.

My knees grow weak as Asmodai grows near, I can feel my tail shake and I coil it around my leg to calm myself.  I am horrified he has come in his full regalia, even carrying all six of his swords at his side, as if he were going to war.

Asmodai looks directly at me, and his voice is loud and shakes me to my core as he addresses me, "**Sara**," I can hear his disappointment, "**You have failed me**."

I can do nothing but fall to one knee, bowing my head, my wings shivering, "Master... Forgive me."

"**Forgive**?" His voice is deep, loud, and shakes the air violently.

I can only shiver in fear more, I've never heard him this angry. He is furious.

"**You dare ask your Master forgiveness for your failures... Wench**?" Asmodai says coldly, loudly, the power of his voice rattles through my body.

I whimper meekly in response to this, mostly because I hate the word 'wench', and it hurts, even more, when it comes from Asmodai. I feel like he means it too. I've let him down, I failed him. I feel a pang in my chest, a lump in my throat as if I'm dying all over again. "Please Master Asmodai..." I stutter.

I can hear him removing his helm, and I look up to see his green and black eyes, the green is swirling in a maelstrom of anger.

He speaks again, his voice shaking my heart as he does. "Oh dear, sweet Sara. You are so young, still so very human." His gauntlet-clad hand moves under my chin, tilting my head up.

I follow his instruction, his hand guiding my chin up further as I rise up to stand on my hooves.

"It is why I favor you. For in you, somehow, you still have hope to break," Asmodai said softly.

I'm on the tips of my hooves, shaking like a leaf when suddenly Asmodai draws me in close for a kiss. My shaking turns to a tremble as I press against him, our armor unyielding against each other. I shut my eyes and feel the raw power of my Master pulsing through my body. His armor-clad hand caressed my own armor-clad thigh and I let a moan escape my lips as he held me tight. My passions surge through me and for a moment I consider that everything might work out. Maybe Asmodai is going to let me off easy? Maybe he arranged something with Lucifer.

Asmodai breaks the passionate kiss, "I knew you would fail." His voice is calmer now, but still powerful, shaking me to my core. "I hoped Immunda would have summoned anyone but you. You are nothing more than my sex toy. Something for me to fuck when I am weary of rending flesh."

I shiver as he speaks to me this way, so crass and cruel. As we're in mixed company, I take most of it as him being facetious.

"I had hoped the hapless summoner would have called Ubiel, or even Kaskus, that woeful simpleton would have opened the gate faster than you." He sighs heavily. "But alas, the fool reached too high, he was not powerful enough to draw me, so he only drew you, the one who leeches off my grandeur."

I lay my head against his right hand, nuzzling it sweetly, "I am so sorry Master," I smile, kissing at the palm of his gauntlet, "I'll make it up to you, I promise to please you in every way."

Asmodai doesn't seem to react to my sweet caresses, "Yet I had desired that maybe, in the least, you would put yourself to the task. But nay." He moved his hands to my horns, grabbing them firmly in each hand, "You tarried.

In a moment that went from calm and serene to nightmarish, Asmodai snapped both of my horns with a flick of his wrists.

The pain seared through me, the likes of which I've never felt. It was as if someone jabbed two knives into the top of my skull. Blood rushed down my face and I screamed. I screamed uncontrollably. I reached up to the rough and bloodied stumps trying to stem the bleeding but I accomplished nothing.

"That," Asmodai's voice rumbles through the air, loud again, quaking through my body, "Was for asking me forgiveness." His voice is cold, measured, but still powerful and horrific.

It's at this point I notice one of his hands moved to my shoulders, the right hand twisting my arm more and more. A very gradual, but relentless pressure. "No! No no, Master, Please!" I beg, blinking blood from my eyes. I can't keep one opened, the blood stinging it too harshly.

The next moment, my arm is twisted to its limit and dislocated from my shoulder. I scream again, my free hand clawing desperately at Asmodai's gauntlet, "Master Please! Mercy! I beg your Mercy!" The words come out of desperation, without any thought.

Asmodai only grows more furious with me, "**Mercy**?" His voice makes the ground shake and I can feel the force of it in my bones. **"You dare ask me, Asmodai, Lord of Wrath, Mercy?"**

Before I even know what's happened, my arm is ripped from my shoulder. I scream as I watch it sail through the air, armor and all, landing uselessly on the ground. My free hand reaches to my now bleeding stump.

Asmodai releases my other shoulder, letting me fall to the ground.

Blood rushes from my shoulder, I can feel the blood drying on my face, tears steam off my cheeks, "No more! No more!" I scream, hoping that mere begging will suffice now. This is worse than the first time he brutalized me. Suddenly I feel his hand on my left-wing. "No no no!" I scream.

"**This...**" he starts again, anger pouring from his body like heat from a fire, **"is for your idleness**." He whispers in my ear, "**Reflect on this pain.**" His voice is still booming, ringing my ears as suddenly I feel my left-wing, torn from my back.

I fall forward, screaming, dragging myself away from him, hoping to somehow escape. My mind is in a panicked state, I should be trying to accept my punishment, I should be apologizing, but there's so much pain my mind is barely functioning. I look up, seeing Father Thomas on his ass, his face in shock and horror at seeing my dismembered body. I whimper, "Father, save me!" This was right about where I made my biggest mistake.

I can feel Asmodai walking behind me, he grabs both of my hooves right above the hock and drags me towards him. I'm hanging upside-down, suspended by his grip alone. He then stretches his arms apart, forcing my legs far apart in the air. I feel the pressure mounting in my hips, he keeps pulling, slowly, but forcefully.

Oh my God, he's going to rip me in half. My heart sinks, he has never been this rough, this violent in his torture of me. A slam here, a stab there, sure, but not like this, not ripping me to pieces. I wonder if he has any feelings for me at all now, that my failure has broken what small reprieve I had in Hell. "No, Master, No!" I scream, hoping for some reprieve in the torture.

"This... is for your failure." He growls as he pulls harder.

I can feel my joints cracking and popping all through my legs and hips. My muscles scream as they're stretched beyond what I could possibly imagine. I try to beat at his hand with my left hand, but soon I focus on the pain in my hips, gripping at it uselessly with my hand, feeling my legs scream in pain as the pressure mounts more and more. I can feel my armor beginning to stretch and break. I scream as the pressure keeps increasing.

Asmodai looks to Father Thomas now, "Place your bets Papist, how will she breach? Left or right?"

My heart skips like it's been ripped from my throat. He's using my torture to torment Father Thomas as if I was a prop. As if I meant nothing. Tears stream down my face as the pressure becomes unbearable. Suddenly I feel something slip in my hips, the pain sharpens.

"Make a wish," Asmodai says wickedly.

The pain spikes through me, worse than anything else I have ever felt, and I scream as my left leg is finally torn from my hips. I scream louder than I ever have before, so loud I feel my vocal cords break, I feel my throat start to bleed. I screamed so hard, so powerfully, that my throat feels like I have something stuck in it like I swallowed something long and stringy, but it's stuck. I'm choking on my own destroyed throat. I'm dangling from my right leg, shivering, shaking, screaming in pain, now silently. Mostly silent, anyway, I'm making some sort of horrific gurgling noise from what's left of my throat.

Asmodai then drops me, landing me on the ground, head first, my neck snaps.

I lay there, writhing and twitching in pain as best I can. Choking on blood from my throat, half-blind by blood from my head, gaping screams like a fish out of water. I wish I could pass out, I wish I could die all over again, but I'm already dead. Is this my punishment?  To be ripped apart by the man who I honestly love?

Asmodai draws a sword from his belt.

He's not finished.  I whimper.  Feeling the horror come anew, the pain not yet ending.

"Enough!" Father Thomas shouts.

I look to him, as best I can, I try to say "Thank you" but all that escapes my mouth is gurgling whimpers.

Asmodai then stabs his sword into my heart.

I look up at him, screaming, my eyes begging him for release.

"Wait for me here, Whore.  While I converse with our uninvited transient." Asmodai walks off, leaving me there as if I were nothing but garbage.

I whimper, ache and sob as I hear the worst words from Asmodai's mouth I ever heard in my afterlife:  "My Master will undertake a far worse fate for her, Papist, I assure you."

# CHAPTER 17

## *Old Wounds*

---

**"Hell holds many sinners, some of various degrees of sin."**

---

Asmodai and Father Thomas are now far away.

The pain is blinding, all I can do is suffer through it. While my neck heals, my arm, wing, leg, and horns don't. I can't drag myself to them to reattach them, because the sword Asmodai stabbed into my chest has pinned me to the ground.

Asmodai flies off with Father Thomas. I close my eyes tightly, trying to ignore the pain unsuccessfully.

After what feels like hours, suddenly, I feel my leg shoved back into my hips. I scream, my throat now having healed.

"...My love," Asmodai says weakly, softly.

The blade is pulled from my chest as he pushes my arm back into place.

I cry out in pain again, looking to see Asmodai, his face fallen, as he carries my wing over to me. Not knowing quite how to put it back, he shoves the end into the stump on my back. I scream again as I feel my bones and muscles slowly heal.

Finally, my horns are placed back on my head, painfully, as blood clots are forced into the tender flesh at the center of my horns.

I'm still shaking as Asmodai picks me up in his arms.

"...It wasn't enough. I'm sorry," Asmodai whispers.

I feel tears stream down my face, "I-I'm sorry Master... I-I'll never..."

Asmodai shakes his head, "I'm not angry with you, love."

I wrap my arms around his neck and pull myself tight against him. I sob into his shoulder.

Asmodai is silent for a moment or two before I feel his voice through him and into me, "We need to go to the Blade of Pride. Lord Lucifer wishes to see you."

I sob more, "L-Lets go to the void!" I shout, "Please... Asmodai... let's hide there... together... you and me, forever, please?"

"I wouldn't mind spending eternity alone with you, but..." Asmodai shakes his head, "Lord Lucifer would tear into the void to find us. There's no running from him." He sighs as he walks towards the cliff, carrying me in his arms.

"Can't we delay?" I ask.

Asmodai sighs, "If it didn't work for you, it will not work for me."

With that Asmodai takes to the air and heads towards the Blade of Pride, carrying me in his arms all the while.

Asmodai lands on the massive balcony and lets me down from his arms.

I look around, and notice Belial standing near the entryway, "What are you doing here?"

Belial grins, "You watched me suffer, wench." His eyes light up with joy, "I'm merely returning the favor."

From inside the massive throne room, Lucifer slowly walks out, his arms behind his back as he appraises the three of us standing there.

I fell to my knees, "Lord Lucifer... I'm sorry I failed."

I hear Belial and Asmodai drop to their knees behind me.

Lucifer's voice ripples through me, "Sara." He starts, "You know I had plans for today. Did you know that, literally as you reached the seal, my daughter launched an attack on Jerusalem?" He says, placing his hand on my still tender head.

I shiver, feeling him pressing more and more firmly as he speaks.

"All that shaking was my daughter hurling helicopters through the air as if they were mere toys," Lucifer takes a moment to consider this, "...I suppose they are, come to think of it."

I whimper.

"Of course, that brings me to you, my dear." Lucifer pushes slightly harder on my head, "You robbed me of a chance to unite with her!  It would have been perfect, my kingdom rising before her and I, stepping down from the Blade of Pride to take my daughter under my wing, and prepare her new kingdom for her." He sighs, "Father's would give the world to their daughters, After all, and I planned on giving God's little blue marble to her." He removes his hand, "But... seems you failed to deliver on this lovely reunion."

Tears drip down my cheeks, burning into steam as they hit the air, "I'm so sorry Lord Lucifer."

"I know." He says, removing his hand from my head. "You know, for a moment I truly believed that perhaps you'd prove my prejudice wrong.  That maybe the Succubi were useful and could perform tasks requested of them." He growls, "of course, you merely confirmed my suspicions.  You are, when the chips are down, an utter failure." He takes a deep breath. "You were not up to the task."

"My Lord, she did not choose to be summoned," Asmodai spoke up in my defense.

**"Did I speak to you, Asmodai?"** Lucifer shouts, the Blade shaking as he did so.

"No, my Lord." Asmodai lowered his head.

"Now then..." Lucifer begins, "How to do this. You have failed me, After all." He snaps his fingers, a chair rising next to me, "Sit."

"Y-yes my Lord..." I say, rising and sitting in the chair, "I-I'm so sorry to have failed you, my Lord."

"Enough!" He growls, snapping his fingers again, a pair of restraints snapping over my wrists and shins, binding me to the chair. "You won't be hung from the ceiling as I had done with Belial, that is a traitor's punishment and though a traitor may betray my trust at least he can be counted on to do so. You? You're lower than that." He explains. "I will not poison you with the Puriel Blade either, physical pain is something you've already experienced. While draining... it is not adequate to deal with the likes of you." He turns away, but glances back at me, "No I think, despite you robbing me of a reunion, I'll be kind enough to grant you your own." He walks off into his throne room.

I turned to Asmodai, "Master, what is he going to do to me? Please tell me, I'm terrified."

Asmodai looked briefly at Belial, then back to me, "I don't know Sara."

"I do wonder," Belial began, "The hanging curse was..." Belial shudders, "well, I am curious what's worse than that."

A horrible scraping noise echoes across the balcony.

I look up to see Lucifer dragging a high-backed chair towards me. The chair legs scraping loudly against the floor, clearly making noise as awful as possible. After what feels like an eternity of horrific noises assaulting my ears, he stops, dropping the chair to stand upright.

I cannot see who's sitting in the chair, not yet, as Lucifer stands next to it.

Lucifer smiles at me, and a chill runs down my spine. It's a wicked, vicious, and predatory grin. "Sara, you robbed me of my reunion, but allow me to be the bigger man, and give you a proper reunion with your father. The one you robbed from me and my own daughter." With a flourish, he turns the chair around with one hand, bowing down low so his head is level with the man in the chair.

My eyes go wide and my stomach drops through the floor as I see my father strapped to the chair. His face is disheveled and his eyes glassy. He's barely there, swaying back and forth, bound to the chair in the same manner I am, "No!" I scream, struggling at my bonds, trying to free myself.

"Say hello to your dear father, Hank Baker," Lucifer introduced tauntingly.

I shake my head, closing my eyes tight, "No no, this can't be! He can't be here! He's not!"

My father's eyes slowly clear as he sees me, "...Sara?"

"That can't be him! He never," I heave, as I realize only now I'm sobbing, "he never did anything wrong!"

Lucifer smiles at me, "Didn't he now? Oh..." He trails off, his hand resting on my father's shoulder as he stands up, "Hank... confess."

My father gasps, his mouth moving seemingly without his consent, "I lusted after my daughter. I assaulted the men she dated.  I usually threatened them if they touched her, I would tell them I'd kill them.  I beat one kid so badly that he... he died in the hospital." He groaned, "I... On the night I died I was going to...." He whimpers, "please... d-don't... make me..."

"Confess..." Lucifer hisses.

My father has tears dripping from his eyes, "I... I was going to find her... pull her from her boyfriend, and on the way home I was planning on... on forcing myself on her."

"What do we call that, Hank?" Lucifer asks, grinning at me.

"Rape.  I was going to rape her..." my father whimpered. "I-I'm S—" Lucifer's grip tightened on my father's shoulder, his fingers digging into his flesh, causing him to scream in pain.

I shake my head still, listening but not seeing, "No!  No, that's not possible!"

Lucifer spoke now, removing his hand from my father's shoulder, "It was your beauty, Sara, which seduced him. Belial's gifts were not physical alone, you were a fledgling succubus, lacking some powers, yes.  But you still had some of them, like your ability to instill lust in any man you met. Even..." Lucifer paused for effect, "Your dear father."

My father now speaks, groaning as his wounded shoulder heals, "That's not my Sara!  My daughter isn't one of your whores!"

Belial laughs behind me.

Lucifer glares at Belial and then looks to my father, then to me. "Let's clear the air then, Hank." He smiles at me, "Sara, would you do the honors?  Please clue dear ol' dad in as to how you wound up here."

I clammed up.  I couldn't tell my father how I ended up here, I couldn't possibly.

Lucifer's gaze then moved to Asmodai.

I heard Asmodai stand, and move next to me, he looked at me, our eyes meeting.  "Explain," Asmodai began, oddly unsure at first, but quickly recovering his stern voice, "Explain it to him.  Explain how you're..." he hesitated briefly, "A succubus."

My eyes watered as I faced my father, "I was thirteen..." I whimpered, "I sold my soul to someone who told me they were an Angel." I can feel a lump in my throat as I speak, my will overridden by Asmodai's command.  "H-He said if I cured a disease by the time I was twenty-one, he would let me keep my soul and make me beautiful.  But if I didn't he'd take my soul."

My father shook his head, "Lies!  You were always beautiful!  I should know..." he frowned, looking down, "I desired you..."

I frowned back, "No daddy... I was an ugly kid growing up. I got diagnosed with ALS when I was thirteen and I was afraid I'd end up in a wheelchair or worse."

"You never had ALS baby-girl..." My father said softly.

Belial interrupts, "Oh but she did Hank.  Until your daughter here, Sara Baker, sold me her soul.  Then, with the power of the pact at hand, I cured her and made her the ravishing creature you so desired."

My father looked at Belial, then to me, "...You sold your soul?"

I nod, tears turning to steam on my face, I could feel the salt fall from my cheeks.

"To Belial?" My father clarified.

I continued, "After that, I-I was pretty.  Once I got older, and discovered my sexuality, I... I had sex a lot.  As soon as I could, with almost any guy I wanted."

Lucifer chimes in now, "How much Sara, how many men in high school alone did you bed?"

I looked down in shame for the first time.  Explaining it to my father felt so horrible, "I... I can barely remember... at least fifty.  Probably more."

Lucifer chuckles, "What a busy little bee."

"Please let me stop," I beg.

"No." Lucifer's voice growls, I look up to see his violet eyes swirling intensely at me.

I frown, glaring back at him, continuing my story, "I went to college, and I kept having sex.  Probably more freely."

"Let's back up a moment," Lucifer smiles, "Did you stop when daddy rammed himself into a tree?"

I look to Asmodai, hoping for some reprieve.

Asmodai looked at me, "Tell..." he pauses, "Tell him."

"I did," I say, hoping for no further details.

"How long did you stop before you started fucking again?" Lucifer asks knowingly.

"A week..." I said, now glaring at Lucifer.

"Careful now my little inquisitor..." He narrows his eyes, "Things could get much worse than they already are."

"One week?" My father shouts, "You mourned me for a week before you started slinging it around town?"

I frown, looking away from him. "I used the sex to cope with his loss. I was addicted."

"To dick," I hear Belial taunt.

I turn my ire to Belial, glaring at him.

Belial just snickers at me, pointing to my father, "You're in the middle of a story, whore."

"Yes, dear Sara," Lucifer adds, "It's been so long since you've seen your dear father. You two have so much catching up to do."

I looked back to my father, who seemed to be more shocked than anything so far, "I met David, my husband, he was one of the men I was... screwing on a more regular basis."

Lucifer stopped me, "Why did you marry David?"

I looked down to my hooves, "He had money, he was a nice guy, and he had a promising career." I looked up at my father, "I did like him!"

My father glared daggers at me, "I loved your mother. That's why I married her. Money was never a consideration."

I frown, "You're a man, money was always a consideration for mom, she just never mentioned it."

"How dare you act like your mother is anything like you! You shallow, gold-digging whore!" My father shouts, "Your mother is a saint!"

Tears welled up in my eyes anew as my father's biting words cut deep into me.

For a moment my father seems ready to say something kinder before Lucifer grabs his shoulder again.

"Continue, Sara." He turns to my father, "Hank, listen to your daughter, she's pouring her heart out to you."

I tried to steady my nerves, "I got knocked up. David and I had a kind of shotgun wedding.  I stayed faithful to him, I did... while I was pregnant and through our marriage. Granted I kept him very occupied in the bedroom." I frown, "When I turned twenty-one, Belial took my soul that very night.  He made me drink myself to death and Jenny blamed herself because we were partying at the time."

My father doesn't seem to react much to this, his gaze moves to Belial.

"Belial turned me into a succubus after that... I got cast down here by some woman who burned me on holy ground. I took her with me but, I guess she didn't come down here." I finished.  "Satisfied?" I said flatly to Lucifer.  I felt emotionally drained.

"Almost," Lucifer says, smiling, "How many men have you sucked dry while you were on earth?"

I frowned, thinking of Terry, the Coffee Shop Guy, the Fishermen, and all the others I came across, "Fifteen." I confess.

"And exactly when was it you last killed a man by fucking him to death? How did you go about it?" Lucifer pried.

I frown, thinking of Saleem. "Just a couple of days ago. I took a rich businessman into a lavatory and drained him with sex. I knew he was going to Hell, so I taunted him."

Lucifer nods, "Yes, Saleem... Lovely of Sara to send Mammon a new soul to torture. What a fitting way for such a man to die."

My father narrows his eyes, "You can't be my daughter... This is just a new form of torture! You're just a succubus who's lying, faking it to look like my Sara! Taunting me by having her tits on display!"

I looked down at my cleavage, I was still clothed, mostly, just my usual girls partially on display. I guess my father was leering one way or the other. That made me sick to my stomach.

Asmodai looked at me, "Convince him that you are indeed his daughter."

I frowned, looking to my father, "Ask me something only I would know." I said defeated.

My father glared at me, "What was your favorite cereal as a kid?"

He had to pick the trick question no one would ever guess wrong if it was me. I speak, my voice cracking slightly, "I didn't like cereal as a kid, because you always said it was just sugary garbage and unhealthy. I didn't eat cereal, even after you died." I explained. I looked to my father, hoping that maybe he could find it in his heart to forgive me. I never intended for him to wind up here because of me.

I watch as my father's eyes tint green for a moment. Soon they grow glassy, "You... You are Sara..." he looks me up and down, now shouting, "You're... the reason I'm in here!" He tries to get out of the chair. "I cannot believe you! How Sara? How could you do this to me?!"

I tried to say something, but he silenced me as he yelled more.

"You destroyed me! Seduced me! I shouldn't be here!" He growled, "Your poor mother! Sara, she has neither of us with her! All alone thanks to you!"

My lip quivers as a knot forms in my throat.

"If it wasn't for you and your damned deal with that monster I would never have been enticed by you! By my own daughter..." His eyes meet mine now, and I see nothing but hatred behind them, "I don't have a daughter!"

It's like a knife sliced my heart in half and powered deeper into my mind. I feel the color drain out of me, I shake, and I try to speak something in my defense, but I can't. My voice won't come out.

For a second it seems my father has pity on his face, he opens his mouth to say something but, in an instant, he's engulfed in flames. He screams in agony and then vanishes before me.

The restraints are released and I rush to the burned spot on the balcony floor, "No! Father!" I scream, "Daddy no!"

Lucifer looks down at me, "Love hurts, always." He reaches down, tilting my chin up to meet his gaze, "He will suffer twice as much for your failure. While you sit in comfort in the Halls of Wrath. Understand?"

"Burn me!" I scream, hysterical, "Please!  Please make me suffer!  H-Have Asmodai tear me apart again and again!  Hang me from the ceiling!  Impale me on that horrible sword!  Feed me to the beasts!" I rant and rave.  "Anything just please…" I whimper, "Please don't punish him for my failure…"

Lucifer's gaze is cold, unmoved by my pleas.  "Sara… where is it you think you are?  You're in Hell, my dear, or have you forgotten?"

I feel something snap inside me, a despair I've never felt, and I collapse at his feet, sobbing and holding myself.  A pain so deep I cannot fathom it, as if my heart had a million holes drilled deep inside of it.  I try to hold myself together, fearful that I'll break apart.

I notice, at this point, someone has walked over to me.  I look up to see Belial right in front of my face.  He grabs my chin roughly and licks my cheek, his tongue sliding up and over my eye, catching under the lid.  "Delicious." He mocks as he literally tastes my tears.

I'm shaking and hysterical, I can't even process the fresh horror.

Lucifer then speaks to Asmodai, "Asmodai, you may carry her to the Halls of Wrath, that is all.  Do not discuss your own punishment with her."

"Yes, my Master," Asmodai says as he picks me up and takes to the air.

I wrap my arms around Asmodai's neck, sobbing uncontrollably.  All I can see in my mind is my father's flesh being burned off his body, replaced, and burned again.  His screams echo in my ears as I sob so hard my body shakes in Asmodai's arms.

When we finally land, Asmodai takes me inside and lays me on the bed.

I continue to wail in absolute despair, thinking of my mother missing both of us, wondering where we are. I imagine her sobbing at hearing we're both lost souls being tormented, and a new wave of despair wraps itself around my body. I coughed and choked as I lost total control over myself.

Asmodai pulls me close against him, kissing my cheek. "...The moment he shows weakness, the absolute second he turns his back and underestimates us..." he pulls away.

Through tears I see the swirls of anger in my Master's eyes, even if it's not enough to console me.

"I will kill Lucifer for what he has put you through," Asmodai promised.

# SERIES THREE

**Jason Miller**

# **Introduction**

I'm a detective for the Boston PD. I've been on the force for a long ass time. I was born in Boston, raised in Boston, both my parents are buried in Boston. Outside of that, there's not much to tell.

I've got a wife, a kid, a dog, and I think we have a cat somewhere. The wife won't stop feeding the stray outside, so yeah, we have a cat because it comes inside during the winter. Summertime, the fucking cat goes outside, because I actually hate cats. You let a stray inside, and it thinks it lives there. Somehow I have a dog that doesn't hate cats. I got the one dog in all of Boston that doesn't mind cats.

I had a day off. That's a poor way of saying it. There was some kind of union strike or something and they told us not to show up today. Whatever, I'm not standing in a Pickett line, I've got things to do. So I took the day to make all the calls my wife refuses to make. Husbands, you feel me right?

On the list is what I'm dreading.  The doctor's calls are fine, my son, Jason Jr.?  Yeah, he's been sick lately. Insomnia, vomiting, night terrors, and some days he just stares at the wall.  Currently, I am on the phone with doctor number three.

"Mr. Miller..." He starts.

"Detective." I correct, "I'm sure you don't like folks not calling you doctor."

The doctor sounds rather exasperated, "Detective Miller."

"Yes," I answered, allowing him to begin again.

"Your son is perfectly healthy," he explains.

I roll my eyes, "So, what, the vomiting is...?"

"The vomiting is self-induced," he explains.

"What, my kid has an eating disorder or something?" I shout.

"That's unlikely for a six-year-old.  He may just be seeking attention," the Doctor asserted.

I grumble to myself. Figures, I get the six-year-old drama queen.  "And the rest of his behavior?  The nightmares?  The insomnia?" I demanded.

The Doctor begins, "If your son is not eating properly and vomiting what he has eaten, then insomnia and night terrors can easily be part of his being malnourished.  I have prescribed some vitamins, and a mild -- I need to stress this -- mild sleep aid."

I sigh.  "So, what, I just have to talk to him?"

The Doctor was silent for a moment.  Then he asks, "Detective Miller, how often are you at work compared to home?"

I frown.  I get enough of this from the wife, I don't need it from a doctor.  "Depends how much the mortgage likes to get paid.  I hear it's every month," I quipped.

The Doctor lets out an exasperated sigh.  "Well, this is a situation where the child may simply want your attention.  He may merely want more time with you.  I suggest you make that time.  Some parents take their child to work with them when they can."

"I'm a detective.  Even deskwork isn't the greatest thing to show a six-year-old.  'Daddy, why is that lady with the fishnets and the black eye in the holding cell'?  Well, Junior, that's because she's a hooker and a John punched her in the face because he didn't want to pay," I mock.

The doctor whistles.  "I hope that's not a real thing but something tells me..."

"That was yesterday, Doc.  Welcome to the real world." I hung up.

I hate that I have to pull so much overtime just to make ends meet.  Makes me wish my grandfather hadn't lost all his cash in the '80s.

My grandfather *was* a multi-millionaire, maybe even a billionaire.  However, when 'Black Monday' rolled around, he was one of the suits who chucked himself out of a fucking window.  The dot com crash took care of any remaining inheritance I might have been privy to.

I close my eyes and lean back in my chair. When Junior comes home, I'm going to make sure to take plenty of time with him. I remember my father. Failing law firm, even with a Harvard education, trying to make ends meet and build up enough clients. Heart attack at fifty, dead a year later. All from stress, I knew that.

Bad enough that I know that on any given call, I might just get shot. I constantly remind myself not to dig myself an early grave. The overtime I take is all deskwork, and because of my wife, I've taken more deskwork than fieldwork in recent years. This hasn't helped my prospects lately as far as career advancement is concerned.

Granted, you can't ignore some of the crazier stuff.

Yesterday, there was a homicide--some guy was found dead in his own house. Though he wasn't just found dead, it looked like the poor bastard literally had the life sucked out of him. The coroner had no clue what to make of it. The guy looked like he was mummified and then someone threw a shirt and socks on him for shits and giggles. We live in a fucked up world, my friends.

The phone rings and it's my wife.

"Hey Marie, how's junior?"

"This isn't some sickness, Jason!" She shouts.

I roll my eyes. "The doc just told me it's because Junior needs attention."

"I'm calling a fucking priest! Do you understand me? This isn't normal! None of this is normal! He told some old woman at the doctor's office that her husband wasn't going to come out of the damn doctor's office!" She shouts.

I sigh. "That's mean of him but I-"

"Jason, he didn't! The doctor came out and from the look of it, she was just told the man was dead, understand? This is some fucked up shit--I'm calling the church!"

I rub my forehead. "Marie... listen, he's being a little prick, okay? You see an old lady in the waiting room and you want to piss her off, you tell her something like that if you don't know any better."

"He laughed." I can hear Marie on the verge of tears.

"What?"

"When the woman was crying... he was laughing. He kept saying 'he's gonna burn up real good' and kept laughing, Jason," Marie cried.

I frown. "Marie..."

"I don't care what you say, or what nonsense you can use to justify this behavior! Something evil has infected our son. If you won't call the church, I will!"

I grumble, "Marie... the church is the last place I want our six-year-old boy right now, okay? No offense, but have you seen the news?"

"Oh, fuck you, Jason!"

The line goes dead.

I was about to try and call her back when the doorbell rang.

First off, who rings a doorbell? I haven't had a UPS or FedEx guy ring my bell in forever. They just dump the package off in front of the door and walk off.  Regardless, I pop up and check the door peephole.

There's a woman standing there.

A woman is an understatement.

There is a drop-dead, gorgeous woman with the face a supermodel would probably kill for standing on my front porch.

I swear to God, if one of the guys at the precinct paid for a stripper or escort as a gag, heads are going to roll when I get back.

Then again, if this girl is only a stripper, she's wasting her talents.  She better thank God for those looks.

I open the door because I'm an idiot.

"May I help you?" I ask her.

She smiles.  It's a beautiful smile with perfect teeth.  Her green eyes light up as she beams at me, sliding a hand through her auburn hair. "Hi."

While I am enjoying the show, I have to ask, "And you are?

She laughs.  Her voice sounds sweet like honey and smokey like a campfire all at the same time.  I can't really describe it well right now because I'm kind of infatuated. "Are you Jason Miller?" She asks.

Someone comes to your door with your name in this day and age, they already know too much about you unless they're carrying a package.  This woman isn't delivering anything I can see, so I'm on guard.  "Detective Jason Miller." I clarified.  This usually stops most scam artists, salespeople, and anyone else who happens by uninvited.

Her eyes sparkle. "Detective?  Oh!" She smiles. "That's wonderful, Jason... Can I come in?  It's been a very long time after all."

I shake my head, having to stop her from walking past the door, "No... you can't come in.  Mostly because I don't know who the Hell you are and that is sort of an important prerequisite for coming into my house."

She frowns at me, her eyes still sparkling, "So... you wouldn't let me in, no matter what?"

I shake my head. "There are three reasons I can't, sweetheart." I stick my hand in her face, raising my index finger. "One? You're too fucking pretty.  So no matter what you're selling, I'll never hear the end of it from the Misses."

She blushes at this.

I pop up a second finger in her face.  "Two, I have no fucking clue who you are."

She frowns at this one.

A third finger goes up. "Three, see reason two.  Now, have a nice life."  With the message received, I slam the door in her face.  I also deadbolt the lock, just in case.

I check near the kitchen window to make sure she has left.  She takes her sweet time.  I think she stared at the door for about two minutes.  From the looks of her, you wouldn't think she's touched in the head, but something was definitely off about her.

I head upstairs to check in my office to see if there are any more phone calls I need to make.

I notice there's a message on the answering machine. Yes, I still have an answering machine. I like them compared to voicemail. I hit play.

"Hello, Mr. Miller? This is Mrs. Goodall, your son's English teacher? I need you and your wife to come by sometime so we can discuss Jason Jr's behavior. He has become increasingly disruptive in class over the last week or so. I know he's out today, but his behavior is unacceptable. Please call me back at 617-555-8573." The message ends.

I sigh and dial the number.

I hear the woman on the other end pick up. "Mrs. Goodall speaking."

"Hey, Mrs. Goodall, this is Detective Miller, Jason's dad?" I began.

"Oh, yes... uh... how are you?" She asks.

"Well, I could be better... you said Jason was acting out in class?" I questioned.

"Yes. That's one way to put it," Mrs. Goodall says. "Yesterday in class we had a chance to draw some... uh... doodles and such. Mostly just free drawing time, you know, for expressive purposes..."

"Yeah?" I continued.

"Your son... he drew one of his classmates, Jessica Sanders," Mrs. Goodall explained.

I frown, not liking her tone, "I mean, kids do that all the time right?"

"He drew her with... uncanny accuracy... naked," Mrs. Goodall said apprehensively.

I shift in my office chair nervously. "Naked?"

"Yes... in a very questionable position. I am not sure what to make of it. I've not seen a student draw something this... accurate... but it's disturbing, to say the least. When I asked him about it, he-he said... well, I don't feel comfortable repeating what he said."

How accurate can a crayon drawing be? I cleared my throat, "What did he say? I promise you he'll never say it again."

Mrs. Goodall takes a deep breath, "He said 'I bet Jessie's cunt smells much better than yours.'"

I was stunned, "He said... what?"

"When I asked him to repeat himself, he-he just looked down at the picture and started crying. He said he didn't remember drawing it or saying that to me," Mrs. Goodall stammered.

I leaned back in my chair. "Yeah, I bet... probably wants to stay out of trouble."

"Mr. Miller, I'm-"

"Detective," I corrected out of habit.

"...Detective Miller," she corrects, then continues, "I am not, by any means, a child psychologist, but I have been around many children throughout the years. I would honestly suggest that you consider taking him to a therapist of some sort."

I crack my knuckles in my free hand to calm my nerves. "You're right about something, Mrs. Goodall."

"Hmm?"

"You *aren't* a child psychologist." I hung up. This is getting out of hand. I need to talk to Junior when he gets home.

Just then, I hear something downstairs get knocked over.

I swear to God, if it's that damn cat, I'm going to kick it right out of the house and hope it runs away.

I walk downstairs and you won't believe it: it's the woman from before! She's rummaging through one of my closets. I haven't confronted her yet. I go upstairs to get my service pistol first. It doesn't seem like she heard me the first time I told her to get lost.

I get my piece, load a full clip, and with the safety on, head down to the main floor. The closet isn't being rummaged through anymore. I keep walking through the house, checking each room.

That's when I spotted her at the kitchen table with my family album in front of her.

I pointed the gun at her. "Don't fucking move."

She looks at me, unphased by the fact I have a loaded gun trained on her. She actually looks annoyed. "You don't have a single photograph of me, Jason," She admonished.

"I can't imagine why I would. You see, that's a *family* album. If you're looking for photos of yourself, most people just check their fucking Instagram.  So, get up, and get out, and maybe I won't call the cops on you."

She huffs, flipping through the book some more, "Somewhere in here you must have a photo of your father and me from college or our wedding day?  I rocked that wedding dress."

I pull the hammer back on the gun, "Lady, put the fucking photo album down, and get the fuck out of my house."

She turns to me again, looks at my gun, and rolls her eyes, turning back to the album.  "That won't work on me."

I am standing there with a loaded firearm and she's telling me it won't work on her--yeah, she's nuts.  "Okay, lady, why don't I just call the police, and maybe we can get this straightened out."  The police... who are on strike. Yeah... hopefully they'll swing by for a B&E if it's for a fellow officer.

She shakes her hair, beautiful hair swaying back and forth, "That's no way to speak to your mother, Jason."

I raise an eyebrow, "What?"

She beams at me, "Jason, I know it's been a long time, but it's me, your mother."

I'm shocked by her assertion because my mother died when I was three years old.

# CHAPTER 1

## *Reunion*

“**J**ason, I know it's been a long time, but it's me, your mother.”

Yeah, okay, the nut job just crossed a line. “Get out now, or I'm going to shoot you. Do you understand? I'm a cop-- I've seen cops shoot for less and get away with it. I've given you plenty of warning.”

She looks at me with a bemused smile. “Jason, honey, you can pull the trigger if you really want to, but I don't think it's a good idea.”

The safety goes off, “Oh, it's not a good idea? What's not a good idea is breaking into a cop's house, claiming to be his dead mother, who died thirty years ago, I might add, and then bluffing about not getting shot.”

"Twenty-eight." she corrects.

"What?" I ask.

"I died twenty-eight years ago."

I frown, not sure what to do, but at this point, I have given her plenty of warning.  My finger moves to the trigger.  "I'm going to do it if you don't get the Hell out of here."

She turns to face me and stands up.  "I'm telling you the truth." She suddenly looks serious.

"Get down on the ground!" I'm starting to panic a little. Normally you catch someone in the middle of a B&E,  they get nervous, or they freak out.  She has to have a piece on her. She's not talking like some lunatic, she's forming coherent sentences.

"I just want you to hear me out," she says. "It's me, Jason, it's mom."

I'm pissed now.  "My mother's in heaven, Bitch, but if you want to meet her, keep talking."

She frowned when I said that. "Oh... well... about that..."

I am not sure if it was the insinuation that my mother was in Hell or just the continued lack of following instructions, but I pulled the trigger.

She doesn't move.

Did I miss?

Instead, she picks an intact bullet off her chest, looking it over, "Wow.  Last time, they at least broke the skin."

Did I have rubber bullets in there by mistake?  I check the magazine, confused.  Nope,  those are my .40 cal rounds.

She takes the bullet and tucks it onto her thumb, flicking it at me.

It spins in the air and I catch it before it hits me. It's still hot, not terribly hot, but still pretty warm. I look at her in disbelief.

"Will you start to believe me now?" She asks.

"I'm gonna start to believe they're making fake tits a whole lot more sturdy." It's about the only rational thing my mind can make up. Is Silicon a non-newtonian fluid? I've seen shows on the Science Channel about that stuff, but I don't even see a bruise.

She glares at me. "These are real!" She then crosses her arms over her chest, pouting. "Is that any way to talk to your mother?"

"No, because you ain't her!" I shout, putting the Magazine back into my pistol.

She sighs. "Haven't we been over this?"

I unload the magazine this time.

She moves, or at least, something moves...

As I fire, I smell sulfur, not from the gunpowder. Some kind of black shadow moves around her in the blink of an eye.

I keep pulling the trigger until I'm out.

She hasn't moved. "I know you're scared... but I can prove it if you just get a photo of me... er... a photo of your mom."

I'm slightly freaked out now. "I just... that was a full clip... what-"

She opens up her hand and lets the spent bullets fall to the ground, from her palm. "Mortal weapons don't work, Jason. Now, if you'll go get a photograph of your mother, I can talk with you." She smiles, "I just want to catch up."

Rational explanations are all out. I need to figure something out, "Okay... uh... I'll be right back." I head up the stairs. I headed into my office and grabbed my cell, and I placed a call into the police dispatch.

"District B-3, Dispatch line, how can I help?" I hear a young woman ask.

"This is Detective Jason Miller - I've got a B&E on my hands, in my house. Female, about five-nine, green eyes, auburn hair, caucasian."

I hear rapid typing. "Have you attempted to subdue her, detective? I could send Unis to you in about twenty minutes."

I try to salvage some pride and still remain calm, "No. I haven't been able to subdue her."

There's silence on the other line, "Detective I can send Unis but, for a B&E, you can't handle one woman?"

I clear my throat, "She's very unstable and dangerous, okay?" I fib a bit. "I don't want to shoot someone in my house, okay?"

"10-4 on your 10-25. I'll have a couple of unis out to Charlie in 20. Hang tight."

"Thanks a lot," I say as I hang up.

Come to think of it, I don't have a whole lot of photos of my mother. My father didn't really have a ton of pictures.

One thing I do notice, as I look at my office desk, is my handcuffs. I grab them and slip them into my back pocket. I leave the gun on the desk. Apparently, it's useless.

When I get back down to the kitchen, she's sitting at the table, flipping through the photo album again.

She looks up at me, tilting the album up and smiling wide. "How old?"

The photo is of me, Marie, and junior at Dorney Park. Junior's posing with Snoopy.

"Last year," I say, walking closer to her. Maybe I can cuff her to the table? Jesus, how is Marie going to react to that? She should be home any minute.

She rolls her eyes at me. "I was talking about the boy here, how old is he?"

I narrow my eyes. "Listen, that's my kid, don't you dare try anything…"

She smiles. "I know… you've got that protectiveness from me. I was like that with you, you know?"

"Oh?" I am done. "So 'mom' I have a question for you, if you were so protective, why did you kill yourself?"

She frowns, "I didn't… I… well okay, I did drink that stuff but I was forced to, okay?" She sighs. "I know how to handle my liquor and I know my limit."

I was expecting her to go the route of, "I did it because I couldn't take it." or "I didn't kill myself". Officially, my mother didn't. But since I went into the force, I pulled her file out of curiosity.

If I was on the case initially, I'd have never labeled it a suicide. They treated it like an open and shut case, but there was some weird stuff. Like why she waited for Jenny to pass out before drinking three entire bottles of booze on her own. No note either, that was odd. Also, suicides on your birthday are an odd thing to come by. The strangest part is... I always thought something was up with it. But I also chalk that up to the victim being my mom.

But why did this woman have the cause of death down? If she was pretending as a scam, she would just say she didn't kill herself. That's what's filed.

I decided to try and humor her and take a seat next to her. "So, if you didn't kill yourself, what did happen?"

She looks away, "I'm... listen we... we could talk about me all day, I want to know about you." she looks at me, misty-eyed. "I've missed you."

I know she's full of shit now, "Oh, you miss me? Do you?" I laugh. "Listen, lady, I am not your kid. You have to be attached to something to miss it, and you only had me for three years before you croaked."

"Three years and four months." She corrects.

This is getting really fucking eerie, how she has the dates spot on. I have to throw in some misinformation, something that can prove to me that she's a fake.

What the Hell am I talking about? Of course, she's a fake, she has to be! She looks no older than twenty-one and my mother would be almost fifty by now.

Regardless, it's good enough to start throwing shit out there for stalling purposes. "So... you're saying that you're somehow my mother?  A waitress at Denny's named Daisy who picked up my dad one night?"

She narrows her eyes, "I will smack Dave upside the head if he ever said I was just some fucking waitress!  I was going to Harvard with him, dammit!  Did he say that to you?  That I was some waitress?  Who the fuck is Daisy?  My name is Sara, you damn well know that!  Oh... you better know that or I will sock Dave right in the balls."

What the actual fuck?  Mom was a Harvard student in the Molecular Biology Department.

This seriously cannot be fucking possible.  Also, how does she not know my Father is dead?

She continues, shaking her head.  "Listen if you're trying to probe me, I get it.  But I was in Harvard, with your father, I majored in Molecular Biology, my best friends were Jenny and Beth from South Side, and your Grandfather's name is Hank Baker."

I really wish she wasn't right about all of that.  Granted I didn't know of a Beth.

I knew a Jenny that was a friend of the family.  We called her Aunt Jenny.  She now works at a local suicide hot-line and does volunteer work at the church over the weekend. Sweet woman, honestly, she's like a Grandmother to Junior.

I'm a bit stunned, not sure what to do or how to react.

"Mind telling me why you became a cop?" She asks.

"I... uh... Well, I wanted to help people." I say, looking her over.  My father never talked about my mom outside of saying the typical 'oh she was beautiful' and about her academics. I don't remember seeing pictures of her.

She smiles at me, "That's so nice, so how did you decide on being a detective though?" She frowns. "You don't put yourself in danger much, do you? You have a family, you know."

She does sound like a mother, it's just that she cannot possibly be my mother.

There's another knock at the door.

She looks to the door curiously and as she does, I cuff her and slide the other cuff to the table leg.

She looks at me exasperated. "Really Jason?"

"Yes, Really. Those are probably the cops I called who can take you away to a nice padded room somewhere, you loony."

Her face falls as I leave the table.

I walk over to the door and open it, thinking I'm going to see a pair of officers.

Instead, standing at the door is a Priest and some Matrix reject standing next to him.

"Ah, yeah listen we already go to church so if–"

Before I finish the priest starts talking. He's got dark hair, brown eyes, and looks to be in his mid-fifties or so. "They told us that there may be a possible possession here?"

Marie called almost an hour ago, these guys move fast. I roll my eyes, "Oh Jesus Christ, fucking Marie--" I stop as I realize I'm cursing in front of a priest. "Sorry, Father. My son's been acting up, playing hooky and shit. She called the church and I have more pressing matters in the house. I have a few units on the way to button it up, we didn't mean to trouble you."

"Jason?" He asks.

"It's nothing the church has to worry about. Just caught this prowler out in the backyard. A mental health patient or homeless person, she's harmless," I lie, not wanting to admit a woman broke into my house, a detective's house, and is currently unable to be subdued. "I have her cuffed in the dining room. As I said, cops will be by to take care of her." I'm kind of done with uninvited visitors today.

"Mr. Miller, if I may, the possessed child is one reason we're here, but the woman is another."

Why will no one leave when I tell them to leave today? "Father, listen, now isn't a good time."

The priest fixes me with a stern look. "She claims to be your mother, yes? That she has been... away for some time and has wanted to see you?"

What the Hell is going on today? I look both of them over, "How the fuck..." maybe these two can take care of the issue, and I don't need a report saying I can't handle this on my own for the boys to laugh at all day long, "Listen, if she's yours then... ah, Take her I guess?" Please take her.

Both of them walk in, heading toward the woman handcuffed to my table.

She looks to the men coming in and frowns, "Not here... please? You know why I'm here. No one is getting hurt."

I frown, as the Matrix-reject sits next to her.

"And you know why I'm here," He states assertively.

I see the woman close her eyes on the verge of tears. "Just leave me be, okay? I have no desire to open the gate, I just want to be with my family."

I'm just hoping this fiasco can leave my house by the time my wife gets home so I can never tell her about any of this. I'm starting to feel bad for this woman though. Should I have played along with her game?

"So, eh, 'Sara', these nice folks from the Church said they know you. Maybe you can head back with them?"

She gives me a sweet look, drying her tears quickly, "Jason, honey, you haven't finished telling me about how you became a detective."

I glance at the priest, a bit exasperated, "See what I mean, Father? She's claiming to be my mother. Who died right after I was born, I might add."

The woman looks at me again. "What about your father? I'd like to see him. I'm sure he could also prove who I am to you."

This woman is pushing every one of my last nerves. "Yeah, sure, why not go visit him, he's out in Forest Hills."

I almost feel bad, her face looks like I just kicked her puppy across the room.

I'm a bit concerned now too because it really seems like she looks saddened by the news.

"Where is Forest Hills?" The dude in the trench coat asks.

The priest answers while I appraise the woman's reaction, "It's a cemetery."

Just then I hear the front door open.

Oh sweet God, it's Marie. My wife, she's home, and there are three insane strangers in my house, only one of them is reputable, and I do not think anyone can explain why there's a beautiful woman handcuffed in the kitchen.

I can hear Marie chastising Junior, "Junior, please, for the love of God…"

I head towards them, and by the looks of Marie's blonde hair and her tired grayish eyes, she's been having a wonderful day so far.

Junior gives me a weird grin, the kind of grin you expect some little psychopath to give you right after he snaps the neck of a bird or something. "Hello, Father."

What is it about kids and saying things slowly and with no emotion that just kind of creeps you out? I try to pick him up so I can take him into the next room, though he doesn't budge, "Junior, stop this bullshit, okay?"

"Lazy whore," is all Junior says.

Between this and what his teacher told me, all I can say is I've had it with his behavior. "Watch your mouth there, Junior, don't make me pop you one in front of the Father, okay?" I want to clarify that 'pop you one' is just a slap on the back of the head. I'd never sock my kid.

At this point, my world spins and I find myself staring up at the kitchen ceiling before my head cracks on the table and everything tunnels to black.

Next thing I know, I'm in the hospital.  I sit up, my head killing me.

I hear Marie sobbing, "Oh, Jason!" She hurls herself at me, hugging me tightly.  "You... You're okay!"

I rub my head, looking her over, "What happened? Where the fuck are we?"

She frowns. "The hospital,  Jason... Junior too."

I look around. "Where is Junior?"

She turns from me.  "When you were out, Junior was talking to that Priest, he was saying terrible things to him, and then threatened that if that woman didn't leave our house, he'd break all his fingers! Jason, Junior broke one of his fingers."  She then glares at me, "He kept calling her a whore and she was handcuffed to the table.  Jason, who was that woman?"

I rub the back of my head, feeling a pretty decent lump, "She was just some crazy person who claimed to be my mother."

Marie frowned.  "Yeah, okay.  Your mother would be in her sixties."

I don't bother correcting her, mostly because she'd just get angry, and a few years doesn't change the point, "Right. Wait, so where is Junior now?"

Marie helps me out of my hospital bed.

I get my shoes on and follow her to another room.

Junior is laying on a bed with some splints on his fingers. He's just staring at the ceiling, not moving, barely breathing.

Marie frowns. "He's been like that since we brought him here."

Junior then turns his head to face us suddenly.

Marie lets out a scream.

I jump from said scream. "Jesus Christ, Marie!" I look at her. "He's our son!"

"That's not our son!" She shouts, pointing at him.

Junior speaks slowly, "But Mother. I am your son. That is, inside. I'm inside your son. You should come inside too."

What the fuck is going on? "Let's just... go home, okay?"

Marie nods. "I would love nothing more than to go home. I called your work and told them you'd be out for the next week."

"Marie..." I am about to protest before she continues.

"Doctors orders."

"Always follow orders, father." I hear Junior say.

I frown, looking at him oddly.

"He had a knife," Junior smiles wickedly. "He had to shoot him."

My eyes go wide as my son looks me dead in the eyes.

"He had to shoot that Nigger."

Marie looks at me in shock. "What the Hell is he talking about Jason?"

Junior smiles wide, "It's not the first time he shot one... but this made the news... so you had to strike, right? Had to..."

I moved to Junior and grabbed him firmly by the shoulders, "Junior, you can't talk like that! Those are terrible things to say, who taught you to say those things?!"

Junior laughs in a really weird way. "Abaddon has a place for your sort. For the complacent, Daddy. For those who look the other way. He's waiting for you in Hell... with Grandma."

# CHAPTER 2

## *Night Terrors*

So my kid has gotten worse.  To the point where we had to pull him out of school.

A priest came by from the church to do what they called a "preliminary evaluation".  Our local priest swung by, announced this time and we went from there.

Father Walsh was the first one to visit.  Father Walsh was the local Catholic priest, or at least local to us.  Marie and I had gone to his church since before we were first married, and Father Walsh officiated our wedding.  Father Walsh is probably the happiest guy I know, and generally why when I joked about the whole child molestation thing, Marie hung up on me.

Father Walsh was smiling brightly.  The lines on his face were old and deep from years of smiling, it seemed.  He looked very happy to see us, as always.

"I thought that Father Thomas had come by here before...?" Father Walsh asked as we led him to Junior's bedroom.

Marie answered for him. "Father Thomas was attempting to help but apparently got side-tracked by some woman." Marie glared at me. "Managed to get him arrested. Then Father Thomas and that Timothy fellow went off after her and we haven't heard much since."

Father Walsh just nodded. "Well, I did discover Father Thomas was here on other business. I believe he's been called to the Vatican at the moment."

I frown. "How did that woman get the Father arrested?" I asked.

Marie scoffs. "Father Thomas was giving mouth to mouth to Junior because he had stopped breathing and when the police you called showed up, she claimed that he was molesting him."

I shook my head. "Well, we have Father Walsh now, so he can bless Junior, and then we can move on?" I ask hopefully.

Father Walsh sighed. "First, Detective Miller, we need to determine the health of the child. Now you did the physical examinations?"

"Three of them." I explain as we climb the stairs to Junior's room, "They all said he was healthy and just gave us some very mild sleep aids."

Marie sighs. "He's at least been sleeping a little bit better."

I get to the door and open it.

Junior is sitting on the bed, smiling, staring directly at us.

I look at Father Walsh, "He, uh, probably heard us coming."

Father Walsh turns to me. "Denial, Detective Miller, is unhealthy at this stage." He turns to Junior. "Good afternoon, my boy, I am Father Walsh." Father Walsh gets down on his haunches in front of Junior, smiling wide.

Junior just looks at Father Walsh, unblinking.

Father Walsh's smile fades as they stare at each other in silence.

Behind us, I hear our dog, Trooper, run down the hallway and hide under our bed.

Trooper is a German Shepard but you wouldn't know it by the way he acts. Friends with the damn stray cat and now currently cowering in our bedroom.

Marie holds my hand tighter as the tension between Junior and Father Walsh seems to grow.

Suddenly Junior just starts screaming. He doesn't blink, he just starts to scream at Father Walsh.

Father Walsh steps back and remains silent as he pulls out his rosary beads.

Marie covers her ears as Junior continues to scream.

I flinch a bit as his scream rises in pitch. His scream goes on for a solid minute, maybe two and he hasn't taken a single breath. His face is getting redder and redder as he keeps screaming.

"Enough!" Father Walsh shouts.

I've never heard Father Walsh shout in anger.

Junior's scream stops.  He just closes his mouth, still staring at Father Walsh.

Father Walsh flinches and drops his rosary beads.

As they hit the ground, the carpet smolders from the heat.

Father Walsh bends down slowly, picking up the beads and frowns, looking at the crucifix which is now glowing red. He turns to leave, saying nothing else.

As we follow Father Walsh, Marie and I close the door to Junior's room.

Marie has tears rolling down her cheeks. "Please!  What is it?"

Father Walsh is no longer happy-sounding nor is he smiling as he usually does.  "I will contact the Vatican right away.  I will reach out and see if there are any exorcists in the area.  I am going to expedite this.  Normally it takes a week or two." He looks to Junior's door.

As he does the cat, Mittens walks by his door.  Yes, Mittens.  I know.  Mittens hisses at the door and runs off to join our dog, Trooper.

A few minutes after Father Walsh left, Marie finally became slightly less hysterical.

"Did--did you hear him scream?" Marie asks.

"No, Marie, I didn't," I say sarcastically as I check my e-mails for any updates on this stupid police strike.

Marie shouts at me, "Damn it, Jason, I'm being serious!" She's glaring at me now, "You don't always have to be such an asshole, you know!"

I figure if Marie is mad, she's not going to be worrying about Junior. I'm worried sick but I can't show it. We can't both be beside ourselves. When Junior screamed, it was the most horrifying sound I'd ever heard in my life. It was barely human. "Yeah, well, we can't fight what we are."

Marie punches my arm. "Our son is being possessed! Don't you get that? There's--There's something evil here! In our house!" She shouts.

I look at her, looking her dead in the eyes.

I see her eyes are still tearing up, and she's shaking.

I hugged her tight to me. I kiss her forehead as she sobs. If Father Walsh is going to take a week to get an exorcist, I don't know how we're going to last.

Marie and I are holding each other for what seems like hours before my phone starts to ring.

Marie pulls back. "You should take that. I'm going to get dinner going."

I sigh and look at my phone. It's my Sargeant," I picked up, "Hey Sarge, what's up?"

His gruff voice comes over the phone. "Evidence C7. Where is it, Detective?"

I walk into my office, out of earshot from Marie. "I did what you told me to do, Sarge. I removed it from the logs."

Sergeant Trent Collins isn't too pleased with this response. "Physically, Miller, where is it now? Right now, where is it?"

Evidence C7 was a cell phone, locked in my desk, that was involved in a recent police shooting. The one there was a strike over.

The union felt that this was the last straw in a long line of "over the top" police inquiries where they were stopping us from doing our jobs.

One of our officers, during a traffic stop, was accosted by some guy. The officer said he had a knife, and kept threatening him. So he shot the guy. The guy was black.

I ran the paperwork and did the initial investigation. I'm not supposed to be the guy to do that, but my Sergeant was adamant about it. Evidence C7 was the black guy's cell phone. From my investigation, it was the object mistaken for a knife.

At the time, I got why the Sergeant wanted it under wraps. It was dark, phones were small and slim-- I could see how it could be mistaken for a knife.

But as I looked over the case more and more, I wondered why the Hell this idiot was walking towards a cop in the first place. Something didn't add up. But all I was told was to keep my head down and bury the evidence.

So I didn't log it. But I didn't destroy it, either. I locked it in my desk instead of the evidence locker.

"Should be in the rest of the case file's evidence," I lied. He clearly wanted the evidence so he could destroy it.

"I checked. It ain't there," he growled.

I sigh. "So you're saying you were looking for a dead guy's phone that can't be unlocked because it had biometrics and... well, the guy is dead."

"Watch it, Detective.  I don't have to say why it's important we get rid of that damn thing, you understand?" The Sarge then gets very testy, "You aren't going to the press, are you?"

"For fuck's sake Sarge!"  I shout, "It's in the evidence locker and if it ain't... maybe someone else got to it first."

He's silent for a moment, "You thinking Sanders?"

"It is his ass on the line,"  I reminded.  Officer Andy Sanders is the officer who pulled the trigger.  "I'd check with him."

The Sarge is quiet.  "I'll check with him in the morning."

"Yeah, you do that," I say, looking to the kitchen as I see Marie stirring in some pots and pans.

He hangs up on me.

I frown.  I need to get back into the office and move that thing before the Sarge gets wise to me hiding it.  I don't know why I'm sticking my neck out like this, I don't know either the officer or the victim, but something seems off about the whole thing.

That night, as we were sleeping, I had a new horror.

I wake up short of breath.  I open my eyes to see Junior sitting on my chest.

Junior places both his hands on my mouth and whispers into my ear, harshly, "If the bitch fails... I get to slit all your throats... I want her to fail." He sniffs next to my nose, "I wanna smell your fear... like now... it smells so delicious."

I try to push Junior off my chest but I can't move him at all.  His hands on my face feel like lead weights; the cold metal of his splints on his fingers aren't helping.

He suddenly starts to push my head down deeper into the pillow, my vision blurring as the pillow rises up around my ears, muffling what he's saying.

"My Master said I can't yet... but I want to... I want so badly... to tell your whore mother that I slaughtered you all." He grins sickly. "But he only talks about not killing you..."

I passed out.

I wake up to Marie screaming.

I bolt upright and run towards her yells.

As I get to her, I stop dead.  On our door is Mittens.

I don't mean at our door either.  I mean nailed to the door, crucified upside down, is the poor cat.

The cat's throat is slit, blood running down the door and staining the carpet.  There's a pentagram carved on its stomach.

Trooper is whimpering under our bed.

Marie runs downstairs.

I try to pull the thing off our door, not having much luck. I spend way too much time with pliers and my hammer pulling the cat off the damn door.  I also spent the next day cleaning up cat blood from the carpet.  Repainting the door was the next fun thing.

Marie and I started to put a door stopper on our bedroom door for the next few nights.  Trooper continued to sleep under our bed.

Marie and I slept in shifts, making sure Junior didn't get his hands on Trooper like he did Mittens.

Three days after Father Walsh had shown up, Marie was at her wit's end.

"I can't get a decent night's sleep, I don't know if Junior's going to kill us or the dog in our sleep..." Marie cried.

I frown. "Marie... he's not going to kill us.  He loves us."

"He loved the fucking cat too, Jason!"  She shouts, "For fuck's sake, he crucified the thing!  He nailed it to the door!  Our door!"

I didn't tell Marie about him straddling my chest the other night.  "Maybe I can call Father Walsh, see if there is something we can do."

"Maybe we can find our own exorcist?" Marie asks, "I mean... we're looking for one from the Catholic Church.  Maybe we can find someone else who can do it?"

I frown, "Marie..." my phone rings.  I curse under my breath.

It's the Sergeant again.

"What's up, Sarge?"

"Sanders doesn't know where C7 is, Detective," he accuses. "Where the Hell is it?"

I frown.  "I don't know then Sarge, if it's not in the evidence locker, and isn't logged, maybe it was just mishandled by someone?"

Sarge shouts, "I am in on this thing, you little shit!  If you got rid of it, tell me so I'm not chasing my own tail!"

I decide to see how far lying can get me, "Sarge, trust me, there is nothing you need to worry about, okay?  The evidence is gone."

The Sergeant is calmer now. "How gone are we talking?"

"As in there is no chance anyone is going to find the damn thing, okay?  The less you know, the better." I figure this might be my only way to placate him for now.

"You come into the precinct tomorrow, strike or not, and look me in the eye and tell me that C7 is gone, you got that?" The Sargeant demands. "Internal Affairs is going to take the case in two days - I don't want them finding *anything*, okay?"

"They aren't going to find shit," I clarify. This isn't a lie.  If they did take the evidence and the file, they wouldn't think to look in my desk.

"Good." Sarge hangs up.

I sigh and look at Marie. "Sorry, babe."

Marie frowns. "Doesn't sound like things are going over well at work..."

I shake my head.  "We're on this stupid strike because Sanders shot some guy and the media is demanding we produce a weapon and have the feds investigate.  The Mayor is on their side so the precinct is all on edge.  No one wants

Internal Affairs up in our business and any missed paperwork or fuck-up could get the whole precinct in hot water."

Marie is about to say something when there's a knock at the door.

Marie looks to the door, "Who could that be?"

I get up and head to the door. I check the peephole first, as has been pretty common, and I see the priest who had come by when that crazy woman had broken in. Father Thomas. Someone else is with him.

I open the door.

Another beautiful woman is at my doorstep. She's short, about five foot six. She has fire red hair, I mean out of a bottle red. Her hair is short but the front is cut like Jessica Rabbit from that old movie. Her hair is combed over the right side of her face, obscuring her right eye and cheek entirely. Her other eye, however, is red as well. Her lips are full, though she is clearly not wearing any make-up.

She's wearing a turtleneck shirt of some kind, completely covering her up to her chin, and over that, huge white robes. Even with the robes, I can tell she has an amazing hourglass figure. A simple brown rope is tied around her slim waist. The contrast between her waist and her bust is almost identical to that of her waist to her hips.

Adding to the white robes, she has on a pair of white gloves. In her gloved hands, she's holding a large and old-looking bible.

She smiles at me. "Hello, Jason Miller, my name is Lady Tasha Crestfall." Her voice is soft, gentle, and soothing.

Standing next to her is Father Thomas, wearing his vestments. He has a bag in his right hand. He fixes me with a stern gaze. "I am here to fulfill a promise I made to your mother."

I am about to ask a question before Father Thomas even finishes.

"I am here to exorcize the demon Ubiel from your son," Father Thomas stated matter-of-factly.

# CHAPTER 3

## *Expulsion*

"**W**ait, a promise to my Mother?" I ask, surprised.

Father Thomas walks in along with Lady Tasha. He looks around as Marie takes his coat.

Lady Tasha smiles as she looks around the house. "You have a lovely home."

I raise an eyebrow. "I've paid for about five doorknobs in the place so far, but thank you."

Lady Tasha smiled warmly at me. "You're a very funny person, Jason." She gave me an odd look. "He loves that in His children."

Marie frowned, "Excuse me, miss. My name is Marie-- his wife."

Lady Tasha vigorously shook her hand. "Wonderful to meet you, Mrs. Miller! Is it okay if I call you Marie?"

Marie is taken aback by the strange bubbly gesture. "Uhm, sure."

Lady Tasha keeps her eye on us as Father Thomas closes the door behind them. "How long have you two been married?"

I gaze fondly at Marie, smiling, "About eleven years, this May."

Marie smiles back at me, but then worriedly glances upstairs. "We had a heck of a time conceiving Jason Jr." She looks at Father Thomas and Lady Tasha. "Are you sure you can help us?"

Father Thomas pulls out a pair of black gloves and an iron-clad Bible, "As I said, I made a promise to your mother. I will cast Ubiel out of your son."

Lady Tasha's face is rather serious as she turns to us. "Is he your only son?"

Marie and I nod together.

Lady Tasha took a deep breath and turned to Father Thomas. "We should get started then."

Marie chimes in, "So is this like an old priest and a young priest thing?"

Lady Tasha smiles again, "Yes. I'll be sure to help Father Thomas with my experience."

I don't think I pegged Lady Tasha as the 'old priest' but it seems both aren't surprised. Tasha doesn't look older than thirty.

Father Thomas asks, "Where is the boy's room?"

"Follow us," I instructed as I walked towards the stairs with Marie.

I heard both of them following close behind me as we made our way up the stairs.

For the first time ever, Trooper happily ran out of the bedroom. His tail was wagging as he ran over to Lady Tasha and started sniffing her.

Lady Tasha smiled and pet Trooper, "What a sweet puppy."

I raised my eyebrow. "He usually barks. Or lately whimpers."

"I love dogs," Lady Tasha said as she happily scratched him behind the ears. As she bent over, I flinched a bit. Her hair fell forward from her face slightly and I could see a hideous scar running from her forehead down over her eye, ending at the top of her cheekbone. The scar seems to even pull her hairline downward.

I look away. No wonder she grows her hair over her right eye!

We get to Junior's door.

I knocked, "Junior, you have visitors." I open the door and he's sitting on his bed staring at us again.

Father Thomas walks in, fixing Junior with a stern gaze. "Hello, Ubiel."

Junior tilts his head to the right slowly, appraising him.

Lady Tasha walks in next.

Junior's head goes rigid and straight, trying to stare Lady Tasha down.

Tasha keeps eye contact with Junior while addressing Father Thomas. "You have restraints?"

Father Thomas nods. "Yes." He digs into a bag and pulls out a set of medical straps with padded cuffs and sturdy velcro.

Lady Tasha takes them, walking toward the bed slowly, keeping her eye on Junior.

I chime in trying to warn her, "He's stronger than he looks!"

"So is Lady Tasha." Father Thomas stated.

Lady Tasha grabs Junior's arm gently, sliding the cuff over his wrist and tightening the cuff firmly. She starts to fix the strap down to the leg of the bed closest to his hand.

Junior takes his free fist and slams it down on Lady Tasha's shoulder.

Unfazed by his strike, Lady Tasha secures the velcro, "That was very rude, young man." She slips another cuff onto his free hand. "The less you struggle, the easier this will be for everyone."

Junior spits in her face.

Once more unperturbed, not even bothering to clean it off, Lady Tasha secures the other strap to the opposite bed leg. She walks over to Father Thomas who has a small cloth towel ready in anticipation. "Thank you, Father."

"Always be prepared." Father Thomas says as Lady Tasha takes the towel. "Are you alright?"

Lady Tasha rotates her shoulder a bit, where Junior slammed her, "I'm fine. I hope those restraints hold."

Father Thomas nods, "They should."

Lady Tasha gets another pair and gets Junior's legs tied down.

Marie complains, "Why do we need to strap him down?"

Father Thomas answers as he helps Lady Tasha with the straps for his legs, "To keep him from further hurting himself. Like before when he broke his finger."

Marie frowns. "Just... Please don't hurt him."

Lady Tasha finishes securing him and fixes Marie with a warm smile. "Hurting young Jason is the last thing on our mind. Do not worry, we will pull the demon from him."

Can't say I'm not nervous either. "What if you can't?"

Father Thomas interjects, "Have Faith, Jason."

Lady Tasha nods. "Yes. Put your trust in God. We are." She smiles and then turns, suddenly looking sternly at Junior. "We will expel you and send you back to your masters. The process of Exorcism is painful for a demon. I am sure you are familiar with pain, being in Hell, but you can spare yourself some pain if you leave this boy's body now."

Junior opens his mouth and vomits on Lady Tasha.

Marie gags.

Lady Tasha's white robes are stained brown and red. She turns to Marie and I and simply asks, "Do you have any *larger* towels?"

Father Thomas walks over to Tasha and says, "And this is why I wear black vestments to an exorcism." He uses another towel to clean her up as best he can.

Tasha fixes Father Thomas with a stern gaze before a half-smile creeps across her face. "I'll remember that."

Junior is laughing hysterically. "The whore's covered in puke!"

"I am no whore, demon," Tasha says, sighing as the towel Father Thomas provided has reached its limit.

Marie comes back with more towels and I step back. "We should, um, probably let you get to it."

Father Thomas agrees with a nod. "Shut the door. Do not open it regardless of what you hear, understand?"

Tasha looks at me to explain. "The Demon will pretend to be your son, he may call to you, he will only do this in hopes that you interrupt the exorcism."

I nod. "Okay. We're trusting you. If anything happens to him, we're holding you responsible."

Tasha gives me a warm smile again. "Your son is in *excellent* hands."

Marie and I head downstairs, shutting the door. Trooper follows us.

I sit at the kitchen table.

Marie gives me a puzzled look. "What did he mean? That he was keeping a promise to your mother?"

I sigh. "The woman who came into the house, the one handcuffed to the kitchen table? She claimed to be my mom."

And then, without a word, Marie gets up and heads to our bedroom, rummaging around for a few minutes.

I sigh and start checking my Facebook and emails on my phone.

Marie comes back down, empty-handed. "I know we had something....oh! Hold on, let me call Jenny."

I sigh. "You don't need to bother Aunt Jenny."

Marie scoffs. "Yes, I do." She picks up the phone.

I lean back and study the ceiling. The lights suddenly flicker and I frown, hearing a deep growling noise from upstairs.

Father Thomas is shouting out some kind of prayer and I think I can hear Tasha doing the same.

I close my eyes, trying to ignore it as the lights flicker more and more.

Marie seems more focused on her phone call. "Yes, Jenny. Any old photos. Wait, Dave gave them all to you? Really? Wow, okay. Do you have them? Would you mind... oh great! Yes, we're... We're free... uh... well..." Marie sighs, "It is kind of important. We have company over at the moment but... Okay, thanks so much." Marie sighs, "I forgot that Jenny will invite herself over no matter what."

"Jenny's a lonely woman," I quipped.

There are the sounds of heavy crashing, thumping, and screaming upstairs, the lights flicker, and I look at Marie.

Marie sits next to me and hugs me tight.

I hug her tighter.

I see Father Thomas walking down the stairs, sweat on his brow.  Tasha followed closely behind him.

Hopeful, I stand up with Marie. "Is it done?"

Father Thomas frowns at me.  "Not yet."

Tasha adds, "Your son is strong."  She gives a sigh.  "But the demon is stronger."

Father Thomas walks to the kitchen and splashes some cold water on his face.  "We should reach out to Timothy--" He gives a sudden groan, clutching his side.

Tasha walks over to him, concerned. "Father, you're hurt..."

Father Thomas conceded with a nod, "Well, I was thrown against the wall..."

Tasha closes her eye and whispers, "Our father who art in heaven, Hallowed be thy name, Thy kingdom come, Thy will be done, As in the sky and on the ground. Give us this day our daily bread; And forgive us our debts; as we forgive our debtors; And do not lead us into temptation, but deliver us from evil."  She then takes a breath and continues, "Heal the wounds Your servant has received in your service, O' Father, and protect his spirit from fatigue and duress in these troubling times."  Her hand moves to Father Thomas's side. "Amen."

Father Thomas straightens up, rubbing his back, his pain suddenly gone.  "Thank you," he nods his thanks to her as he dries his face with a towel.

Tasha uses the towel next, adding some soap in an attempt to clean her robes.

Marie whimpers, "So, you're saying he's still not cured?"

Having gotten most of the stains out of her robes, Tasha murmured, "Father Thomas, I dislike black robes but I will agree with you that white robes are a drawback for this sort of work."

Father Thomas ignores her complaints to once more suggest, "I think we need to contact Timothy."

"Who's Timothy?" I ask.

Father Thomas explains, "He was the man who had come with me earlier when we were following your mother."

I try to ignore that even Father Thomas felt that woman was my mother!  "Okay, why and how could he help?"

"He's an Ang–" Father Thomas starts.

Tasha cuts him off.  "We don't need my little brother, Father Thomas."  She turns to beam at me.

I step back as I notice Tasha is staring at me oddly.  It's a very intrusive look like she's staring looking deep into my eyes, as if she's searching for something.

Father Thomas confronts Tasha, "But you said we needed someone to stop Ubiel from interrupting our efforts. Someone to guard us."

Tasha removes the staff from her back.  It's a simple whitewashed wood, with a pair of tarnished iron end caps. She pulls it out of its sling and smiles at me.  "Here, Jason. Catch!"

I grab the staff as she throws it at me.  "Okay."

Father Thomas stares at me in disbelief. "How is he holding it?" He asked, shocked.

Tasha smiles brightly. "Because he is the son of Sara Baker."

I frown, tightening my grip on the staff. "Why are you both talking about my mother that way?" I growled a bit, confused. "She died when I was only three."

Father Thomas frowns "I can explain later, Jason. But we're going to need your help."

Tasha continues beaming at me. "Most certainly! Follow me and I'll explain what you must do, okay?"

I look at Marie and she just nods. I follow Tasha as she goes up the steps, Father Thomas in tow.

"You need to look past the physical. It will be difficult for you now, but if you see any shadows moving toward Father Thomas or myself, you need to stop them from touching us," Tasha explains.

"How do I stop a shadow?" I ask.

Father Thomas interjects now, "With that staff." He is staring at it in awe. "That staff--"

"--is a very powerful holy relic," Tasha interrupts. She smiles at Father Thomas. "That's all he needs to know for now."

I consider the staff in my hands. It feels light but sturdy. Outside of the iron caps it seems indistinguishable from a normal white rod.

Tasha opens the door and my eyes grow wide at what I see.

My son is still tied down on the bed, vomit on his shirt. But the room is a mess. Papers fly around the room. A large dent is in one wall, presumably where Father Thomas was tossed. Worse and most disturbing--Junior's eyes are rolled up into the back of his head.

Tasha moves to the side of the bed while Father Thomas moves to the foot.

Father Thomas begins, "Ubiel, you have no right to this child. Leave now! By the authority of Jesus Christ, I compel you to leave this innocent child of God!"

The bed starts shaking.

Tasha places her hands on the bed and begins to pray the Lord's prayer from before, but unceasing, constantly saying the prayer in a loop. As she does this, the bed shakes more.

"In the Name of the Father, and of the Son, and of the Holy Ghost. Amen," Father Thomas begins.

Tasha then changes from the Lord's prayer to another: "Most glorious Messenger of the Heavenly Voices, Saint Gabriel the Archangel, defend this child in our battle against corruption of his spirit, against the rulers of this world of darkness, against the spirits of wickedness in the high places."

As Tasha begins her portion, I notice Father Thomas begins reciting the Lord's prayer again.

However, in the middle of Tasha's chanting, I see it. Rising off my son's chest, a shadow of some sort. It's faint, so faint if I wasn't looking for it I'd have missed it.

I move to the other side of the bed slowly, and just before it makes contact with Father Thomas, I jab at it with the staff.

To my surprise, I feel the staff connect with something.

The bed shudders, jumps, and shifts forward.

Junior's eyes roll forward from the back of his head and he glares at me. "Daddy... you're not playing fair." His voice then becomes guttural as he begins to chant himself.

Father Thomas is now speaking while Tasha continues to pray, "Come to the assistance of men whom God has created to His likeness and whom He has redeemed at a great price from the tyranny of the devil."

I notice a lamp is flying towards Father Thomas--I knock it out of the way and the lamp sails past Tasha's head, shattering on the far wall.

Entirely focused on her prayers, Tasha doesn't even look up.

All this time, Father Thomas has continued, "The Holy Church venerates you as her guardian and protector; to you, the Lord has entrusted the souls of the redeemed to be led into heaven. Pray therefore the God of Peace to crush Satan beneath our feet, that he may no longer retain men captive and do injury to the Church."

I see a shadow moving behind Father Thomas. I run towards it, smacking it down with the staff.

Junior starts to convulse on the bed.

I watch as Tasha gently places her hand on Junior's forehead, keeping his neck from violently whipping back and forth.

Still, Father Thomas continues: "Offer our prayers to the Most High, that without delay they may draw His mercy down upon us; take hold of 'the dragon, the old serpent, which is the devil and Satan,' bind him and cast him into the bottomless pit that he may no longer seduce the nations."

Suddenly something whips me backward. I hit the floor, and feel something choking me.

I hear Tasha start to chant, "In the Name of Jesus Christ, our God and Lord, strengthened by the intercession of Mary, Mother of God, of Blessed Gabriel the Archangel, of the Blessed Apostles Peter and Paul and all the Saints, and powerful in the holy authority of our ministry, we confidently undertake to repulse the attacks and deceits of the devil."

All this time I'm on the floor, choking. I pull the staff against my throat and I hear an inhuman scream from somewhere. I smell something burning.

"Okay, motherfucker." I get to my feet, "You might be from Hell, but this is how we do things in Boston!" I see the shadow on the wall and rush at it, swinging the staff like a baseball bat.

Another good hit! I watch as the shadow flies to the opposite wall and cracks through the sheetrock.

"God arises; His enemies are scattered and those who hate Him flee before Him. As smoke is driven away, so are they driven; as wax melts before the fire, so the wicked perish at the presence of God," Tasha continues. She checks on me as Father Thomas begins the next set of prayers. "How are you holding up there Jason?"

"I'm peachy!" I shout as I feel the shadow pull my feet out from under me. "Fuck!"

Tasha speaks right before she starts to pray again. "Okay, let us know if you need any help."

I grumble, hitting at my feet with the staff. "Oh, will do, ma'am!" I shout as I get back to my feet.

"Behold the Cross of the Lord, flee bands of enemies." Father Thomas shouts, thrusting his rosary beads over Junior.

I manage to spot the shadow heading towards Father Thomas again. "Oh, no, Asshole, I ain't done with you yet!" I swing the staff down and feel like I'm pinning something to the floor. I feel the shadow struggle underneath the staff. "Get the Hell outta my kid!"

Tasha speaks next. "The Lion of the tribe of Judah, the offspring of David, hath conquered."

Father Thomas starts to throw holy water on Junior. "May Thy mercy, Lord, descend upon us."

Tasha does the same. "As great as our hope in Thee."

I pin the shadow down with Tasha's staff, as I do I feel it writhe beneath me as it weakens. I can feel it tugging at my feet now, weaker than before.

Tasha continues, "We drive you from us, Ubeil, unclean spirit, all satanic powers, all infernal invaders, all wicked legions, assemblies, and sects." Using the holy water she draws a Cross on Junior's chest. "In the Name and by the power of Our Lord Jesus Christ, may you, Ubiel, be snatched away and driven from the Church of God and from the souls made to the image and likeness of God and redeemed by the Precious Blood of the Divine Lamb."

"O Lord, hear my prayer," Father Thomas shouts as he throws more holy water on Junior.

"And let my cry come unto Thee," Tasha continues.

The shadow manages to push me away, almost knocking the staff out of my hands.  As it does, the Shadow becomes a huge figure rising up before me and starts to solidify.  The thing is huge, filling the space between me and Father Thomas.

The shadow starts to look reddish, and I see a pair of horns manifest, as well as green glowing eyes.  I see a muzzle of some sort start to stretch out and dark black teeth filling its maw.

"You're one ugly motherfucker," I say as I thrust the staff at its throat.  The room shakes as the figure slams to the floor once more.

Father Thomas speaks next, "May the Lord be with thee."

"And with thy spirit!" Tasha shouts, her hand still on Junior's chest. "Let us pray!"

The shadow starts to fade off the floor, causing the lights to flicker.  Suddenly the wind picks up around the bed.  It's so intense, it makes it difficult to breathe.

Tasha and Father Thomas now chant in unison.  "God of heaven, God of Earth, God of Angels, God of Archangels, God of Patriarchs, God of Prophets, God of Apostles, God of Martyrs, God of Confessors, God of Virgins, God who has the power to give life after death and rest after work: because there is no other God than Thee and there can be no other, for Thou art the Creator of all things, visible and invisible, of Whose Reign there shall be no end, we humbly prostrate ourselves before Thy Glorious Majesty and we beseech Thee to deliver us by Thy Power from all the tyranny of the infernal spirits, from their snares, their lies, and their furious wickedness."

Holding the staff tightly, falling over the bed and grabbing Junior's restrained right hand. Trying to look at his eyes as they roll back and forth in his head. "Come on kiddo... Get that bastard out of yah!"

Father Thomas and Tasha continue their shared chant, "Deign, O Lord, to grant us Thy powerful protection and to keep us safe and sound. We beseech Thee through Jesus Christ Our Lord. Amen"

Tasha looks at Junior, running her hand over his forehead, "From the snares of the devil."

Father Thomas is next, "Deliver us, O Lord!" He throws holy water into the air over the bed, splashing Junior and me in the process.

"That Thy Church may serve Thee in peace and liberty," Tasha shouts over the roar of the wind.

"We beseech Thee," Father Thomas shouts, "hear us!"

Junior suddenly starts to convulse.

Tasha places her hand in Junior's mouth, I think to grab his tongue. "That Thou may crush down all enemies of Thy Church!"

"Begone, Ubiel, the predator of the meek and mild, the enemy of man's salvation!" Father Thomas shouts.

Junior soon opens his mouth wide, I can hear his jaw crack and snap out of place as it opens wider than should be humanly possible. The air no longer swirls around the bed, now the room is still. Rising out of his mouth comes a small solid black and red ball. The orb has steam coming off of it, as if it were a chunk of dry ice floating over Junior's gaping jaws.

Tasha quickly grabs the orb in her hand. As she does, I see her glove start to burn at where it comes in contact with the orb. "Most cunning serpent, you shall no more dare to deceive the human race, persecute the Church, torment God's elect, and sift them as wheat!" She looks at me and commands, "Strike it, Jason!"

I take the staff and pull it up over my head, "Tell Satan that God sent yah screaming outta Boston, you sorry son of a bitch!" I swing the staff down on the orb and I hear a bone-chilling roar. A white light flashes from the orb, and I'm tossed back across the room.

I'm thrown so hard I smash into the next room, Marie's and my bedroom, and I find myself in the bedroom closet. Sheetrock and old dresses Marie hasn't worn in years bury me as I try to get a handle on what the Hell just happened.

I struggle for a bit, my feet stuck in the wall, the rest of me stuck in the closet. I see Tasha cross into my vision.

"Nice swing!" She smiles at me, offering me her gloved hand. I notice her right hand is bare but doesn't appear burnt like her glove.

I take it, and grunt in surprise as she pulls me out and onto my feet, "I'll try out for the Sox next year," I groan.

I see Father Thomas slowly removing the restraints from Junior. "It's going to be alright, child. You're safe now. Drink this, hmm?" He hands Junior a small round bottle.

Junior drinks it, coughing, "My jaw hurts.."

I run over to him, "Hey Junior... you okay?"

Junior shakes his head. "I want a juice... an' I wanna watch Paw Patrol."  He gives me a look, "You have dust on you, daddy."

I hug him tight and kiss his forehead, not caring about the bits of sheetrock I have all over me.

Tasha opens the bedroom door, and on the other side, I see Marie.

Marie looks at Tasha, "Is... is he...?"

Tasha just beams at her. "He's clean now."

I'm staring at the broken wall while Trooper sniffs at it.

Marie walks up behind me, "Please tell me Junior didn't put you through that wall."

I turn to her, "I'm going to the Home Depot tomorrow to buy stuff to fix it."  I pick up the staff that's stuck in the closet, heading downstairs to where Tasha and Father Thomas are packing up their respective items.

Father Thomas finishes packing his ironclad Bible into his bag, "While the house and your son has been blessed," he says to us with a smile, "I would suggest you all start going to church.  Think of it as a vaccination against unholy spirits."

Tasha laughs, "You did your job of protecting us perfectly," she rolls her eye a bit, "though a bit crass."

I shrug, handing her the staff, "That's just me."

Tasha smiles as she takes the staff in her bare right hand, which I notice has sharp red nails. Very sharp-looking nails, almost like claws. I see her eye flash for a second and I swear I see a pair of reddish bat-wings and rose colored horns on her, but only for a second. I blink and everything is normal, however, she's not smiling.

I let go of that staff real quick.

Tasha starts to slide it onto her back, "Do you know the difference between a good man and a righteous man, Jason?"

I shake my head. Father Thomas is already heading out the door.

Tasha fixes me with an intense gaze, "A good man looks out for his family, for his fellow man, and does good in the community whenever he can," she explains gathering up her Bible, "but a righteous man? He does what is right, what must be done, even if it's a detriment to his own self-interests."

I frown, my heart rising up in my chest. She knows about the cell phone, somehow.

She heads to the door; I follow her.

Out the door, I see Father Thomas holding open a cab door for her.

Tasha turns to me right before she gets in, "You're most certainly a good man, Jason Miller." Then she beams again, "But if you're also a righteous man... I'll see you again soon."

I walk towards her as she gets into the cab, Father Thomas getting in from the other side. "Why would I be seeing you?"

Tasha just beams at me again. She brushes her hair off her face briefly, showing that hideous scar. "Because you are the son of Sara Baker." She closes the door, rolling the window down. "See you soon, Jason."

# CHAPTER 4

## *Corruption*

You'd think exorcizing a demon would be the most traumatic thing to happen to me this week.

Seems a guy can't even get a decent night's sleep.

I passed out after a long day of explaining that our cat, Mittens, ran away... yeah, don't judge me, you want me to tell the six-year-old boy that he was forced to nail his cat to a door by a demon?

Well, anyway, I didn't have the best night's sleep.

I heard a woman's voice and she sounded like she was crying.

"Haven't I had enough?  Please... stop...!" She begged.

I looked around, slowly opening my eyes to see a black void surrounding me.  "Hello?"

I heard chains rattle. From above, I saw a figure drop down right in front of me.

I'm face to face with my mother. I can't deny that at the moment. But her face is slightly different.

She has a pair of extended canines, goat-like horns, and I spot leathery wings on her back.

I stagger back in surprise, seeing she has a thick metal collar around her neck. Attached to it is a long heavy chain.

Tears run down her face as she gasps for air. She managed to say one word to me: "Run."

I turn and try, but I hear the chains falling again as I turn around.

Behind me, a dark figure lands on the ground. It lands hard enough to shake the ground and I lose my balance.

The figure is obscured, covered in shadows. I can only make out glowing green eyes at the top of what is a monstrously tall creature. It has black wings and looks like there are two other heads on the damn thing: one animal head is on one shoulder and another on the opposite side, their eyes glowing as well.

The chain is pulled and I watch as my mother is yanked upright. I can see her fully now.

She has a purple tail coming out of her back, a pair of purple furred goat hooves, and her hands seem normal up to her fingernails, which look long, black, and almost claw-like. Come to think of it, they look familiar.

My mother screams, trying to pull her feet, or her hooves, under her and hide herself from me. "Not Jason too... Master! I can't tell him too!" She gasps.

The chains are pulled upwards, lifting her up until she is dangling in the air.

A deep rumbling voice shakes the ground around me "Who do you belong to?"

She looks at me. "I'm yours, my Master...always and forever."

"What are you?" He growls.

She starts to sob. "I'm... a Succubus... Bu-" she gasps as the collar suddenly tightens.

"Enough from you." The dark figure growls.

I clench my fists. "Ma!" I run towards her.

A massive gust of wind then knocks me to the ground.

I get to my feet. "Let her go, you son of a bitch!"

My mother is clawing at her collar. She gasps as I watch the collar grow tighter on her neck to the point where I see blood around the top.

The dark creature spoke. "She is mine, boy, in every way: body, mind, and soul, to do with as I please."

I get to my feet slowly, staring him down.

"Do not trust the crimson whore." He says plainly. "Your so-called 'Righteousness' will bring you to ruin... upon you... upon your home..."

I narrow my eyes at it, "Oh? And why should I believe you?"

"I made a promise..." He looks at my mother.

I turned to her as well.

Her eyes are pleading, tears streaming down her face.

His green eyes become fixated on me, everything glowing greenish. "If you do this thing, you will be sought out... and destroyed."

"Oh yeah?" I walk towards them, looking at my mother. "I kicked Ubiel out of my house, so I don't think I'm too concerned with your shady ass."

The figure chuckles. "My servant Ubiel is but a flea compared to me!"

"And who the fuck are you?" I demanded.

The ground shakes, his eyes burning green, green wisps of smoke rising out of them. "I am Asmodai! Lord of Wrath. Prince of Hell."

"Only a prince and not a king huh?" I taunt.

"Silence, mortal!" The ground quakes and I fall to the ground again.

My mother's eyes are wide in terror now.

"Even with your stick of Cedar, Pine, Cypress, Bronze, and Blood of the Lamb, you could not hope to harm me, boy!" He shouts.

"So what do you want then, huh? Why bother me?" I glare at him, "If you're here to kill me for knocking your flunky out of my kid, then get it over with!"

"I have come to warn you, as I said. Do not follow the path of the righteous as the crimson slut has requested of you." His voice rumbles.

"Her name is Lady Tasha... and why the fuck should I listen to you?" I demanded.

The figure seems to grow larger. "I have promised Sara protection for your family and my word is law in Hell." I see large feathery black wings spread behind him. "If you do this, then I cannot offer my protection any longer."

"Your *protection*?" I mock. "Oh, the protection that got my son possessed?  Or my cat fucking crucified on my fucking bedroom door? The protection that terrified me and my wife for the past week and a fuckin' half?  Oh, I sure as shit wouldn't want to lose that!"

"I will set your mother free.... For a price," The voice rumbles.

My mother's eyes go wide and she turns to the dark figure.  She gasps, trying to speak, but is unable to do so.

"You want my son, don't you?" I ask.

The head in the middle shakes.  "No." His other hand points to me. "I want you.  Your soul... for myself."

"So you'll take me in exchange for my mother?" I ask.

"I will release her soul.  She can go wherever she desires... but I will take your soul in exchange.  You will be my... mole... my informant." The creature's voice rumbled.

I look at my mother, her eyes are red from crying and she looks to be begging.  "Will she still be a Succubus?"

The middle head shifts to the left slightly, "...Yes?"

"So you can't change her back, can't let her out of Hell-- what good is letting go of her soul?"  I ask.

There's an angry roar, and I see my mother dropped to the ground. The world spins as I'm tackled and then checked into a wall of some sort, the wind getting knocked out of me.

I hear the massive voice roar again; a black sword is shoved into my shoulder. "I offer you more than just her freedom. Ubiel told me of the issues you face. I can make no man cross you, no man question your authority, I can make them all your servants who would bow to your grand power!"

I wince, looking him in the eyes. "Go back to Hell..."

"I will take her with me," he growls.

I look to my mother, remembering what Father Thomas said. "You already have her. There's nothing I can do about it..."

The creature roars. "What is it about you--you people-- your family..." Putrid breath scoffs into my face.

My mother is in tears, on her hands and knees.

I look past the huge dark figure and I see her look at me, smiling.

"Good job, baby... Good job..." I see her mouth silently. The black creature picks me up and throws me across the black void.

I feel myself spinning, faster and faster through the air. The point hits where it feels like my stomach is about to tear out of my body before I wake up with a start, sweating profusely.

Marie gasps, "Jason? Are you okay?"

I groan, "Yeah... Just a nightmare." I turn to get out of bed and wince as I feel a pain in my shoulder. I frown, hoping that's the last visit I get from that creature and my mother. I shudder as I remember the look on her face. I hope this was nothing more than a horrible nightmare.

After my lovely evening, I'm getting ready for work.

Marie's phone vibrates. "Oh, Jenny is sending those photos over."

I walk over to Marie as she looks over her phone.

There's a photo of my Father in a dorm room somewhere, and my Ma, who looks just like she did when she came by the house a few days ago.

"That--did--did your mom have another daughter? She's the spitting image of that woman who was here the other day," Marie says in shock. "What was her name?"

I frown as the phone vibrates again, more photos coming. "She said her name was Sara, my mom's name."

The next photo is of Jenny, my Father, and Ma.

Marie shakes her head in disbelief, "This can't be real!"

A text shows up afterwards from Jenny.

"That's me, your father, and your mom. Isn't she beautiful?" The text reads.

Another photo appears: it's my Ma in a bikini, inside a dorm room, striking a sexy pose.

Marie scoffs, "I think I envy your mother!"

Another text rings: "Be happy you have a son and not a daughter--you'd have to shoot every boy in Boston!"

I raise an eyebrow.  Another photo of my mother in a slinky dress shows up.  "Is it me... Or does Aunt Jenny have a whole lot of sexy pictures of Ma?"

Marie punches my left shoulder.  "Enough... who knows, maybe they experimented with each other."

I rub my shoulder as one more photo comes in.  It still hurts from this morning.

The photo is of Ma:  She's doing a shot in a bedroom, a few candles lit.  Behind her is a balcony and sheer curtains.  I swear I see something in there.

"Marie, let me see that," I say as I take the phone from her gently.

Marie frowns. "What is it?"

I zoom in on the photo, moving toward the balcony. Behind the curtains, there's a figure.  It's faint, but it's there. A figure of some man, his face is smiling wide and his eyes are fixed on my mother.  I don't know if it's the transparency or not, but his eyes look black, save for a pair of yellow irises.  I noticed some distortions behind him as if there was something covering the balcony view.  Looking closely, they almost look like wings.

A text comes from Jenny.  "This is the last photo I ever took of your mother, Sara.  It was her 21st birthday--just a few drinks, we told ourselves."

I frown. "That's a photo of my mother a few hours before she died." There wasn't any kind of debate--the woman who showed up at my house? It was my mother.

Marie looks it over, frowning. "Why did you zoom into the balcony?"

I motion to the face in the curtains. "You don't see that?"

Marie shakes her head. "Nothing seems unusual."

I look at the time on the phone, handing it back to her. "If Father Thomas left his number, you gotta call him and ask about my mom, okay? I gotta get to work."

I finally got back to the precinct. Things haven't entierly blown over but the strike is over at least, for now. The entire precinct is talking about turning their back on the Mayor the next time he shows up in public. Most of us are against it because the NYPD did that already, and personally, I hear the 'Discount NY' bullshit enough.

For the record: New England Clam Chowder is better than Manhattan, the Yankees suck, and go Pats. Yeah, I said it, six rings, what do you wanna do, fight about it? But I digress.

I unlock my desk drawer and see it. Item C7, one cell phone, sitting in an evidence bag. Still has blood on the top of it.

Tasha's words bump around in my head: "A *good man looks out for his family, for his fellow man, and does good in the* community whenever he can, but a righteous man--he does what is right, what must be done, even if it's a detriment to his own self-interests."

Detriment to my self-interests is an understatement.  I take the phone and slide it into my coat pocket.  I close and lock the drawer.

As I do this, the Sarge barges over.

He's about forty, big fat belly, gray hair, and burly hairy arms, "Detective, I'm gonna need you to open up that drawer."

I roll my eyes, "Sarge, I tol--"

"I don't like locked drawers, you understand me, Detective?  Open it." He barks.

I take out my key, and I unlock the drawer, opening it. "Have fun in there."  I get up and start toward the door.

The Sarge rummages through my desk as I head out of the building.

I know my captain is dirty.  He likely told Sarge to send the evidence to me before Internal Affairs got to it for 'political' reasons. So, I'm heading out to West Roxbury.  The captain at the local precinct there I've heard is a real Boy Scout.  Well, a Girl Scout.

I'm sitting outside Captain Rebecca Louche's office, staring at the ceiling.  On my way over, I had gotten an external battery pack for the phone.  I also had some packing tape.

My left arm is killing me all of the sudden as I sit there waiting. I feel it throbbing like a bastard and I glare at it, "fuck off." It doesn't relent.

Almost an hour passes by when the Captain finally heads to her office, "Detective Miller I assume?" She offers her hand. She's a stout black woman, curly black hair, brown eyes, fairly dark skin.

I shake her hand, "Captain Louche."

We head into her office and I sit across from her as she moves behind her desk.

"I was a bit surprised to hear you wanted to speak to me. Specifically me." She says, taking her hat off. "Especially since your precinct is a bit of a vault right now."

I take out the evidence bag with the cell phone and place it on her desk.

She picks it up, making sure it doesn't move too much inside the evidence bag. "What's this?"

I take a deep breath. "It's the 'Knife' that Mr. Brown had on him when he was shot by Officer Sanders."

The Captain places the evidence bag gently on the desk. "One phone found at the scene of the accident doesn't clear nor condemn anyone. I can't call this damaging evidence." She stands up and reaches onto a shelf, producing a box of latex gloves. "Allergic?"

I shake my head.

She takes out two pairs, putting her own on.

I slide the gloves on, popping the bag open. I connect the external battery and power the phone up.

"Seventy percent of all cellular phones shipped last year contain biometric security measures.  Most popular are fingerprint readers," Captain Louche flatly states.  "Assuming there is important evidence on this smartphone, how do you expect to bypass the biometrics?"

I place the packing tape on the desk.

She raises an eyebrow, "That might work--but it's not 100%."

I nod.  The phone boots up, and sure enough, it is asking for a fingerprint.  I take the tape and affix it over the fingerprint reader, pushing down hard.

The captain opens her desk drawer, pulling out a small bottle of baby powder. "This should make the prints clearer."

I nod, gently pulling the tape off the phone. I have a print.

"Also it won't stick when you try to unlock it," she continues.

I coat the tape in the baby powder and then blow on it gently.  I put my finger behind the tape, wrapping it around my gloved finger.  I press my finger onto the fingerprint scanner.

Click.  The phone unlocks.

"I'd check the camera first, see if there's a recording." She says.

"Everyone's got a camera on these days," I say as I navigate to the camera.

"Yes, they do." She says as she watches me.  "That looks like the last recording."

"And it's exactly 10 minutes long,"  I point out.

"Standard timeout of a phone recording to conserve disk space," she states flatly.  The Captain seems extremely focused on details.  It's clear to me that she used to be a detective.

I hit play on the recording.

A man's voice is on the phone's speaker.  "Officer! I have the whole thing here, why won't you listen?  I want to give you the video as evidence!"

I can see Sanders and another officer milling about. Sanders is very close to the guy.

"I said we have it covered, sir.  Now please step away from the scene," Officer Sanders orders.

"I have a video of that white bitch running that brother over man!  I am trying to help you!" Mr. Brown shouts.

The Camera shakes around now, there are sounds of a struggle.  "Give me that fuckin' thing!" Officer Sanders shouts. The phone is now sitting on the hood of a car somewhere, looking down on the metal.  The screen is almost black.

A woman's voice is heard.  "Uncle Andy, my mouth is dry."

Sanders responds.  "Becky, please be quiet and sit in the car, sweety."

"That bitch is your... oh hey!  Hey! Hey, now stop it!  I'm showing you my hands!" Mr. Brown shouts.

"Put the knife down!"  Officer Sanders shouts.

The other officer's voice is heard, "Andy--calm down, man."

"This girl is too smart to have a simple DUI ruin her whole life, okay? She's a good girl!" Sanders shouts.

The phone is picked up, and there are the sounds of running. Mr. Brown's face is seen briefly as everything jostles around.

"Stop!" Officer Sanders shouts.

There are no signs of stopping.

"Drop the knife!" Officer Sanders shouts.

The other officer is heard, "Andy, he doesn't have a --"

A clip is emptied out entirely.

The image flies around and stops, the phone having traveled at least fifty to sixty feet from Mr. Brown's body.

It's fallen in a position that is good enough to see Mr.Brown's chest moving up and down over grass blocking the rest of him.

Officer Sanders is moving towards him, gun still trained as he drops the clip, and reloads.

Mr. Brown wheezes, "If I... survive... it's... gonna be... your ass... motherfucker..."

Officer Sanders finishes reloading. "Guess what, you fuckin' spook? You ain't survivin'."

"Andy, don't--" another two shots ring out.

Mr. Brown's chest is no longer rising and falling.

Officer Sanders holsters his gun and searches Mr. Brown. "Where the fuck is that fucking phone?" Sanders kicks Mr. Brown's corpse. "For fuck's sake..."

The woman's voice is heard, though what she's saying is not decipherable.

"What the fuck, Andy!" The other officer shouts.

"This girl isn't getting her life fucked up because of one mistake!"

"She killed a guy! She ran him over Andy! She's not getting out of that!"

"It was self-defense, these guys tried to carjack her! She ran one over, and the other guy came at us with a knife."

The other officer protests, "Andy, I can'--"

Officer Sanders grabs him by the shirt, "He had a knife... and we stopped a carjacking. Do you understand? Or do you want to join him?"

"A-Andy--"

"I swear to God; Rick, if you roll over on me, you'd better hope they toss me into supermax because I will fuckin' bury you, do you understand?"

The other officer just nods.

"Good." Officer Sanders picks up his radio. "Dispatch, I've got shots fired, need an ambulance, intervened in a possible carjacking, the victim is okay, perps are down."

The radio clicks back but isn't decipherable.

We sit watching the scene as another car arrives and eventually, an ambulance.

A CSI truck rolls in near the end of the video before it cuts out.

"CSI must have found the phone." Captain Louche states.

I flip to the previous video.

It's a video of the sky and the street below it.  Mr. Brown's voice is heard. "Praise the *Lord*!  Look at that sunset!"

Admittedly the clouds and sky do make for a pretty impressive scene.  Yellows, purples, blues, all mixing together behind fluffy clouds, the city skyline in the foreground.

Another black man is walking on the sidewalk.

Mr. Brown calls out to him, "Yo!  Francis!  Ain't it a beautiful sunset?  What a beautiful day!"

The black man walking presumably, Francis, turns, and waves.

Suddenly tires squeal.

"What th-- Francis, look out!"

The man on the sidewalk tries to jump away.

Suddenly a red sports car hops the curb, inches away from the man.

The camera focuses on Francis and the car.

"Francis?  You okay?"

Francis gets up with a limp and groans.  He stands up and slams his fist on the hood.  "What the hell do you think you're doing, you crazy bitch!"

The car starts to back up.

"Oh, Hell no!  Get your little white ass back here!  I gotta get your insurance, you done fucked up my leg!" He shouts.

Mr. Brown chuckles. "You fuckin' asshole, Francis--your leg's been fucked up for ten fuckin' years."

Francis remains on the sidewalk, shouting. He pulls out his phone. "I got your plates, bitch! I got your number!"

The car is now on the street. Then suddenly the engine revs loudly and the car slams into Francis, knocking him over.

The car continues to hop the curb and runs him over with both sets of tires.

"Francis! Oh my God!" The camera is moving rapidly before the car backs up, running over the man, again with both sets of tires.

The car stops. "What the fuck are you doing?" Mr. Brown shouts.

The car seems stuck on something, the tires spinning in some muddy portion of the grass. A young blonde woman staggers out of the car. "Gimme... Gimme that fookin'... camera... old man... you... oh... oh, fuck..." She passes out.

"Sweet Jesus..." Mr. Brown says before the video stops.

I put the phone down, making sure to keep my finger on the screen to stop it from locking. I look at Captain Louche.

Her eyes are slightly glassy as she looks at me. "What were you told to do with this phone?"

I clear my throat. "I was told to get rid of it. I left it out of the report."

"Why did the report go to you and not Internal Affairs?" She asks.

"I don't know. But I locked the phone in my desk drawer before the strike. My Sargeant ordered me to get rid of it. I told him I did. I don't think he believes me," I explain.

"And you came here because you're pretty sure your Captain and Sergeant don't want this getting out to the public?" She asks.

I nod.

"I'm going to call the Commissioner, we're going to show this to him, and get this logged." She stands up. "Thank you for doing the right thing."

I lean back in my chair as she picks up her phone.

It's less than twenty minutes when Commissioner Harris walks in.

He's a pretty tall white guy, harsh blue eyes and a squared jaw. "Detective, Captain. I understand you have some evidence regarding the Brown case?"

We show him the videos.

Commissioner Harris nods. "Excellent work... Captain, I'd like you to go over to the Detective's precinct, go over all the procedures their captain has implemented and assume temporary command of his precinct. I'm going to get Internal Affairs all over this. He'll be relieved until a later date."

Captain Louche nods. "Yessir. I'll head right over." She gets up and shakes my hand. "Detective," and leaves.

The Commissioner sits at her desk. "You can hand that phone over to me."

I looked at him incredulously, "You'd need gloves first, Commissioner."

"Son," he says, leaning forward. "I will fire Sanders, that's a fact. But I don't want the press to see any of that, do you understand? I'll make sure Sanders never becomes a cop... Hell, he'll be lucky if he can find a job in mall security." He clicks his tongue at me. "I can't have the press knowing about suppressed evidence in such a high-profile case. You understand, right?"

My thumb's been on the phone the entire time. I purse my lips as I move my finger discretely over to the 'share' button. Seems Mr. Brown's Facebook is still logged in. I look to the Commissioner. "Sanders is a murderer," I accused, trying to buy time.

Commissioner Harris narrows his eyes at me. "He is also a cop. A fellow officer. His reputation reflects on you, reflects on every last one of us. I will make sure that Sanders doesn't disgrace this uniform. That is what I am aiming for."

I tap the share button on the first video, keeping my eyes locked on the Commissioner.

"Now--if you want to keep your job, you will give me that phone, Detective Miller."

# CHAPTER 5

## *Justice*

As far as stress is concerned, I've never felt more of it. That includes when I was fighting my *first* demon. But looking back, I wouldn't have done anything differently.

The Commissioner couldn't see the screen. He was just staring me down, maybe he wasn't tech-savvy. He was certainly an older guy, closer to his fifties, but you could never be certain.

My finger slips over the 'post' button on the first video. It starts to upload. I keep the screen at the edge of my vision, keeping my eyes locked on Commissioner Harris's eyes. I hit share on the second video. As I do I feel the pain in my shoulder intensify.

"How do I know Sander's is going to get shitcanned?" I ask, stalling.

The Commissioner huffs at me, "Because this is strike three for the little prick.  Do you think this is the first time he tried to bail out that little trust-fund lush niece of his?"

I whistle, 50% uploaded on video one.  Damn it, I should have kicked the small video out first.  "What else did the little lush do?" All the while the pain in my shoulder is throbbing harder.  I tough it out though.

The Commission rolls his eyes.  "Drunk and disorderly, which I could give two shits about... but vehicular homicide? I don't feel much like getting my hands dirty covering that up. That bitch will likely get what's coming to her as well."

I look at the phone.  I think that if I smash the screen, it should still upload. It will look like it's inoperable, but it should still work.  I hope it will anyway.  With my free hand, I pick up a paperweight.  I see the phone is done uploading the first video, now it's on video number two.  I move the paperweight over the screen.  "So what?  just smash it?"

The Commissioner glares at me now. "I will do it, Miller."

As I see the 50% mark for video 2, I lock the screen, handing it over to the Commissioner slowly.

He takes the phone and looks it over, trying to unlock it. "What did you do?"

I shrug. "The phone was a bitch to unlock."  I show him my finger with the tape on it. "It has a fingerprint reader we had to get around.  It locked the screen while we were talking."

The Commissioner looks at my finger and shrugs, then snaps the phone in half slowly, bits of glass spraying into the air like glitter as he does. "You breathe a word of this to anyone and I'll have you terminated, do you understand me?"

"What about the Captain?" I ask.

He chuckles. "Captain Louche? Don't worry about her, she won't sell you out. She may be a straight shooter but everyone has something to protect, everyone has a weak spot."

I nod. "Well, Commissioner, it's been a treat. I'll head back to my unit then." I remove my gloves and toss them in the trash.

It's a twenty-minute drive back to my precinct and my desk. It felt like three days.

The Sarge slaps me on the back as I walk in. "There you go, Detective! I shouldn't have doubted you! But man, you did have me worried. What did you do with the..." he looks around and whispers, "Trash?"

I look at the Sarge, not feeling like lying, "It's snapped in half if that's what you're asking."

He laughs and walks back to his desk.

I sit down at what is my desk until someone in Mr. Brown's family, first name Andre by the way, discovers two new videos uploaded to the deadman's Facebook. I started writing an email.

I write about the Sarge, I write about the orders coming down from my captain. I even write about me and Captain

Louche and the Commissioner. I use the special "Do not use ever!" e-mail distribution. The one that sends an email to literally everyone in the Boston PD. I also CC a few reporters I know of, and an old FBI contact I made a couple of years back on some interstate murder case. I sigh, looking at my phone as a story pops up about the video.

I see the headline: "SHOCKING FOOTAGE OF BOSTON COP KILLING UNARMED BLACK MAN."

Why are they always in caps?

I hit send on the e-mail.

I promptly start to clean out my desk. I place my gun and badge on it and I shut down my computer. I figure I'm at least getting suspended, so I should save them the trouble and start to get the Hell out of dodge.

My Captain and Captain Louche are arguing in his office. I mostly just take a few photos of Junior and Marie off the desk. A few magnets here and there. My coffee mug, "Best Husband..." The back reads "...so far."

That's when I hear the sound of the inevitable.

"Miller!!" The Sargeant storms over to me, "You little shitstain!"

Sanders runs over to me, grabbing me by the collar. "I want a go at him first, Sarge! You son of a bitch! What the Hell is wrong with you?" He pulls his fist back like he's going to deck me.

I lock eyes with Sanders. I'm not even mad, I just stare him down, my photos and personal items in my hands. I guess after you stare down a demon possessing your kid, and a supposed demon prince, some pissy beat cop, isn't that terrifying.

Sanders backs down immediately.

I keep my eyes on him. "You're a disgrace to the uniform." I've never felt so calm about something I shouldn't be calm about. "Go ahead, rough me up. Hell, kill me for all I care. I'm sure the papers would love to hear that a whistleblower got his ass kicked or was murdered on his way out the door. That'll be really good for PR, huh? I bet it would help your defense out a lot." I look to the crowd growing around us, "Which reminds me, shouldn't you be lawyering up right about now?"

The Sarge pulls Sanders away from me.

Sanders runs his hands through his hair, walking back to his desk. "Fuck, Fuck, Fuck..." he says as he sits down.

I head for the door.

Captain Louche shouts at me on my way out, "Detective Miller!"

I turned to her.

She smiles at me, "When this blows over, you come to my precinct, you understand?"

I nod, walking out.

Marie is getting her coat on and zipping up Junior's jacket. "Well, you're a popular man."

I shake my head. "Yeah... Officer of the fuckin' year.  I'm everyone's friend." I say sarcastically.

Marie sighs. "You just... Please be safe okay?  I'll call when Junior and I get to mom's house."

"Tell your mother 'Hi' for me," I say.  "I'll call you when the heat dies down."

Marie nods. "I'm enrolling Junior into some e-courses anyway... So we can get him up to speed at school.  This works out nice."

Junior frowns and hugs me tight, "Daddy, I don't wanna go to Grandma's!  I wanna stay!"

I hug him tight.  "Me too buddy.  I want you to stay too, but right now there are some bad cops out there who might want to hurt us."

Junior sniffles, looking up at me worried.

"But you know they can't hurt me, right?  I kicked that demon's butt so I'm not afraid of them!" I boasted.

Junior smiles at me.

I ruffle his hair.  "But those bad men might try to hurt you and your Ma, and I can't risk that.  Okay?"

Junior sniffles again, hugging me tightly.

"You have fun at Grandma's, buddy, okay?  I'll call you every day.  I promise." I kiss his forehead.

Junior nods.  "Okay, daddy.  Beat up those bad cops!"

I stand up and give Marie a passionate kiss, more so than usual.  Hell for all I know, it might be the last one I give her.

"Ewwww!!" Junior shouts.

She gasps when I'm done. "Oh… You keep that up, Junior might have a little brother or sister soon."

"EWWWW!" Junior shouts in mock disgust, covering his ears.

I smile. "Yeah, maybe." I sigh, looking at Trooper as he stares at Mitten's little bed sadly. "Maybe we should get another cat."

Junior gasps in excitement. Funny how he hears that right away!

Marie looks at me, eyebrow raised. "You hate cats!"

I chuckle. "Yeah, well. Trooper needs his feline friend, right?"

Marie sighs. "When we get back, we can hit up a shelter, okay?"

I nod. "We aren't naming this one 'Boots.'"

Marie laughs. "Then don't let Junior name him!"

"I wanna name the kitty! I won't name him 'Boots', I promise!" Junior's more excited about a new cat and hopefully he never learns the truth about what happened to the last one.

I look down at Junior. "Okay, when we pick one out, you give me some ideas for names and we'll make a decision together, okay?"

Junior smiles at me and gives me a thumbs up.

I hear the taxi beep its horn.

Marie smiles at me as she takes Junior's hand. "Jason, I'm proud of you. You did the right thing." She gives me one last kiss before she and Junior head out, getting into a cab bound for the airport.

I spend the rest of the day watching TV, having a beer, and trying to decompress. Trooper is up on the couch, laying on my legs. I checked that Marie and Junior got to the airport via a text message and another text message once they were on the plane. I relaxed a bit. I flip on the news, and there's our story.

The anchorwoman is pretending to be shocked but you know she's super hyped to report on the scandal.

"An incredibly disturbing pair of videos have been leaked by an officer within the Boston Police Department, showing that Andre Brown Sr. was viciously murdered after he attempted to provide police with evidence of a vehicular homicide. The video also seems to prove a direct motive for the murder. Officer Andrew Sanders, the police officer shown in this video here..."

The video pops up on the side, Mr. Brown and Sanders's niece faces both blurred out.

"...Apparently is related to the female driver. He attempted to cover up what was an apparent DUI and Hit and Run. Officer Andrew Sanders and the female driver are now in police custody." The camera turns. "And the story keeps unfolding. Several officers have been suspended and charged with conspiracy and tampering with evidence.  One officer, who wished to remain anonymous, however, is speaking up."

A distorted voice is on the line, "I was there at the scene. I wish I could have stopped him.  I'm glad this happened. Officers are supposed to uphold the law, we aren't above it. Some are calling Detective --" thankfully my name is censored, "--a 'snitch'.  A 'snitch' is a term for someone who rats out their friends. We need more officers like Detective--" and my name bleeped out again.

I close my eyes and lean back.  Relaxing for the first time in a while.

"In other news, the terrorist threat made days ago by the man calling himself 'Xyphiel' has many government officials..." is the last thing I hear before I drift off.

Later on, I wake up to Trooper whining.  I hear the TV playing infomercials in the background.

I sit up.  "What's wrong, boy, you gotta go out?"

Trooper is sitting up on the couch, looking at where the TV should be.  Instead, something is blocking it.

I must be dreaming again.

In front of me are a pair of doors.  They're a pair of large double-hung doors; they look like stone.  They're huge, almost ten feet tall and twelve feet wide.  They barely fit in my living room.  I walk towards them.

"Hello?" I ask.  No answer.  But the pain in my shoulder kicks in again.

I put my hand on the doors, and I feel them slide open easily.

Trooper's ears perk up and he wags his tail excitedly.

"Stay, boy," I say.

Trooper whines, laying down and plopping his head on the couch.

I slowly step inside the otherworldly doors.  I hear voices, a few men and women. They echo through the huge entryway from various hallways.

As I walk in, I look around.  The floor, walls, the ceiling-- everything is a pristine white marble.  The ceilings are at least forty feet tall, maybe higher.  In front of me is a pair of huge statues.  They're of a woman, or an angel, anyway.  The sculpture is amazingly detailed.  A flowing gown covers her from shoulders down to her bare feet.

The other statue is also of an angel, wearing a cowl and holding a sword, pointed down at its feet. Though there are no feet to see, only long flowing robes cast in stone.

I hear a voice that I think is Lady Tasha's, "I am still apprehensive about having Zephrina here..."

Not wanting to be rude, I close the doors behind me.

I hear another voice that I believe is Father Thomas "Did you hear something?"

I called out, "Hello?" My voice echoes through the halls.

I hear a clip-clopping noise like high heels running on a wood floor echoing through the massive room. I spot Tasha running up a set of stairs to the right of the entrance.

I think it's Tasha anyway. She's got the same face, the same robes, the same hair, but she looks taller. Her robes are much longer, covering her feet. Behind her are a pair of pinkish leathery wings. They start out red towards their base and turn white at the tips and edges. On her head are a pair of short straight horns, the base of the horns are red, and they fade to white tips, pink being the predominant color in the middle.

Tasha smiles wide. I can see a pair of white fangs as she does. "Jason! You're here!" She walks towards me quickly, the clip-clopping growing louder.

Where before she was a good head shorter than me, now we're eye to eye. Those are a hell of a pair of heels, apparently. Though I can't see what she's wearing on her feet.

"My brother Timothy is getting our sisters all set with their lodgings right now. So you need to follow me right away!" She beams at me, taking my hand in her gloved one.

If I had not met her before, I'd be worried, but she's the same woman who cared for Junior during his exorcism, the same who held his tongue when he was seizing, the same who kept his head from jostling too much, the same who held her hand on his chest while she and Father Thomas cast out the demon that had possessed him.

Still, I couldn't help but stare at her horns.

"Uh... Tasha... I... what are you?" I asked.

Tasha looks up and sighs. "I guess I should explain... but follow me while I do, okay?"

I nod. "Y-Yeah... seriously though... What are you? Because... you kind of look like-"

"A Succubus?" Tasha's face falls. As we walk toward some stairs, she keeps her eye on me. "My father Xyphiel? Well, I carry a curse from Belial thanks to him. When I turned thirteen, my sister and I changed. I became... well, this." She smiles. "But I turned to God, fought my instincts, and was blessed." She smiles at me again. "I prefer to look human, of course, but the temple... well, despite my blessings, my disguise is still... at its core, a deception. This temple removes all deception, brings out the truth in all of us, and brings us all together."

I frown. "Xyphiel... that... that name was on the news recently, yeah?"

Tasha frowns, nodding. "You can't choose your family, as they say."

We finally get to the base of the staircase and as we turn the corner, we come to a fountain, where I see Father Thomas sitting next to it.

Father Thomas smiles at me. "Welcome to the Guardian Temple, my son."

Tasha clip-clops over to the fountain. I notice the "belt" that she has across her waist is actually a thin tail wrapped around her, connecting at the end of her tailbone from her back. She takes a seat near the fountain across from Father Thomas. As she does, I see she has red cloven hooves that peek out from under the robe as she settles in on a seat at the edge of the fountain.

Okay, the fountain doesn't really describe it well enough, so let me give this a shot:

From somewhere above the ceiling, cascading down the entire wall, and ending in a huge basin stretching out almost thirty feet wide, is crystal clear water. The marble it's running down doesn't appear to be worn or eroded, and I cannot tell where the source of the water is, or where the water is going after it touches the basin at the bottom. The marble is so smooth that I can see my reflection in the wall itself.

Tasha removes her glove and as she places her bare hand into the water, her horns glow brightly. "This is the sacred water of the Guardians. Long ago, this was where Guardian Angels came to receive orders from God, which came from the Guardian Council, led by the Metatron. They would take these waters to heal themselves, and bless others. The waters are incorruptible and very potent."

I hear footsteps behind me. I turn around and spot the Matrix guy from before.

Only now the guy has white feathery angel wings tucked behind his back, his trenchcoat is off, and his arms crossed over his chest. I must be dreaming again. As if to remind me, my shoulder stings again, painfully.

"How is this guy here?" The Angel asks.

"Wait, what the Hell!" I shout, "You had an angel and you didn't bring him to the exorcism? Why?" I turned to Tasha for some kind of explanation.

Tasha smiles broadly, running over to him and hugging him tightly, "Timothy! Oh, this is wonderful! Father Thomas doesn't think I'm right but I know it, I feel it!" She glances at me as she hugs Timothy. "The doors showed themselves to him because Sara Baker's name was on that list. That's why we didn't need Timothy--we had you, Jason."

The Angel, Timothy frowns. "What do you mean? He's the son of that Succubus? But, what of it?"

Tasha smiles. "Sara Baker." She pulls a tattered bit of paper from her robes. "You remember? The first time you sat in Saint Dinah's throne, you babbled for a day and I wrote down as much as I could. At some point, you started to list names." She looks at me, happily. Her tail twitched about her waist excitedly.

Timothy nods. "I remember but...No, I don't... I was speaking in tongues, at the time? It was the first time I tried to listen... I couldn't make anything out. It was all jumbled."

"Wait, wait! Okay, listen! " I shout as Tasha seems about to say something else. "I need an explanation!"

Everyone is silent now. Only the running water is heard.

"How did my mother, who's been dead for twenty-eighty years, show up at my house? How is she a Succubus? And who the fuck is Asmodai?" I demanded.

Father Thomas runs up to me, his eyes wide, and grabs me. "You saw him...? Asmodai? When? Where?! Is he here?!" Father Thomas is visibly shaking.

I shake my head. "I had this nightmare... it seemed so real, my mother was in this guy's clutches and she looked... well, like a demon." I turn to Tasha, "Like you."

Father Thomas lets go of me, composing himself a bit. "I'm sorry, it's just... I too have seen the demon prince

Asmodai." He sighs, "But I must tell you: your mother was led astray as a young woman, Jason." His eyes seem saddened now, his shaking ceased. "She sold her soul to a fallen angel who promised her beauty and good health, but his promise was misleading." He says as he walks away from me.

"She... Wait, if she sold her soul...?" I ask as I remember when I shot at her, the black shadows that swarmed around her, the smell of sulfur.

Father Thomas makes the cross over himself, whispering a silent prayer. "She's lost, for now... All we can do is pray for her soul, Jason. But Lady Tasha's presence is clear evidence that a demon *can* be redeemed."

Tasha scoffs, "I was *never* a 'demon'!"

Timothy laughs, "You only look like one, have the powers of one..."

Tasha narrows her eye, playfully pushing Timothy away from her. "You should be one to talk. You have a little *gift* from our father as well, remember?"

Timothy frowns, then looks at the list in Tasha's hands. "That is fully under control."

"It doesn't need to be. It's not what you believe it is." Tasha smiles at him.

Timothy glanced at the list. "So... Getting back to the succubus, her name was on this list...? I don't see how this helps us. She's in Hell now, how can it matter?"

Tasha is overly excited again, downright giddy. She goes over the list briefly, smiling at me, "The problem was the list was supposed to come out decades ago, to help the Guardians mark future people whom God had chosen. But..." Tasha clip-clops over to me, "Every time I tried to find one of them, they had met an untimely demise. Some explained, some unexplained. As if dark forces had found them first. I had crossed them off the list as I went, but I never thought to seek out their children!" She looks at me with a nearly insane level of happiness. "I never thought that maybe... just maybe the gift would be passed down." She beamed at me, placing her hands on either side of my cheeks, squeezing my cheeks like an old aunt at a family reunion. "He's the son of the same Sara Baker that was on that list! She was chosen by God--but she fell before she could receive her gift."

Timothy turned to me with a sympathetic look. "What gift?"

Tasha releases my face, and clip-clops over to the fountain, flipping over a cup near the basin and filling it to the brim. She walks over to me. "If the doors opened for you Jason, then you *are* a righteous man, as I believed."

I take the cup she offered me, looking at the crystal clear water. If I didn't know any better, I'd think the cup was empty. I look at Tasha suspiciously.

Tasha's hands are clasped together, her smile so wide that her fangs are showing. "Drink, please! The suspense is killing me!"

Father Thomas takes a sip from the fountain himself, nodding at me, "It merely purifies. I have drunk it many times, with no adverse or divine result. Honestly, I do not think it will do what you think it will do, Lady Tasha."

"Humbug!" Tasha scoffs at him. "You're too green yet, Father Thomas."

I look at the cup.

Timothy is smiling at me.   "Well, it might explain this." He hands me a small scroll.

"What's this?" I ask.

Tasha looks at Timothy with an almost mean look, but it comes across as far too soft, almost cute.

"It's an edict." Timothy faces Tasha. "For him, from **Him**."

Tasha's eye grew wide. "What's it say?"

I place the cup down, trying to avoid drinking it, for now, opening up the small scroll.

It reads: "The Corrupt claim to be The Peacekeepers of the Puritan City.  The Peacekeepers must be cleansed and made righteous again.  The corruption shall spread if not halted, or it shall fall to Wrath.  This task must be taken by the Guardian Jason Miller," I read out loud.

I glance at Timothy, "I'm sorry, 'Guardian'?"

Timothy looks to the cup. "Drink."

I swear I hear little clip-clop noises as if Tasha is tapping her right, then left hoof on the marble floor, impatiently.

I frown, picking it up.  I sniff it and shrug, knocking the whole thing back like a shot.

I feel dizzy for a moment and then incredibly calm.  As if my whole body just got a massage or I didn't have a single care in the world.  I stumble backward a bit, my balance shifting after I hear a ripping noise.  The dull ache in my shoulder is gone, finally. I even give it a good rotation to check.  But no, the ache is gone.  Thank God!

Tasha cries out happily. "Timothy! We can restore the temple!" She sequels with joy. "Oh! I have to go find the children of the chosen on the list! There *is* hope! Hope to stop Father and Aunt Ragna! Oh, I am so happy!"

Father Thomas seems to be in shock. "By God in heaven--she was right!"

I look at Tasha oddly. "I just took a drink. I don't see how I'm going to clean up the Boston PD on my own. They all hate me."

Timothy chuckles. "I'm sure you are more than capable... Brother."

I turn to look at Timothy to ask why the Hell he's calling me 'Brother', but as I look up from the cup, I spot my reflection on the wet marble wall of the fountain.

Behind me are a pair of large feathery white wings. They rise and fall as I breathe.

They're angel wings.

They're *my* angel wings.

# Epilogue

I t's been a few days since I got my wings.  Let me tell you, being a Guardian Angel isn't a walk in the park-- it's more like a sprint.  The good news is, I'm a bit of a runner these days.

I'll give a little example: As you can imagine, I'm the most unpopular cop in town.  That being said, Marie and Junior are still at her mother's.  Trooper needs to stay with me, of course, mostly because Marie's mother is allergic to dogs.

Trooper and I are taking a walk when I notice I've got a pair of guys tailing me.  Two guys wearing hoodies and face masks.  Not suspicious at all!  I turn down an alleyway and I notice another two guys who were walking in front of me turn around and follow me into the alley.

Seems fair enough, to be honest.  Gives them a fighting chance.

I kneel down and whisper to Trooper to meet me at the house.  I don't know if Trooper just behaves better now or if this is another angel power, but I let him off the leash and he runs past the four guys walking down the alley.

"Yah, should have made like yer bloody dog and runoff, yah fuckin' rat," one of my pursuers hisses at me.

I shrug. "Fellas, I feel like we could resolve our differences without violence."

Guy number two pulls out a gun. "Aye, but I choose violence."

"Suit yourself," I say, cracking my neck.

Two of the guys move in with nightsticks. Apparently, the idea is they're going to beat the living shit out of me and then shoot me? This is going to be fun.

The two nightstick guys both come right up to me and try to hit me at the same time, trying to club me on either side of the head.

I manage to grab both of them and pull them into each other, knocking their heads together. The rest seems to happen in slow motion. I hear the hammer get pulled back on guy number three's pistol, watching him getting ready to shoot me. Seems the last guy is still reaching for his piece.

I jump up over the two knocked-out thugs and plant my foot against the left wall of the alley. To say I feel lighter on my feet these days is an understatement. I get a good six feet over the rather stunned guy before I manage to land a punch right on his shoulder.

The gunman stumbles against the first guy and they both tumble into the wall.

I turn to my left and spot that one of my wings slid out of my coat. I have to laugh a bit. The first guy who was all talk, his eyes nearly bug out of his head before I knock him out. Lucky for me, not a damn soul is going to believe him. As I head home, I call it in. The unis can pick up these idiots later. I have some business to attend to.

Timothy might be mad, but I don't care. I'm pretty resolved to fix up Timothy from his sad sack of a self. Ever since he faked his death to vanish from earth, the guy hasn't been looking good. He looks ten years older and he's not been himself. At this point, I need drastic measures. Here's hoping my little plan works out.

To add some context: This girl, Sofia, is Timothy's girlfriend. However, Timothy decided to protect her by faking his death. Problem is, Sofia keeps calling his phone, leaving frantic voice messages for him, and it's tearing Timothy up inside.

I've got a minor hairbrained scheme to get her to The Guardian Temple. Timothy might be pissed, but I'm willing to deal with his temper versus his moping.

That being said, I have some business at the Suffolk County House of Correction. I'm visiting our mutual friend Officer--well, I guess now it's just--Andrew Sanders. The guard pats me down, luckily not on the back, just my sides, and sends me in. Benefits of being a cop, or maybe just divine intervention? Hard to tell these days.

Having wings is wicked but honestly, it's also a bit of a pisser. I took Timothy's advice on wardrobe and wear a trench coat now. Not black, however. I don't want to look like a Matrix reject or some shit. Tasha had offered some kind of other method but it seemed too far off for me.  Regardless, if I hold them tight enough to my back, under the coat, it just looks like I'm fat, or that the coat is just bulky.  Choose the wrong one, win a prize!  Likely a punch to the face.

Oh yeah, fun fact: Apparently there are different kinds of Angels.  Timothy is a messenger angel?  I mean, he talks to God, directs us where to go, tells people omens and shit.  Me? I'm a Guardian Angel, which means I handle things in a much more, let's say, *direct* manner.  Aka: I beat the devil outta yah, as our four buddies discovered earlier today.

Because of all of that, I'm in the best shape of my life, literally.  I'm stronger than before, look a couple years younger, and I've noticed I have stamina for days.

The last part I figured out with the wife.  However, when I mentioned this to Timothy, I had a rude awakening.

I remember discussing it with him in the Temple.

"Marie can't get enough of me.  Talk about a wife who got her prayers answered." I boast.

Timothy stares blankly at me, clearly not entirely used to locker room talk.  "I... see."

"I'm thinking of naming the girl; if it's a girl, Lara, or maybe Angie.  Would Angie be too cliché for us?" I asked, looking at Timothy.

His face falls.  "Oh... uh... I guess there is... well."  He clears his throat.  "There's a minor issue with that."

I raise an eyebrow at him. "What do you mean?"

"As a Guardian Angel... You're sterile." Timothy says abruptly.

Well, my hopes were dashed for a second kid, but you know what?  It's all right.  Oh, another bad part about this Guardian Angel gig?  You'll like this...

Marie and I were having dinner at her mother's house.  I just smiled at her as she gave me a mischievous look.

"So... Jason,  think you and I can try for another kid after dinner?"  I don't know if it's the angel presence, the ten years younger thing, or the increased stamina.  Whatever it is, count Marie as 'Luckiest Wife' because she basically got a whole new man without the divorce and custody battles.

"Well, I certainly wouldn't mind making love to you Marie but I found out I'm shooting blanks today."  I blink for a second.  I had *wanted* to say 'Sure thing Marie, I'm gonna try to put a kid in you for the next two hours,' as I didn't want to disappoint her right away.

"Wait, what?!" She shouts.  "When did you find this out?"

"Today," I say.  I'm still confused about exactly how everything is just sort of coming out of my mouth without me really meaning it to sound that way.  "They never told me beforehand. I was talking to Timothy today and that's when he told me about it."

Marie frowns.  "I was looking forward to a little girl."  She pouts.

I nod.  "Me too, to be honest, I would have liked another kid but... well, at least you and I can continue to have fun, right?"

Marie raises an eyebrow.  "Jason, I have a question for you."

"Hmm?" I ask, food still in my mouth.

"Do you find my sister attractive?"

Trap questions I've dealt with in a marriage plenty of times. Marie's sister looks almost identical to her in every way, yet somehow she feels the need to hear that I find her unattractive or that I wouldn't touch her. "Yes, I find her attractive--you two look almost identical, I couldn't find you attractive without finding her attrac--hold up!" I shout, hand going over my mouth.

She stares blankly at me and then grins. "You can't lie."

"What?"

She grins wickedly at me. "You cannot lie to me, Mr. Angel." She sauntered over to me, sitting in my lap. "Do you want me right now?"

"Fuck yeah." I grin.

She laughs. "Well, that's all I need to hear..."

I'm not detailing what happened next, use your imagination.

Today, I was checking on a few things before my 'flight' to New Hampshire. I am mainly checking because Anderson's niece somehow got off scot-free! I checked with every DA and they all told me the same odd story: "Insufficient evidence." Worse yet is they told me that while having a weird look in their eyes--and I knew something was off. Maybe it's my new instincts, but something foul and maybe even demonic was afoot.

I walk into the visiting area and make my way to the booth the guard points out. I have a seat, thank God it's a bench.  Do you know what a pain it is sitting in a high-backed chair with these wings?  Swear to God, it's a pain in the ass.

I heard about all of this from my new Captain, Captain Louche of course, who informed me of the recent goings-on of the case.

Captain Louche had pulled me aside on my way in. "Detective Miller, a moment of your time?"

I head into her office. "What's up, Captain?"

She looks me over, noticing my brown trench coat. "Detective, is it that cold out there for you?"

I shrug.  "Is it against regulation?"

She gives a deadpan expression.  "Well no, but you look like some sort of noir gumshoe."

I clear my throat. "What is this about?"

"Rebecca Anderson?   She's free as a bird," Captain Louche informed.

"Till she hits a pane glass window. " I frown, "How?  The DA had her dead to rights on manslaughter and a DUI.  The girl was more lit than Charlie Sheen."

Captain Louche nods. "She did test for just about every substance there is--the more impressive thing is that she managed to survive."

I frown. "So, how did she manage to get off the hook? I'm going to do some digging."

Captain Louche stops me before I head out.  "Some more information for you: Andy Sanders?  He's not out, but he's taken to prison really well.  I have sources there telling me he's running a gang."

"Running a gang?" I ask, rather surprised, "Andy Sanders? What gang?"

Captain Louche frowns. "Seems he's in charge of the Aryan Brotherhood inside. Not only did he manage to take over--he's recruiting."

"I knew he was a racist prick but I didn't think he was a card-carrying Neo-Nazi," I commented.

"He wasn't.  Sure as shit wasn't in the force.  Maybe a racist, sure, but no affiliation with any hate group."  Captain Louche looks concerned, the first bit of emotion that has come over her.  "It's very disconcerting."

"I'll check it all out, Captain."

With that, I had headed off to the DA's offices, and gotten the same answers: "insufficient evidence."

When I checked the evidence, any mention of Rebecca Anderson, or even her voice, her face, her license plates, all of it was missing from the video.

We couldn't even pull what was leaked from the news because all the stations blurred out her information, and Facebook had removed the video for some terms of service violations.

That leads me here, sitting in the visiting cubical of the local prison.

Out of the blue, Sander's hand slaps onto the glass from the other side as he walks over, shaking me out of my reverie. I assume he's trying to startle me.  He is staring at me with wide eyes and a sick grin. His eyes look sunken, and I'm not sure if they've always been that green before.  He has a seat and picks up the phone to his left.

I pick up the phone on my end.

He starts, "Miller, you ol' son of a bitch.  What a nice surprise!  How the Hell are ya?"

I look him over, and from the start of it, he doesn't seem right.  Something's truly off about him.

"How's prison treating ya?" I ask.

"Wonderfully," he says, leaning close to the glass, "I'm havin' a fucking ripper in here every night, you should come, get that stick out of yer ass."

I nod. "Sure, I heard you're best friends with the Aryan Brotherhood on the inside."

Sanders nods. "Yeah, I get along with all those hateful bastards.  I'm a fuckin' celebrity in here as far as they're concerned." His eyes look kind of crazed as he says this, "I fuckin' run those sons of bitches."

"I bet," I say as I look him over, "So, your niece somehow got off.  I was surprised.  Figured you had something to do with it."

"Me? Oh, no. I ain't got nothing to do with that. Though it was a favor to me from... A mutual friend." He smiles with a wide and demonic grin at me.  "You were warned, Miller.  He warned you before you started this shit show.  He told you to leave it alone."

Now I can tell something is way off.  "Who warned me, Sanders?  Who have you been talking to?" I think back to what

Father Thomas said about my Ma's soul and what she sold it for. "What did you do?"

"Me? Oh, I didn't do much Miller, not much at all, not *yet* anyway. Just wait until I do though... just wait," as he starts to rant, I see something dark coming from him. I see an aura surrounding him as he clenches his fist, his forearm and bicep bulging with dark veins and swelling in size. "Maybe if I do well, he'll let me have a go at your mother."

I narrow my eyes. "What do you know about my mother?"

"Your mother sucks cocks in Hell!" He punches through the glass, cutting his arm up pretty good as he does.

Alarms go off, but he manages to grab me and pulls me close, his other hand still on the phone.

Several guards rush over to him and try to pull him off me. They aren't making much progress.

He glares at me, eyes burning with some kind of green energy. "I'm going to run this joint, I'm going to take every hateful motherfucker in here, and I'm going to enlist a fuckin' army to tear your life to shreds. Because that's all I need to do to keep being able to do shit like this."

I narrow my eyes at him, moving my hand over his. "And what did it cost, Sanders?" I crack a small pouch of sacred water over his hand, holding him tight.

He reels back, screaming as the guards tackle him, but he doesn't budge.

"What the fuck did you do, Sanders?!" I demanded.

He grins. "I just--" He starts to chuckle, then transitions into maniacal laughter, shouting at me, "I made a deal!" His mad eyes fixed on mine.

The guards are struggling to even move him.

I give them a hand and pull Sanders quickly against the glass.

To Sander's shock, his forehead smacks right against the glass in front of me and as he stumbles back, the guards manage to get a handle on him and finally subdue him.

"Who'd you make a deal with Sanders?" I shout as he's dragged off.

Sanders starts laughing again. "Who?" He laughs. "No, Miller! It's What!"

Our eyes lock hard as he's pulled around the corner. The alarms seem to fade into the background and it's as if no one else is in the room but us.

Sanders shouts, laughing maniacally, but just before he disappears around the corner, he manages to shout, "I made a deal with an Angel!"

**To Be Continued...**

# **About the Authors**

Jordan and Mimi have written together for the nosleep and Reddit community in the horror genre for a few years. New to the scene as submitters but not as avid readers, the pair have found great success in presenting the Guardian Temple Universe to the reddit community and beyond.

Each from different backgrounds, the pair bring their shared experiences, talents, and perspective to a diverse and passionate cast of characters, scenery, and events. Jordan and Mimi strive to show a world that reflects that of reality, both the gritty truths and the indomitable spirit of the world. With the goal of showing an uncensored slice of the world in every story, be it large or small in scope.

Jordan & Mimi have been contributing to the r/nosleep Reddit community since 2017. Since then, the story has grown and expanded to encompass far more than just the Boston area of the United States. Writing a long and interconnected series spanning many timelines, events, and international locations, the Guardian Temple Series is a labor of love from two writers who focus on a character driven story that mixes the themes of Theology, The Supernatural, Mythology, and Science Fiction into an expanded universe unlike any other: The Guardian Temple.